ALSO BY JAN CASEY

The Women of Waterloo Bridge

This edition first published in the United Kingdom in 2021 by Aria,
an imprint of Head of Zeus Ltd

A CIP catalogue record for this book is available from the
British Library.

ISBN (E): 9781838930752
ISBN (PB): 9781800246034

Cover design © Lisa Brewster

Typeset by Siliconchips Services Ltd UK
Printed and bound by CPI Group (UK) Ltd, Croydon, CR0 4YY

Aria
c/o Head of Zeus
First Floor East
5–8 Hardwick Street
London EC1R 4RG

www.ariafiction.com

WOMEN AT WAR

Jan Casey

An Aria Book

For my daughter, Kelly and my son, Liam.
With all my love.

I

July 1939

Many days have wonderful moments within them. Some are so good they allow us to hold fast to the feelings of well-being they create for longer periods of time; twenty minutes, half an hour, an hour or two. And on a few, which can be counted on one hand, time ticks by in what promises to be a coming together of perfect unison amongst oneself, others, the surroundings, the light and the atmosphere. And then there is the disappointment that inevitably ensues when those promises fail to come to fruition.

But today would be different. Was different. Nothing could sully or defile the cloudless, crystalline sky, so clear as to be almost translucent. Try as she might, Viola could not blink open her eyes for longer than a second to follow the flight of a collared dove or a blackbird, chaffinch, goldfinch or some other bird that appears on matchless British summer days, like smudges on the palest of blue china.

The boys were hitting a tennis ball back and forth in

a half-hearted, laconic way behind the greenhouse and sheds that stood beyond the small orchard. The dull thump of their plimsolls on the lawn and the ball meeting taut racquet strings came to her in a muted, rhythmic pattern; she was sure she could smell the dust they kicked up. Laughter carried over as they taunted each other with jibes, then one or another shouted a congratulations of 'Shot!' followed by twigs snapping as they retrieved the ball and lined themselves up to start all over again.

There was the cushioned thud of a plump apple falling into the grass; the leaves of a tree quivering as another was plucked by one of her brothers. On their way to inspect the hollyhocks or roses or foxgloves, bees swooped in and out of earshot. As a warning, she flapped her hand when one of them buzzed too close to her face.

Under the willow, she felt shaded and cool even though the heat found a way through the lustrous branches that swayed almost to the ground. Mum had left an earthenware jug of elderflower cordial and three glasses on the table. Viola filled one and sipped the sweet juice that always reminded her of summer as it ran down the back of her throat, leaving her tongue tingling.

Pitch lay beside her, his eyes closed, his coat sweltering when she parted it with her fingers. She poured cordial into his bowl and pushed it under his nose where he lapped it without moving his head an inch. 'Lazy Pitch,' she murmured, laughing out loud at the irony. 'Lazy Vi, too,' she said. But the day, she decided, was made to be lackadaisical.

She flopped back against the canvas deckchair and thought about Fred speaking to her father in his study at this very moment. This perfect moment. On this perfect day. She smiled when she imagined him, tall and determined with eyes as blue and pellucid as the sky, striding across the lawn to her any minute now, telling her it was all settled.

Fred. Who would have thought she would find herself in this position with Her Fred as she now called him? She hadn't. Not when the other girls working in the university library started to giggle and nudge her when he came in yet again asking for her, and only her, to assist him in finding more and more obscure books to help with research for his thesis. Not when he happened to be propped against a tree next to the side entrance of the grey building when she finished her shift, frowning into a book on his open lap – a book he fumbled with and let fall the minute she appeared. And not when he turned up in the pub with his friend, George, asking if they could sit with her and her crowd although they were surrounded by a number of empty tables. She smiled to herself.

He made her laugh on those occasions, but he was also a thoughtful and rational conversationalist – everyone listened when he spoke. On one particular day, he didn't come to the library to look for her over the heads of those in front of him in the queue and she felt deflated. Another time, she caught herself turning towards the door of the pub every time it was pushed open and realised that her heart dropped when a shorter, darker-haired man with less of a well-built presence appeared.

But still she dismissed that she felt anything for him until he asked her to meet him one evening. It was early autumn, so she decided to wear a light jacket and she remembered now how giddy and girlish she felt when deciding which brooch to pin on it – like an agitated bottle of champagne that was ready to pop. She thought she'd be nervous alone with him in the pub, in the Arts Cinema, on the walk home. Instead she felt the fizz of anticipation and a deep comfort, both at the same time. When they said goodnight, she knew they would see each other again as he had wrapped his college scarf around her neck against the first frost. Disappointment had overwhelmed her when he hadn't kissed her goodbye, but he soon made up for it. That thought caused as much heat to rise from her skin as did the blazing day.

Sunshine and contentment allowed the book she was holding to slip from her fingers to her lap to the ground where it lay, cover up, next to the sluggish dog. She gave up the battle with her weighted eyelids and succumbed to sleep.

Gooseflesh spotted her arms when she woke. The boys had retreated to the house and her book was wet and sticky from the cordial that Pitch must have upended when he refused to be left behind. Gusts of warm, damp wind ruffled the branches of the willow and tossed the hollyhocks from side to side as if they were lost at sea.

The air had become heavy and burdensome and it felt as if she alone were holding up the sky with her head and shoulders. Fred was standing next to her, his jaw set stiff and tense. She looked down at his hand on her shoulder, moulded into a rocky fist, and wondered at how swiftly a day such as this could deteriorate. Because she knew with certainty that it had.

'Fred, whatever has happened?' Viola asked, rising to face him. 'What did Dad say?'

Fred placed both his hands on her shoulders and eased her back down into the deckchair, the bright yellow and blue stripes mocking her with their frivolous reminder of a seaside holiday. She sat and looked up at him, her mouth agape and heart pounding.

'Fred,' she demanded again.

He pulled his hands through his dappled brown hair. 'He said no.'

'But I... I can't... How could he? Fred, why would he?'

Fred sat on the grass next to her, his shoulders sagging in his summer-weight jacket. He plucked up handfuls of grass and weeds and earth and slung them towards the root of the tree. 'He's taking care of you,' he managed at last, each syllable delivered in a concise, controlled way.

Viola stared at him. Fred kept his eyes down. 'If, Frederick Albert Scholz, this is your idea of a joke it's not at all funny. Not at all.' A drop of tepid rain glanced across her cheek as she waited. 'Fred,' she hissed. 'Please tell me you're winding me up.'

'Viola Victoria Baxter,' Fred said, lifting his head to look at her. 'I wish I was.'

'But... But...' Viola rose and pushed away Fred's hand. She felt for the collar of her blouse and pulled and scrunched at the soft material. The garden seemed to tip on its side and blur around the edges. There was nothing to hold on to, nothing stable under her feet. Everything that existed in concrete terms was bound up in Fred.

'Viola, sit down.' There was an edge of alarm in Fred's voice.

5

'The countless times he's made you welcome here.' She began to pace in circles. 'Both he and Mum. What did they think was happening between us? How could they think we were not leading up to this? This... hope for a future together.' Her head was spinning and she clutched at it to steady the turmoil that made her want to be sick.

Fred grabbed her and held her against him. Viola could feel the shallowness of his breathing, the banging of his heart, the tick, tick, tick of his quick pulse. She put her arms under his jacket and his shirt was slick with sweat. 'I cannot tell you now.'

Viola pulled back and scoured the lines around his eyes, the trimmed beard, the streak of sunburn on his straight nose. 'I don't understand,' she said.

'After dinner,' he said. 'When there is more time I will tell all that was said.'

As if she'd been waiting, Mum appeared on the terrace. 'Dinner in twenty minutes,' she said. 'Just enough time to freshen up.'

Viola could not believe what she was hearing. Her eyes, she knew, pleaded with Fred for an explanation, but he placed a hand under her elbow and steered her towards the house. She could feel that every step he took was charged with bridled anger and she was frightened for him. And for herself.

As they stepped into the house, she looked back over her shoulder into the garden. What remained of her perfect day was nothing more than a spurious shambolic mess. Roses and hydrangeas bounced down towards the dry earth as they were bombarded by fat raindrops; apples lay rotting on the patchy, brown grass; a ruined book; an abandoned jug of sugary water; a muddy tennis ball under a fuchsia bush. If indeed the perfection she had perceived, or conjured up, had existed at all, she knew it had disappeared and would never be restored.

2

The powdery blue silk stared at her from its padded hanger at the front of the wardrobe. She and Lillian had taken hours to find it, traipsing up and down Oxford and Regent Streets arm in arm, weighing up the pros and cons of silk versus taffeta, short sleeves rather than three-quarters, a full or fitted skirt. Lilac or grey. Burgundy or blue.

It had been a lovely day. Viola thought back to meeting her friend at Paddington and how they'd thrown their arms around each other after they'd alighted from their respective trains, happy to be together again after five weeks apart.

'So,' Lillian said, 'the time has come, has it? Fred is going to ask your father for your hand. How quaint of him.'

Viola elbowed her friend. 'Don't tell me you wouldn't like a man to be as courtly and well-mannered on your behalf.'

Lillian put her hand on her heart and said, 'I would not like a man to be as courtly and well-mannered on my behalf.' She pursed her red lips and raised her dark, sculpted eyebrows. 'And neither did you until Fred came along and flexed his muscles at you.'

'I know.' Viola sighed. 'But the courtliness is something that goes with everything else about him and that everything else is just right for me. Perfect, in fact. And I don't think he in any way takes away from my independence. Or wanting to be independent as much as possible.' She peered at Lillian for her approval and understood that the gesture was none too independent either. 'Do you? Or are you telling me now that you aren't accepting of him?'

Lillian smiled widely, wrinkling her nose in the charismatic manner that won over everyone she met. 'Of course I do,' she said. 'You know that. He's a fine young man and I'm sure you'll be very happy together. Now, what's first: the shops or tea or a drink?'

They discovered the perfect dress in Selfridges. Lillian said the cornflower colour would contrast splendidly with Viola's dark green eyes and also be a good match for Fred's pair of icy blues. Viola was taller than average and the way the fabric draped accentuated her long slender arms and legs. 'I especially like the belt,' Viola said, studying herself in the full-length mirror. 'It gives me more of a waist.'

Lillian laughed. 'You'll be pleased with your slim figure when you get older. I'm going to look lumpy and bumpy like my mum when I get to her age.'

'Yes, but now when it matters you go in and out in all the right places. I look like one of my brothers. And what twenty-four-year-old woman wants to look like a thirteen-year-old boy?'

'Well, that's what you get for running around playing tennis with them all the time.'

The assistant drew back the curtain and looked Viola up and down and up again. Then she nodded. Behind her back Lillian crossed her eyes and did the same. Viola had to stifle a guffaw.

'You look stunning, my dear,' the assistant said. 'Is this for a special occasion?'

'My engagement.'

'Your fiancé is a very lucky man,' she said, the bun at the back of her head bobbing.

Lillian stuck her fingers in her mouth and feigned being sick.

'Don't you agree?' The assistant turned just as Lillian ceased her theatrics.

'Absolutely.' Lillian snapped to attention. 'They make a lovely couple.'

The dress would be wrapped and delivered to Cirencester. They spent the rest of their time browsing the jewellery counters in a number of stores, scrutinising shoes, stockings and undergarments. When they parted after dinner and a couple of drinks, with promises to write until they saw each other again when the new term started in Cambridge, Lillian leaned in close to Viola's ear and said, 'Although it really is a load of old tosh, I do think I could get used to a man being courtly and well-mannered on my behalf. At least I'd like to give it a go.'

Viola laughed out loud then kissed Lillian on her cheek. '*Auf Wiedersehen, meine Liebe*,' she recited her customary goodbye.

As she sprinted for her train, Lillian chanted her usual '*Au revoir, mon amour*,' over her shoulder.

Viola watched Lillian rush towards her platform, her sturdy legs in their seamed stockings moving in between wandering passengers with confidence. They blew one last kiss towards each other, waved with curled fingers and then Lillian was gone.

Now Viola balled the silk in her hands and threw it into the dark, dusty depths of her wardrobe. An immediate rush of guilt made her scramble for the creased garment and press it to her chest. She started to cry, not soft, feeling sorry for herself tears, but a hot, angry flood that she had to use all her willpower to subdue.

With the same self-control, she stopped her tears and stood, putting the dress back on its plush hanger. It was beautiful. Sniffing, she wiped her nose on the handkerchief she kept up her sleeve. She could feel the muscles of her face harden one by one. With resolve, she smoothed the fabric as best she could with her damp hands. She would need to wear it *when* her engagement went ahead. Her engagement to Fred.

Viola heard Mum's refined, measured footsteps making their way across the landing to the stairs, followed by the light scuffle of her brothers. 'Boys,' Mum scolded. 'How many times must I tell you? No playing on or near the stairs.'

'But he pushed me,' Robert said.

'Only because he shoved me first,' fired David.

'Neither of you should be pushing.' Viola could picture Dad hurrying to catch up, his hands going through the motions of knotting his tie. 'And don't give Mum your cheek.'

Their chattering faded and she recognised the sharp click of Fred's steps as he trailed behind the rest of her family, not wanting – she imagined – to put himself in the awkward position of having to make small talk with them. She listened as he slowed down near her door and knew that, if he knocked, she would not dare allow herself to answer only to be told again she would have to wait until after dinner for an explanation. Fred, too, must have understood the futility of their meeting at this stage as his footsteps resonated momentarily then became muffled before the landing was silent again.

Viola flicked through her wardrobe for an alternative ensemble, but nothing seemed appropriate. All the items she should wear were too dressy, too full of carelessness and fun; they all spoke of celebration or at least happy, optimistic times. She crossed her arms and determined that she would not be made to reflect what she most certainly did not feel. At the back of the rail, where they had been since the end of term, hung the two outfits she alternated for work: a knee-length, box-pleated tartan skirt and another of grey serge that she mixed and matched with either a cream or grey blouse topped with a bottle green or black cardigan.

They were drab and serviceable and looked like they meant business in the library where she dragged out books from long-forgotten shelves and put them back in place when students had finished their research. It was a standing joke between her and Fred that he could ever have found her attractive when he first saw her behind the desk and asked her to retrieve a manuscript about Medieval German literature for his doctorate paper. He liked to tease her that he had found it difficult to see beyond the high necklines, the buttons, the thick material, but his eyes and in time, his hands and mouth, told her a different story.

What were they to do now? Go back to those days when they did nothing else but flirt with each other? When they danced and skirted around their feelings? They had been lovely times and she would treasure the memories, but they were ready to move things forward and she couldn't imagine them living in limbo for long.

Viola sat on the edge of the bed to pull on badly mended stockings. They were, she decided when she looked closer, the very pair she'd been wearing when Fred proposed. But they weren't in such a state then. They'd been brand new and had felt silky and lustrous next to her skin. 'I'm going to take you somewhere very special for your birthday,' Fred had said. 'I've booked a table for half seven this Friday.'

She knew he didn't have a lot of money, so wanted to show how much she appreciated the gesture by looking as pleasing as she could and the stockings, along with an evening bag and new lipstick, had been her purchases for the evening.

She remembered how handsome Fred looked when he'd turned up in his college tie, his shoes gleaming – she'd felt so proud on his arm. The Bull Hotel was beautiful; the food and wine excellent; the pianist unobtrusive. But she smiled when she thought of how disappointed she'd felt when it seemed as if the Fred she knew had been left behind in his rooms and in his place was a stammering, fidgety, uncomfortable Fred. 'Are you quite alright?' she'd asked several times.

In reply he'd either said, 'Yes, of course,' much too quickly or somehow nodded and shook his head at the same time.

Before dessert was served, Viola had excused herself and when she returned Fred looked so serious and distracted that she'd feared she was going to be cast aside. Fred had reached for her hand and said, 'Vi.'

'Yes, Fred?' she'd said, bracing herself for the worst.

'There is only one thing that could make me happier than I am at this moment in time. And that is if you will agree to be my wife.'

For a moment she had been so stunned that she couldn't speak.

'Vi?' Fred had said again. 'If you need some time…'

'No,' she'd blurted out. 'I mean yes. I mean no to the time to think. And yes to be your wife.' And she'd burst out laughing, all tension magically lifted.

Laughter was the farthest thing from her mind now as she chose the grey skirt, the grey blouse, the black cardigan, the flat, black lace-ups. She used two combs to scrape back her hair, lank from the rain and wind, behind her ears. There would be no jewellery tonight, she thought, but pulled the cardigan together with a dull chain.

Through the dining room door, Viola could hear muted discussion but couldn't make out the gist of the conversation beyond a few scattered words that filtered past the wood and fittings: Germany, the situation, German, the papers, the news, Parliament. She watched herself place her palm on the door handle, but somehow, she could not bring herself to apply pressure and enter the room. There was what seemed to be an inept and artless silence, then one of the boys, probably Robert, said something and the others laughed in an overblown, unnatural way. At that exact minute in time, frozen in inertia, she felt isolated. As if she didn't know any of the people beyond the door and perhaps never had.

'Ah, Miss Viola.' Abigail walked towards her, a steaming

bowl of something in her hands. 'You're here. Shall I serve or wait for Mrs Baxter's say-so?'

Still her hand felt immovable. 'Please wait for Mum,' Viola said, wary that her thin, tremulous voice might give her away.

'Of course.' Abigail looked at her more closely. 'Are you quite well, Miss? The heat is oppressive. Perhaps you would like me to call your mother. Or young Mr Scholz?'

Viola shook her head and pressed down with determination on the handle. 'No, thank you, Abigail. I'm fine.' She smiled to prove the validity of what she'd said and Abigail carried on to the kitchen from where she could enter the dining room behind Mum's place at the table.

'A-ha.' Dad rose from his chair as did Fred, who within three strides was by her side offering his arm to support her. 'Boys.' Dad looked at Robert and David over the top of his spectacles as they clamoured about and rose to their feet.

'We thought perhaps you'd changed your mind about dinner.' Dad turned his head and coughed into his hand to cover, Viola thought, his embarrassment at the lack of courtesy she displayed in her careless manner of dress. Fred led her to her chair, next to his, his hand rigid on her forearm again, as if he was trying to contain the vast dimensions of the anger they both felt within his grip. Well, it would take more than that gesture to quash the exasperation that was swelling inside her by the minute. She knew it had nowhere to go other than out into the open. She waited for Dad to comment on her appearance, but in what was an uncharacteristic act of defiance towards his own strict code of etiquette he turned to his wife and said, 'Edith, shall we start?'

Fred eased her into her chair whilst Mum looked on. For a beat or two her mother's eyes were round with incredulity and alarm. 'Edith.' Dad peered into his wife's face. 'Will you call on Abigail?'

Mum peeled her eyes from Viola and said, 'Yes. Yes, of course.' She picked up a tiny brass bell from the sideboard behind her and holding it between a trembling thumb and index finger, tinkled it twice with habitual delicacy.

Abigail glided in with the lightest of footsteps and the occasional swish of white apron fabric. Backwards and forwards she marched with bowls and platters of food that Viola, in her distraction, could not name and could not imagine tasting. 'Thank you, Abigail,' Mum said when the young woman went to dish up onto the plates. 'We'll help ourselves. And please thank Cook. It all looks lovely.'

Mum proceeded to pass the carrots, cabbage, peas and steaming new potatoes to her right and Dad held the serving plate piled with lamb for Fred who helped Viola and then himself. Viola looked down at what was usually her favourite meal and her stomach turned. The slices of meat that were not drowning in a bed of greasy, gelatinous gravy were turned up and greying at the edges. Running through the slabs of meat were strings of white fat that reminded her of the thin spittle that drooled from Pitch's mouth.

Viola looked from her plate to Fred and wondered what Mum's reaction would be if she emptied the contents of her stomach all over it. 'Here,' Fred said softly. 'Allow me.' He pushed back his chair and walked around the table to hand the platter to Robert.

Except the occasional 'thank you', 'yes please' or 'it smells lovely', no one spoke until each dish and accompaniment had been around the table and placed to rest on the sideboard.

'I do hope no one minds not having soup?' Mum asked, looking at each person around the table in turn. 'I thought it wise to abandon the idea on such a humid day. Robert,' she addressed her older son, who was always hungry. 'Do you mind awfully?'

His mouth full, Robert shook his head. As he swallowed, the protruding Adam's apple that had lately made an appearance bobbed up and down. 'No, I don't mind, Mum,' he said. 'As long as there's seconds and a good lot of pudding.'

Mum and Dad laughed. 'I'm sure you'll have plenty,' Dad said. 'And if not, you'll have to raid the orchard before bed. But I don't think it will come to that as Viola doesn't appear to be the least bit enthusiastic about her dinner, so you could always have hers. Come now, Viola, you must eat.'

The wide-eyed look Mum gave Dad implored him to desist. Fred nudged Viola with his foot. The curtains blew out then bulged in through the half-open French doors. The clock in the hall chimed eight and Abigail entered to turn on the sidelights. Rain drummed against the windows.

But Viola had had enough. 'Must I, Dad?'

The boys stopped eating and stared at their sister and parents in turn.

'Yes, my dear.' Dad's voice was gentle and kind, not at all what Viola had been expecting and the sudden change made tears throb behind her eyes. 'You must. I insist.'

She picked up her cutlery and cut a small potato in half, speared it to a slice of cabbage and dangled it in mint sauce and gravy. 'Why must I?'

Dad sighed. 'Because, my dear. Because…'

'Because if you don't, you won't grow big and strong,' David said. 'Like Dad. Or Fred.'

Viola managed to smile at her little brother, who hated bad feeling and would do anything to please; she was sure he had been a Labrador in another life or would be in the next. He smiled back, revealing teeth still too large for his mouth, his dark, silky hair streaked red from the sun skimming his forehead. Then he reattacked his meal with gusto as if he had put all that was wrong in the world right.

'But I am grown as much as I will ever be, David,' Viola said, the food on her fork growing cold. 'In fact,' she addressed Dad. 'I am a grown woman and therefore have a right to—'

'Oh, can't we eat in peace?' Mum pleaded. 'We never argue at the table. It plays havoc with the digestion.'

'We never argue full stop,' said Robert. 'So why—'

'Enough,' said Dad, throwing his serviette next to his plate. 'You must eat to keep up your strength. As must we all.'

Mum reached for her wine glass; Robert shovelled in the last of what was on his plate.

'Another war will soon be upon us. It is imminent.'

Viola cried out, 'But what has that to do with me and Fred and our engagement?'

'Everything,' Dad said, pushing his plate away and leaning back in his chair. 'I'm afraid that it has everything to do with it. Besides the fact that he is German…'

'Mr Baxter,' Fred blurted out, unable – Viola thought – to hold his peace any longer. 'I must protest. We have been over this many times. I am a British citizen.'

'Yes, Fred and also a German citizen. And—' Dad turned to Viola '—a German citizen who is going to Germany tomorrow when the situation is so highly unstable.'

'Yes, I know that.' Viola could hear the growing frustration in her voice.

'But I don't think you know that he is going against the advice of the British government who have announced that they cannot, after today, guarantee safe passage back to England from Germany.'

All Viola could manage was a feeble and tremulous, 'Fred? After that news, surely you must reconsider.'

'Viola.' Fred raised his hands towards the heavens in a gesture of helplessness. 'You know the dilemma with my sister.'

Dad interlaced his fingers and turned to Fred. 'One thing we haven't addressed, Frederick, is why Annaliese is in Germany at all. Given the volatile crisis between our two countries.'

Fred's discomfort was plain for all to see in the dark purple colour on the tips of his ears. He stammered and slipped over his words. 'I have explained. She is caring for our dear grandmother.'

'But there are other family members you have mentioned?' Dad said. 'Aunts, uncles, cousins. Surely…?'

Fred sighed. 'We received word that Oma was on her deathbed and Annie insisted on travelling to Ulm for her final moments. She very much loves our Oma.' His voice caught. 'We all do, but they have a special bond and Annie was desperate to be at her bedside. I advised her not to go, but I did not forbid it as that is not my way, although in hindsight I wish I had. And nor is it hers to do as she's told, I'm afraid. My sister is an extremely strong-willed and tenacious young woman.' He looked around the table, then chuckled without humour. 'Not unlike Oma who happily pulled through, although I have been made aware that she is fast approaching the end of her time.'

Fred lifted his cutlery, scrutinised his plate and replaced his knife and fork without eating anything. Under the table, Viola found his sturdy hand and intertwined her fingers with his, seeking the callus that had formed from holding his pen against his middle finger. He made to wipe his sweating palms on his trousers, but she held fast, refusing to allow him to feel embarrassed.

How hard this must be for him, Viola thought. After she had started to mention Fred in her letters home, Mum had written back that she and Dad wanted to meet him, but every time Viola tried to broach the subject with Fred, a shyness that she wasn't accustomed to experiencing overcame her. He hadn't declared himself at that stage, although she thought that was merely a lack of putting words to emotions so she tussled with herself about whether he would think she was presumptuous about his feelings. But during a picnic next to the river in Grantchester, she managed to invite him home and he was delighted. His eyes lit up and his smile was broad. 'I would be honoured,' he said. 'When will this happen? Easter Break or a weekend before then?'

Viola had laughed more from relief than anything. She curled her toes underneath her and said, 'You're very eager.'

'I want to know everything about you.' He sprawled out with one hand supporting his head and traced the outline of her jaw with a blade of grass.

She toyed with the ends of his brindle-coloured hair. 'Well, if you're game, I suppose there's no reason not to go this weekend.'

He smiled and kissed the end of her nose. 'I'm definitely game,' he said. Then his face pulled downwards and he sat up, hugging his knees with his arms.

Viola shivered, wondering if this was when he told her something she didn't want to hear. 'What is it, Fred?' she asked, reaching to stroke his back.

He turned away from her and gave his full attention to the river, moving in lazy swirls and eddies towards The Orchard. 'I cannot return the invitation, Vi, as you know.'

She did know, as he had no parents, no family home, just a younger sister named Annaliese at boarding school and an elderly, eccentric aunt who he had not deemed capable of looking after Annie. Fred could have made the decision for both of them to live in Germany, but he was passionate about England being their home and the country where they would stay. Viola pulled him back to her, cradling his head in her lap, and dared to hope that one day she could provide him with the family ballast he lacked. And Annie would be part of that, too.

Now he was being asked to talk about his Oma, whose impending death must feel, to him, like another empty hole in the already pitted landscape of what used to be his close family. Viola squeezed his hand again and felt pressure back from him.

Fred cleared his throat, shuffled in his chair and continued. 'So, some would argue that I should not have let Annie go, but I did and now I must bring her home. It is my duty and responsibility and I...' He faltered again and

Viola could tell he was playing for time to steady himself. 'I cannot lose her, too.'

The boys had stopped eating and were still, probably not wanting to bring attention to themselves and the fact that they were privy to an adult conversation. Mum was florid, her chest rising and falling with each agitated breath. As for Dad, he was leaning forward and taking in every word Fred uttered.

'Thank you, Fred, for clearing the air about that situation,' Dad said, then carried on without pause. 'But I am afraid my answer is still no. And whether you both choose to believe me or not, the decision has been made with responsibility and care. And love.'

Viola had to bite down hard on her lip to stop tears forming; iron flooded her mouth and she wiped the blood away with her tongue.

No one else said a word and Viola became aware of each person's oppressed breathing. The air was thick with the smell of lamb fat and cold potatoes in butter. Abigail stepped into the room and began to say something about dessert, but Mum waved her away.

'Well, if Fred really is going away,' Robert broke the silence, 'a jolly last meal this has been.'

With affinity, the wind seemed to be escalating in fury and cruelty. A gust caused the French door to bang outwards and then rebound with a crash. From somewhere deep in the house, Pitch howled and barked then howled again. Mum caught her breath and, drumming her hand on her chest, rushed to secure the lock. 'Robert, David,' she said. 'You can take your dessert in the kitchen with Abigail and Cook.'

The boys seemed grateful to leave the dining room and the adults behind. When they reached the door, David turned and said, 'Vi, does this mean our game of tennis at the Club tomorrow will have to be cancelled?'

Viola hated to disappoint him, but she couldn't lie. She had to tell him the truth. 'I have absolutely no idea.' Her stringy hair slapped her cheeks as she shook her head from side to side. 'No idea at all what is going on either today or tomorrow or the next.'

Silence hung over the room like an old, fusty curtain. An image flashed through Viola's mind of her trying to fight her way out of it, whilst it wound and wrapped itself ever more tightly around her, trapping her arms, her legs, covering her nose and mouth, clogging her lungs. She looked up from the table and noticed, for what seemed to be the first time, the powdery lint that swirled towards the ceiling in chaos and then drifted back down to settle on the sideboard, the carpets, in the chinks and clefts of silly ornaments and fussy serving spoons.

Viola thought the suffocating taciturnity said more than any amount of noise. Yet she knew that one of them would have to cave in, say something to get the argument going again, as that is what would surely follow.

She could hear a hammering in her ears and was aware of the blood moving fast through the overloaded rhythms of her heart. The residue of cold, clammy sweat under her arms began to slip and slide as it turned hot and sticky again. *Say something*, she willed her father, who sat with one arm over the back of his chair, his tie loosened at the neck; a man who thought he had said all he needed to say. Mum had lost what was left of her composure and was checking her earrings, bracelets, necklace with busy fingers as if finding her jewellery in place would give her a sense of comfort and security.

Speak; one of you speak. Her lips twitched; she rubbed her tongue raw against the back of her teeth. Next to her, Fred sounded as if he was breathing through an underground grate. The wind shifted direction and rain hurtled against the glass, puddling around the French doors. For a moment, they were all mesmerised as a thin stream meandered towards the middle of the room, yet none of them made an attempt to stop the flow.

Look at us, Viola thought, a sense of disgust akin to nausea overwhelming her. *Look how foolish we are. Standing on ceremony. Waiting to see who will go first and what they will say. Not wanting to offend when we are already deeply offended. Lacking the courage or wherewithal to give a voice to our thoughts; our feelings; our fears; our betrayal and bewilderment.*

Leaning across the table, Viola grabbed the water jug and filled her glass. She drank in slow, steadying gulps then put the glass down with care. 'Well,' she was able to say in a controlled voice, 'I suppose I will have to start, as no one else appears to want to step up. So, needs must and all that.'

'Viola,' Dad said. 'I ask you to listen to me.'

After a moment, Viola turned to him, but made no response.

'Very well,' Dad continued. 'I will begin by repeating what I stated earlier. We are on the cusp of another war. It is looming and inevitable.'

'But—'

'Sssh.' Dad's command was sharp. 'I cannot allow you to become engaged to a man who is a citizen of Germany and that is that.'

Viola was distressed to see Fred hang his head, as though ashamed. and she placed her hand on his.

'Not because I don't think the world of him. We do approve. Don't we, Edith?'

Mum nodded in agreement.

'But because…' His grey eyes narrowed and became hard and obdurate. 'Your life will be a misery if we allow an engagement to go ahead.'

Viola sucked in her breath.

'Arthur, really,' Mum said. 'I think you're being a bit…'

A hiss again from Dad. 'That is not a harsh statement, it is a matter of fact. I'm sorry for it, Fred, but my daughter must be my first consideration.'

Fred did not raise his eyes from his lap.

'You would be vilified and called names. Traitor, renegade, turncoat. And worse. Believe me. And it pains me to say this, but I must. People will accuse Fred of absconding in order to avoid his responsibility as a young British man. He will be denounced as a deserter. We would be subject to white feathers through our door.'

At this, Viola, Mum and Fred all drew a gulping breath. Viola and Fred both rose to their feet, their palms planted on the table; Mum sunk lower in her chair.

'Sir, I must protest,' Fred shouted. 'I would give anything to stay here and fulfil my duty.'

'Dad, you must rescind that statement. How can you even think it?' Viola shouted.

Dad raised his flat hand to each of them in turn. 'I don't,' he said. 'But others will. And I will not subject my beloved daughter to that kind of abuse.'

'I don't care,' Viola said. 'I only care about being married to Fred.'

'I care,' said Dad. 'And your mother cares.'

'So do I,' Fred added, his voice a harsh whisper.

The rain had let up to a steady drum on the terrace. Apart from the occasional barb of lightning, the sky was dark. Mum picked up a serviette and flapped it in front of her face. They sat in silence.

If this was a play, Viola thought, the musty, velvet curtain would close now and everyone in the audience would feel terribly sorry for all of them.

It became clear that none of them had anything else to say. There was a bit of shuffling and coughing and then Viola asked her parents if they would give her and Fred some time on their own. They did not hesitate and Viola could sense relief in their brisk movements toward the door.

'Use my study,' Dad said. 'And the port. Please.'

Fred stood and said, 'May I say goodbye to both of you now?'

'Why, yes.' For a moment Mum looked confused. 'Won't we see you for breakfast?'

'Sadly, no,' Fred answered. 'I must be on my way very early.'

The leave-taking was fumbling and clumsy. Hands and arms and cheeks that had met and fit comfortably together on numerous occasions now looked awkward and unfamiliar.

As soon as the door closed behind them, Fred turned

to Viola and put his arms around her. 'The study,' he said, taking her hand and leading the way.

Viola shook her head. 'We have a few hours left. Quietly,' she said, a finger on her lips. And they crept up the stairs to her bedroom and locked the door behind them.

The many times Viola had daydreamed about sharing a bed with Fred, she'd imagined herself waking and reaching for him in one fluid movement before she allowed the moment to pass. But whether because his presence the previous night had been unexpected or because his being next to her was not a habit ingrained in her psyche, as she hoped it would be in time, her first action of the day was to sit on the edge of her bed and lift a corner of the curtain to establish the weather.

Cooler this morning and fresher after the storms of yesterday evening. Movement around the tennis court should be easier and she smiled when she thought David was in for a good thrashing. Then: Fred. She turned and reached for the outline of him on the sheets, but the cotton was already cold.

Then a violent surge of dread started in her stomach and spread, like stabs of electricity, to her limbs. What was she doing sitting here wasting time? They had murmured promises and shed tears before they fell asleep last night, but if she was quick... She fumbled for the skirt and blouse, cardigan and undergarments she'd discarded under the bedclothes and on the floor. Feeling under her pillow for a misplaced stocking, her fingers touched something small and round. When she drew it out, she was holding a dainty ring with one tiny diamond inlaid flush with the gold. She'd seen it before. Fred had shown it to her and explained that it was his mother's engagement ring, but Viola had presumed it was for Annie in time. With trembling hands, she tried to push it onto her ring finger, but it wouldn't go past her knuckle.

The rush of adrenaline was ebbing, but she was left with wobbly limbs that made piling on her things difficult. Clutching the ring in her fist didn't help. The hooks refused to find the eyes on her brassiere, her vest went on and stayed on back to front, she missed a button on her blouse and fumbled to rectify the mistake but gave up, stockings would have to wait.

Flinging open her bedroom door, she hurtled herself down the landing to the top of the stairs, where she watched her feet descend two at a time. Mum was passing through the hall and caught her by the shoulders. 'Take a deep breath, my dear,' she said softly.

When Viola looked up Mum shook her head and pulled her daughter's head onto her shoulder. There she stroked her hair and Viola could hear the sort of soothing noises her mother had used to pacify her when she was a child; how very many years ago that seemed now. Prising themselves apart to wipe their noses, Mum unfurled each of Viola's fingers to reveal the ring, twinkling on her palm.

'It's beautiful, Vi. But you know you can't wear it yet, don't you?'

Viola nodded, her eyes fixed on the unbroken circle that encompassed so much promise. 'And even if I could, it doesn't fit.' She demonstrated by trying the ring on her finger again.

Mum took Viola's hand and led her upstairs to where she found a delicate linked chain amongst her jewellery and threaded the ring onto it with care. Then she clasped it around Viola's neck and burrowed it under her vest.

3

3 September 1939

Perhaps it would have been better to do as Dad had tried to insist and stayed at home to hear the inevitable declaration of war when it was transmitted over the wireless. But Viola had been more adamant, arguing that if the announcement was imminent and certain, then they were already informed and she would be better off heading back to Cambridge to prepare for the new term. So she sat in a threadbare, overstuffed armchair opposite Lillian, each of them with a gin in one hand and a cigarette in the other, silently listening to the news.

Viola tipped her glass towards the ceiling and said, 'Cheers,' in a flat tone.

Lillian drained her drink and reached for the bottle on the low table between them. She filled her glass and the one Viola held out to her.

'No ice? No slice?'

'Neat or nothing,' Lillian said.

'Shall we turn him off?' Viola nodded towards the radio.

'Now then, Miss Baxter, enough of your cheek. Don't be disrespectful to old man Chamberpot.'

Viola flicked her snake of ash into a saucer and turned the dial on the wireless until it clicked, putting a stop to Prime Minister Chamberlain's voice. The room was hushed and empty although the last words they'd heard him speak hung in the air with ever-diminishing reverberations. 'Now may God bless you all.' His voice had been grave. 'May He defend the right. It is the evil things that we shall be fighting against – brute force, bad faith, injustice, oppression...'

Viola breathed deep into her lungs and felt the cold in her nostrils; she shivered and wrapped her cardigan around her chest. 'Shall we light a fire, Lil? What do you think?'

Lillian looked startled, as if she'd never before laid eyes on Viola or the minuscule flat they shared. 'It's a bit early for that, isn't it?' she said at last. 'Third of September? Besides, it's really quite warm.' She walked to the window and pushed aside the net curtain. 'But pouring horribly. Warm rain, the most annoying and irritating of all weather systems.'

Viola threw back her head and laughed out loud. 'You sound like a report from the Met Office,' she said.

Turning, Lillian smiled. 'It's so nice to hear you laugh,' she said. She tossed her own cardigan towards Viola and said, 'It's probably the shock, but this should help. Pop it on.'

Viola did as she was told and layered up with Lillian's brown, many times darned, buttonless woolly. She brought a handful of the material to her face and sniffed Vol de Nuit, tobacco and Pears: the comforting blend that belonged to her friend. She paced around the room from the window to the fireplace, the door to the narrow hallway that led to the bedrooms; opening the concertinaed door to the cupboard that served as both larder and kitchen, she perused their provisions, but couldn't remember, when she turned her back, what she had seen. 'These flowers have had their day,' she said, pointing to a vase balanced on top of a pile of books. 'Who were they from? Remind me.'

With a wave of her hand, Lillian dismissed the question. Her light grey eyes, dark hair against fair skin and that way she had of puckering her nose meant she was used to attracting so much attention from men that she could afford to forget the names and faces of her suitors. Viola, too, had engendered her fair share of male interest and like Lillian she'd played around with courtship rituals until Fred had come along. She stared down at the wilting bouquet of red roses, tied with a blue ribbon, and felt a stab of loneliness.

Once, Fred had arrived at the library with an arrangement large enough for him to hide behind. When she came close, he'd bobbed around the pink and white blooms and said, 'Boo from the bouquet.' She had laughed until her stomach ached and whenever she thought about it she smiled, although no one else she told seemed to think it was amusing in the slightest. Now there wouldn't be any more flowers or shared jokes or surprise visits for what might be a very long time. The lump in her throat seemed to increase in size until it threatened to choke her and she turned away from the vase and reached again for the gin.

'Let's have a cup of tea instead,' Lillian said. 'My shout.'

'All the cups are dirty.' Viola attacked her drink. 'And there's dust all over the books and we can't get to the rug to sweep it.'

'I know,' Lillian said. 'And there's mildew around the windows.'

'And in the bathroom. Is it our turn to clean it?'

'Probably, but stuff and nonsense to housework.'

Jumping up again, Viola said, 'I think perhaps I'll go for a walk. Clear the cobwebs.'

'Oh, Vi.' Lillian's voice had a pleading edge to it. 'Are you sure? I'll come with you.'

But Viola needed to be alone. She felt a crushing urge to get out of the claustrophobic flat and stride across the parks and commons and think – or not think, if she could possibly help it. 'No.' She shook her head until she could feel the chain that secured Fred's ring trembling against her neck. 'I shall be just fine, thank you.'

'Well, take your coat at least. You have been shivering after all.' Lillian followed Viola to the hallway and watched as she put on her outdoor things. 'Shall I meet you at The Eagle? In say, thirty minutes' time?' Lillian checked her watch.

Viola hesitated, then thought the atmosphere in the pub might be cheering. Everyone in the same boat and all that. 'Can we make it an hour?' She managed a much too thin smile, which she knew would probably worry her friend rather than bring her the reassurance she had been aiming for. She was sorry for it, but that was the best she could manage.

Lillian had been right; the day was unseasonably warm, but the rain fell in droves. Viola made no attempt to shield herself from the relentless downpour, shaking her head and letting fat drops cover her eyelashes, cheeks and shoulders with muffled plops.

She strode across Lammas Land with purpose. Rain clung like a shroud over the river, but she could make out the form of a punt gliding across the Cam, the punter bending and straightening in rhythm to the projection of his pole in and out of the water. Cadences of laughter rose and fell from what sounded like two young women who were probably languishing in the body of the punt and being answered by a male voice, which only served to incite the girls to giggles again. She wondered if they were aware of the news that had been announced or if they were making an almighty effort to rise above it. Either way she could not stand their joviality that sounded forced and contrived to her ears.

Waiting for a chance to cross Fen Causeway, she stamped with conviction into a filthy puddle and dirty brown water soaked her stockings and brogues. She studied her lower legs for a minute and the muddy blotches she saw gave her a sense of satisfaction. 'Hit,' she mumbled, stomping down again. 'Ler.' This time she aimed her heel with vengence at the dead centre of the quagmire and shouted. 'Bloody—' her foot hit the puddle '—Hitler.' She pounded again and again until the mucky pool was no more than a thin veil of scum and still she carried on, the sole of her shoe scraping across the asphalt.

The screech of a bike reached its maximum pitch in front of her and came to a stop. 'Viola, what on earth…?'

Viola looked straight at a young woman, her face framed with a tartan headscarf tied under her chin. At the same moment they both looked down to take in Viola's stockings and the hem of her mackintosh, now caked in thick, sludgy slime.

'Oh dear, Amanda,' Viola said. 'What a dreadful sight I am.' When she peered at her friend's worried face, it was through a film of tears that had collected more in anger than in sadness. She pushed a sopping strand of hair behind her ear.

Amanda hesitated then replied, 'Don't be silly. We're all the same in this deluge. Where are you off to?'

Viola shook her head and shrugged.

'Well, come along with me,' Amanda said, flinging her leg off her bike. 'I'm on my way to the office to sort out some files. We'll have a nice cuppa there and get dry.' She scooped Viola's elbow into her palm with a bit too much force for Viola's liking. 'What do you say?'

Viola shook off Amanda's stranglehold and made to cross the road without looking either way. Another bike swerved to miss her, the rider calling out a piercing, 'Oi!' and two pedestrians tutted loudly from under their umbrellas. She jumped the puddles slopping around the kerb on the opposite side and made towards Coe Fen and the Cam. 'Viola,' she heard Amanda shout. 'Wait a minute. Let me...'

But Viola didn't hear the end of Amanda's plea as she found her way through the overgrown cow parsley to the footpath. She batted her way through damp grasses and around squelchy cow pats until her way was blocked by the river. She stopped, hands on her hips. From here, the swish of traffic was muffled and she was aware of her own blood drubbing in her temples, wrists and against the sinews in her neck. Breathing in time to the rhythm of the arterial beat, she felt the anguish pass, followed swiftly by embarrassment and guilt. She looked around to see if Amanda had followed her, but all she saw was a small herd of cud-chewing kine, observing her with non-judgemental curiosity, a couple in the distance walking arm in arm, the pinprick of a few bicycles close to Silver Street Bridge and an elderly professor-type muttering to himself.

She sighed and reached for the tip of a reed, thinking it would break under the pressure, but it bent until it pinged back and spattered drops of rain over her face. Closing her eyes against the shower, the tears that welled up again turned, unnervingly, to laughter and oh well, she thought, what are a few more splotches of mud?

Hugging the river, she made her way towards the bridge. Fighting the urge to stamp in more puddles, she walked around them instead with studied decorum and headed towards the Backs. The view of King's College Chapel, always sombre and imposing, was now bleak with the effects of the weather and, she supposed, the grim news. War. The country was at war. Pins and needles attacked her arms and legs and her breathing accelerated. She hesitated for a minute as the realisation hit hard. When, she wondered, would it become commonplace to refer to the state of the Empire as: at War. Part of her wished she could be that matter-of-fact soon – now. But another part was appalled to think that she would ever consider war as routine or anything other than a heinous aberration.

The rain was slowing and a minute break in the clouds flashed momentary light across a few of the stained-glass windows. It made her sad to think their beauty would soon be boarded up or removed from eyes that needed nothing more at this period of time than a glimpse of the splendour and elegance humans could create.

The lawn leading down from the grounds to the river was lush and thick and verdant. A secretary at the department told her that she had gone to the May Ball at King's a couple of years ago and run through that grass in bare feet, down to a waiting punt to be whisked away for breakfast in Grantchester. Viola could picture the joy on the girl's face as the blades of grass tickled her feet.

Two years previously, Fred had been asked to chaperone at Emmanuel's May Ball and she had gone along for a few hours as his sidekick; they'd made time for two or three dances across the polished floor of the ballroom. So many different bands played myriad types of music from waltzes to foxtrots to jazz. Buffet tables were laid out with salads, cold cuts of meat, breads, cheeses, pyramids of fruit, meringues rich with cream. And the flowers. If she breathed deep into her lungs and closed her eyes, she could smell the lilies, the roses and lilac; it had been intoxicating. All the girls were lovely in their ball gowns, and the men handsome in their dinner jackets. It had been delightful. If she'd known then that a war would stop them all in their tracks, she would have held Fred closer as they danced, savoured the mountains of food and stayed until the bitter end. Now she doubted there would be any semblance of a May Ball any time soon. And if there was, she would never attend without Fred.

Viola looked behind her and there was a bench not too far away – soaking she presumed. But her face was damp, her light brown hair darkened with dripping rain and her legs and feet drenched and bedraggled. So what were the odds?

She smoothed the back of her mac and sat on the wet bench, shivering when the cold hit her flesh through her thin dress and undergarments. The streak of sunshine had passed and the façade of King's was grey and stately and shadowed again. There weren't many people about although a few young men hurried, heads down, backwards and forwards to the university library, books and notepads under their arms; next month when Michaelmas Term began the crossing would be packed – the students jostling, laughing and shouting out to each other.

Then she wondered if that would be the case or if by October the students would have left this self-indulgent place to selflessly do their bit. She imagined that the transition would hit them hard. When she looked at the crossing she could see their ghostly images moving in obscurity, their limbs and torsos transparent and unearthly. There was Fred and hurrying behind him a taller, broader Robert. Then there was David in brown corduroy trousers, a smile on his face, books in one hand, a tennis racquet swinging from the other. She wanted to reach out to them but knew that if she did, her hand would slip through a gauzy haze. Another shudder ran through her when she remembered the generation lost during the Great War. But the thought came and went and she dreaded to think that complacency was becoming her standpoint so soon.

Her handkerchief was quite sodden when she fished it from the depths of her pocket, but she found a corner and wiped it with harsh, rather unkind sweeps over her face. She fidgeted around for the shape of the ring under her clothes, but was glad she hadn't grabbed the letters from Fred that she'd read numerous times and usually kept about her person; they would be as saturated as the hanky and that would have caused her spirits to plummet, if they could drop any further. Three had arrived from him since he'd crept from her bedroom last July and made his way to Germany to try and bring Annie home. The first two had been six or seven pages long and full of hope about him and his sister setting foot on British soil again very soon, despite politics and bureaucracy and combative officials tightening their grip around them and doing their best to cut them off irretrievably.

The last letter, which had arrived a week ago, consisted of one paltry, dog-eared, censored page and in it Fred made no bones about the fact that there was now no way or means for them to return. He was blunt and in a sentence that finished abruptly, said there was no point in deceiving themselves that a passage would be clear for them to cross the Channel. Then nothing more than a blank space where words had been cut raggedly from the paper. She supposed, hoped, that he'd stated he would not stop trying, no matter the circumstances, to find his way back to her.

Annie had written once, or at least one letter had arrived from her; many more might have been sent but become victims to interdiction. In it, she wrote about late summer in Ulm and Munich, how lovely it was to have Fred around despite the fact he seemed distracted and rather frantic for much of the time, their Oma's declining health, salad from the garden and pork schnitzel for dinner, the doctor's son who seemed to be naïvely courting her and so on and so forth. So vivid were Annie's descriptions, that Viola felt as if she were there with her sister-in-law-to-be. She smelled the sap and vegetation of the forest as they walked through it together, looking for a knoll on which to spread out their picnic of bread, cheese, tomatoes and thin, leftover slices of beef. They lay on soft dandelions and read, shielding their eyes from the glare of the sun.

She imagined Saturday mornings, choosing a hen for Sunday's dinner from the flocks flapping around the outdoor market in the shade of the Minster then meeting Fred in a café for coffee and a slice of Bundt cake. An afternoon holding Oma's hand, offering her tea or soup from a spoon, talking to her about anything that came into her head. Could Annie's reality be so idyllic? Hers wasn't and she didn't know anyone in England who could claim that it was for them either. Like the girls on the punt, Viola thought Annie was either oblivious to what was happening or was blocking out the truth of the situation. She had read the letter over and over again, wondering if there was a cryptic message in amongst the sentences that spoke of an indolent Indian summer; but she could not decipher any such thing.

The rain had settled into a constant, fine drizzle and was soaking through her mac and dress. She pushed back her sleeve and looked at the dainty gold watch on a jewellery bracelet Mum and Dad had given her for her twenty-first birthday and was surprised to see she'd been almost an hour and a half. Holding the watch to her ear, she could hear it ticking faithfully, so knew the time was correct. Great St Mary's should have alerted her to when her hour was up and it was time to head to The Eagle; the reliable church bell could be heard all over the city. Then she remembered and anger bubbled up again. St Mary's was silenced for the duration, as was every other public bell and chime in the country, including Big Ben. How dare he? Bloody Hitler.

*

The Eagle was heaving. Academic types of all ages spilled from the door onto the pavement, from the side entrance onto the flagstones of the sheltered courtyard with its lush bountiful summer flower baskets hanging like the Gardens of Babylon. Viola excused herself through the assembled crowds of people talking in earnest close to each other's faces. She caught the occasional word, all of them connected in some way to the war: Chamberlain, Germany, Hitler, troops, bombs, strategy, Parliament, announcement. Intermittent laughter volleyed from the shadows of one or two cubbyholes, but for the most part the atmosphere was sedate and fervid. No one gave her a second glance or seemed to notice the mess she was in, everyone looking as if they had rushed to be together in a familiar setting without a care for their hair or clothes or makeup. She heard snatches of conversation. 'Thank heaven the suspense is over,' from a man with dark green patches on the elbows of his worn brown jacket. Momentarily wedged between a group of women on one side and a group of men on the other, an older woman in wire spectacles said, 'At least now there will be a clear-cut contest.'

'Yes,' one of her drinking companions said. 'And however distant victory may be, we must be intent upon that end.'

Peering between arms and over shoulders, she tried to glimpse Lillian who, she knew, would be fretting about her tardiness. Finally, Viola spotted her friend, her back to the fireplace in the dark, low-ceilinged bar; Lillian raised her hand in exasperation. Viola didn't recognise any of the others gathered there, so presumed they were acquaintances.

Viola watched as Lillian extracted herself from the group who immediately closed ranks around the gap she left to carry on their discussion without missing a beat.

'Where have you been?' Lillian grabbed Viola's arm. 'I have been so worried. I was about to go out and look for you.'

'I'm sorry, Lil,' Viola said. 'I was depending on St Mary's for the time, but forgot the bell had been silenced. Sorry.'

'Well.' Lillian looked a bit put out, although her voice was forgiving. 'I'm glad that's all it was.'

'What else could have possibly happened?' Viola's laugh sounded dispirited. 'No bombs have fallen yet, have they?'

'Don't make fun,' Lillian said. 'It's not a laughing matter.'

'No, you're right. It's not.'

'But this is.' She glanced at a group of young men and said, 'Do you think we can get them to buy us a drink?'

That had been one of their favourite sports when they were out together, no dates in tow. But that had been before Fred and the thought of batting her eyelashes at a strange man in return for a gin or lager tops or whisky and soda made Viola shudder with repulsion.

Lillian waited for her response, her face bright and her eyes twinkling.

'Perhaps not today,' Viola said. 'It doesn't seem appropriate somehow.'

'Oh, tosh,' Lillian countered. 'Especially today. We're a distraction.'

Giving in, Viola followed Lillian to the to bar and lingered behind her at the back of the three-deep pack. Shuffling forwards when pressed, Viola felt a tap on her shoulder. It was George, Fred's closest friend. He raised his eyebrows, put his fist to his mouth and mimed drinking. 'Thanks, George, two Gin and Its, please.'

Lillian cleared her throat behind Viola's back. 'See?' she whispered. 'It'll take more than a war to stop us.'

'Stop you,' Viola said. 'I have Fred to think about and besides, it's only good old George.'

'Well, let's see what good old George thinks about you calling him that.'

'No, don't, Lil,' Viola said. 'At least let me have my gin first. Besides, you were the one who started it, ages ago.'

Turning, George smiled at them and pointed to a crammed table on the other side of the room, where a fair few members of the Modern Foreign Languages teaching staff, assistants and lectors were gathered.

Lillian made her way to join the others, but Viola hung back and squirmed through to George. 'Can I help you with the drinks?' she asked. 'I doubt if there will be any trays available.'

'Thanks, Vi,' he said, strands of his dark, wavy hair sticking to his forehead. His spectacles had fogged up in the mugginess and he wiped them with care on his hand-knitted waistcoat. 'I was going to ask Matteo to help, but as you're here. You won't tell Fred I've been using you as a packhorse, will you?'

Tears sprang into her eyes at the exact moment an elbow in her back sent her stumbling forward. 'Ouch,' she said, grabbing George's jacket sleeve.

'I felt that.' He glowered in the direction of the man attached to the responsible limb. 'Oh, you're crying. That must have been some jab.'

But Viola knew her tears had nothing to do with the

dig in the ribs. They were brought on by the thought that it should have been Fred's arm she clung to for support. 'Don't worry about it, George,' she said, not looking him in the eye. 'Can't be helped in here on a day like this.'

He reached the bar at last and reeled off his order. Handing the first two drinks to her, he smiled and told her to join the others, which she did without arguing. The floor was sticky and uneven and she watched her steps.

'Oooh, thank you,' said Lillian reaching for the drink as if she and Viola hadn't been knocking it back for the best part of the day.

'Thank George.' Viola nodded towards their friend who was somehow carrying two glasses in each hand.

'Here, let me.' A young man who might have been Italian or Spanish – if his swarthy skin and dark, oily hair were anything to go by – leapt towards George to help. Viola recognised him, but they had never met.

'Lillian, Viola.' George nodded to each of the women in turn. 'Matteo,' he said gesturing towards the young man. So, Italian then.

One of the men stood and offered Viola and Lillian his chair and they squeezed into it together.

The tiny table they shared was chock-a-block with drinks and empty glasses. The pub staff seemed to be much too busy supplying alcohol rather than cleaning, but that was the least of any of their worries today – or should have been.

She looked around at the milling crowds, talking about such a critical event and yet appearing to be so confident and rather smug with themselves, their surroundings, their safety, their ideals, their rights. How long, she wondered, could it remain so? How long would the alcohol last out?

And their food? Electricity, running water, institutions such as Cambridge, hospitals, medicine. How long could all of those things and more exist in their present state? A day, a month, a year... Gradually it would all be eroded away. That thought was too gloomy to dwell on. She set her drink on the table, but picked it up again right away and took a deep draught. Better make the most of things whilst she could. When someone called for another round, she didn't hesitate.

'What do you think, Viola?' George was trying to get her attention. 'Vi?'

'Fine, as I said, George,' Matteo, in his benign accent, answered instead. 'Some, like you, Viola, Lillian and many others, have British passports or dual citizenship, so will, inevitably, not be worried about the department being disbanded. You will get jobs elsewhere.' He shrugged. 'But us?'

'Vi...' George's eyes were imploring, as if he was determined to get her to join in. 'Do you think the whole department will be dissolved?'

Viola thought for a moment about what Matteo was suggesting, based she guessed on the premise that the vast majority of staff in the Modern Foreign Languages department were from other countries in Europe, which indeed complicated the matter. 'It will, of course, depend on so many factors,' she said, making an effort to be thoughtful and measured.

Matteo spread his palms skyward, a gesture that seemed to be universally accepted to mean, *but of course – that is a given*. Or: *please tell us something we don't know*.

'And those being?' George asked.

'First and foremost must be call for the subject,' she said. 'If no one wants to study languages, or if there aren't any students available to study, then the department would have to go, I suppose.'

'That is what I mentioned,' said Matteo, nodding his head. 'And next there would have to be staff, like us, available to teach. But many of us are without British passports. Well…' He shrugged again. 'Who knows?'

'The university may very well honour your contracts,' said George.

'Surely,' said Viola, 'that would depend on what the government decrees should happen to non-citizens.'

Matteo's voice rose to a passionate level. 'They will round us up like animals and pen us in together somewhere like a camp… or a prison.'

'Steady on, old chap,' said George. 'I don't think the British government would think of—'

But Matteo was in full flow, other groups close by quietening their discussions either in alarm or to listen in with curiosity. 'But what I say is true. We will be no more use to them than that.' He blew on his fingers and shook them as if trying to shift something distasteful. Viola pushed her chair away from the table and snatched her drink to safety. 'They will throw away the keys and forget about us. Or worse, trade us for British citizens held in their camps.'

'Hang on,' George said. 'Who are they?'

'They,' Matteo said, less animated now, 'are the authorities. The government. Or governments.'

'I think you're speculating wildly,' Lillian said. 'The truth of the matter is we have no idea what is going to happen.' She looked around the table. 'Have we?'

But George seemed not to have heard her and continued to address Matteo. 'Surely you're not suggesting the British government would negotiate with the Germans in order to swap detainees?'

Viola interjected, 'And if they did then Fred might...'

George looked down at his thumbs; Matteo used his hand to wipe the condensation from his glass; someone coughed and a Frenchman who had been listening in turned to greet a man at a table behind him.

Matteo opened his mouth to speak again, but stopped suddenly and rubbed his calf. 'What was that for?' he said, accusing George with a dark look.

Viola knew it was something to do with her. Or Fred. And she wanted to make it clear, in a general way, that although she appreciated their concern and discretion, she didn't want anyone to adjust their thoughts and words to spare what they thought might be her discomfort. Drinking the last drop from her glass, she felt emboldened and said, 'Oh dear, there's something heavy hanging in the room and it needs to be aired. And that something is named Fred.'

Lillian nodded.

George slumped back and said, 'I suppose you're right, Vi. But we just don't want to upset you any more than you must be already.'

'Dear George.' Viola raised her glass to him. 'Dear friends.' She saluted the others, too. 'How compassionate and gracious all of you are. But we must continue speaking about Fred as if... as if... well, not as if he's here but as if we are thinking of him constantly and willing him to be here.' She looked from one to the other. 'Does that make the slightest bit of sense?'

George nodded along with Lillian and Matteo managed a thin smile.

'I mean, none of you must be embarrassed or frightened to speak of him for fear of offending me. In fact, I want to know what you think about the situation. I need to hear your frustration and fears for him as well as yourselves. Listen, I'll go first. Fred is in a very different position from those of you who are here on a visa or work permit. He is in Germany on his German passport.'

'But does he not have a British passport in addition?' asked the Frenchman.

'Yes,' Viola said. 'He's a dual national.'

'But he left it too late to get back,' said George. 'Isn't that right, Vi?'

'That's exactly it, George,' Viola said. 'He left it too late. Or rather, family circumstances dictated that he could not return earlier, although he wanted to. And now he's well and truly stuck in Germany. Of all the dreadful bad luck.'

The group was silent again. Then Lillian said, 'Let's raise a glass to absent friends.'

'And,' George added, 'their swift return to our fold.'

'Hear, hear.' Her friends clinked their glasses to Fred, and Viola was grateful that the discussion reverted to the war as a whole and was no longer centred on her situation in particular.

★

They were amongst the last to leave the consoling confines of the pub, tipsy and holding on to each other. George guided them in the direction of their flat, but Viola put her hand up to stop him. 'No. Thank you, George,' she said. 'We're going this way.' She pointed with a wavering finger in the opposite direction.

'Are we?' Lillian asked.

'Yes,' Viola slurred, her head nodding in an exaggerated movement.

'Oh, alright,' Lillian said. 'George. We're going that way.'

'Then I,' George said, equally squiffy, 'will accompany you.'

Viola drew her shoulders back, looked at both of George's faces, one more blurry than the other and said, 'We are intrepid adventurers, George, and as such we're going to strike out on our own.'

'Indeed. We are,' said Lillian.

George sighed and blinked several times, as if to clear his eyesight. 'And I, like the Germans soon will be, am defeated.' He waved a hand in front of their faces. 'Goodnight, ladies. You know where I am if you need me.'

Viola looked down to find her footing on the cobbles and began to walk as gingerly as if she was skirting unexploded bombs.

Lillian stumbled, giggled and tried to match Viola's hesitant stride. 'Where, Vi, are we going?'

'Emmanuel.'

Lillian shook her head. 'He won't be there. You're just, I don't know the word... torturing yourself, that's it.'

'I am already a tortured soul,' Viola said, hand on heart. 'I know.'

'I just want to see what's going on there, so I can tell Fred when I write to him.'

'Yes, Vi,' Lillian said in a sing-song voice, as if she was talking to a child. 'Whatever you say, Vi.'

Anyone out and about like them walked with their heads down and their collars up, making themselves as inconspicuous as possible as if to practise tucking themselves away from searching spotlights. Downing Street was quiet and dark; all streetlights Stygian, no flicker of a desk lamp or candle could be seen through windows. *What an awful way to live*, Viola thought, *in the dark like scuttling rats. But this is how it is going to be; how it is. And we must get used to it.*

Pearson came out of his post, tipping his bowler to greet them. 'Good evening, Miss Viola,' he said. 'What brings you out so late?'

With great effort, Viola controlled her speech and said, 'I. Well, we—' she nodded at Lillian '—would like to have a look around.'

'May I ask why, Miss? I'm afraid I can't allow you in at this hour.'

'Just the grounds. Please? So I can write and let Fred know that all is well.'

Pearson raked his thick moustache into place, turned to the door in the gate and opened it with a key from the ring on his belt that was otherwise hidden underneath his long porter's coat. 'It's not possible for you to enter,' he said. 'But peer through and you can observe the firefighters valiantly guarding the Westmorland Building.'

Across the Front Court Viola could see two figures sauntering backwards and forwards in front of the portico and entrance gateway. Sandbags lay at intervals along the base of the brickwork, buckets positioned in between. Viola followed the progress of one of the men as he made his way towards the East Range and Chapel, then turned and promenaded back; he looked as if he didn't have a care in the world or if he did, it was how to word his thesis, nothing more.

'So,' Pearson said, pulling the gate closed and locking it. 'You can tell Fred that his college is in good hands. Now, safe home with you, ladies.' He tipped his hat again. 'Goodnight.'

Viola began to feel less addled, although her head was beginning to pound and she watched her feet carefully; Lillian clung to her arm and didn't say a word. The night smelled of late summer – the end of blossom hanging heavy on the trees; a whiff of vegetation drifting from the Fens; smoke from smouldering fires; wet wool from coats drenched by the earlier rain.

When Lillian opened the door to their flat, she turned to Viola and laid a hand on her arm. 'Vi,' she said in a soft voice. 'I don't want to be cruel, but anything you write to Fred along the lines of security will be censored. At least I think it will be. And perhaps it will be much more than security issues that are a no-go.'

Viola told herself she knew that; of course she did. But still it came as a shock. 'So soon?' she said.

'I'm afraid so.' Lillian's voice was heavy with sympathy. 'Do you want me to bunk in with you tonight?'

'No, thank you, Lil,' she said, making her way straight to her bedroom. 'See you in the morning.'

Her postage stamp of a room was cold and when she

climbed in between the sheets in her petticoat, they felt chilly and unforgiving against her bare arms and legs. She fumbled for the warm comfort of the ring, cupped it in her hand and shivered. The alcohol caused the room to spin slowly and rhythmically; her thoughts spun, too, with images of Fred, letters he wouldn't receive, sandbags, college architecture, detainees watching from behind barbed wire fencing. An owl hooted and she knew that if she could see it, its eyes would be the brightest entity in the void of night. There was not the tiniest chink of light to be seen; the world indoors and out was as dark and foreboding as the very essence of her being.

4

Oxblood leather. The smell was fierce and overwhelming, the colour earthy and warm. Annie opened the packaging and peeked in at her new notebook. She could have chosen blue, but that seemed too ethereal; or green, too lush and verdant. And she could have picked out a more refined grain of material, one in which the animal skin had been beaten, stretched and treated until the cover was as thin and elegant as a lady's glove. But the oxblood leather spoke to her as raw and down to earth – a reminder of how she wanted to write in her journal – with truth and straightforward honesty. Taking a quick look around at the other passengers to make sure no one was watching, Annie stuck her nose into the brown paper bag and breathed in the pungent smell.

Satisfied with her purchase, she lifted her face and re-tucked the ends of the bag around the book until it was hidden from view then, to be on the safe side, she wrapped her scarf around it twice and put it right at the bottom of her bag, under the apples and bread and beetroot. All of these precautions were necessary because if Fred saw the notebook he would be most upset. He would huff and puff and berate her for going into Munich against his wishes. Then probably, like any sensible person, he would dash the book into the fire if he thought for a minute she was going to use it to write about her thoughts and feelings now that Britain had declared war against Germany and their passage home was blocked.

Picking up the bag, she inspected it from every angle to make sure the outline of the large, red rectangle would not be a giveaway. If discovered, it would give Fred more upset and anxiety than he was already experiencing and she couldn't bear that thought.

'Why?' he would demand. 'Why did you defy me and take the train to Munich when I said you must – we must – stay as close to home as possible until we have decided and agreed upon our plan?'

Her stomach dipped and she felt a surge of nausea when she pictured how he would nurse his head in his hands and claw through his hair until he looked quite mad. Then he'd turn away from her and once again become immersed in the other problems that occupied so much of his thoughts. He hadn't mentioned it once, but Annie felt sure he blamed her for both of them being stranded here when she had gone against his wishes that time, too and travelled to be with Oma when she had taken a turn for the worse.

Poor devoted Fred, he did everything he possibly could to protect and care for her, Oma and Viola and it must seem to him that she threw that loyalty and devotion back in his face. That was why she had to get the journal into the house and hidden before he discovered it. If they were well and truly stuck, and it did appear that every avenue to return home had been closed, then after this she vowed she would make it up to him with kindness and food and washing and tending the garden and reading aloud to him, which used to give him so much pleasure.

One woman, hunched in a corner seat, gave her a quizzical look, the deep lines on her forehead furrowing when she frowned at Annie's endless fussing with the notebook and the shopping. In return, Annie flashed one of her best broad smiles and the woman deigned to turn up the corners of her mouth before being distracted by a barn swallow, gliding at a pace with the train window.

A small child sitting on the edge of his seat next to an older man, who was probably his Opa, shrieked out loud at the sight and watched as the bird turned its head to the left as if it was taking in the forest and then to the right, observing the passengers in their maudlin attitudes. Despite being shushed repeatedly, the child continued to loudly enjoy the flight of the bird until it flapped its wings frantically and dropped behind. The dear little boy rambled on, trying to tell anyone who might listen about the miracle he had observed, pointing towards the window and looking from one to other of the passengers as if they were insane not to celebrate such a sight with him.

His Opa grabbed his wrist and told him in a quick, sharp voice to be quiet. The boy's eyes filled with tears, but he set his trembling mouth and stared down at his hands like the adults around him.

None of the other passengers looked haughty or self-righteous as they might in thinking the start of war was not the doing of their beloved Fatherland. Instead, a sense of foreboding pervaded the atmosphere like a huge, thick cloud bearing down on all of them and Annie felt the dread, too. She had expected that everyone would look defiant, their chins in the air, swastikas on their lapels, shoulders back. But, and she might put this in writing later if she dared, people looked defeated before any shots had been fired. Necks were rounded down into upturned collars and mouths followed suit.

Munich had been the same, but the emotions, or lack of them, were intensified by the swelling of the crowds. No one was wearing anything bright and cheerful; everyone was awash with grey, black, brown, the occasional splash of a white shirt. Trees drooped with rain and the first shedding of leaves. Clouds scuttled across a drab sky. She had no way of knowing, but Annie guessed people in England would mirror them here. None of them, here or there or, she presumed, anywhere in the world, were happy. How awful, she thought, a world full of wonderful things, like birds in flight and not a living soul able to appreciate them. They were too burdened and distracted by another hideous war and would have to put their lives on hold before they could view the world as it deserved to be appreciated.

Whilst the woman next the window was busy tutting at the little boy's every fidget, Annie checked her bag from the corner of her eye and decided that no one would discern a notebook hidden in its depths. When she arrived home she would take out the vegetables then run upstairs to her room with the bag, telling Fred if he asked that she had personal things to put in her drawers. Being such a gentleman, he would not enquire further. She congratulated herself on her plan and was determined to make it work as she had no intention of telling her brother that she meant to write with great candour about everything she observed and heard and experienced from today on. The announcement yesterday warranted her defiance as she wanted to give credence to the terrible magnitude of the news. It felt unreal and completely unbelievable. The two countries that were in her blood and that she loved and respected were at war – again.

How could this be? she wondered. The sun still rose and set, as it did before the announcement; the grass was patched with autumnal brown as it always was at this time of year; the kettle had not changed its position on the range; Oma was as bedridden as she had been these last seven months. Dogs barked, trains hooted and slid along the tracks, the aroma of fresh bread remained intoxicating. And yet Annie's head told her that despite what she saw, heard, smelled, touched, everything had changed irreversibly and irredeemably.

After the announcement, Fred had gone to church as it was Annie's turn to stay with Oma. But she wished it had been the other around as Fred stormed back into the house livid with anger. 'Fred,' Annie had said, 'please calm yourself. Think of Oma.'

Fred had reached for the schnapps, even though it was before noon, and poured himself a large glass. Then he'd steadied himself. 'How dare they, Annie. How dare they,' he'd said time and again.

Annie had waited patiently, although her palms were clammy and she fiddled with the hem of her skirt.

'You will not believe what Pastor Otto said, in church, where everyone could hear and where everyone, or so it seemed by the subtle nodding of their heads, agreed.'

Annie had waited another few minutes during which Fred became quieter then carried on, saying that now he'd had time to think, it was not so much what the pastor had said but what he hadn't said.

Very interested to hear what was coming next, Annie could not contain herself any longer. 'Well what did he say?' she'd blurted out. 'Or not say?'

'He said that Britain had declared war on Germany.'

'Yes, that is a fact,' Annie had commented.

'I know,' Fred had continued, agitated again. 'But what he failed to iterate was that Britain had no choice and had given Germany so many chances to divert this crisis by leaving Poland alone. But no, Hitler decided to invade and Britain and France were left with no other option open to them.'

Annie had agreed with Fred but was surprised that he thought the pastor would say any different. After all, no newspaper article or radio announcement would tell them that Germany was to blame. That was not what the people were meant to believe, although they must have known, in their hearts, what the truth of the matter was. Or perhaps they didn't; they might know, or only want to know, what they were fed by the regime.

'Also,' Annie had reminded Fred, 'the German Christian Group is aligned to the Nazi party.'

'Along with many other organisations.'

They had read about a number of them over quite a few years, but had never worried, as they were known in the town for being as German as they were British, even though their visits to Oma and their cousins were confined to school holidays. Fred must have read Annie's thoughts as he'd turned away and muttered, 'Only during the school holidays. Until now.' He'd then shaken his head from side to side like a poor lost puppy. 'At this most dangerous juncture in time to be stranded on German soil,' he said. 'I cannot believe our terrible luck.'

All her life until now, Annie had felt comfortable and rather proud of her dual nationality, being equally enchanted with both German and British languages, culture and history. Perhaps she had also been a bit guilty of arrogance or pomposity in her knowledge of both countries. But she had always thought of herself as absolutely accepted by both sets of relatives, friends and authorities, as had Fred. A chill spread through her when she predicted that they would become abhorrent and suspicious to both countries, if they were not so already. That was indeed very worrying.

To change the subject, Annie had told Fred they should come up with a plan of action that covered their behaviour, their movements, the story that they would feed others about their presence in Germany. Fred had agreed that they would sit down together the following day and do that in great detail, but until then, he instructed her to stay close to home and try not to engage in conversation with too many people. But she had ignored him and could now, as the train pulled into Ulm, picture him watching the clock for her return so they could get on with that task. As soon as she was out of the station, she ran all the way home.

Out of breath and nursing a stitch in her side, Annie opened the front door and waited for a chastising call from her brother. Nothing reached her ears. He wouldn't have gone out and left Oma, but he might be sitting with her upstairs. She kicked off her shoes and tiptoed towards the kitchen. Pushing open the door, she saw him on his knees, turning the dial on the wireless at the pace of a snail, listening as it crept from crackle to crackle, hoping to find a British transmission.

'Ah, Annie,' he said, not looking up from his task. 'I gave Oma her soup, but she has been asking for you.'

Annie put the vegetables on the scrubbing board, 'I will go up to her now,' she said.

'This blasted wireless,' Fred said, giving the radio a good slam with his hand. He stood up and glanced at the clock on the sideboard. 'Where have you been?' he asked, looking at her at last.

Not telling Fred she had defied him, yet again, was one thing. But lying to his direct questions was something she could not bring herself to do. So she evaded the question. 'Tonight, I am going to recreate a roast dinner for us with your favourite Yorkshire puddings,' she said.

His eyes grew wide, then he wiped at them with his fist and Annie supposed his tears were for the idea of Englishness encompassed in the dish. She laid a hand on his arm and said, 'Save your tears for the impending disaster when I try to cook them using the wrong flour and powdered egg.'

Fred smiled at that. 'Here,' he said. 'Let me take your bag.'

But Annie slipped it behind her back. 'Personal things,' she said, lowering her eyes. And it wasn't a lie; the journal was and would remain her personal property. 'I'll take them upstairs then go in to Oma.'

'Of course. Yes. You must.' Fred nodded with his eyes closed. 'We will get on with our plan when you come back down.'

'Yes, of course,' Annie said, heading for the safety of the stairs. 'I haven't forgotten.'

Burying the notebook beneath her undergarments in a drawer of the tallboy, Annie let out a sigh of relief. She felt sure that was the best hiding place as Fred would never go in amongst her private possessions and Oma was not able to do so. If warranted, she would come up with an alternative in the future.

She straightened her hair and clothes then went across the landing to Oma. Every time she opened her grandmother's door and peered at her, she had to steel herself to be faced with the worst. Herr Doctor repeated every day that they should be prepared as the end could come at any time. But Annie didn't know what she could do to prepare for that kind of heartbreak. Oma, once so robust and energetic, was becoming more frail and fragile before their eyes. It was often difficult to tell if there was breath left in the elderly woman, so Annie had to creep forward and, dreading not finding any evidence of life, place a hand on her grandmother's chest or under her nose.

This time, Annie could detect the gentle rise and fall of Oma's nightgown over her heart, so put her lips to Oma's hand then placed it back on the counterpane.

'Oh, Liebling Annie.' Oma stirred and opened her eyes. Her voice was thin and sounded painfully rasping. 'The market was busy?'

'Not too crowded, Oma,' Annie answered.

'Fred brought me lunch and told me about the war. Terrible,' she said.

Annie sat in the chair that was nestled next to Oma's

bedside. 'Yes, it is,' she said. 'But you must not worry about it. We will do the worrying.'

'It seems as if I have nothing left to do now but worry,' Oma said. 'Will you turn me, Annie?'

Annie leaned over her grandmother and placed one hand under her waist and the other on her shoulder, feeling the brittle bones and wasted muscles under her hands, nudging and adjusting inch by inch as Herr Doctor had shown her. Oma landed, with a sigh, on her side. 'Are you quite comfortable, Oma, or do you need to be a bit more towards me?'

'No, this is good. Thank you, Liebe. I will close my eyes for a moment or two.' But Annie knew it was more likely to be hours, as the elderly woman couldn't stay awake for more than a few minutes at a time.

She sat and watched over Oma, curled on her side as if protecting herself from the suffering and outrage of the world, and longed to talk to her as they had done so often, about everything and anything. Now Oma was too feeble and infirm and besides, it would not be fair to burden her. What she needed and deserved was quiet calm, tenderness, patience, care and love. But that didn't stop Annie from thinking of all the things she would dearly love to chat to her about.

What would Oma say if Annie admitted that she fretted about her identity and how it would now be viewed here in Germany, where she had felt accepted and safe for large chunks of her life? Or about how people would see her in Britain if she was there? With an intake of breath she realised she and Fred could be accused of being spies by either country or sympathisers to the other side from whichever country they were residing in. They had gone from having a foot firmly in each country to finding themselves with nowhere to place their feet and with their legs trembling in fear.

One thing she was sure about was that she did not want the Fatherland to count her amongst those who agreed with the pastor and the Nazi party. That was an aspect of this country she would always reject. And she refused to be brainwashed into believing that the ordinary, everyday, commonplace German, like Oma, wanted to be thought of in that way either. It was not within the scope of the German people she knew and loved. They were innocent of crime and wanted to do nothing more than get on with their lives.

Vati had been outraged at what was happening in Germany from the end of the Great War. He could have so easily up and moved them here, to be with his family when Mum died, but thank goodness he hadn't as they might well have become entrenched in the Nazi way of life and become victims of their propaganda.

Annie vividly remembered Vati's shock and contempt when Onkel Niklas suggested – no, strongly advised – that she should join the Young Girls' League with her cousins when she was twelve or thirteen. Fred, exempt from Hitler Youth at seventeen, had dropped his jaw in horror. 'I do not think so.' Vati had sounded unshakeable.

'But, Franz,' his brother had said. 'Better for Annaliese to join voluntarily than be conscripted.'

'Enough,' Oma had interrupted. 'No such thing is about to happen.' She'd dismissed the idea with a wave of her ringed fingers.

'No, it will not,' Vati had said. 'I would not allow Annie to be conscripted. If such measures are taken, then we shall leave for home at a moment's notice and not return.'

How wrong Oma had been. By December 1936, all eligible youths in Germany had to belong to either the Girls' Leagues or Hitler Youth. As it turned out, Fred and Annie did not qualify as ethnic Germans so were considered ineligible. Instead, they were able to stand back and watch their cousins going off to their gatherings in blue skirts or brown shirts, heavy marching boots clumping their path to the meeting halls and back.

Amongst the photos on Oma's dresser, Annie picked out various of those cousins during different phases of growing up. She spied Werner, who had refused to join any Nazi group. His parents had begged and scolded, pleaded and tried to reason, but he would not be drawn. They thought his resolve would cave when he began to be taunted by fellow pupils and one of his masters set him an essay entitled 'Why am I not a Member of Hitler Youth?' But he merely set out his arguments in paragraph form, handed in the essay and steadfastly dug in his heels; Fred and Annie both admired him for that. Then, the poor lad was told he would not receive his school leavers' diploma unless he joined the wretched organisation and that would, in effect, bar his entrance to university. Their own dear Vati had stepped in and said he would ensure Werner could study at Oxford and live with them but, lo and behold, when Werner gave that piece of news to his school, it was confirmed that he would receive his diploma along with the rest of his class. They wouldn't have wanted to lose a brilliant architecture student to Britain, although she would take bets he was being watched very carefully at the university in Hamburg.

Vati had taken such good care of them. He was so confident in himself and his beliefs that it seemed as if he didn't have to think before he made what was always the best decision. Annie knew that Fred tried so very hard to be like him – strong, decisive, trustworthy and reliable – but sometimes she saw terror in his eyes, for a fraction of a blink, that she had never seen in Vati's. But perhaps she would now, were he here with them in this situation.

Enough about the past, Annie thought. They must think about the future and to do that they must have their plan in place. Her eyes strayed to the door beyond which was her room and the brand-new notebook ready and waiting for its first entry. She knew Fred would not disturb her, so took the journal from the drawer and sat back down next to Oma. For a few minutes she chewed the end of her pen and deliberated about whether or not she was doing the right thing. If uncovered, the book could get all of them arrested, imprisoned, sent for trial or executed. But Werner stuck to his beliefs as did Vati and she felt compelled to do the same.

She dated the page then set down how she had disobeyed Fred's decree, what she had seen in Munich and on the train, Oma's struggle, her sympathies with both the German and the British people and her ever-increasing fears of alienation from both sides.

But now I am determined to give my brother as little cause for worry as possible, she wrote. *I will tend to Oma and the house, the shopping and cooking. I will make a start by coming up with a plan for our safety, which I will present to him so I can take the pressure of that responsibility off his shoulders.*

We must inform each other of our movements, intended destinations when we go out, who we are meeting if anyone, what time we will return and we must keep to this at all times. (The irony of this is not lost on me, but I do understand the necessity of adhering to this in the future.)

In public, we must appear to agree with the status quo. How we go about that in practical terms will have to be discussed. However, we will have to be prepared to wear masks of alliance and affiliation when our heads and hearts will be rejecting the regime in no uncertain terms. We will have to learn the jargon that goes along with being good, upstanding German citizens. We will have to practise the Nazi salute and use it. We will have to Heil Hitler in response to others and perhaps instigate the greeting if necessary. We must stay away from the truck and diesel factories, the barracks and depots in Ulm, which will be under heavy surveillance. We will have to avoid gatherings if we can or perhaps go to a few to show our faces.

In private we can vent our anger, frustration and antagonism. But what if we are asked to join the party? We will have to go along with whatever is required to save our own and Oma's lives. I suppose. But I am not sure I would have the stomach for that if the situation arises.

Now our plan is going to get more and more complicated. For what about all of the above in regard to other members of the family? Those, for example, who happily sent their children, our cousins, to the wretched Hitler Youth Clubs. My deep concern with this is that amongst them there might be some who have willingly joined the party and would be delighted to give our names to the authorities as dissenters and troublemakers. In other words, should we trust anyone at all? Probably not. And that includes, and here I have to steel myself, the very handsome and charming Walther who will be taking over from his father, Herr Doctor, when he has completed his studies. The thought of that makes me fume with anger.

We must not purchase anything that is likely to cast aspersions upon our loyalties, for example books or newspapers or pamphlets that do not toe the party line. It causes me great dismay, though, to know that if one so desired, it would be beyond difficult to get one's hands on any books other than those approved by the Nazis since they have either burned or banned any type of literature that goes against their regime. All my favourites are no longer available: DH Lawrence, Upton Sinclair Jr, James Joyce, Trotsky, Tolstoy, Vicki Baum and Hermann Hesse; they are ash. Ash that has by now dissipated into the air or been ground into the earth. I like to think that some of the powdered embers have lodged themselves in the cracks of walls and pavements, or in the roots of trees that continue to grow strong, still nourishing the world we live in. It's an idealistic hope, but even if it were true it could never make up for the ideas that were razed to the ground when those tens of thousands of pages were set alight. I remember verbatim Helen Keller's response that Vati read aloud at the time: 'You can burn my books and the books of the best minds in Europe, but the ideas in them have seeped through a million channels and will continue to quicken other minds.' How we clapped and cheered, never imagining that we would be in the position we're in now where we have to live without the freedom of reading what we want when we want.

We must take care of our health – eating the right foods, taking exercise, sleeping well. We must take care of each other.

Annie snapped the book closed and placed it on the dresser behind her when Oma stirred.

'Annie?' Oma's voice quivered.

'Yes, Oma, I'm here. Do you want to be turned again?'

'A sip of water, please.'

Annie helped her grandmother to sit up and held a glass to her mouth. A sip was all she could manage, then she fluttered back, exhausted, against the pillows. 'Annie...' Oma reached out her hand. 'You do know I loved your mum, don't you?'

Annie was taken aback. Why would Oma ask that now? Because Mum had been British? 'Of course,' Annie said, finding it as painful to utter her words as her grandmother did.

'She was like a daughter to me and to your Opa. Our very own English rose.'

'Yes, she was beautiful,' Annie said. 'Everyone loved her.' Oma slept again, and Annie added that exchange to her journal. Then she returned the book to its hiding place under her knickers and vests and went down to Fred.

Lining up potatoes, cabbage and carrots to peel, Annie started to tell Fred about the plan.

'Where is it then?' he said. 'I'll read through it whilst you do that.'

Annie pointed to her temple. 'In here,' she said. 'So you'll have to put up with me reciting it.'

Fred popped a round of carrot into his mouth and studied her. 'Why were you such a long time today?' he said. 'Buying a few items from town never usually takes you that long.'

Annie turned to the sink on the pretence of rinsing the vegetables.

'Did you meet Walther?' Fred asked.

Annie felt her face turn as puce as the beetroot she'd bought earlier, but she knew this turn in the conversation would detract from the truth so let her brother see her chagrin. 'No.' She shook her head. 'I didn't meet Walther today.'

'Are you telling me the truth?'

'Yes,' she said. 'You know about every single time we've seen each other.'

'And I'm begging you to keep it that way.'

Annie sighed. 'Yes, I will, even though I was never privy to the same information about you and Vi.'

'Don't be childish,' Fred said. 'You know the situation is completely different.'

She did, but felt aggrieved regardless. 'Besides,' she continued, 'I think Walther must have returned to university.'

'Without saying goodbye to you?'

Annie shrugged and thought that perhaps this was the beginning of being alienated by people they had known and been friends with all their lives.

'I am sorry, Annie,' Fred said. He sighed and gazed into the distance, a glaze covering his eyes that Annie guessed meant he was thinking about Viola.

Fred agreed with all the points Annie had thought about to keep them safe and was grateful to her for devising them, but the Yorkshire puddings were not such a success, as they were flat as pancakes and would have been inedible if they had been living in a time or place or position to waste food.

Oma managed a bit of gravy and mashed potato, then Annie settled her before going to bed herself. She lay awake and listened to Fred pacing the floor below, as he did most nights, and was so grateful that the notebook was secreted away and could not add to her brother's restlessness and disquiet.

5

November 1939

Matteo had been right. Despite his academic career as a specialist in eighteenth-century Italian literature, government officials came knocking on his door to announce that he would be rounded up, with thousands of others, to an internment camp on the Isle of Man. Viola was initially flustered, then moved enough to take him in her arms and comfort him when he tried, and failed, to contain his emotions as he told her the news.

'But,' she said into the collar of his coat, 'can't the university or the department or the college write and tell them how...' She searched for the correct words. 'How respectable you are?'

Matteo stepped away from her and rubbed his eyes. She could see this wasn't his first bout of tears. 'They have interviewed everyone here who could be of help.' He shrugged, then dejectedly dropped his shoulders. 'It appears there is nothing left to do. I have been ordered to go. And at least I will be spared having to bear first-hand witness to what is going on in my beautiful country now that Mussolini and the Fascists have got their hands on it.' Matteo looked sadder than when he'd been crying. 'It is like finding out that your cultured, sophisticated, beautiful wife has been unfaithful. Everything you built your life on has given way beneath you.'

Viola flopped into her office chair and thought about how terrible that must be. For Fred, too. And if he were here would he also be imprisoned? Or perhaps he already was in some cold, damp cell or overcrowded, stinking camp in Germany.

'But the British government is unjust to intern you merely on the grounds of your nationality,' she said.

'Yes,' Matteo agreed. 'But I suppose it is beyond their means to delve into the beliefs held by each of us, so we will be lumped together until we can be trusted again.'

Now tears flooded Viola's eyes and her throat constricted. She leaned towards Matteo and covered his hand with hers. 'You are an incredibly brave person,' she said.

To which he whispered, 'No, that is not so. I am very, very frightened, Vi. If you pray, pray for me. If you don't, keep me in your thoughts.'

When Viola put her hand on his shoulder, she could feel him trembling under her touch.

At the end of August, Cambridge took eight bombs. None of them hit university buildings because, it was rumoured, Hitler thought if he spared the academic city, Britain would in turn veer her planes away from Heidelberg, the equivalent German university town. Who knew if that was true? Viola wondered how the powers-that-be could possibly gather enough evidence to conjecture that as truth. She reasoned to Lillian that if that were the case, then the British government would have to be in some sort of communication with the German authorities to the degree where they could strike deals and bargains about certain aspects of the war. And they had dismissed that theory during their debate in the pub the night war was declared. Besides, that made the whole thing seem like a game.

Lillian agreed that the whole thing was probably a strategic game and that the general public was, in reality, told very little about tactics, manoeuvres and outcomes.

But of course it wasn't a game to the poor people who were bombed out of Pembleton Terrace and Shaftesbury Avenue. And she felt for any young boys boarding over the summer in the Leys School who must have had such a fright when they found out that an unexploded bomb had dropped within yards of their safe haven. Then she smiled to herself because she knew her brothers would have been more excited than scared and probably tried to climb a fence or two to have a closer look at the incendiary. They, and it seemed all their school friends, were in awe of the men in uniform a mere few years older than them and couldn't wait to join their ranks in action. Viola shuddered at the thought. *It will all be over by the time they reach that age,* she told herself. *It must be. Fred and Annie will be back and we'll all be together again in the garden at home on a perfect summer's day that never ends.*

When Viola heard about the solitary victim of an attack on a house in Barrow Road, she was overcome with sympathy not so much for his death, but for facing that demise in isolation and loneliness. She thought about him and his plight for days after the news, wondering whether he lived alone or if his family happened to be out when the bomb hit, or if they had been at home with him but were lucky enough to be unscathed.

Still, she told herself, whatever conspiracy or under-the-table agreement might have been reached between Britain and Germany, Cambridge was getting off lightly in comparison with other parts of the country. Mum and Dad told her many times over how pleased and relieved they were that she was safely cocooned away from the chaos in London, in particular. She wrote to them that when she cycled along the Cam or walked to the Department of Modern Foreign Languages, she was struck by how the ivory tower of academia seemed to be trying to keep the continuity of its culture and traditions safe and secure, although her guess was as good as anyone else's about how long that would last. And perhaps that was a good thing, Viola thought, as there would have to be doctors, barristers, engineers, politicians, vets and writers of poetry to ensure the country got back on its feet when the whole thing ended.

'And also,' Lillian said to her and George one evening in The Whim, 'what are we fighting for, if not our traditions and ways of life? And that includes Oxbridge.'

'Hear, hear,' George banged the table until his cutlery jumped.

The waitress placed plates of shepherd's pie in front of Viola and George and a bowl of chicken soup on Lillian's placemat. Steam from the food wafted up to meet their faces, obscuring George's eyes behind his spectacles, but none of them rushed to start eating their meal. George sighed. 'Is it my imagination or have you noticed the portions getting smaller?'

Viola loosened her scarf and tied it around the handles of her bag. She nodded. 'Yes, I've noticed.'

'And,' said Lillian with a lack of enthusiasm, 'everything is somehow… I don't know. Greyer?' She looked up at her friends for affirmation.

'That'll be the rationing kicking in,' George said, picking up his knife and fork at last and tunnelling into the lumpy mashed swede and potato on top of the greasy mince.

'Here goes,' said Lillian, following suit.

Viola laughed. 'When did we stop saying bon appetit?'

'When, my dear ladies,' George said, 'bon was the first ingredient to be completely rationed from every meal.'

They ate in silence for a few moments. George nodded to a couple of men he recognised; Viola asked the waitress for three more cups of tea. The windows onto Trinity Street were opaque with streaming condensation.

'Are we going for a pudding or shall we skip it and head straight to the pub?' Lillian asked.

'Well, I tried the marrow jam tart yesterday in Halls and it was atrocious,' George said. 'The chap I was sitting next to described it as "one of the foulest dishes of food within human history". We'll be better off sticking with alcohol.'

Viola rocked back with laughter. 'And someone I spoke to said their college was serving up a lunch of either kidney omelette or calf's head vinaigrette.'

'Vile,' said Lillian. 'That beats the egg cutlet I tried to force down my throat the other day.'

'If you were hungry…' George sighed. 'You'd be grateful.'

'I don't think we're quite there yet, George.'

'At least there's Formal Hall,' said Viola. 'Despite the tapioca pudding it's still a wonderful occasion.'

George lowered his voice. 'Apparently, the Ministry of Food is sending directives to the university left, right and centre. They're controlling the minutiae of the quantity and elements of all our food. But I think the cellars of these colleges are very deep indeed.' He stopped to look over his shoulder, then carried on. 'And it will take a lot more than a war to stop the top dogs from adding all the lovely gravy they want to their dogs' dinners.' He signalled for the bill and when the waitress brought it to their table, he signed the bottom of the chit and asked her to put it on his tab.

'Too bad we can't get to Formal Hall more often, Vi,' said Lillian.

'You're always welcome as my guests,' George said. 'But I'm sorry that can't be more than once a month.'

'We're grateful for that, George. Thank you,' said Viola.

George helped Lillian and then Viola on with their coats, held the door open for them and helped them down the three steps to the narrow pavement.

As soon as they turned left towards The Anchor, Lillian and George started an animated conversation that left Viola behind both in proximity and from the cosiness of their chat. She knew they didn't mean to exclude her, but it was happening more and more frequently and Viola wondered if something deeper was burgeoning between her two friends. Something even they might not be aware of yet, or perhaps they were and had decided to keep it to themselves for a while, although she and Lillian kept very little from each other.

She trailed behind and looked up at the sky, mist swirling

around the bricks of Caius and the Senate House, eerie and looming in the blackout.

Looking back, she wondered if she and Fred had unintentionally left out Lillian or George or any of their friends whilst they were so cosied up with each other. A tinge of shame spiked her when she remembered a concert that she, Fred and Lillian had attended together. During the interval, she and Fred had been so wrapped up with each other, standing close and exchanging news of their day, that neither of them spoke a word to Lillian. When Fred delicately brushed a stray lock of hair from her forehead, she had caught a glimpse of Lillian, holding her drink and looking lost and awkward. Of course, Viola was stunned into reaching out for her friend and drawing her into the conversation, but she supposed that wasn't the only time she had been oblivious to others.

But circumstances were different then. None of the others had had their intended lifelong companion ripped from their side, and that was exactly how it felt, as if Fred had been torn from her and the place where they had been joined left raw and weeping. She tried not to be too dependent on her friends for company and diversion, yet she knew she was. And she was also aware that she was not always convivial to be with. Often she was distracted or less confident than she had been on Fred's arm, which probably gave her crowd too much to worry about on her behalf.

On a laugh, Lillian turned to her and said, 'Alright, Vi?'

Viola nodded. 'Just trying to watch my footing on these cobbles. If I twist my ankle, I can say goodbye to beating my brothers at tennis.'

Lillian waited for her to catch up and they threaded their arms together.

At The Anchor, George was holding the door open again like a faithful pup. They found a table and he went to the bar to order their usual.

'How are the two little herberts?' Lillian asked.

'Growing up way too quickly,' Viola said. 'But not maturing very much as they can't wait to jump into uniform and join the scrum. They think they're missing out.' She looked up and George was watching them, half sitting on a stool with one foot on the foot rail. Well, she thought he was looking at them, but his eyes were trained on Lillian who smiled when she caught his eye.

'Lil,' Viola whispered. 'Are you and George…?'

Lillian waited without saying a word.

'You know…'

'Know what?' Lillian looked confused, her lovely dark brows forming hoods over her eyes.

'Well,' Viola said. 'Involved with each other? Romantically linked?' She lowered her voice. 'Lovers?'

Lillian's eyes grew wide. 'Good old George? And me?' She shook her head. 'Whatever gave you that idea?'

George set their drinks on the table and chose to sit on the stool closest to Lillian. And when he produced his cigarettes he offered them first to Lillian before turning to Viola. *Yes*, Viola thought. *You and good old George. We'll see.*

They talked about the terrible bombing in Coventry; Hungary joining the Axis; Matteo; George's thesis on Shakespeare and War. George asked if by any chance Viola had heard news of Fred. No, Viola had not. And she would of course let them know if and when she did. In fact, they would hear her shouting in the streets, waving the letter above her head so they would know such a wonderful thing had happened.

'But I write to him all the time,' she said. 'Every other day. Share all the news I think I can get away with.'

George nodded. 'I write to him, too,' he said. 'Not as often as you, but once in a while.'

Viola's tummy took a little tumble. She felt so grateful to George. 'Thank you,' she said. 'That is so kind of you.'

George shrugged as if dismissing his gesture of friendship. 'Well, the man has to have more than one perspective. You know, another chap's point of view.'

Viola rubbed the coarse material of George's sleeve. 'He will really appreciate that, dear George.'

The door opened on a gust of wind and Amanda appeared, as neat and well-turned-out as ever despite the damp and cold. She gave her umbrella a good shake, then nestled it amongst the others in the stand by the door.

When she saw them, she gestured with her finger to an empty chair, asking through the pantomime if she could join them. They nodded and beckoned her to their table. She sat with a straight back and crossed her legs. 'I thought I might find you here,' she said, smiling at each of them. 'Good to see you.'

'And you,' said Viola.

George and Lillian nodded in agreement.

'Let me get you a drink,' George said.

'Thank you, George.' Amanda shook her head, her sleek auburn hair moving like a rippling wave against her cheek. 'I'll get one for all of you in a minute as a goodbye.'

'A goodbye?' Lillian parroted. 'What can you mean?'

Amanda sat back and looked rather smug. 'Well, it's taken me a while, but I've come to a decision,' she said, leaning into the table.

Viola pressed her face closer to Amanda's. 'Oh, do tell,' she said.

'I've decided...' Amanda looked from one to the other of the faces around the table, drawing out her answer for dramatic effect. 'To decamp to London to do my bit. As a translator and interpreter.' She sat upright again, her face giving way to a full-blown haughty expression.

Viola slumped back in her chair. She felt she had to concede that Amanda was doing something principled. 'Well, good on you,' she said. 'You'll be welcomed with open arms, I'm sure. A few others have already gone that way, haven't they?'

Amanda nodded. 'Yes, a number from every language base have moved for the same purpose and a friend of mine, who teaches in a private girls' school, has followed suit. Have you given it any thought?'

The table was quiet. Viola could almost read the others' thoughts and they were the same as her own. It seemed like the right thing to do, but it was hard to make that final decision.

'I've been considering it,' said Lillian. 'Two other French assistants left for London last week. But then that only leaves me and one other.'

'Vi?' Amanda turned and faced Viola with unblinking brown eyes, as if she was accusing her of not being patriotic. 'Anyone as fluent as you in German must be needed by the government.'

Viola fidgeted. She felt a film of sweat blossom on her

lip and under her arms. 'I am thinking about it,' was all she could muster. But there were so many things to consider, not least of all how hard she would find it to leave behind the place she had met Fred and fell in love with him. His spectral presence on familiar streets and in comforting haunts provided her with warmth and safety. Maybe she would talk to Lillian about all of this at some stage, but she had no intention, here in the pub in front of Amanda who was looking more and more supercilious by the minute, of opening up her feelings for debate.

The ever-chivalrous George, who must have felt her discomfort said, 'Well, I'm sure the government won't want me. What good is Shakespeare to them at this point in time? But my thoughts are leaning towards joining up. As an officer, I hope.'

They drank a rather sombre round and said their goodbyes and good lucks to Amanda, then George saw them to the door of their small flat before heading back to his rooms in St John's.

As soon as they lit a fire and made a cup of tea, Lillian asked Viola what she thought about following Amanda's lead and giving up Cambridge for war work in London. 'Have you thought about it, Vi? I certainly have.'

Viola curled up in an armchair and blew on her tea. 'A bit, but then I dismiss it, telling myself that what we're doing here is important, too.'

Lillian nodded. 'I know what you mean, but the same level of importance?'

'In the long run, yes. In the short term, of course not.'

'It's the immediate crisis that matters now, isn't it?'

Viola had to concede that it was. 'I also have to consider

Mum and Dad, though, and how relieved they are that I'm in a relatively safe place.'

'Oh, stuff and nonsense.' Lillian put her cup on the floor and fished a packet of cigarettes from her bag. 'Your parents would soon get used to the idea and I dare say their pride in you would overrule their anxiety. And who's to say Cambridge won't take more bombs tomorrow than London has done since the beginning?'

'Lil.' A thought struck Viola and made her sit up straight. 'Have you made up your mind to go to London? It sounds very much as though you have.'

Lillian took in a lungful of smoke, held it, then blew it slowly towards the ceiling. She shook her head. 'Not completely, Vi. But I am thinking about it very seriously.' From the corner of her eye, she looked at Viola. 'And I think you should, too.'

Viola gave her friend a wan and forced smile. 'Can I tell you something else, Lil? But please don't be judgemental about my silliness.'

Lillian chuckled. 'If we judged each other by how silly we are, we would never have remained such great pals.'

Viola laughed, too, then told Lillian about her reluctance to leave Cambridge because she felt Fred was there with her – waiting for her on every street corner, keeping a seat for her in the pub, asking for her help in the library, striding towards her across the common. Lillian didn't say she was silly, although she sounded it to herself.

'I know how much Cambridge means to you,' Lillian eventually said. 'With the connection to Fred. But don't forget that Fred isn't here in Cambridge. And he won't be in London.' She lightly touched the left side of Viola's chest, causing the little ring to press into Viola's skin. 'But he will always be with you right there.'

A few days later, Lillian announced that she had made her decision to move to London and George had made his to join up. But Viola continued to ruminate over all the options.

Pearson sent her a sweet note telling her the college had determined that enough time had passed and Fred's rooms needed to be cleared to make way for another student. Viola had never been to Fred's room, ridiculous as that seemed, the antiquated laws of the university dictating that women were forbidden to visit men in their private spaces. So many times she and Lillian had fumed about how absurd that was, but not as ludicrous as women not being able to gain a degree. As if they weren't capable of reading, researching and writing at least as competently as men. So Viola had been left to imagine the rooms as cosy and comforting, packed with books and lamps, papers, teacups, bottles of whisky and packets of biscuits; a college gown and hood hanging on the back of the door.

When Pearson unlocked Fred's rooms for her and crept back down the staircase to his post, she did see all of those things lying about, if not in the same positions she had imagined. If she had not believed that Fred had every intention of returning to her as soon as possible, the manner in which he'd left his possessions would have reassured her. A book face down on the bed; laundry in a sack waiting to be collected by the bedder; cufflinks on a shelf; an opened packet of tea, the fragrant leaves spilling out next to a teacup; a ticket for dry cleaning; a straw boater on the floor; sealed post. His latent presence sent a frisson of intimacy and connection through her core.

She spent a lonely afternoon, her eyes cloudy with tears, sifting through his things. Folding and smoothing his clothes into a suitcase, she released the smell of him, which made her sink to her knees and softly call his name. She remembered when he had worn his linen jacket and how it felt under her fingertips when she stroked his arm; the gaberdine trousers she had mended after the right turn-up tore on a bramble during a blackberry forage; the college tie he'd been wearing when he said he wanted to marry her. All the memories crowded in on top of her and she rushed to open the window, gulping in the cold, autumn air.

She hadn't wanted to disturb his books or his papers, knowing how precious his research was to his PhD. But she read through the top page of the pile on his desk, the ink long dried where the writing stopped halfway down the page. She was so used to proofreading all of Fred's essays and papers, helping him to edit and order his work, that her hand automatically reached for the fountain pen that lay discarded, as if it thought it would be picked up again after a mere day or two. Little did it know, and nor did she, when either of them would next feel its master's touch. She boxed the pen, with the other academic papers, but pinned together the draft thesis with a treasury tag and put it in her bag. Books, shirts and tea could be replaced, but Fred would be grateful to her for protecting his doctorate so that he didn't have to start from scratch when he came home.

When the rooms were empty, Viola stood at the door and impressed on her mind the floor layout, the slant of the sun through the window, the height of the desk chair, the ashtray and paperweight, the bookcases askew on the canted, timeworn floor, the musty smell of her Fred. As if she would ever forget. She sniffed and rubbed the skin under her eyes. Then she closed the door behind her.

Sometimes she would stop by to have a chat with Pearson. Over a cup of tea, he told her that B12, or Fred's rooms as Viola always thought of them, were now occupied by a Physics scholar who would, like other science and engineering students, be allowed to gain his degree in two years. After that, the Forces would be waiting to snap up him and his expertise.

'The Arts and Humanities students graduate after one year,' Pearson said, his voice rising on a note of disbelief. 'Can you believe it? Things certainly are changing here,' he said, 'like they are everywhere.' And North Court, Viola knew, was now for the exclusive use of men already in the RAF, or Navy or Royal Engineers who were undertaking so-called short courses that the Forces had written specifically to benefit the war effort. Still, Viola thought, it was rather lovely to see the various uniforms out and about and the men seemed to be enjoying themselves, taking advantage of everything on offer – squash, rowing, running, debating, music, rugby. Well, who wouldn't relish six extra months of fully-endorsed freedom before facing the total barrage of war?

'Did you notice the missing railings out front?' Pearson asked, taking their cups to the sink.

Viola nodded. 'Hard not to,' she said. 'Do you know where they'll end up?'

'No idea,' Pearson said. 'There was a backwards and forwards with some Ministry or other. Works and Buildings, I think. The college didn't want to give them up, but...' He shrugged.

'I know, I know,' Viola said, as if trying to comfort a child who had lost a beloved security blanket. 'But the idea of the vegetable patches instead of flower beds is a good one, isn't it?'

'I'll say.' Pearson brightened. 'Much more productive and there's nothing like a plateful of fresh sprouts or a good head of cauliflower.'

Yes, thought Viola, *to go nicely with the boiled sheep's brains or pigs' trotters or cuttlefish in aspic or whatever delicacy some creative cook comes up with for dinner.*

That was the last time she shared a cup of tea with Pearson, as the following week he told her he had made the decision to retire. 'Spend more time the grandchildren, Miss,' he'd said. 'And tend to my allotment.'

'It sounds blissful,' Viola said. 'Good luck.'

It looked as if a gale had blown through the tiny flat, with Lillian's belongings strewn everywhere whilst she packed for her big move to London. Every time Viola returned home she had to negotiate piles of books, teaspoons, vases, pictures and cases. And every day Lillian tried another tack to get Viola to agree to move to London with her. Often, she concentrated on painting a picture of how much fun they would have together in the capital. 'We could share a flat again, Vi. Think how exciting it would be.'

'Yes, it would be,' Viola conceded. 'But have you thought

about how much more horrific life will be in London? All the bombing and gas mains exploding and crowds of people sheltering in the underground.'

'I have thought about that, Vi.' Lillian's shoulders went back and her chin jutted out. 'But I think it's worth it in order to do something useful.'

'Are you taking this old thing with you?' Viola held up Lillian's worn, brown house cardigan.

Lillian shook her head. 'It's yours. If you want it. But,' she added, 'if you come to London with me, we can carry on sharing it.'

Viola looked at her friend's hopeful face and sighed. 'The only decision I've made, is that I'm going to take the Christmas break at home to decide.'

Lillian nodded and they didn't mention it again after that.

Christmas came and went. Cook did wonders with rations for dinner and laid out a cold buffet for their Boxing Day supper so she could spend the day with her family. Although Viola knew it wouldn't be such a lovely occasion for her as her son was away with the army.

Robert and David talked non-stop about every detail of the war that they followed without fail on the radio and in the newspapers. Dad, of course, joined in and like them, couldn't wait to hear the next development. Mum listened with great concentration, but insisted they have at least one course every mealtime when they discussed other subjects, saying that constant war talk was not conducive to good digestion. Try as she might, Viola could not get her brothers to discuss tennis or any other sport with the same enthusiasm they had once possessed. They thanked her for the snowy white tennis socks she gave them, but left them hanging over the back of a chair until Abigail took them to their rooms.

Their annual New Year's Eve party, for the good and great of the Cotswolds, went ahead but was a more subdued affair than usual. The lively music was replaced by oppressive, indistinguishable background compositions, the sit-down meal by plentiful but plain finger food, and the dancing by mingling. At midnight, the gathered joined hands for a slow, bittersweet 'Auld Lang Syne'. When the guests left, they wished each other a better New Year.

Mum had arranged a number of social calls over the festive period and she expected Viola to accompany her or be available to sit with other ladies and gossip about the intricacies of country life and whose son had joined which regiment or what each daughter was doing for her war job.

On one such occasion, in the company of four women Viola had known for years but couldn't claim to know, the spotlight turned on her. She could feel Mrs Bishop's gaze turn from soft to harsh, her voice from sugary to acidic. 'And how is the war panning out in the refined air of Cambridge?' she said, tilting her head to one side and arranging her face to look terribly interested.

Viola placed her half-nibbled fondant fancy on a side plate and cleared the icing from her teeth. Her face was hot and angry from everyone's fixation on her. 'Things are much the same as here,' Viola answered, hoping Mrs Bishop and the others would realise she was alluding to the fact that they didn't have it too bad, either.

'But...' Mrs Bishop glanced from one face to another,

ensuring she had everyone's attention. 'What are you doing, dear, exactly? I mean to support the war effort. Surely you're not still helping professors and the like with their research in the Languages Library?'

Viola started to defend herself. 'Well, what I actually do is—'

'And what about your friend?' Mrs Carter interrupted.

'Lillian?'

'No, no. Your man-friend. Or is he now your fiancé? I can't quite remember.'

'German,' Mrs Slade said, as if her mouth was full of sauerkraut that had been too heavily doused with vinegar. 'Isn't he?'

During the whole of this exchange, Mum had been looking with great interest at the tassels on the curtain ties, the flowers on the piano, the pattern on the rug, the curved legs of the coffee table. When at last she looked up, Viola could see an agitated spot of colour high on each of her cheekbones; her hands playing restlessly with each other. 'His name—' Mum forced a smile '—is Frederick Albert Scholz, as I believe I've mentioned many times. That is the name of Viola's soon-to-be fiancé who is half-British and half-German.'

Viola fumbled for Mum's hot and bothered hand. Pride welled inside her chest for her mother, who could so easily be dismissed as immersing herself in the trifling, domestic side of life, of having no interest in the world beyond her family, her home and the small circle of flower-arranging, coffee-drinking women she moved in. Part of her longed for Mum to continue, the other half willed her to stop before her connection with these women was severed beyond repair. 'Mum, perhaps we should...' Viola pressed her mother's hand towards standing.

'No.' Mum sounded determined and sure of herself. 'No, I want to tell everyone. All my... friends.' Mum smiled her most disarming smile and enunciated each word. 'That Fred is an honourable man. Through no fault of his own and whilst on a mission to protect his grandmother and sister, he has become stranded in Germany.' Viola looked from one woman to the other, each fidgety and flustered; together they were a herd of animals awaiting their fate in a holding pen. 'Were he not quite so principled, he would be here now. Doing his bit. As it is, I am in no doubt that he will return as soon as he possibly can to perform his duties and responsibilities.'

Viola pressed her mother's hand again. When she'd gained her attention, she could see how this outpouring had exhausted the woman who would rather be in the background, encouraging from the shadows, smoothing over any sense of discord. She thanked her with her eyes, from her heart.

'Now, Vi.' Mum stood. 'I think we should take our leave.'

When Viola helped her mother with her coat, she could feel her shoulders shaking under her hands and her own legs felt wobbly.

All the women seemed sincere with their goodbyes, except Mrs Bishop whose eye contact was as cold and steely as her handshake.

The minute they were behind their own front door, Viola took Mum in her arms and whispered thank you. Mum clung to her daughter and sobbed in a way that Viola had never experienced.

Then there were her own thoughts and memories to deal with. The shadowy visions of Fred that haunted her in Cambridge had followed her home; she saw him in the dining room; in Dad's study; sitting on the chaise longue waiting for her; standing with his back to the fire in the parlour; bending to stroke Pitch's silky head; joking with the boys; reading the papers after breakfast. Looking out on the garden caused her enough pain to take her breath away. How different it all was from the lush, verdant scene last summer that she foolishly thought had held the key to her future happiness.

Now her naïveté made her blush with chagrin, even though she was alone in the sitting room, gazing out on the wintry scene. Absolutely nothing was left of that summer's day – the bare trees reached up to the ash-coloured sky with branches like beseeching limbs. Any fruit left rotting on the ground had long dissipated into the mud. Not one flower or tennis ball was left to brighten the dull, sleeping scene. In the distance, she could hear the sound of the chainsaws that Dad had ordered landscapers to use during these cold months to thin the trees in the orchard and mend any gaps in the fencing.

And yet, to some extent, Viola found a glimmer of comfort in what she saw and recognising that, held on to it and encouraged it to flourish. After all, wasn't it heartening that in spite of everything the war threw at them, here again was winter? Before that, autumn had materialised and in a few months, if they lived to see it, spring would reoccur. The earth would continue to spin, the tides would ebb and flow, stars would emerge and the sun would try, at least, to make an appearance during the day. When Abigail tiptoed in with a tray of tea and left it on the side table for her, she felt somewhat consoled by the thought that there would always be greater forces than human beings at play in the universe.

But if the garden caused her consternation, her bed held a helter-skelter ride of emotions. She remembered every detail of the one night she and Fred had spent together. His hands on her skin, his flesh under hers. How perfectly they'd fitted together, which was a wonderful affirmation of their relationship. She missed him so much and felt cheated at how they had been forced apart.

Of course, she reasoned with herself, if he had stayed he would be away with the war by now or interned along with Matteo, so she still would not have him safe in her bed. But at least she would know where he was and how he was, to a certain extent. It was all so awful to dwell on. Lillian's words whirled in her head. Fred was not in Cambridge. He was not with her in the Cotswolds. He was not away with the forces or in London. By some unfortunate quirk of fate he was marooned in Germany. But he was with her in her heart.

That thought followed her to bed where she tossed and turned and fretted. The scene with Mrs Bishop and her cronies plagued her, too. What was it Mum had said? That if he were not so morally upstanding, Fred would be here now happily doing his bit. Of course, that phrase was bandied about interminably along with doing something worthwhile, engaging in one's war work, performing your duty. During that horrible dinner last summer, Fred had faced up to Dad and said as much himself. He'd wished more than anything that he hadn't had to go to Germany, but that he could have stayed in Britain and lived up to his responsibilities.

Well, she was here and her knowledge and proficiency were valuable assets that she could use to contribute to the fight against Hitler. Dawn was breaking across a pink-tinged slate sky when at last her arms and legs felt heavy and she began to fall asleep. In the morning, she would tell Mum and Dad she was moving to London to begin her war work. The thought jolted her with the first semblance of excitement she had felt for months.

6

It is an understatement to tell this journal that things are not going well in any aspect of our lives. The fact is, life is barely tolerable. Oma has become increasingly unwell. Four times we have had to get Herr Doctor to her and twice he has called for the minister. But each time just as we thought we'd lost her, she rallied. I cannot begin to fathom how strong, physically and mentally, she must be.

One of us is with her at all times; either me, Fred or one of our uncles or aunts or cousins, when they are on leave from the war. I can see etched on each of their faces the pull we all feel to will Oma to stay with us and the push to let her go from the agony and heartbreak of her sickbed. It's good that they come; it's right that they come. And it gives me a chance to get on with other things that I need to do or to have a little bit of respite for myself. But I hate it when they are here in my house, Oma's house, all puffed up in their vile uniforms. Clumping

*about in their shiny boots, designed to intimidate. Well,
they certainly don't daunt me. Horst needs to remember
that I helped potty-train him, so no amount of boot will
make up for the fact that I've chased him around this
house with nothing on his bottom half.*

Annie refilled her pen and looked out of the window at
the rain. She could hear the deep murmur of Fred's voice
from across the hallway as he read aloud to Oma who
would be asleep but hopefully comforted by her grandson's
soft mumble. Thank goodness it wasn't Horst again with
his loud, grating honk. Just last week he had come in, a
patronising smile on his fresh and inculpable face. Annie
had to remind him to take off his ridiculous boots and leave
them on the rack by the front door. 'Do you want to drag all
manner of filth into Oma's bedroom?' she had said, hands
on hips.

He'd sat down with a heavy sigh and started to tug at the
heel of one of the cumbersome things. Annie had chuckled
to herself at the sight and imagined all the German officers
having the same problem with their footwear during critical
moments in the war proceedings. Perhaps their awkward
boots would be the secret weapon that allowed the Allies to
win. She had loved the thought of that.

'They're new,' Horst had offered by way of explanation.
Annie stood and watched him strain and yank. His cheeks
had grown red, but she'd noticed that he hadn't lost the
sly smirk plastered on his face. With a whoosh, first one
boot then the other was heaved off. He'd sighed with relief.
'Why are you speaking English?' he'd asked. 'Please change
to German.'

A visceral chill had travelled up her spine and spread into her arms and legs. No, she'd wanted to say, the half of her that was British wanted to speak English today. And she would have liked to remind Horst that he had begged her to speak English with him in the past as he was desperate to learn the language. But she had pretended to have been muddled by pulling her hand through the ends of her hair and looking confused. She had acquiesced to his request and reverted to the mother tongue, not wanting to draw further unnecessary attention to herself.

Standing back from the stairs, Annie had made room for him to pass so he could get to Oma's room. But he had diverted to the kitchen, touching Oma's curios and whatnots on the way. Annie had shaken her fist behind his back and felt better for it. 'I will have coffee first, I think,' Horst had said, opening cupboards and drawers with a familiarity she found offensive. Of course, he had as much right to be in their grandmother's house as she did, although that fact had caused her to snub her nose behind him.

She had grabbed the coffee and set water to boil on the stove. 'I'll make it for us,' she had said. 'You sit.'

But he had continued to unlatch doors and stare at the shelves within before closing them and moving on. He had turned over the contents of the cutlery drawer; picked up a jar of pickles from the larder and placed it back in exactly the same position; inspected the matches next to the stove. 'What are you looking for, Horst?' Annie had forced herself to laugh, as if he was still the mischievous child and she the older cousin visiting from abroad.

'Something sweet,' he had said, not taking his eyes off his search. 'Have you baked today, Annie?'

'Sorry, not today.' Annie had mimed scrubbing. 'Wash day.'

At last he had looked at her and made his way to the table. 'Any bread?'

'I think I can find a slice for you. But what about Oma?'

He had shrugged. 'I will go up in a minute.' Then he had beamed, showing a mouth full of bright teeth. 'So, Annie. What do you think of the bombs we dropped on London, huh? A few weeks ago. Parliament was damaged. Most probably beyond repair.'

She knew it was a mercy that her back was to him or the involuntary flare of her nostrils and the deep pucker of her lips would have given away her outrage. She had been surprised he hadn't seen the jets of steam spurting from her ears, but then again he was too arrogant to notice. She was aware, as she knew he was, that Westminster Abbey, St Paul's and The Royal Mint had taken hits too, along with countless numbers of people and their homes, pubs, churches, shops and places of work. Fred had been so grateful that Viola was in Cambridge, which rarely got a mention in the news.

As she'd fussed with the coffee and cups, she'd managed to say that she had heard about the bombs dropped on London, but couldn't bring herself to utter a jubilant comment. She wasn't very good at putting on a front, as she and Fred had decided they must do. 'So,' Horst had challenged her, 'great news for the Fuhrer, don't you agree?'

Annie answered him in German with words to the effect of – *it goes without saying*. Perhaps she was getting better at hiding her true thoughts and feelings after all. That had seemed to satisfy him, although she had felt his huge blue eyes boring holes in her back, trying to see beyond her skin, bones and muscles into the heart and spirit of her being. By the time Horst had finished his coffee and bread and went upstairs to sit with Oma, she had felt drained of all energy.

But then she'd remembered her journal and the ensuing anxiety mobilised her again. He might be opening cupboards, drawers, dressers and presses upstairs; looking under the beds and in between the sheets; continuing his search for whatever it was he had been hunting for in the kitchen. There had been nothing downstairs to condemn them, she had known that, but upstairs there was the notebook. Hidden, or so she hoped, in between her knickers. Once upon a time, Horst would have been mortified at the thought of rooting through any woman's private articles of clothing. But now? How could she have been so stupid, she'd chastised herself, to try to conceal the book in such an obvious place and then to let Horst go upstairs alone?

She had stood like a statue at the bottom of the stairs, holding her breath to see if she could hear the creak of the loose floorboard in her room, the scritch of Horst's uniform as he crept across the landing. But there had been nothing until she caught his low resonant voice as he said a fervid, throaty goodbye to Oma.

He'd left soon after, saying he would return when he was next on leave. He had grabbed her in a hug and told her to let him know if Oma needed anything at all – extra rations, brandy, dispensation to have hot water more than the regulatory twice a week. Hanging in his arms like a rag doll, she had thought she would rather starve than ask him for a single thing, but perhaps for Oma she might. Feigning interest, she'd asked him if he knew where he would be posted. He'd touched the side of his nose in an oddly English gesture, then had said that all he could say was that the Fatherland need not worry about the Edelweiss Pirates any longer. She'd nodded as if she understood, although she had never heard of that appellation before.

The rain was slowing to a steady drizzle and the pavements outside Annie's window were dark and slick. People under black umbrellas hurried past. Tears filled Annie's eyes because she knew it was possible that Horst's visit could have been his last with Oma. She could not imagine how she would go on without her beloved grandmother. How would she define her days without Oma to look after, to shop for, to wash, to read to, to worry about? Oma was the reason she and Fred were here in Germany and without the protection of her existence, would they become more susceptible to being searched and questioned or worse? Annie was frightened to think that, after Oma was buried, she and Fred would be looked upon with greater suspicion than they were now. She felt sure the authorities would and could find some other crime to pin on them – the journal for one.

She dried her tears and picked up her pen again, then began to write about her grandmother.

Oma's life had been eventful and beyond Annie's realm of understanding during her twenty years. Although she looked forward to adventures in the future, she also hoped that she would never have to experience some of the things that Oma had to go through. She married when she was eighteen and Opa was not her choice, but that of her father. It was so hard to take in that her love life, or lack of it, was set in stone when she was younger than Annie was now. That must have been so difficult for her.

Once, quite a while ago, when Oma could still communicate and was full of stories, she told Annie that over a period of time she did fall very much in love with Opa. And that love was built on respect, honesty and patience. 'Let that, young lady, be a lesson to you on what to look for in a man before you agree to marry him.' Annie wished she had asked how the transformation took place, and at what stage of their marriage Oma realised that the shift in their emotions had happened. She liked to think it had occurred when Oma told Opa she was expecting their first child, but perhaps that had been too much of a shock, so early on in their marriage, for it to be a moment of celebration for Opa. It might have had the opposite effect and caused him to resent her for tying him to a life that in all probability he hadn't asked for either.

Or maybe it was after the birth of the baby, a little boy, that their love burgeoned – or when the child died at eleven days old. They went on to have nine living children, two more who died soon after they were born and another who lived until her teens. What an inventory of joy and despair. Each and every one of those incidents could have caused them to realise, as they drew strength and courage from each other, that they were in love. But equally the traumas could have severed them.

By the time Annie was old enough to be aware, Oma and Opa seemed almost to be one person, so alike were they in their opinions, their attitudes, their mindset and their values. They used the same vocabulary and even spoke with the same inflection and tone in their voices. Opa did well with his job at Kässbohrer, the diesel factory, clawing his way up from the factory floor to be a manager. He was respected by everyone in the vicinity, until a heart attack took him eight years ago. Oma had grieved for him every single day of her life since then, proving her love to the world.

And she lived through the War to End All Wars and was now in the middle of this one, although she didn't know much about it or so they thought. During that war she worked in a factory that made army uniforms as well as tending to her own family. If only Annie could always remember Oma as she had been – a whirlwind of activity, pulling everyone into the cyclone with her where they felt cared for and loved and special. Even now, when she was so weak, Oma would caress Annie's arm or reach out to touch her hair. One day last week, she had opened her eyes suddenly and said, 'Annie, are you crying?'

'No, Oma,' Annie had said, although she had been.

Oma's gnarled finger had brushed a tear from her granddaughter's cheek with pressure that Annie could barely feel. 'No more tears,' she'd said. 'There is not much in this life that is worth it.'

You are, Annie had thought, before smiling as best she could.

From across the hall there was the soft click of Oma's door. With well-practised efficiency, Annie replaced the notebook in its hiding place, opened her reading book and studied it as if she had been doing so all along.

'Come in, Fred,' Annie called in answer to his knock.

'Annie,' Fred said, his head appearing in the doorway. 'There is no milk to heat for Oma. And only a heel of bread left. Will you bake a loaf?'

Annie thought about these small requests that had become huge missions to fulfil. Shopping for anything could take hours and then, more often than not, she would come home with nothing she went out for. They were told by the regime to take heart from the fact that as a nation they had copious amounts of food, in comparison to the Allies. What they did have was bread, potatoes and preserves and more bread, potatoes and preserves. The party line was that as they had been victorious against France, they had access to the wonderful French cuisine. Well, someone might be getting escargot and champagne and foie gras, but it wasn't them or anyone else they knew. She suspected that if it existed, it was saved for those high up in the Gestapo or Wehrmacht. And their floozies, of course. Well, good luck to them. None of it would pass her lips. All the indoctrination and brainwashing. She wondered how many German citizens, in reality, believed in this Nazi regime, or if they, like she and Fred, had one side of their faces for the authorities and another for the truth deep inside them.

All they knew about how the Germans were bombarding Britain was from the German point of view. An article in the newspaper said that the destruction of Parliament was extensive, but the one and only photograph they had seen showed minor damage so they had no way of verifying that what they were told was the truth. The radio told them that the British were on their knees, crumbling and collapsing as a result of the bombing, rationing and blackouts. Then always in the next breath they were told to compare themselves to the Allies and be grateful. Germany, allegedly, had taken very little damage. Well, that might be true here in Ulm, but she knew from other reports that Cologne, Dresden and Berlin were devastated.

'Annie?' Fred stepped into her room, taking in the open book and his sister, sitting with her chin in her open palm.

'I will go and get some.' Annie sighed, dreading the queues and the downturned look on the other shoppers' faces. 'Just let me kiss Oma goodbye.'

Annie headed straight for the dairy and could not believe her luck when she saw the dairyman's wife, in a dirty white coat, arranging a row of full milk bottles in the shop window. She raced to be third in the queue outside the door but was soon joined by a long line of women who stood behind her. They alternated between gabbling to each other and gawping at the display through the window. The woman in front of her, who was wearing a stained pink cardigan and a shawl around her shoulders, nudged Annie over and over saying, 'Look, what a wonderful sight. Is it real?'

'I hope so,' Annie said, noticing a thin stream of drool escaping from the other woman's mouth.

But it wasn't. They were told the bottles were full of salt and being used for decoration only. Annie could feel the excitement drain from the crowd like smoke from a bomb. They didn't know whether to laugh or cry.

Before they went their separate ways, the woman who had dug Annie in the ribs said, 'You can't trust anyone or anything these days.'

No, Annie thought, *nothing is what it seems.*

Although the rain had stopped, Annie walked with head down like all the other women searching for rations. She passed the Minster, looming in shadow, and remembered

Oma and Mum swinging her between them in the sunshine on a visit to the cathedral many years ago. They had been happy, laughing and chatting about which cake they would choose from the bakery, how Annie's socks wouldn't stay up, the stories Vati told from his school days. Then the mood shifted when they saw Fort Oberer Kuhberg in the distance and Oma whispered to Mum that it was a concentration camp for political dissidents. Annie didn't know what any of that meant then – and she didn't have much of an idea now. But what all of them sensed was that something sinister was going on in the depths of the party and that people had been feeling intimidated by the authorities for some years. She'd seen the yellow stars sewn onto the heart side of Jewish people's coats and the stamps in their ration books that meant they were given less than others. She'd seen those things and averted her eyes, much to her shame. But what could she do? Confront the authorities and risk her tenuous freedom and that of the poor starred people?

Anyway, she had milk and bread to find. Bread was easy enough and she bought a loaf of rye with her rations from the bakery that nestled in the gloom of the Minster. Milk was harder and after trying five different shops, she had to settle for the less than satisfactory powder. Wondering if she should try to get a bit of fruit from the greengrocers, she came face to face with Walther's mother.

For a reason she couldn't pinpoint, she felt flustered and tongue-tied. 'Frau Wilhelm,' she said. 'I beg your pardon. I was so busy looking for milk or fruit or… Oh no.' She made to brush water from Frau Wilhelm's otherwise immaculate coat. 'Was that from my hair? Here, let me…'

Frau Wilhelm laughed. 'Annie, don't worry. There is rain

everywhere. It is a rainy day. Are you well? How is your Oma?'

'I am quite well, thank you, Frau Wilhelm.' Annie tried to stop fidgeting. 'But Oma is very weak.'

'Yes.' Frau Wilhelm nodded slowly, her eyes hooded in sympathy. 'Herr Doctor has kept me informed. I am so sorry.'

'She loves warm milk with cinnamon. It is one of the only things she will swallow. But you know that it's almost impossible to find.'

Without hesitation, Frau Wilhelm put her hand in her shopping bag and drew out a bottle of pure white milk with a plug of thick cream on the top.

Annie felt her eyes widen.

Frau Wilhelm pushed the bottle towards her. 'Give this to your Oma with my love.'

But Annie hid her hands behind her back and shook her head, more rain showering around them. 'I couldn't possibly take it.'

'I insist,' Frau Wilhelm said. 'You would be surprised at what people keep under the counter for the local doctor. It fills me with chagrin. Please, save me from embarrassment.'

Tentatively, Annie took the bottle saying, 'Well, for Oma. Thank you. I am so grateful.'

Frau Wilhelm patted her arm and left her standing, rain dripping from her hair onto the bottle of milk she held as if it were priceless.

Annie would probably never know whether it was on the strength of that meeting that a few weeks later, Walther came calling. Fred was out and she had been feeding bedsheets through the mangle when there was a knock at the door. *Oh no*, she thought, hoping it wasn't Horst again. Still wiping her hands on her apron she pulled open the door and there stood Walther, holding a small bunch of flowers that must have been from his mother's garden.

'Annaliese,' he said, drawing out the last part of her name. He presented the flowers to her with a huge smile on his face.

'Oh, thank you, Walther.' She looked down at her apron and indoor clothes. 'As you can see, I wasn't expecting anyone.'

They shuffled around and looked at each other for a few minutes before Annie asked him in and he looked very happy when he crossed the threshold. He followed her into the kitchen and watched her put the flowers in a vase and make them both a cup of coffee. Walther told her he had returned from university the day before, but would not be going back there for some time as he would have to continue his medical studies in the army. 'So,' he said, 'I have had to trade my white coat for a uniform.'

He didn't look or sound proud about that, but Annie was reluctant to question him in more detail. Instead, she enjoyed looking at him whilst he talked. He wasn't very tall, but his muscular frame lent him presence, as did his dark hair and pale hazel eyes. The ridge between his nostrils and the deep dimple in his left cheek made him appear playful and boyish.

She liked everything she saw very much, but more than anything she loved that they shared the same sense of humour. The last time they had met in Ulm for a walk and a drink, he'd told her that he thought her laugh infectious.

'That,' she had said, 'is good use of vocabulary for a doctor's son.' And they'd both laughed until tears ran down their faces.

As always he was gracious and gentlemanly, other attributes she found extremely charming. He asked after Oma and Fred. They talked about the weather, football and swimming, the beautiful tree his neighbour had chopped down for firewood. His voice became hoarse when he told her that his beloved dog, Ulfie, had died. They laughed about a couple of things, but not as heartily as they had a while ago and they never mentioned the war.

Walther was awkward when he stood to leave and Annie felt stiff and artless, not knowing where to put her hands or how to position her feet. She knew what was coming, but still his question caused her to feel deeply unsettled. 'May I call again, Annaliese?' he asked softly.

In her mind she stamped her foot in frustration. She was a young woman who was possibly under constant surveillance and suspicion, neither wholly rejected or accepted. And he was a young man who was about to join the military, albeit the medical corps, but perhaps he had been asked, or been commanded, to get close to her – to them. Annie stuttered and faltered and had no idea how to answer him for the best.

He looked so hopeful and eager standing there waiting for her reply, but the longer she hesitated the more his face fell. Eventually, his hands hung limp at his sides and he looked as though his balloon had been popped.

She didn't like this turn of events at all, so without thinking any further about the myriad of possible consequences, she said that yes, yes of course he could call again. She would look forward to his next visit.

He closed his eyes for a moment and smiled. When he bent and kissed her on the cheek they bumbled and shifted and somehow ended up with Annie against the wall and Walther leaning into her, their mouths open and their tongues pressed hard together.

When they prised themselves apart, Walther said, 'Thank you, Annaliese, I will see you very soon.'

'Why,' Annie said, wanting to clear up a mystery, 'are you calling me Annaliese all of a sudden? You know everyone calls me Annie.'

For a beat he looked shy, then said, 'I don't want you to think of me as just anyone, Annaliese. I want to be someone different to you.'

When he left, Annie thought the soaking bedsheets could wait. She raced upstairs, checked on Oma, then put everything down verbatim in her journal.

That evening, she related almost the whole episode to Fred. Instead of being angry or worried, he said she should encourage Walther to call on her. 'He is your childhood friend and an upstanding citizen. I think it will be good for others to see him coming and going.'

Annie nodded, but hugged close the thought of her and Walther's kiss, knowing that his visits would be about much more than a good word around the town for her and Fred.

Of course, there was a lot more she worried about after

that meeting with Walther. She knew she would have to ascertain whether or not he had allegiance to the party. If he did, she would have to try, if she could, to rebut him. It would be very difficult to do, but the image of him in that abhorrent uniform and clumpy boots would help her to reject him if she had to. But oh, how she hoped it would not come to that.

As she went about her daily chores, she felt growing resentment as endless questions crowded her mind. How would the childhood rapport between her and Walther have developed if it had been allowed to evolve seamlessly? If the war and the mistrust that was part of it had not happened? She daydreamed about living, in due course, in the doctor's house here in Ulm with Walther; about him working alongside his Vater until the practice became his to run; about taking it in turns with Fred and Viola to visit each other in their chosen countries. She imagined them, as a couple, eating together, sleeping together, making children together, creating a garden together. But most often, and this made her want to sit and cry, she pictured them laughing together. That was how their lives could have been. That was how they would have faced everything and anything together. Hitler had so much to be ashamed of and robbing people of their laughter was not the least of his guilty actions.

It was late and Annie had no idea where Fred was or when he would return. She was fuming and frantic. They had an agreement, they had discussed it, drawn it up and promised each other they would abide by it. She had kept her side of it, but was convinced Fred was hiding something from her.

Three weeks ago, Fred had told her he was finding it difficult without the direction of a job or studies to attend to. Also, he said, people were beginning to question why he hadn't joined the army. Two members of the SS had stopped him near the rail station and asked him why he was not in uniform. Fred told her that he began to sweat like a pig; he was sure the officers could smell his fear. Whilst it might excuse him to say he was half-British, that would only have made matters worse. So he told them he had been unwell and was waiting for permission from the doctor to be able to join up. He said that in his alarm he forced himself to cough and rubbed his knee with vigour at the same time. That sounded hilarious, and she hoped that one day Fred would mime the incident to her and Viola to make them rock with laughter, but in this time and place it was not funny at all and she had been unnerved by it.

They let him go without asking for his address or proof of his temporary dispensation, but who knew about the next time.

After that, he said he'd been thinking for some time of trying to get work at the university in Munich. He wasn't sure if there would be anything available for him there that might render him exempt from fighting, but he was going to try. He came home on time after his first visit, sounding heartened and looking more galvanised than he had since the war started. The rest of that week followed the same pattern, although his reports became more and more vague. The second week he said he had made good contacts and thought there was something for him in the pipeline. This week, his movements had been worryingly erratic and underhand. If he came home tonight, and how could she be sure he would, she determined to confront him until he told her what was going on. It would be most unfair of him not to do so.

It was 1.30 a.m. by the time Fred tiptoed into the house and made straight for the stairs and the sanctuary of his bedroom. He must have thought she was tucked up and oblivious to his recklessness. When she flung open the living room door he looked as though he was being faced by a harridan – she was wearing a nightdress with one of Oma's shawls over her shoulders; her hair was unpinned and she was shaking with anger and worry. They stood and stared at each other for a minute until Annie put her finger on her lips and pointed upstairs, then beckoned him to follow her to the living room.

She closed the door behind them, stood in front of it and faced Fred with her arms crossed over her chest. Fred fiddled with the buttons on his jacket, smoothed his beard, looked towards the kitchen and then at the curtains. It became apparent to Annie that she would have to start the conversation, but try as she might, she couldn't hold her nerve and started to cry instead. Fred took a step towards her, his arms wide but she couldn't bear it and batted him away. He closed his eyes and when he opened them he looked helpless.

'Fred,' she said at last. 'Why are you doing this? After all our plans to keep safe.'

He stood mute in front of her.

'Fred,' she pleaded with him. 'Please try to think how I feel. Sitting here night after night, wondering and worrying. You must tell me what's going on.'

He fidgeted a bit more then asked if they could sit. Annie

was too exhausted to do anything else, so flopped onto the couch, pulling a blanket over her legs. Fred sat opposite in Oma's overstuffed chair. He took a deep breath then said he was ashamed of breaking his side of their agreement but had done so to protect her.

'From what?'

By way of a reply, he looked away and shook his head. 'I am sorry for upsetting you so much, dear Annie,' he said. 'But I cannot tell you what is afoot. I will not implicate you.'

Her feelings of frustration increased until she could feel them boiling over. 'I am implicated regardless,' she exploded. 'As you are in everything I say and that's why we agreed to keep each other informed of our whereabouts. Remember,' she shouted, 'we said that we would stand together and if it came to it, go down together.' Besides, she thought, not knowing was so much worse. The anxiety, the vivid imaginings, the restlessness, the panic that froze her to the spot.

Fred did not rise to her anger, which only served to inflame her. His hands were folded in his lap; his legs were crossed at the knees. Again he shook his head. They sat in silence for a few minutes, then he leaned towards her and said he understood her grievance and that yes, if circumstances were the other way around, he would be deeply offended. So he would compromise.

'I do not want a compromise,' she huffed.

'It is the best I can do. At this point.' he said. 'And keep your voice down, I implore you.'

He explained that from now on he would tell her where he was going and what time he would be back, but would not always be able to tell her who he was with. 'I am sorry, Annie, but for your safety I cannot disclose more.'

'But you expect me, I suppose, to stick to all our rules like a little servant girl?' she spat out.

'Yes, I do. And one day you will understand,' he said, standing to bring the argument to a close.

But she had to ask him one more thing. She had to know if who he was seeing and what he was doing involved the Edelweiss Pirates.

'Similar,' was his simple reply.

She wasn't sure if this information made her feel better or worse. But the knowledge ignited a tiny shard of pride in her chest.

Probably hoping to muster some solidarity after their battle, they went together to tend to Oma before they went to their beds. The minute Annie saw her, she knew something was very wrong and rushed to her side. 'Oma, Oma!' Annie flung herself at her grandmother, terrified to feel her sweating and to hear her mumbling and calling out the names of her husband and children, the clatter in her chest worsening with every breath she fought for.

Fred ran for Herr Doctor and Annie held tight to Oma's dear parchment-thin hands, listening as her out-breaths became more and more shallow and her in-breaths like pebbles being slung around in a bag. She told herself she must remain calm and controlled and help Oma to feel safe and comfortable as she slipped from this world to the next – as Oma had helped her so many times in the past.

In Oma's last moment she opened her eyes, looked at Annie with recognition and affection and smiled. She would hold on to that forever.

The funeral was arranged. All the family attended, most of her cousins in some kind of repulsive Nazi uniform, goose-stepping behind the coffin and giving each other the hideous Heil Hitler salute. Annie and Fred never initiated the ridiculous one-armed address, but they had to return it many times over the course of the day. Whenever Annie was backed into that corner, as she thought of it, she inwardly counteracted the salute with a rebellious action – an imaginary raspberry, a two-fingered wave, a cross of the eyes, a swear word. She knew it had no effect whatsoever, but it made her feel better.

In a blur, family, friends and neighbours filled Oma's house for food and drink, provided by the regime, after the ceremony. Annie was so distraught that she went through the motions of being hostess as if in a fevered dream. Whilst wiping her nose with one hand and clearing away plates with the other, she became aware of Horst touching everything once again, opening and closing cabinet drawers and cupboard doors. He sidled up to her and asked what she and Fred planned to do now. Annie couldn't think what he meant; all she could think about was how she was going to miss Oma, and said so.

'Will you stay here?' Horst asked. 'Or can the house be put to better use?'

Fred must have overheard because he came to stand beside her. Horst repeated his question.

'Do you mean Oma and Opa's house should be handed over to the Party?' Fred asked.

'Perhaps,' Horst said, his hands behind his back. 'It would make a wonderful billet. And...' He looked from them to Herr Doctor and Frau Wilhelm with an almost imperceptible narrowing of his eyes. 'You could live elsewhere.'

Annie opened her mouth to ask what he was alluding to, when she felt Fred's elbow brush hers. 'Well,' Fred said, 'if that is what the entire family agrees, then of course it must be so. Shall we start by asking your father's opinion?'

Horst reddened and his nostrils flared. For a beat he was silent, then he acquiesced with a slight nod. 'It was merely an idea, my dear Frederick. Of course the house is yours to live in until...' He waved his hand aimlessly, turned on his heel and made for the buffet table. Annie was beginning to see that perhaps Horst was full of bluff – all mouth and no trousers. At least until such time as he became so confident that he followed through on his threats.

The reception finished and everyone went home. Annie and Fred sat and stared at each other, their eyes red and handkerchiefs soggy. Annie knew the flowers would wilt very soon. The neighbours would stop bringing them meals to heat on the stove. Oma's bed would be changed and remade for visitors. Fred would resume his daily journey to Munich and Annie's grieving would begin.

At last Fred took Annie into his confidence. Late one evening he took a wad of well-thumbed papers from his inside pocket, unfolded them and without a word, placed them in front of her. She looked at him for explanation, but he left her alone with the typewritten pages. Reading through the top sheet, she gasped aloud and clutched the essays to her chest. Her heart was pounding and she felt both terror-stricken and overjoyed at the same time.

Three powerful sermons written and delivered by a Catholic bishop were in her hands. She read one after the other, then started the first again. She could not believe it; someone in authority was protesting about Gestapo terror, condemning euthanasia, forced sterilisation and the concentration camps; attacking the regime for their part in the disappearances of countless people without trial, and the trepidation the Party had instilled in everyone. Most of all, he vilified the Third Reich for reducing decent and loyal citizens to inertia for fear of ending up in a prison cell or concentration camp and thus undermining belief in justice and reducing the German people to cowardice.

This wonderful man, who she hoped in time would be honoured as a saint, went so far as to write that the German people were not being destroyed by Allied bombing but by negative forces from within their own government.

In her reverie, she did not hear Fred come to stand behind her, until his hand on her shoulder made her jump. When they looked at each other, she could see the tears in his eyes that mirrored hers. 'Fred,' she whispered. 'How did you get these documents?'

He sat next to her. 'They are being copied and circulated widely.'

'Legally? Surely not.'

He shook his head. 'No, they are being moved secretly from one underground group to another.' He lowered his voice. 'I even heard that the Allies got hold of some copies and have dropped them amongst German troops, but I don't know if that's possible.' He shrugged his shoulders.

'Has this hero been arrested? Or executed?'

Fred rubbed his hands together and smiled. 'No, and that's the most marvellous thing. The regime dare not as it would completely alienate the Catholic population and they do not want to risk that. But he is under what can only be called house arrest.'

Annie flipped the pages over again and reread parts of the sermons; every sentiment in each sentence was inspiring. Fred watched her in silence. Then he coughed and said, 'That is why we must do all we can to spread and expand upon what he has started.'

Annie's head jolted up as if pulled from behind; she could feel her eyes bulge. 'We?'

'Are you in?' her brother asked.

Images of Oma and Opa went through her mind, followed by pictures of Walther and Horst, Nazi salutes, salt in milk bottles, the Edelweiss Pirates, Viola, the Allies, bombers, her secret journal and the brave Catholic bishop. But they were mere flashes and Fred would have only been aware of her immediate nod of absolute and complete conviction.

7

Viola stubbed out her cigarette with force until she was satisfied that it was beyond revival. She sat and watched it smoulder and took a deep breath past the heaviness in her chest that she'd felt since seeing Mum off at the train station. She had always hated saying goodbye to anyone she loved, but it had become much harder since Fred left and the war began. Now she had to work hard to keep her emotions in check.

Dad had not wanted Mum to spend a long weekend in London. He said it was ridiculous enough that Viola was living in the capital when she could have remained relatively safe in Cambridge, or moved back home to Cirencester, let alone having to worry about Mum becoming an easy target for Jerry bombs as well. But Mum had insisted, in her quiet manner, that she wanted to visit her daughter and Dad had given up and acceded. The weekend was arranged and what a marvellous time it had been.

Mum had not been the least bit anxious or daunted,

certainly not that she'd let on. Carrying herself with calm dignity, she stepped around bomb debris and burst water mains, sheltered in doorways during air raids, showed an interested sympathy for the grotesque damage to buildings and people, paled a bit when a hit was taken close to the Savoy where they were having a lovely high tea and concentrated on Viola and their time together. Viola aspired to be the image of her mother in those respects.

Most of the artwork and exhibits had been evacuated to places of safety, but they visited what was left to browse in the British Museum and the V&A and Viola was most surprised when Mum said she was interested in seeing a small exhibition at the Tate: Paintings, Drawings and Sculptures of Nudes by Contemporary Artists. When they began, arm in arm, to make their way around the gallery, Viola could feel a flush blossoming under her collar. She and her mum had never discussed the differences between the male and female anatomy, or what happened between men and women, or how babies were conceived and born or any of the intimacies of life. But she appraised the artwork with cool objectivity in contrast to the heat Viola was sure her mother could feel rising from her cheeks and under her arms. She stood in front of one exhibit for what felt like ages, taking in a pen and ink of a young man lying on his back, his hands under his head and his knees splayed in a devil may care attitude; despite the cool, preserving temperature in the gallery, Viola had to remove her coat and gloves and surreptitiously wipe the glow from her face.

During all that, Mum kept up a commentary about the artwork, as was her habit when visiting museums, but Viola could not manage to join in with her usual studied remarks, as was hers. Instead, she hummed and hawed in what she hoped were the right places and felt like an absolute fool. But that particular drawing received no judgement or dictum from Mum until she peered closer, then without taking her eyes from the sketch, said, 'Well, you'd need Dad's magnifying glass to see that young fellow's manhood, wouldn't you?'

Viola couldn't quite believe she'd heard correctly and stood stock-still, as if in shock until Mum turned to her with a huge, brazen grin on her face and said, 'Don't you think so, Vi?'

After another minute of inertia, Viola began to giggle. Mum joined in and they had to leave the museum before their shrieks of laughter got them thrown out. Viola had thought the subject matter might re-emerge in a more serious manner, but the incident was never mentioned again. What a wonderful moment it had been and things between them seemed to shift slightly after that. Viola couldn't quite pinpoint the difference, but decided it was something to do with Mum perceiving her as a woman in her own right, not merely as her daughter.

Viola was pleased that they chose the Wigmore for a concert rather than the RAH as Fred had been given the second name of Albert after Queen Victoria's consort and that raw reminder would have put a damper on the evening for her. She would have been unable to think of anything except the fact that Victoria got to have her husband, so why couldn't she?

They walked in Hyde Park, bought a few little things in Selfridges and Harrod's, slept together in Viola's single bed, talked about books and the boys and Fred. Once, Mum asked about her job, but Viola had to remind her, with a fingertip on her closed lips, that she had signed the Official Secrets Act.

And then the weekend was over. Neither of them would allow themselves to cry or be sentimental when they said goodbye at Paddington, most certainly not when the station was packed with mothers leaving their tots to be evacuated to the safety of the country. But they hugged each other for longer than usual and pressed each other's hands through the train window until the last possible moment.

And now Viola was alone in the flat, lighting another Player's Navy Cut to help take away the pain of missing Mum – and Fred.

Making the most of the last hour or so before the blackouts needed to be drawn, she parted the curtains and looked down on Tottenham Court Road. So many people out and about and not all of them hurrying to and from work; they looked too happy and excited for that to be the case. The war had not deterred people from having a good time, quite the opposite – it seemed to have boosted their capacity for amusement, especially in London. *Look at all of them*, she thought, *walking with great determination to who knows where to meet who knows whom to do who knows what*. A woman on the opposite side of the street threw herself into the arms of a man in uniform who returned her public display of affection without any sign of chagrin. In fact, if his roaming hands and dappy grin were anything to go by, he was relishing the attention. When they drew apart, they linked arms so tightly it was difficult to tell one of their ashen-coloured coats from the other. A group of girls laughed their way in the other direction, flipping their hair and flinging their hips from side to side as three American soldiers gave them the once-over.

Sighing, Viola stepped back from the window and into the dull room. She had recently finished *Faro's Daughter* by Georgette Heyer and the next book waiting for her was *Frenchman's Creek*, Daphne du Maurier's latest. Or she could reread the partially completed thesis Fred had left behind in his Cambridge rooms. She knew all the idiosyncrasies of his writing; his rhythms and cadences and turns of phrase and having the manuscript close at hand gave her much comfort. But she'd read through it, corrected and edited it so many times that she wasn't sure she could face it again. Not tonight.

She wondered where all those happy young people were going. Dancing, she supposed. That was all the girls at work seemed to talk about. Even Lillian, who Viola had never before heard mention a waltz or a foxtrot or a jive, regularly joined one or other of their many colleagues on a dancing night out. They had persuaded her to join them once or twice and the music was good, but the endless garrulous talk about who was dancing with whom and who they hoped to dance with and who had the best footwork and who had asked for whose address did not interest her in the least. Lillian said it was because she was so faithful to Fred. Well, of course she was and that made her feel guilty when she did agree to dance with a few select young men who asked.

Viola remembered a gangly man with fleshy earlobes who took her for a twirl after asking three times. Afterwards, he bought her a drink and they stood together at the bar. There were a few grey hairs at his temples and his hands were clean and looked strong. 'I work in the War Department,' he said. 'In a reserved role. For now. And you?'

Viola put her finger on her closed lips and said, 'Shhh.'

'Oh, I see.' He nodded to let her know he understood she could say no more.

Then, before he could waste any more time or money on her, she thought she ought to tell him about Fred. 'And I have a fiancé. Or at least, someone I've promised myself to.'

He didn't look disappointed at all, but smiled in a way that led her to believe he thought her unworldly. 'That's a rather old-fashioned expression,' he said.

Viola chose not to reply and thought about how to move the conversation on, but her admirer got in first. 'So, which regiment does he belong to? Or is he in a reserved occupation like me?'

'Neither,' she said. 'He's stranded in Germany.'

The young man moved backwards sharply, as if avoiding a punch. He paled and his eyes narrowed. His features could no longer be described as nice. 'Germany?' he repeated. 'How did that happen?'

When Viola finished explaining with sketchy details, the man straightened his tie and said, 'So, your fiancé-to-be is part German.'

'Yes.' Viola nodded. 'But he's also…'

'Excuse me,' the man said and turned his back on her. Viola followed him with her eyes and watched as he chatted to a group of young men who stared in her direction without compunction then closed ranks.

★

When she had returned from Paddington the flat was cold and empty, Lillian having left for a night out with June and Harriet. They had been getting ready around Mum packing to leave and Mum had seemed to enjoy the ensuing chaos. 'Will you be joining them later?' she'd asked. 'I would in your position.'

'Probably not,' Viola had answered, feeling a wash of loneliness at the thought of being on her own. 'They're going to a dance hall and I don't always like to... I can't always... join in, I suppose.'

'Does dancing make you feel disloyal to Fred, dear?' Mum had said. Then with a small touch to Viola's hand she'd added, 'None of us wants you to be a martyr. Or a saint. Especially not Fred.'

Hurt had stabbed at Viola but it dissipated in the bustle of getting Mum to the station and on her train. But alone in the darkening flat, Mum's words came back to her and she allowed herself to feel the full throttle of offence. Surely that was not how she came over? As a persecuted, tormented sorry-for-herself soul? If that was the case, Lillian would have mentioned it, wouldn't she? Viola would ask her at the first opportunity; Lillian would tell her the truth. But Mum would never be cruel in what she said, Viola knew that. The words she used were always well thought out and meant to steer her children through the pitfalls in their lives. Perhaps she merely hated seeing Viola so desolate when Lillian, Harriet, June and everyone else out there was making the best of a horrendous situation.

Retrieving Lillian's old brown cardigan from the back of a chair, Viola wrapped it around herself against the chill. So this was the exciting life she'd entertained hopes for in

London: the occasional night out to the pictures or the pub, looking at what little there was in the shops, mending and making do, trying to be creative with rations, being evasive about Fred. She shook her head to clear her thoughts. *But there is always my job*, she rationalised, *and the fact that I am doing the right thing.*

The thought of getting back to her office created an invigorating energy strong enough to cause a grin to spread across her face. She took down the du Maurier from the shelf for later and stretched out on the couch, an ashtray and cigarettes close by. Wriggling her toes in her stockinged feet, she pictured how she had left her desk on Friday evening. Neat piles of fresh paper, her pens and pencils in a pot, envelopes of various sizes in a tray. In a locked drawer there were documents that were not regarded as highly secretive and could wait until later to be dealt with; her personal things like lipstick and a hanky; a list of names and numbers of the government officials who worked from offices close by. There were two typewriters side by side, both cleaned and covered with care. A piece of equipment that enabled someone to record their voice into a machine for her to listen to and transcribe was equally pampered with its own grey dustcover.

Then there was the miraculous machine that recorded the relentless sound of the voices of Hitler, or others from his mob, proselytising on German radio that she had to listen to and interpret for the government. And oh, if they could be believed one would think the Axis was winning in the most glorious manner, with the plump, well-fed civilians of Germany skipping and dancing around towns and fields untouched by Allied bombs. But of course she didn't believe a word they said. Nor did anyone. It was all disgusting propaganda.

The large office was manned solely by women, most of them quite young and from a background of assisting with foreign language teaching. They were, of course, managed by men who rushed in and out all day with documents that needed to be translated urgently. There were also telegrams, propaganda leaflets, foreign news, radio announcements and newspaper articles that needed to be transcribed to English. And in between, the inexorable tirade of news from Germany to be typed up and sent to the higher-ups. Each document had to be stamped with the time and date and initialised by the translator and strangely, the constant thunk-thunk was reassuring rather than intrusive. The office was a hive of activity, but like a swarm of bees they each knew their role and went about their business in a structured manner with the lowest level of buzz possible.

Lillian's desk was next to the boarded windows amongst those interpreting French. Amanda was on the wall at the back with the Italian speakers and whenever Viola heard them talking, she thought of Matteo and hoped his life was not too dreadful in the internment camp. June sat in the same section as Lillian and Harriet was one of the four who translated Russian. The largest and busiest area belonged to Viola and the other German analysts who sat closest to the door and were kept occupied without respite every day.

Hours went by without her thinking about anything else but the job at hand, which was an enormous relief. As soon as she took off her coat in the morning, a document would be propped in front of her and she was asked to translate, as a matter of urgency, a newspaper article that quoted verbatim a speech by Hitler. Throwing aside the cover of her typewriter, she would begin to hit the keys in time to the rhythm of the German that she read; there was but a moment's delay between the two activities. When she was halfway through the article, another man would appear with a radio transcript that he said should take priority over what she was doing. Leaving the page in the typewriter, she moved to her other machine, banged out the document, then went back to the original article. 'Thank you, Miss Baxter.' 'Excellent, Miss Baxter.' 'Well done, Miss Baxter.' And although she wasn't being singled out by any means, the words were gratifying to hear and affirmation that she was doing a good job.

Closing her eyes, she laid her head back on a cushion and realised that, thanks to the visit from Mum, she had not heard the grating, disturbing, screeching Nazi voices that followed her home and invaded her waking and sleeping moments for the entire weekend. 'Part of the job,' all the girls said. Although it was worse for her and the other German translators as they worked with the enemy's language rather than the tongues of those countries that had merely followed Hitler's lead.

Her packet of cigarettes was empty so she searched the counter and table tops and hunted through a few drawers hoping to find a cigarette or two that Lillian had left behind. But none leaped out at her. And there was no gin in the flat, although she felt very uncomfortable buying that when she was by herself. She would have to go out and face the throng if she wanted to smoke during the long evening ahead with her book. But pride would not let her do so without looking presentable, so she pulled a brush through her thick wavy hair until it was tamed and rather shiny; it had grown to just below her shoulders since she'd been in London and was due another perm, but she quite liked it the way it was. She thought Fred would like it, too.

Looking in the mirror, she put a tortoiseshell comb first behind one ear, then the other. She turned this way and that, took out the second comb and felt happy with the result. Her face had changed shape, she thought, but almost imperceptibly. Where once her cheeks had been round, they were now more hollow and womanly, which in turn allowed her eyes to appear larger and rounder. Perhaps it was the result of rationing or pining or a combination of both. The overall effect might have made her look gaunt and a bit emaciated, but instead everyone commented that she looked striking and sophisticated. She applied eyebrow pencil, one sweep of mascara and a muted rather than siren shade of red lipstick, a tiny touch of rouge on the tips of her cheeks and that was all she needed. Discarding the faithful brown cardigan, she pulled on a cream-coloured blouse and her dark green coat.

Those few adjustments actually lifted her spirits and she wondered if that was why the others made themselves up, or went dancing – to feel better. Could it be that easy?

George regularly spent his leave in London visiting Lillian, even though they both denied there was anything between them. June had a chap fighting in El Alamein. Harriet was fancy free but had lost one brother to the war and another was in the Navy. And yet, they got on with their lives, seeming to make the most out of each other and what they did have here and now. That attitude was probably what Mum was referring to when she said Viola should not expect herself to be a martyr or a saint.

She smiled to herself. Not a huge beam, but enough to lighten her demeanour a tiny bit more. Checking her handbag for money, keys, handkerchief, she made her way down the narrow stairs to the street.

The nearest tobacconist was on the corner of Oxford Street but instead of turning in that direction, Viola turned right towards Soho. Now that she was out, she could do with the fresh air and exercise. If anything, there were more people about than earlier in the evening; all dressed up and full of themselves. It felt good to be out amongst the crowds. There was a lot of laughter and she could hear music from a couple of underground clubs that seemed to be springing up all over the place. It was cold, but not freezing and the earlier rain had left a lovely, freshly washed smell on the air that cut through the smoky residue that lingered day in and day out.

Suddenly, she thought she heard someone shouting her name. But of course it couldn't be. She looked around but didn't see anyone she recognised amongst the throng. Then again, a bit louder: 'Vi, wait.'

Viola turned and there was Lillian running towards her, out of breath and red in the face. Laughing, she said, 'I tried to catch up with you but had to resort to running. How undignified. Where are you off to at such a fast trot?'

'Nowhere really.' Viola shrugged. 'I needed cigarettes and thought I'd make the most of being out with a quick walk.'

'You and your walks,' Lillian said. 'You'll have legs like my tree trunks soon.' Lillian looked from Viola's long, slender legs to her own sturdy pair and laughed again.

The rain had given way to sleet so they moved into the shelter of a shop doorway. 'But what are you doing, Lil? I thought you were going to a dance.'

'The resident band didn't turn up and the stand-ins were terrible.' She pulled a face. 'So we're in The Black Horse.'

'Well, you're not.'

'You are a clever one, Vi, aren't you? I was on my way home to drag you out.'

Viola knew she would never forget the kindness of that simple gesture. She started to express her thanks, but Lillian took her by the elbow and they ran together through the heavy crowds and the light hail; two girls like any others, enjoying themselves on a night out.

They were much more subdued and business-like the next day at work until the office was packed with crowds of men flapping documents and files, waiting to read about how the world had reported the failure of Operation Barbarossa. There was frost outside, but the room was stuffy and uncomfortable and Viola's fingers slipped over the keys of her typewriters. She had two sets of documents on the go, four others piled in order of importance and the unceasing voice of Hitler to translate. All the men were talking in loud, booming voices, calling over each other to colleagues. But she remained single-minded and meticulous and handed over one set of papers at a time to the men who had provided them, then glued herself to her chair and transcribed the broadcasts.

Gradually, the office was vacated of its visitors and she and Lillian sat slumped in their chairs, smiling at each other across the room. The steadier pace was welcome then, for a few minutes or hours, until another crisis would have the office clamorous again. How girls in jobs that never varied dealt with the tedium was beyond her.

It was difficult not to be able to discuss what she did with anyone outside the office, apart from Lillian and the other girls. But they knew it was very dangerous to talk about anything work-related in the pub or a café or taking the air on a park bench or waiting for a bus. One evening, a group of them had been sitting around a table in a quiet pub and a colleague named Phyllis or Peggy or Penelope ducked her head low and started to talk in loud whispers about something she had translated that day. Viola and Lillian and all the others shushed her but she would not be hushed.

'Will you keep your voice down?' Harriet had said.

The tattletale looked over her shoulder and said, 'Why? There's no one here.'

'You never know who's listening,' June said. 'Haven't you seen the posters?'

'Besides,' Viola chipped in. 'We've all signed the Act, haven't we? And we don't want to hear it. Not here or anywhere.' She looked around the table. 'I, for one, will get up and leave if you persist.' The others all nodded in agreement.

The following day at the office, the girl was ignored by everyone who had been out with her the night before. And in a more dramatic turn, she was called into the manager's office and never seen again. Someone had reported her. But whether that someone was one of their number or a big ears in the pub never became public knowledge. But good riddance to her.

Viola had learned, as had her friends, to deal with the situation by either drawing her finger across her tightly closed mouth or holding it against her lips and the pantomime seemed to do the job. Initially, she thought it might be perceived as giving her a certain amount of mystery, but in reality it left her on the side-lines during a number of conversations.

When she was alone in the flat, or on one of her walks, or on the skeleton night shift at work, she often thought about the fact that she really should be used to being on the periphery, but time and time again the reaction she inflamed in others both surprised and upset her.

She liked to sit in a comfy chair in the corner of the ladies' resting room during her break, a book in her hand and a cup of tea on the low table in front of her. There were no windows in the room, so there was no telling what the weather was doing outside, but the first few days of March had been bitter and she could feel the icy cold seeping through the brickwork. Viola shivered and cuddled into herself, the thought of the next chapter of her book making her feel warm and cosy. The door opened and two girls swung in, jostling and laughing. They were dressed for an evening out but had small overnight bags in their hands in which, Viola presumed, they carried more sombre clothes for their shift at work. Viola had seen them previously, but not been introduced, so she marked her page and smiled at them. 'Hello,' she said. 'You look as if you've been having a good time.'

The tallest of the pair, who wore a beautiful, low-cut, shimmering burgundy dress that drew attention to her plump cleavage, extended her hand and said, 'Yes, it was. Pity it had to finish. Ann by the way.'

'Carol.' The other girl nodded to Viola.

'New?' Viola said. 'Our paths haven't crossed yet.'

They both nodded. 'Russian,' Carol said.

'And I'm German,' Ann said. 'Well, not German, thank God. But that's the language I deal with.'

Before she thought better of it, Viola answered, 'Oh, me too. I suppose our shifts haven't coincided yet, but they will do, believe me.' She smiled. 'I'm Viola,' she said.

They both visibly bristled; Viola would swear later to Lillian that she could see the hairs on their arms stand on end. The girls stumbled over their greetings, mumbling something about how pleased they were to meet her when probably they were merely glad to have their curiosity sated about the woman among their ranks who was fretting and worrying about the boyfriend who was living with the enemy.

Still, as the year rolled into spring, Viola did become more accepting of the situation. She practised being decorous and gracious, like Mum, but also aloof towards those who rebuffed her. There was nothing she could do about it, so good luck to them. On the other hand, she took a leaf out of Lillian, June and Harriet's book and tried to enjoy life with what was left at her bestowal.

Living by that premise, Viola made more of an effort with her appearance, as she had done when Fred was with her. As she had proved to herself, months before, that discipline paid off in terms of her self-confidence. Now, she rarely turned down an invitation either, having determined that almost whatever she did in the company of others passed the time in a pleasant and agreeable manner. She danced whenever asked, but followed her own rule not to accept more than two requests from the same man during the same evening.

On some occasions she found she quite enjoyed herself, whether in a handhold with a young man or with one of her friends. It was fun and as she suspected, provided her with a few hours here and there when she wasn't dwelling on circumstances she had no control over. On others, when she left the club on Lillian's arm, loneliness engulfed her and her glow from the lively evening vanished as quickly as a ration of tea.

Lillian looked confused when Viola sat on the arm of a chair late one night and wept. 'Whatever is the matter, Vi?' she asked. 'I thought we'd had a lovely evening.'

Viola accepted the arm around her shoulders and snubbed her nose with the heel of her hand. 'We did. Really.'

'Well, what's brought this on?'

'Everything and nothing, I suppose.' She sighed. 'The contrasts, I think.' It was music followed by air raid sirens. Or silence. Light then darkness. Heads held high and bright smiles that made way for looking down at feet with concentration. Pretty dresses on show that were then hidden away beneath shabby, grey coats. The perfectly acceptable men. None of whom were the perfect Fred.

Lillian rubbed her friend's arm. 'Yes, the contradictions are too stark,' she agreed.

Eisenhower took command of the US military operations from London and in celebration, numerous clubs decked out their shadowy premises with red, white and blue and invited the American GIs to mingle with the locals, as if they hadn't been doing so freely all along. Below stairs in Fitzrovia, Viola found herself enjoying a second dance with a tall, sandy-haired American staff sergeant to a jazz rendition of 'I'll Never Smile Again'. She was wearing her favourite navy-blue dress – pinched in at the waist with pintucks at the neckline – newish faux pearl ear clips, black heels and stockings on which anyone would have been hard-pressed to see the mends. Her hair had recently had that long-awaited perm and she felt good about herself.

'My name's Mike,' the staff sergeant said when the number finished. 'Where are you sitting?'

Viola pointed to a pile of coats, bags, drinks and ashtrays under which there was a table requisitioned by her and her friends. Mike went to the bar to get her a Dubonnet cocktail and when he was walking back towards her, he passed under a sidelight and with a sharp intake of breath, she realised that his hair was made up of the same brindle streaks as Fred's. It was uncanny – she had never encountered anyone else with that colouring.

Taking a sip of her drink, she was mesmerised by his hair and couldn't stop herself from staring at it through the corner of her eye. He asked her about her job and she drew her finger across her mouth. Then for good measure she said, 'And I have a fiancé. Or an almost-fiancé.'

'I thought there might be something like that going on,' he said, nodding towards the ring that had somehow worked its way to the outside of her dress where it sparkled and danced in the light.

Fiddling with the necklace, she repositioned it back into

its accustomed place. 'So,' she continued, 'I never dance with the same man more than twice in one evening.'

'Then I've had it,' he replied, drumming his fingers on the table in a rather arrogant glib manner. Soft tufts of hair sprouted along his fingers and they, too, were the same mixture of red, blond and brown as Fred's.

He produced a packet of Lucky Strikes and holding them towards her asked, 'Well, are you game for one of these?'

She nodded her agreement and when she leaned towards the match he offered, she realised that her head came to the exact spot on his chest where it had rested so many times on Fred. He smelled like Fred, too. Her heart felt it would stop and she didn't so much rise to the thrill of it as sink deep into the comfort.

8

July 1942

When their grief allowed them to feel able, Annie and Fred cleaned every surface and corner and cubbyhole of the house. And the things they found were in turn heart-wrenching, baffling and amusing. An encyclopaedia with a single white rose squashed between two stained pages. An old no-longer-necessary dog food bowl right at the back of a kitchen cupboard. A painting of Neuschwanstein Castle that used to hang, lopsided, at the top of the landing. But still Oma's presence remained – a whiff of her talcum powder, a scrap of her handwriting, a sweater at the back of a cupboard, an echo of her giggle or her last jarring breaths. When they came across a box of letters they had written over the years from England, they read all of them aloud to each other, sitting on the floor, doubling over with laughter which turned, on a childish phrase or misspelling or pencil drawing to tears. Not being able to bring themselves to throw them away, they replaced the envelopes in the order they found them and lifted them into the attic. 'We'll forget about them there,' Annie said. 'And when we next come across them we'll probably feel able to put them on the fire.'

'Yes, good idea,' Fred said.

But Annie doubted that would ever be the case.

Then Fred resumed his daily trips into Munich and Annie waited with impatience to join the group he'd promised to involve her in. She was desperate to know what he did and that urgency made her daily tasks seem more banal. Pushing herself up from kneeling, she mentally ticked off dusting from the list of chores she had to get through every day. She tidied, hung washing on the line, scoured the sink and tackled the shopping that she detested so much, brought it back and tried to turn it into something edible. All of it was undertaken within the dark enveloping cloud of grief.

So Annie pleaded with Fred to allow her to accompany him, but all he said was, 'Yes, yes, yes, Annie,' in a sing-song voice. 'You will be summonsed, but in good time. When I deem it safe.'

'Oh,' she said aloud, washing the frame of the back door. 'The wait is driving me mad.'

She was beginning to feel so irked, that in a moment of bravado she thought she would disclose her writing to Fred, thinking that he might consider her brave and oblivious to danger and would, therefore, beg her to join whatever it was he was doing in Munich.

But thank goodness she gave herself time to think before she acted, as she came to the conclusion that he would take one look at her beloved journal, tear it from her grip and rip it apart with his hands or dash it to the fire. So she would continue to let him think she kept a simple diary and that the entries contained nothing more explosive than the weather, flowers and kittens she might see on her walks into Ulm, recipes and her burgeoning love for Walther.

8 July 1942
We have not seen hide nor hair of the gloating Horst and I hope that means he has had all leave cancelled for the foreseeable future.

But it also means that Walther is away for interminable periods of time. Before he was sent with numerous other medics to the Eastern Front, he called on me a number of times, either to take me to a café or for a walk. We chatted for hours and I felt so proud and important when he took my arm and threaded it through his. Twice he asked me to have a meal with his Mutter and Vater and once he stayed to eat with me and Fred. I can feel him drawing nearer and nearer to me and I can sense he hopes his feelings are reciprocated. Well, they most certainly are. When he turns up on my doorstep, my stomach flips of its own accord and when his gaze meets mine during a conversation round the dinner table, we smile at each other as if there is no one else present.

When Walther received his posting papers, he brought them for me to read. I have never seen him so forlorn, the dimple in his cheek all but flattened against his drooping face, and I thought it might be an opportunity for me to pry around the idea of where his heart lies in terms of the Nazi regime. I feigned surprise at his reaction to the notification he held in his hand and asked him if he were not proud to be doing his duty for the Fuhrer.

He answered my question by asking if it were not for

Oma, would I be here in Germany? I felt the blood rush to my face and tried to give him a sensible reply, but was unable to get past my stuttering and muttering.

He bobbed down so he could look into my face, a gesture I love, and held my hand. He told not to be afraid as mine and Fred's behaviour and demeanour have made it common knowledge that as we happen to find ourselves here, we have become loyal to the Axis. Then he smiled at me and said we may have fooled everyone else, but he didn't believe that to be the case.

I tried to remain composed, my eyes on my lap, but I felt sure he could see my heart thumping against my thin, summer blouse. Other than this journal, which I have faith will stay well hidden, there was not one bit of evidence to condemn me or Fred.

We sat inert for what felt like minutes. I didn't know what to say, so said nothing. Walther watched me, then leaned towards me and pulled me into the deep recesses of his chest, where I am compelled to say I fit perfectly.

He repeated that I should not be afraid and then said he could see into my heart. His heart, he assured me, bears the same witness as mine. He kissed me goodbye, curled his lip in disdain when he looked down at his uniform and left for his posting.

Walther had asked Annie to call on his Mutter and Vater from time to time so she decided, after he'd been gone for a week, to knock on their door and have coffee and a chat with Frau Wilhelm. The older woman looked taken aback to see Annie on her doorstep, but when they got over the preliminaries of whether or not Annie was unwell and needed her husband, she invited Annie into the immaculate house.

'Herr Doctor is in his examining room.' Frau Wilhelm nodded towards the part of the house that served as a surgery, which Annie knew well from childhood sore throats and tummy upsets.

Leading the way, Frau Wilhelm took them past the cuckoo clock and the stairs and into the sitting room – all familiar to Annie, but she felt shy without Walther by her side. 'I hope you don't mind,' she said. 'But Walther asked me to pay you a visit or two whilst he's away.'

'Oh, he didn't say,' Frau Wilhelm said. 'But isn't he a wonderful son? And of course, you are always welcome. Shall we take coffee in the garden?' she asked.

'That would be lovely,' Annie said.

The garden was as neat and tidy as the house, clearly organised and tended by this woman who was as dedicated to being the local doctor's wife as her husband was to being the doctor. Whilst she waited for Frau Wilhelm to bring out the tray, Annie became engrossed in what she would change inside and out if she were to inherit her title. It made her feel naughty, but the daydream was very enticing and entertaining.

The curtains would have to go, beautiful and plush as they were. They must have been expensive when first made, but now they looked much too heavily brocaded and rather dated. She wondered if Frau Wilhelm had thought of changing them for something lighter, but perhaps that wouldn't be wise when they had to black out every night anyway. The carpet was of the same ilk. Swirls of muddy greens and browns and burgundy in a pattern that was difficult to discern. In the kitchen she would have the tinted glass in the cupboard doors replaced with solid wood so that no one could see into the shelving that would no doubt become untidy under her command.

She shielded her face from the strong mid-morning sun with her hand. Frau Wilhelm had given over most of her flowers for vegetables, as had all of them. Hers were weedless and marked with handwritten sticks to delineate one germinating edible from another. If the garden were hers to landscape, she would find room for a willow like the one in Viola's family home; it was the epitome of grace and calm. Other than that, she thought she would be happy to live here and organise the house and Walther's life. The door behind her rattled open and she gave herself an inward slap on the hand. There was so much more to be thinking about than her and Walther – the war, rationing, Fred. But, she reasoned, there was no harm in sometimes giving in to daydreams, too.

'Your hair suits you,' Frau Wilhelm said. 'Walther told me you had it cut.'

She was pleased that Walther was mentioning her to his mother. Her hand wandered to the ends of her hair. A couple of weeks ago she'd taken a pair of scissors to it and watched as each buttery-coloured strand fell to the floor. She was still getting used to nothing hanging below her ears, but she did feel lighter and liked the natural wave that had appeared. Fred said the change made her look more mature and modern and she could see that for herself, too.

They talked about things that women occupy themselves with. Important things that amount to the very essence of life. But how many times could they discuss what to do with rations, how to ensure water is used wisely so that it lasts, ways to tie a scarf to make a jacket look different, the best technique for darning stockings, how to stop germs from spreading after being in public places. She was not getting any sense of Frau Wilhelm's political views, until a Focke-Wulf buzzed through the stark, cobalt sky. They stopped their chitchat and craned their necks to take in the sight. Following the course of the silver fuselage until it became a pinprick, their attention was drawn to another two, flying in tandem behind the first.

When Annie looked down, spots of dark appeared before her eyes each time she blinked and a mechanical rattle lingered in her ears.

Frau Wilhelm tutted. 'The brazenness of them,' she said.

'Do you mean...' Annie pretended not to understand the word that had been used. 'Their bravery?'

Frau Wilhelm turned on her, her usual poised mien replaced by a look of effrontery. 'No, Fraulein. I mean brazenness.' Then immediately her polished veil of tact and diplomacy slipped into place again. 'Pay no attention to me, please, I beg you,' she said. 'Herr Doctor and I are still jaded from the last war. And of course, we are getting old and set in our ways. We had come to enjoy sitting in our garden without crude interruptions.'

'Of course,' Annie said, realising that Fred had been correct in his assertion that everyone was wary of everyone else. No, not merely frightened or scared but terrified, as the Catholic bishop sermonised, that by passing the mildest of comments any one of them could end up betrayed and rotting in a prison cell or concentration camp. So much for justice.

'However,' Frau Wilhelm was saying, 'the garden isn't as pleasant to sit in as it used to be.' She pointed towards the left, where tomatoes were ripening. 'White, pink, red and yellow roses used to grow against that whole wall. The white ones had the most exquisite perfume. They were beautiful and filled the air with the most marvellous scent. Perhaps you remember?'

Annie thought back to one summer when she sat feeling sorry for herself in the surgery whilst Herr Doctor treated her for a blister that had gone septic. The windows of the surgery were open and the smells of summer had wafted in; dry earth, heat on paving slabs, ripening strawberries, wheat and the roses. Oma had been sitting in the chair next to her as Herr Doctor covered her heel with thick ointment and a dressing, Walther was bouncing a ball against a wall, waiting for her to be sent out. Somewhere in the distance a tractor purred and children laughed. She'd felt safe and sleepy. 'Yes, now you mention it, I do.'

'But one must count one's blessings,' Frau Wilhelm said. 'Always. We seem to have gotten off lightly in comparison to Hamburg or Kassel. Have you read about what is happening in our beloved Berlin?'

'Munich, too,' Annie offered, 'is in a terrible state. So Fred tells me.'

'Well, I suppose it's all a matter of comparison,' Walther's mother said. 'I have been to both cities to meet family members and Munich is nothing like the wreck that remains of Berlin.' She drummed her fingers on the arm of her chair and looked into the distance. 'Yes, we are lucky here, so far. Believe me.'

She went on to tell Annie that when Herr Doctor had

been studying in Berlin, she often went to visit him for the weekend. 'What a city,' she said. 'I am sorry for you and Walther and other young people who have never had the chance to see it in its prime. The clubs and music and dancing. Lights everywhere. Beautiful clothes worn by beautiful people. More than plenty of everything. Alcohol, cigarettes, food, passion.' She patted Annie's hand. 'Yes,' she said. 'I am sorry for your generation on that account. And many others.'

They exchanged a smile. It seemed a good point at which to end their tête-à-tête, so Annie rose from her chair. On the way home, she traced three other pairs of aircraft as they left a trail of vapour across the sky and felt bolstered to know she and Frau Wilhelm were in accord about the planes. And leading on from that, she surmised they must be in agreement about every other aspect of the regime.

When Fred announced that Annie must be ready to leave with him at 7.45 the following morning, she was brimming with questions that bubbled over one after the other: Would she be working legitimately or pretending? What should she say if stopped and questioned by authorities? What should she wear? How did the group plan and plot without being overheard? How would she know who to trust? Would Fred leave her on her own or would he be by her side at least initially? How many were in the group? Any women or all men? What would her role be? Would she still be Annaliese Margaret Scholz or would she have another persona?

Eventually, Fred began to laugh until he held his stomach

and buckled over. That was good to see although the laughter was at her expense. When he managed to contain himself, he said, 'Oh, Annie, for all your Walther and logical thinking and grown-up hairdo, you are still a little girl.'

She shammed taking offence but was glad to have been the cause of his temporary joviality.

'Come now, Annie. Perhaps it is not girlishness but youthful enthusiasm and long may it last. It will be an asset to the group. But you must also learn to cultivate level-headedness. Do you understand me?'

She nodded vigorously, then toned down the gesture to a sedate dip of her head. That made her dear brother laugh again.

'Now,' he said in a much more serious tone. 'I will tell you everything that is going to happen and you will listen. Then if you have any questions I will try to answer them, although some situations we have to play by ear. Do you understand?'

'Yes, of course,' she said. 'Please, begin.

He told her that he had an actual job at the university as an academic assistant, which also meant he had time for research. As for Annie she was going to be an administration assistant in the office that recorded degrees, PhDs, theses and the like. Her main duties would be filing, checking for correct spelling on certificates, answering queries and relaying messages from one office to another. That particular office was always very busy, he said, because there were so many new, short courses for those in the Wehrmacht. He told her he had overheard a conversation in the dining hall that another girl was needed there and he enquired on her behalf, saying that she was ready for employment now that their Oma was gone and the obligations that tied her to the house had ceased.

'Naturally,' he continued, 'as you're my sister I will introduce you to the colleagues at the university who I am friendly with and invite you to join us for drinks after work at the pub and to read and discuss poetry in each other's rooms.'

'Poetry?' She was surprised.

'Yes, that is what the founder members gathered to pursue initially. One thing led to another from there. So, I continue. You will soon be one of the group of friends in your own right. We never, and I mean never, talk about our resistance activities at work; we make arrangements to meet for what, to all intents and purposes, are social occasions and that is all. Also, we never talk in public about our ideas, enterprises or planned actions. We only ever discuss those things in the privacy of other members' rooms when there is absolutely no one else around. We never write anything down, although that is about to change.'

Her mouth hung open and her breathing became shallow when she thought of the dangers they were walking into. 'And that,' he said, 'is where you come in.'

'Where?' she echoed.

'You will be involved, with the rest of us, in writing and distributing leaflets to motivate and convince intelligent, intellectual people that together, we can challenge the Nazis.'

He sat back and studied her, one hand on her heart, the other covering her mouth. 'I had no idea...' she said.

'If you feel uncomfortable you must say now, before you become more embroiled.'

'Of course I feel uncomfortable,' she scoffed. 'But I can't wait to meet the others and start helping at last.'

'Any questions?'

She didn't have any, so Fred took some crockery to the sink and swilled the plates and cups around in the soapy water that had to last for two days.

'Oh,' he said, looking over his shoulder. 'Wear whatever you would usually wear to work.'

She felt her cheeks redden with the knowledge that she could have been so superficial a mere thirty minutes ago.

Fred did not look up from his newspaper as the train pulled into Munich until Annie nudged him in the ribs and pointed with her chin towards a cattle train in a siding. Yellow stars were displayed on each of the trucks. A lone sentry guarded the empty platform. She wondered if the train was waiting to be loaded with its oppressed cargo or if it had recently offloaded a pitiful consignment. Frau Wilhelm had told her she once saw a young mother, three toddlers in tow, trying to flee from being prodded into a similar train, only to be smacked across her head with the butt of a rifle. She dreaded to think she might witness such a scene as she would find it almost impossible not to rise shouting from her seat and have to be held back by Fred. Then he would probably put her on the first train back to Ulm and make her stay there.

As it was, he had to keep whispering to her to walk apace with him and act as if she'd seen the havoc in Munich many times before. But it was more than difficult to ignore the devastation, let alone the SS and Wehrmacht on every corner, going into and coming out of cafés, elbowing their way through the crowds, suddenly eyeing a passer-by for no apparent reason, stopping random people, interrogating others, searching housewives' shopping bags. How bad had things become that a cabbage, three carrots and a minute paper bag of coffee were suddenly cause for suspicion? *Bullies, that's all they are*, she thought as she saw two soldiers halt a middle-aged man carrying a couple of books and mumbling to himself. They patted down his pockets and flipped through the books, reading the titles on the spines and consulting between themselves. It dawned on her that they cared nothing for the man, his books or his conversation with himself. All they wanted to do was prove to everyone that they had power. She wondered how they could live with themselves.

'Don't stare, Annie,' Fred hissed. 'Or you're next.'

At once her shoes became very interesting. But she knew that if not today or the next, then someday soon it would be her turn and the first would not be the last.

The university stood like a beautiful, welcoming beacon and its slightly damaged exterior promised calm. But inside, the halls and corridors were streaming with those uniforms; men taking short courses in anything that would aid the war effort. Fred walked her straight to her office, introduced her and said he would come back to take her to the dining hall at twelve. Meeting the manager and other administration assistants was easy, the filing work was easy, learning the layout and routine was easy; she felt as if she had come upon her own private haven.

During the midday meal, she met the six others who made up the band of collaborators and she followed their lead by giving the illusion they were meeting as friends rather than co-conspirators. Annie sat next to the only other girl in the group, a young woman named Ilse. Then there were Carl, Helmuth, Ernst, Otto and Gustav. She had imagined they would be intense and perhaps full of angst, but nothing could have been further from the truth, at least not in that public environment. They greeted her in an effortless, companionable manner, as if she were just another girl to talk and drink and laugh and eat with. There was no mention of anything underhand; no arrangements for clandestine meetings. When the dinner break was finished and they rose to return to their duties, Ilse said she would see her tomorrow and Otto said, 'Good to meet you, Annie. And we will see you Friday evening at the pub. Okay?'

'Yes,' she replied. 'I'll look forward to it.' Then it was back to the painless job in the admin office.

That evening Annie questioned Fred about why hordes of people didn't rush to the aid of the Jews being shoved around like animals on the train platform, if they saw such a scene.

'That is exactly what the Catholic bishop was referring to – we have all been cowed beyond recognition,' Fred answered. 'But we can't act individually or on impulse. That is why our group is advocating mass denouncement and we must voluntarily conscript other like-minded people in order to make an active stand.'

'My goodness,' Annie said. 'That's quite a reply. So Friday night. Is that when we make plans?'

'Yes,' he said. 'It must start in earnest.'

She knew she would find the wait excruciating.

★

It was very late. They caught the last train home to Ulm, laughing and pretending to be inebriated after what they let be known was a sociable, alcohol-infused Friday night with their colleagues. As they presumed, they were stopped on two occasions, but allowed to move on when the soldiers saw the state of them, proving that they had become skilful in the art of cunning.

Annie could not sleep and neither could Fred on their return. They sat up in the dark and drank a glass of schnapps – their second alcoholic drink of the night. They talked about all that had been discussed and decided upon during the evening, then Fred's eyes drooped and he dragged himself to bed. Annie fished out her journal and wavered, stricken with agitated doubts, about the damning evidence she was about to put in writing. She knew what she was condemning them to if found out. Then she told herself that if the activities they were going to be involved in were exposed, then a sure sentence would follow. She was taking a huge chance anyway, so she might as well take two.

She wrote about how they had left the pub after one beer each, laden with bottles to take back to Gustav's quarters in order to make it look as if the party would continue there. In fact, the bottles were crammed unceremoniously in the corner behind a curtain for consumption, Ilse said, at a later date when it wasn't so important to have their wits about them; tonight they needed to be sober.

It had already been decided that the best and most efficient plan of action was to write a leaflet, then copy and distribute it as widely as possible.

'How wide is wide?' asked Ernst.

'Well, eventually throughout Germany and beyond. But initially, perhaps we should concentrate on Munich.'

A consensus was reached on that point. But Annie wondered if even that was too vast an area. 'Would it be safer to confine distribution to the university areas?' she said.

'Yes, safer for sure,' answered Gustav. 'But not as effective.'

It was agreed that they target the university buildings, student neighbourhoods and haunts first, see how that was received and what it produced and decide from there.

Next, they deliberated about the points they wanted to make in the leaflets. Fred suggested Annie keep a list as they concurred each edict so that they were sure they had covered everything they wanted to address. 'Annie.' He turned to his sister. 'Please listen. You must not write anything for the leaflets outside of this room. Do you understand me?'

She promised. The others didn't look surprised at his command so he must have told them about her tendency towards defiance.

'Nor must you take the papers away with you to work on at home or anywhere else.'

'None of us must do that,' Ilse said. 'They must remain here in hiding.'

Again she nodded and felt like a chastised child until she picked up her pencil and they began to draft their leaflet. Hours later the list was ready. In the leaflet they would:

- Ask people to recall images of Germany in past times to stir up action. Inaction would result in the destruction of Germany and of German shame.

- Encourage people to question whether they were willing to give up their free will to the Nazi regime.
- Plead with people not to wait for someone else to make a start, but to be courageous and take the lead. Others would follow.
- Call upon tried and tested intellectual references to rouse people to think about the dynamism of government. The constitution of a nation should develop humanity, not restrict it.
- Quote an excerpt from *The Awakening of Epimenides* by Goethe and from a poem that Otto had written entitled 'Hope'.

'I think at the end we should add a note asking others to copy the leaflet and pass it on,' said Ernst. 'What do you think?'

'Excellent idea,' said Carl.

'And we need a name for this movement,' added Helmuth. 'Something that represents our values.'

'And a symbol,' said Ilse.

'How about a feather?' said Otto. 'A dove's feather. You know, for peace.'

'No,' said Fred. 'That can also represent cowardice.'

An image of Frau Wilhelm and Herr Doctor in their garden, wishing nothing more for themselves and every other German citizen than to enjoy peace, flashed through Annie's mind. 'How about a flower,' she said. 'A white flower. Any other than Edelweiss.'

Everyone was happy with that. 'Next Friday night,' Gustav said. 'We write and copy the text.'

9

September 1942

Another wave of nausea pasted Viola from head to feet in a slippery slick of sweat. She lifted the hair from the back of her neck and tried to control her breathing. Pummelling the cushions behind her, she huffed and groaned. Then she heaved again, retched and wiped her mouth on the back of her hand. But perversely she willed the pain and agony to continue. *Let me feel worse*, she thought. *Much worse. Punish me.*

One morning three weeks ago, she'd woken up to a clear day and a clear image. Fred's face was looking at her – his strong, striking features; sparkling blue eyes; mottled brown hair; neat, trimmed beard; even white teeth. But the beautiful smile that was for her alone was missing – replaced with a look of disbelief and disappointment. So vivid was the fictive presence, she truly thought for a split second that Fred was there, in the room with her. Of course he wasn't, but Mike was and he, Viola could see at last, was nothing like her Fred. How could she ever have been so stupid to think he was?

In the few minutes' respite she had in between dry heaves, she remembered the first night she had met Mike in that sleazy club and how she had taken consolation from the way her head had leaned against his shoulder in the old, familiar position that was resonant of Fred and after that, she filled in all the gaps. With her guard down, she had allowed Mike into her life.

Now she was sure she was pregnant. And the torture of guilt and remorse was harder to bear than the sweaty infirmity of morning sickness. Lillian had asked her, as timidly as a church mouse, if she could please vacate the bathroom so she could have a wash and get ready for work. She'd helped Viola to the sitting room, eased her on to the sofa and tenderly placed a basin in her hands. 'I won't be long,' she'd said. 'Then I'll get you a cup of tea and a slice of dry toast. That's some tummy upset.'

How naïve she is, Viola thought. *How naïve we both are.*

Viola had been adamant that Mike was not allowed into the flat, so they had spent their covert meetings at one of his friend's bedsits. She yelped as another spasm twisted her gut. Then she wondered how, at the time, she hadn't seen how dingy the room was with peeling wallpaper and mould in the corners where the walls met the floors; she shuddered when she recalled the bedsheets, which she now felt sure hadn't been changed from one meeting to the next. And God only knew how many other couples might have been playing out their frantic yearnings in the same lumpy bed. The whole affair had been sordid.

Oh, and the 'how's-your-father' as some of the girls called it. Fresh tears flooded her eyes when she thought about her one night with Fred, which she would only ever coin as making love. He had been so tender and attentive, but then he had wanted to keep her forever and that had never been Mike's intention. Nor hers, she had to admit; she was not blameless in this storyline. But she had fooled herself, whilst the affair was happening, that the sex was wonderful and that they were two sophisticated and mature adults who were doing what everyone else on the run from the war was getting up to.

Now she could see not only the room, but the pair of them in action in the cold, lucid light of day. It was as if wide, dark blinkers had been removed from her eyes. There was Mike, with his clammy, greedy hands all over her breasts and thighs, caring for her only in so far as her actions and reactions would enhance his pleasure – and bring her back for another base tryst. He mumbled constantly in her ear, too, words and phrases she supposed he thought would either excite or soften her; inane, rather than sweet, nothings. How could she have been so blind? How could she have let him anywhere near her? The damning questions, for which she had no logical answers, came thick and fast. She put a hand on her tummy, still flat and taut, and trembled when she thought of his baby growing inside her.

Lillian put her cool hand on Viola's forehead. 'I'll let them know you won't be in for a few days,' she said. 'Well, the whole week by the looks of you.' She filled the kettle and turned on the grill for toast.

The cloying smell of gas made Viola's stomach pitch again. 'Nothing for me,' she managed. 'I can't face it.'

'You must, Vi,' Lillian said. 'Just a nibble. You know, to keep up your strength.'

Just in time, Viola moved the ring on its chain to the back of her neck before another retch sent her head over the basin. She could feel it skimming her prickly skin as it had done when she'd flung it down behind her every time she had lain with Mike. Now she could not believe that touching that treasure had not been enough to break the misguided spell she had been under.

When she resurfaced there were flashing lights in her vision; she closed her eyes against them. There was not one bit of energy left in her to argue with, so she nodded and said thank you to Lillian. And perhaps the sustenance would help the morning sickness in some way, but no amount of tea or toast or kindness would ever ease the burden she would have to carry around in her mind for the rest of her life. The thought made tears spill down her face.

'Oh, Vi.' Lillian put her arms around her friend and held her tight. 'It will pass.'

Viola wiped her eyes on the sleeve of the old, brown cardigan and said, 'No, Lil, I don't think it will.'

Lillian held Viola at arm's length and studied her. 'Stuff and nonsense,' she said. 'Of course it will. Tummy upsets aren't fatal.'

'I'm sorry, Lil,' Viola said as she rushed to hang her head over the basin again. *And this is where my head will be forever more*, she thought, *hanging in shame*.

'Now then, Vi, don't talk tosh.' Lillian's tone was firm. 'I know you must be feeling very poorly because you're not usually this dramatic. And I do understand this has come at an inopportune time what with the party this weekend, but...'

The party. Viola moaned again when she remembered Robert's birthday bash this Saturday that she was expected to attend, looking fresh and glamorous and ready to help her mother with hostess duties.

'...You may well be completely better by then, some of these stomach bugs only last forty-eight hours or so. And if not, well, we will send a telegram to your parents and explain.'

Viola nodded and shook her head at the same time, not able to comprehend Mum receiving a telegram informing her that her daughter was incapacitated with a violent stomach upset. She recalled Mum in the art gallery and her cool, worldly understanding of anatomy and knew she would not be as naïve as Lillian; she would jump to the correct conclusion without a moment's hesitation.

Putting the tea and toast on the coffee table in front of Viola, Lillian said she would come straight home after work, patted her friend's shoulder and said goodbye. Viola lifted a hand and the corners of her mouth in reply.

Much as she loved and appreciated Lillian, Viola felt relieved to be alone in the flat that was now still and quiet. Breathing deep into her lungs, she dared to lean her head back against the antimacassar for a moment but with another violent spasm, her stomach told her it was too soon to become complacent and she sat upright again. 'Oh, Fred,' she called out as her fiancé's face passed in front of her again. 'What am I going to do?' But the warm, affectionate features she hoped to conjure up did not appear and they were, if anything, harsher this time. The image didn't linger but drifted out of sight as if pleased to be shot of her.

Then her mind switched to Robert and his party and she beat her fists on her knees. 'Robert, Robert, Robert,' she sobbed. She picked up her teacup and thought about dashing it to the floor, but couldn't bear the thought of having to clear up the mess. Instead, she put her head in her hands and wept.

Around noon, Viola found that she could nibble on the dry toast and managed a cup of tea. When she kept that down she felt as if she had a bit more energy. This was probably the way it would go every morning now; she shuddered at the thought. After she cleared the breakfast things she managed to wash, brush her teeth, change her clothes and tidy round.

Then an icy fist twisted in her gut and she knew it was nothing to do with morning sickness. She'd been top of her class right the way through school, an assistant in the Languages Department at the University of Cambridge, a model daughter and sister, an excellent tennis player, a voracious reader, almost-fiancé to a wonderful man and now – an unwed mother.

First her hands and then her legs started to shake and again she had to sit down before she fell. The thought that she had allowed this to happen was shameful. Yes, it happened to other young women – she knew it did. There were girls at work who were there one day and not the next and when they left, sniggers followed them and that included her own. Girls like that were considered to be loose or fallen or like hedonistic animals who put immediate pleasure above long-term consequences. Her hands trembled as she touched her face, neck, ears, pulled through her hair. She knew she was not the definition of any of those base, cheap descriptions but no one else would believe that; she would be labelled, maligned, dismissed and damned.

What would Mum and Dad think? And Lillian? She sobbed aloud and covered her mouth when she pictured her brothers being told. And Fred. She grabbed her knees to her chest and rocked back and forth. Fred would never want her now and how could she blame him?

The walls of the flat crowded in on her and she knew she must get away from them. Pulling on a jacket, she checked her pockets for a hanky, tied a scarf around her hair, grabbed her key and headed for Russell Square.

The corner of Malet Street was cordoned off probably due to a burst pipe; the street itself was packed solid with beds, sideboards, lamps, books, pots, pans, shoes, bits of broken crockery, baby carriages and all manner of treasured belongings that made up everyday life. Viola stood and stared at the precious remnants thrown out on the narrow street in the hope that some of them could be salvaged. A little blue slipper caught her eye and she frantically searched the jumble for its partner, desperate to know that the child who wore them in what had been the safety of his own home, would know their softness and warmth again. But she couldn't catch sight of it amongst the mess and appeased herself that the child had probably been evacuated at any rate and would have grown out of them by the time he returned. Carrying on towards the gardens, she reminded herself that if that were the case, there would be a mummy who had kept them as a reminder of her little boy – her most cherished possession. She shook her head, trying to dislodge the thought that one day very soon she might be in a similar situation. It hardly seemed feasible.

Another cordon surrounded what was left of the gate at the Montague Place entrance, so Viola wandered around to Bedford Place and into the gardens from there. Russell Square, that beautiful sanctuary in the middle of London chaos, was not looking its best, but then again nor was she. Trees were down from two hits and had been dragged off the paths to allow pedestrians to pass. All the lovely lamps, devoid of their light bulbs, were blinking blindly. A bench was missing seat rungs, but a courting couple was making the most of the facility regardless to carry out an assignation. Viola hoped that the young woman, encased in the arms of her suitor, had put more thought into her actions than she had. Eventually, she found an empty seat under the watchful stone eye of the Duke of Bedford and sat with a long, drawn-out sigh.

How she would have loved to sit and think about whatever it was she'd thought about before this had happened. Now there wouldn't be room for much else in her life, or the lives of her parents, for years. Already it felt as if her world was becoming much narrower and more confined; she had to make a concerted effort to quell the panic that started in the depths of her stomach and attacked her lungs and limbs, making her whole body quake with fear for today, tomorrow, the months and years to come.

The first hurdle she had to get through was the coming weekend. She could kick herself as she'd been looking forward to seeing Robert and David for the longest time. They had met up at home over the Christmas and Easter periods and from time to time during the long summer break but not as regularly as they had been able to when she worked in Cambridge. On two occasions, she'd made the trip to their school with Mum to take them out for tea, which was great fun, but was also a glaring reminder that they were both growing into young men at an alarming rate. Men with minds of their own. Dad had long harboured the ambition that they would go up to his old Oxford college but they both wanted to join up as soon as they were eighteen. By way of compromise, he told them they could choose any of the Oxbridge colleges but he was insisting, without debate, that they continue their studies.

Mum told her in a letter that during the Easter break, Robert and Dad had argued almost non-stop about the subject. Apparently, Dad said he did not want the boys to miss out on their education because of the war and Robert had shot back with: 'That's all well and good, but I refuse to be thought of as a coward on the basis that I fulfil your aspirations.' Mum said their bickering had been very unpleasant and Viola thought back to the altercation during Fred's last day in England and how unhappy that had made everyone. This bloody war was the cause of so much heartache in so many different spheres – from the minutiae of family life to the workings of Whitehall.

Viola would take bets on Robert agreeing to a short degree course at Oxford or Cambridge in say, engineering or surveying, in order to appease their father, but then joining up the minute Dad left him in his college rooms. She wanted to talk to Robert about all of this, not to nag him but to try to get him to appreciate that his safety was paramount and at university he would not be called a coward because he would be surrounded by other young men who were exempt from the war on the basis that the country needed educated men and women to move everything forward. But last time she had seen him he was so different. All that tennis had paid off as he was wiry and athletic and held himself so well that anyone would think he was already an officer; his hair was thick and shiny, controlled with some sort of grooming aid and there were signs of a shave on his chin and upper lip. His voice had come from his chest rather than his throat.

When they'd gone for a walk together, he'd offered her his arm in a gallant manner and she took it, his bicep as rock solid as a tennis ball. 'It's the RAF for me,' he'd said.

'Please think about it carefully before you decide,' Viola had said.

His reply had been as abrupt and sure-fired as a round of bullets. 'I've had two and half years to think of nothing else,' he'd said. And in an exact replication of Dad's tone of voice when he demanded an end to the discussion he'd added, 'I've made up my mind and that's it.'

But she wanted to give it one more try by appealing to his duty to his family as well as the Allies because she, Mum, Dad and David needed him, as the oldest boy, to be here with them.

Now there probably wouldn't be another opportunity and she was to blame. She pulled her jacket tightly around her stomach and chest as if trying to protect herself from the humiliation and fear that washed over her again. Heat coated her chest, face and scalp when she thought about how she'd made a mockery of all the months and years she'd fended off any man who flirted or made eyes at her. The self-righteousness she'd felt when turning down all the men who had asked to meet her for a drink or a date meant nothing now. The countless times she had explained to anyone who would listen that she was engaged, or almost-engaged, to the most wonderful man were nothing more than a pretence; she would be a laughing stock amongst her friends. And, with a lurch that set her nerves jangling, she realised that if she thought herself ostracised before this, then the visual effects of her betrayal would see her abandoned and isolated without an ally in sight.

She had to think hard and make a decision about this weekend. If she cried off, Mum would suspect something and probably make her way to London after the party to assess the situation. If she tried to get to the Cotswolds, Mum, and perhaps Dad, might ferret the truth out of her and it was too early for that. Weighing up every side of the situation was exhausting and all it did was dig up further complications. She wondered if she could possibly make it home for the weekend and hide the situation from her parents. After all, the house was big enough to insulate the sounds of sickness from them and if her days followed the already established pattern, she would feel better by lunchtime. The more she thought it through, the more she warmed to the idea that she could manage it. And she could enlist Lillian's help as she'd been invited to the celebrations, too. But that meant she would have to tell her friend about the baby. Could she do that and risk Lillian's rejection? She would have to; there was no way around it. And Lillian was her dearest friend. Surely she would help? Yes, Viola decided she would confide in Lillian. If it was the other way around she would want to know and would do whatever she could, no matter the circumstances, to be Lillian's mainstay.

Lillian breezed in looking young and fresh at about six-thirty, with June in tow. 'Vi!' She flung herself at Viola who was fussing with washing up in the kitchen. 'Let me look at you.' She scrutinised Viola up and down and pronounced that she was looking much better. Viola knew this to be stretching the truth as the mirror had told her that her skin was sallow, her eyes rheumy and her hair limp. Viola turned away and continued being busy.

'Sorry to hear you've been poorly,' June said, keeping her distance for fear of picking up something catching.

'Thank you, June.'

'Do you feel like a drink?' Lillian said. 'We're heading to the Jack Horner if you're well enough.'

'I do feel better,' Viola said. 'But I think I'll give it a miss. Look at the state of me.'

'Makeup and a scarf,' June said. 'A girl's best friends.'

'Oh, I don't know...' Viola hesitated. The thought of the long evening on her own was less than captivating. On the other hand, sitting in a sticky, smoky pub filled her with horror; suppose she started her heaving again. 'I think I'll rest tonight. You know, be on the safe side.'

Lillian had discarded her coat for her old navy pullover and stood, hands hidden in the loose cuffs, studying Viola.

'Shall we stay in with you?' she asked, then answered before Viola could reply. 'Yes, I think we must. Sorry, June, but I for one am going to forego tonight.'

'Don't you dare,' Viola said. 'I insist that you don't change your plans for me. In fact, I will be most upset if you do.'

June turned an imploring look in Lillian's direction and after a few more minutes of deliberation Lillian agreed to keep to her original arrangement. June, who Viola thought found her humdrum and mundane, visibly brightened. Whilst they readied themselves in Lillian's bedroom, helping each other with hairdos, sharing lipsticks and advice on brooches, Viola took down her latest book from the shelf and opened it at a random page to give the appearance of being quite content. As soon as Lillian and June shut the door behind them, Viola tossed the book aside with a huff, then began to weep again.

The next evening was the same, except the guest Lillian had with her was Harriet. The night after that, it was both June and Harriet. Every night Viola rolled around in tangled, clammy bedsheets exhausted by thoughts of the predicament she was in and the feelings of electrifying panic that went with them. Every morning she was decimated with heaving sickness and every morning Lillian brought her dry toast and tea. On the third morning, Viola grabbed Lillian's hand and said, 'Lil, I'm pregnant.'

Lillian held her gaze, her soft grey eyes sad and concerned. 'I know,' she whispered, not so naïve after all.

Lillian threw herself next to Viola on the sofa, but didn't let go of her hand.

'Does everyone know?' Viola asked.

'No, I promise,' Lillian said. 'All I've said at work is that you have a violent stomach upset.'

'But what about June and Harriet?'

'You know them.' Lillian shrugged. 'Much too involved with themselves to even notice.'

Sitting up straight, her voice lower and more purposeful, Lillian said, 'Vi, what are you going to do?'

'Oh, Lil.' Viola raked her hands through her straggly hair. 'I have no idea. I've been longing to talk to you about it, but I was frightened you'd turn your back on me.'

Now it was Lillian's turn to cry. 'Don't talk such tosh,' she said. 'As if that would ever happen. I'll make sure I return tonight without any hangers-on so we can talk.'

'Thank you, Lil,' Viola said. She rubbed her eyes with the back of her hand and sighed. 'It's such a relief to tell you.'

Together, Viola and Lillian came up with a strategic plan for the weekend. They would travel to Viola's family home for the party and hide Viola's pregnancy to the best of their ability. If and when Viola couldn't be present, Lillian would cover for her. They would both casually splice hints into the conversation about the various illnesses going about their crowded office, stomach upsets being one of the most virulent.

But, Lillian wanted to know, what was Viola going to do in the long run?

'No idea, Lil,' Viola said. 'I don't even know what I can do.'

'Well, there are things I've heard about. My sister's friend got herself into trouble and...' Lillian scrunched her features together as if in pain. 'What an awful saying. I'm so sorry, Vi.'

Viola shook her head. 'No need to be. That's exactly what this is. Big trouble. What did this girl do?'

Lillian lowered her voice and looked over her shoulder. 'She had an abortion.'

'But how?' Viola asked. The thought made her feel a different kind of sick.

'She did it herself. There are ways.'

Viola knew her wide eyes and slack jaws reflected how appalled she felt. 'I don't think I could,' she said. 'It must be horrendous.'

'But, Vi, it might be for the best.'

Viola put her head on her friend's shoulder and rested for a beat or two. 'I do know that. You're absolutely right. And if I decide on that course of action, Lil? Would you, you know. Help me?'

Beneath the navy pullover, Viola felt Lillian's heart quicken. And it seemed as if she was having difficulty swallowing through a dry throat. 'Yes,' she said. 'If that's what you decide, I would try. Although I believe it's the earlier the better, so bear that in mind. But there are other things you should think about, too.'

Lillian listed her alternative suggestions. Viola could tell her parents, her mum at least, and then be guided by her advice after their initial fallout. Or she could tell her parents she had to go away for work and her work colleagues she had to go home for a family situation then turn up on the doorstep of a hostel. 'You mean one of those dreadful, Draconian institutions like the Loreto?' Viola choked on the word. 'Or the Home for Deserted Mothers and their Infants? Mum and Dad would die of shame. And so would I.'

Lillian was doing her best to sound practical. 'But they'll probably…' She hesitated as if she wished she could swallow her words.

'What?' Viola spat. 'Die of shame anyway? I have thought of that over and over again.'

'But the whole point is that they would be none the wiser. No one except me would know.'

'Oh, just the thought of it makes me cringe.' Lillian put her arm around Viola's shuddering shoulders. 'And then what? What about after the baby's born?'

'Adoption can be arranged.' Lillian's voice was measured. 'Or you could decide to keep the baby. Not at all feasible or workable, but an option nevertheless.'

None of those suggestions seemed the least bit helpful and Viola couldn't imagine herself living through any of them. 'What would you do, Lil, in my situation?'

'You must make up your own mind.' Lillian was adamant. 'But if I had to make a choice, I would risk the abortion. And soon.'

Think, Vi, Viola commanded herself. But she was too drained, her thoughts too jumbled and she knew she could not, should not make a decision yet.

'Vi,' Lillian said. 'Can you tell me how this happened? I mean, I do know how babies are made. June or Harriet, I could fathom, but you? Of all people. Who's the father? You've never touched another man with the pad of your little finger as far as I'm aware.'

Viola pressed herself closer to her friend and buried her

face in her chest. She shook her head and said, 'I'm a vile person, Lil.'

'No, you're not, I won't have you talking about yourself like that.'

'I am.' Viola spat out the words. 'Do you recall that American, Mike, who I introduced you to once? He met us in the pub, had one drink and left?'

'Yes,' Lillian said. 'I think so. Quite tall. A bit nondescript really. You said he kept asking you to dance whenever you happened to be in the same club.'

'Yes, him.' Viola felt the heat of chagrin reddening her face again. 'I was carrying on with him for a couple of months and I hate myself.' Viola thumped her chest over and over again. 'Abhor myself for every single one of those times we met up.'

Lillian tussled with Viola's fist to stop the beating. 'You'll hurt yourself,' she cried.

'I've earned it and more,' Viola shouted back.

Lillian lowered her voice. 'Shh, that's enough. Let's both calm down.'

When the atmosphere stilled, Lillian said, 'And where is this Mike now? Still on the scene?'

'No, thank goodness. I hope never to see him again.'

'But do you have contact details for him? He ought to know about this. And pay to help you out of the situation.'

'No, no, I couldn't bear it,' Viola cried out loud. 'I told him it was over before I found out about the baby and he vanished as swiftly as he appeared. And as for him paying for this, well, I'd rather manage on my own entirely.'

★

Mum and Dad were delighted to see Viola and Lillian when the car that picked them up from Cirencester drew up to the front door. David threw his arms around both of them and did nothing but grin. Robert, too, seemed to be happy but was more reserved and tentative in his approach, which Viola put down to nerves about being the centre of attention.

After the preliminary greetings, Mum didn't waste a second before she began to bustle; Viola was sure she'd been in the same state of perpetual activity for weeks. 'Now, you'll be in your old room, Vi,' she said. 'And Lil, you'll be in the furthest room along the corridor on the right.' She called for Abigail to show Lillian upstairs. Then she hesitated. 'Unless you want to share?' she asked. 'After all, you live in such close quarters in London that you might be lonely.'

'Oh yes, please, Mrs Baxter,' Lillian answered for both of them. 'That's very thoughtful of you.'

'Right you are, then there's no need to drag Abigail away from her task. David will carry your bags up for you.' She headed for the living room. 'Then, please – can you make yourselves available to help me?'

'Of course, Mum,' said Viola, not daring to look Mum in the eye. 'That's what we're here for.'

'It will be a pleasure,' Lillian added.

Bouncing ahead of them, David managed to carry two bags in each hand and keep up a steady stream of one-sided conversation. 'What's it like in London? I want to come and visit on my own. May I please, Vi? I don't mind sleeping on the sofa. I really don't. How long are you staying? All weekend, I hope. We'll get to have a game of tennis, Vi, I know we will.' He held the bedroom door open for them, followed them in and placed their bags down on the floor. Then he stood and stared at them in silence until the atmosphere became uncomfortable. After a bit of shuffling, David grabbed Viola's hand and said, 'Come on then, let's go down.'

Viola laughed for the first time in ages. 'Oh, I see. Well, give us five minutes first.'

'I'll wait,' David said.

'No.' Viola shook her head. 'That's not very gentlemanly, David.'

'Isn't it?' David sounded genuinely surprised. 'What should I do then?'

'Young ladies need a bit of time on their own, especially when they've had a long journey.' Viola softened her voice. 'So we'll be down shortly. I promise.'

David nodded and crept to the door, lifting his hand as his only form of goodbye.

As soon as the door closed behind him, Lillian clamped her hands over her mouth to stifle her giggles, then when they were sure he'd disappeared downstairs, she threw herself on the chintz bedspread and laughed out loud. 'Oh goodness,' she said. 'He's hilariously funny.'

Viola sat beside her. 'I know, but look how tall he is. I can't believe it.'

'Yes, and Robert. He's certainly changed.'

Viola nodded, hoping again to have some time alone with her brother to learn about his plans.

'Well, we got through the first hoop,' Lillian said. 'It would have been much more difficult if we'd been at opposite ends of the house.'

'But I don't know how long I can manage without Mum

noticing how nervous I am. I can't even bring myself to look at her.'

'You must try to be natural, Vi.'

'And another hoop has rolled right into place. Somehow or other I have to get out of that game of tennis.'

'That should be easy,' Lillian said. 'It can either be a hangover or the stomach upset from work.'

'Oh, but David's face when I have to tell him.' Lillian winced at the thought. 'I can't abide it.'

From outside, the sounds of labourers raising a marquee floated up to them. Pitch barked once for effect and then stopped. Viola could imagine he'd decided it was more congenial to wag his tail and lick the workmen's hands. The lush scents of fresh earth, herbs, ripe summer vegetables and lavender wafted through the open windows. It was all so peaceful and calm after London. Under a better set of circumstances, Viola would have loved to sit out her confinement here under the caring eyes of Mum and Dad, breathing in the country air. But that could never happen with this pregnancy and probably never would if there were to be subsequent chances; she had burned her bridges with regard to Mum and Dad's respect and succour.

'I thought you said your mother was paring down the celebrations because of the war?' Lillian asked, rolling over onto her side.

'She is,' Viola said. 'This is going to be a small, select, sedate gathering to salute their eldest son.'

'But it's not even his coming-of-age,' Lillian said.

Viola thought for a few minutes before she answered. 'Perhaps things are too precarious to wait another three years.'

'Revel whilst you can,' Lillian said.

'And look where that got me.' Viola placed a hand on her stomach.

'Vi,' Lillian said, prising Viola's hand away from her belly. 'Break that habit now. It's a dead giveaway.'

All day they were busy. True to their plan, Viola and Lillian dropped hints about the state of health amongst their friends and colleagues, thus excusing Viola every time she had to sit for a little while to recover her breath. Dad and the boys would never have noticed anything untoward and Mum was much too preoccupied to fret about what she probably thought was a gurgle or grumble in Viola's digestive system. Although once or twice, Viola caught Mum studying her for longer periods of time than were comfortable, and at those points in the proceedings Viola would force herself to her feet in an energetic manner and throw herself into tacking up bunting or folding serviettes or inspecting glassware.

At six, Mum sent everyone upstairs for a rest and to ready themselves. Lillian kicked off her shoes and relaxed on the bed. Viola paced the bedroom floor, deliberating between telling Mum as soon as possible and keeping up the charade. Both girls changed, made up their faces and dressed their hair in oppressive silence. Viola knew that probably the last time she had been jolly and enthusiastic had been when she and Lillian shopped for her engagement dress, but this was an all-time low in her countenance and Lillian must be so fed up with her. Then when they made for the stairs in readiness to greet the guests, Lillian took Viola's elbow and whispered to her that she was right by her side. Gratitude washed over Viola and she held firmly to Lillian's hand.

Despite Lillian's protests to the contrary, the party was a rather flat version of the functions Mum and Dad had hosted during the time between the wars. There were too many families with dead or missing young men and women to gloat inappropriately over the ones that households were trying to hold on to for dear life. But there were uncles and aunts, cousins who were on leave or able to get away from universities or schools, a few of Robert's close classmates and their parents and various neighbours and friends.

Mrs Bishop clasped Viola's hand in both of hers and looked straight into her eyes. 'You look wonderful, Viola dear,' she said in a syrupy voice laced with distaste. 'And your dear mother has told me so much about your work in London.' She lowered her tone and moved in close enough for Viola to smell anchovy on the older woman's breath; she turned her face as far away as possible whilst still maintaining her manners in case the whiff started her nausea again. 'Well done, you are serving the war effort and we are all so grateful.'

Viola tried to turn her grimace into a smile, but it was difficult. 'Thank you, Mrs Bishop,' she managed. 'I appreciate the sentiment.' With a bit of a tug, she withdrew her hand and excused herself on the pretence of helping Mum.

Through clenched jaws, Viola relayed the exchange to her mother. 'Obnoxious woman,' Mum said. 'I rarely speak to her after her appalling verbal attack on you and Fred.

Besides, all she knows is that you work in London, nothing at all about what you do.'

The string trio started a rendition of 'I've Got a Gal in Kalamazoo'. 'Thank goodness,' Mum said. 'Something lively at last. Don't pay any attention to her. She puts two and two together and makes five.' Her eyes strayed to the diminishing buffet food and she bustled into the kitchen to consult with Cook.

The evening continued in the established eddy of trying to make conversation with complete strangers or people she knew but was not interested in. She and Lillian checked in with each other at regular intervals and Lillian deputised for her when she needed to lie down for ten minutes or so.

Soon after eleven, Viola found herself alone on the terrace. The palest of pink climbing roses bordering the French doors filled the air with a potent, late summer scent. She squinted to see the blackened marquee in the dark, the only light coming from it the amber flicker of cigarettes. Once upon a time, Mum would have festooned the tarpaulin with lanterns and fairy lights, now the only glow was from the moon and stars, paving slabs and statues. Beyond the canvas canopy was the willow and the orchard. It seemed so long ago that she had sat under that tree, confident and sure of the trajectory her future would take, sure of Fred, certain of her father's answer to Fred asking for her hand, convinced of their life together in Cambridge; that Viola was another person, nothing like the young woman whose future was as dark and shadowy and dubious as the garden in blackout.

She felt a presence come through the door and heard a

long, relieved sigh. 'Robert,' she said. 'It's good to be out of the way for a few minutes, isn't it? Is Mum looking for me?'

He came and stood close to her. 'Not that I know of,' he said.' I suppose we both need a few minutes of peace.'

'If we're lucky,' Viola said, pointing at two spitfires making their way to the channel.

Robert saluted them and said, 'Good luck, chaps.'

It's now or never, Viola thought. *I must give it one more try*. She threaded her arm through her brother's. 'Robert,' she said.

He turned to her and she caught a faint trace of alcohol wafting around him. Putting his finger to his lips, he said, 'Shhh.' Then he took a flask from his pocket and sipped from it. Well, why not? It was his party and he was clearly not enjoying it. Very carefully he replaced the stopper, put it back in his pocket, patted it and gave her a soppy smile.

'Yes, my lovely big sister,' he said.

'Robert, please listen to me.'

'I'm all ears,' he said.

'You must think long and hard before you decide about the RAF…' He pulled away from her in a huff.

'No, Robert, please. Listen to me. Just think about it again. Give yourself time to… be young. Two years at Oxford would be wonderful for you and you will still be doing your duty for the Allies, I promise you that.'

Robert's nostrils flared and he turned from her and looked out over the garden. He was no longer swaying or slurring. 'Viola, you're as bad as Dad. I have made up my mind and nothing anyone can say will stop me.'

'But we need you here in one piece. All of us.'

'And what about what I need?' he grumbled. 'All this fighting for freedom and liberation. What about my freedom to make up my own mind about what I want to do? Are we merely fighting for others' freedom whilst being controlled and confined by our families?'

'Don't dare to be so foolish and idealistic,' Viola said. 'Everyone living under Nazi rule would love to be in your position. Besides you'll have plenty of time for all that. It's called the rest of your life.'

'Life is a very tenuous concept at the moment,' Robert said. 'One can't lay claim to any amount of future.'

They stopped and, breathing heavily, looked out on the inky scene. 'They'll be wondering where I am,' Robert said. 'And you.'

'I suppose,' Viola said.

'Vi,' Robert said softly. 'Please try to understand. I need that from you.'

A mass seemed to congest in Viola's throat and she covered Robert's hand with her own. 'I do understand, Robert. I do. But don't forget us.'

He wrapped his arms around her and whispered, 'Never. I'll never forget you, Vi. My dear, beautiful big sister.'

As he ducked back into the party through the French doors, Viola could feel the imprint of his warm fist under her palm. The fragile, flexible bones and sinews interspersed with those that were more dense and solid; the taut, capable flesh; the hot, eager blood coursing through his veins – it all bored deep into her own hand and she hoped the impression would never leave her.

*

In a blur, the tennis match with David went ahead and her little brother won, three sets to two. David was delighted; Viola was exhausted. She treated him to a sandwich lunch in the club and again, he talked non-stop about what he hoped to do for the war effort when the time came, visiting her and Lillian in London, life at his school, rugby, tennis and long-distance running. She smiled and nodded in what she hoped were the right places, but was distracted with recurring thoughts about her own dilemma.

On the train back to London, she felt guilty about not giving David her full attention and about how sincere Mum and Dad had been when they said they hoped she felt better soon and that Lillian didn't catch the dreaded stomach bug. Guilt upon guilt heaped upon the guilt of her betrayal. Lillian was fast asleep, her head lolling and a soft, snuffly snore vibrating from the back of her throat. Viola knew she should make up her mind about whether to keep the baby or not, but there were two opposing forces working on her – the pragmatic and the idealistic. By the time the train reached Paddington, her heart had won the day.

On Monday morning, Viola felt confident enough to manage her morning sickness and went back to work. Within five minutes there was a stack of documents on her desk waiting to be translated. Paper was ready and waiting in both typewriters. Hitler's voice was droning in her ear and she was aware of snippets of foreign languages from all corners of the office. She knew she would miss this so much.

By Friday evening, she was ready to write to Mum, but her hand shook so violently she had to start four times.

Dearest Mum,
I have some disgraceful news that I must share with you.
But before I disclose all, I am begging you not to turn
me away and desert me, even though I know I deserve
nothing less.

IO

The first leaflet did a good job of challenging readers to think about how they would feel when the crimes of the Nazi regime were exposed to the world and the citizens of Germany had done nothing to prevent them. People were asked to consider the idea that every nation gets the government it deserves. And from that, they gained members, which Annie, for one, welcomed with some qualms.

Of course, Annie explained to the others, she knew the whole intention of their resistance movement was to amass enough support to make a real and convincing stand against the regime, but she worried that they might attract some people who would betray them or who were spying for the Gestapo or who might become spooked for their own safety and run towards the Nazis instead of away from them. Fred said he had also thought of those consequences, but they were the risks they must take or else the movement would become stagnant and ineffective. So, she decided to take her lead from them.

The second leaflet addressed just that conundrum and spoke to the type of person they would most like to enlist – the young intellectual. Not that they wouldn't embrace anyone from any background, but they thought they could instigate a more rapid and committed uprising from the intelligentsia. So, they wrote about the fact that National Socialism could not be defended or engaged with on an intellectual basis because it could not be debated in any kind of logical manner as it was built on constant lies. They quoted Hitler's book, which they pointed out was written in terrible German. 'You would not believe,' Hitler had written, 'how one must deceive a nation in order to rule it.' If she was not already against Hitler and his party, that one quote would have set her in opposition to him with a passion.

They then went on to say that since Poland had been conquered, hundreds of thousands of Jews had been murdered. She remembered that cattle train standing, waiting on the platform in the station and wondered about the fate of all those Jewish people who had been forced to board it. Over and over again in the leaflets they encouraged others to break loose from their chains of apathy and join their movement to fight, passively, for the freedom of all.

The third leaflet caused a lot of debate. 'Perhaps we should narrow our target audience again to devout Lutherans and Catholics,' said Ilse.

'If,' argued Fred, 'we can commandeer the influential religious, we will be heard by untold numbers.'

'Yes,' said Gustav, 'that makes sense. So we would, in effect, have the best of both worlds.'

'Exactly,' said Fred, smacking the table for emphasis.

'I agree and think that instead of quoting Lao-Tse, Aristotle and Goethe,' said Ernst, 'we should concentrate on Novalis and King Solomon's Proverbs.'

Again they begged readers to think about what their religious beliefs demanded of them and asked them to be courageous and not stand back in the hope that someone else would speak out so they would not have to put their necks on the line. They likened Hitler to Satan and said that everything that came out of his mouth was evil. Then they asked two things of people. First, to consider the fact that the numbers lost on the Russian Front were just that to the Nazi regime: numbers. But there were mothers all over Germany weeping for their sons who were the whole world to them. They also asked everyone to be vigilant and note the names of anyone who was the least bit involved with the Nazis; they agreed that no one should be allowed to escape their engagement with the Party.

Whilst Annie did, in theory, agree with that sentiment, she aired her doubts. 'But where does it stop?' she said. 'We all Heil Hitler many times a day. Are we complicit?'

The others put down their pens and were thoughtful. That gave her confidence and thinking of Walther, she carried on. 'I mean, how do we know who is and who isn't committed by the mere fact that they're in uniform?'

'Yes, Annie, you have a point,' said Gustav.

'A good point,' agreed Ilse.

Fred shook his head and raised his voice. 'How will anyone ever sort out the good from the bad? It seems like an impossible task.'

'But one that is not our problem, perhaps?' Otto puffed on his pipe and spoke slowly and deliberately as if he was trying out his theory on himself. 'Our problem is the here and now. Not what happens in the future. We must ensure that we have gathered as many names as we can of possible guilty parties, then trust that justice will once again rule the day.'

'But what if we know, for certain and without doubt, that someone in uniform is not in agreement with the regime?' Annie asked.

'Then, dear Annie—' Fred smiled at her as if he could read her thoughts '—you must not put them on your list. Create another list for them, that of the exonerated.'

Helmuth nodded then put his finger in the air, which was his way of letting them know he had what he thought was a good idea. 'For a closing line, as we are addressing the religious population, how about saying that we will not be silenced and that we are their conscience.'

'Yes,' said Gerda – a new member of their group. 'That is good. Their guilty conscience.'

In the freezing cold of January, with snow on the ground and not enough fat on their limbs or wood on the fire to warm them, they discussed the fourth leaflet. After that, there were no leaflets for some months as a good few of the men were sent off to the Russian Front with the medical corps. And of course, they would all be on the list of the exempt. Those of them who were left behind decided that they would wait until their comrades returned to carry on with their campaign. A certain period of silence might help to assuage any suspicion surrounding them and it would give them time to gauge if their crusade had instigated other similar movements around the country.

When all the medics returned home, they had many

stories to tell about the Front. Annie's heart felt as if it was going to split apart when Otto and Gustav told them about the atrocities and deprivation the soldiers were enduring. Injuries beyond comprehension: a leg completely shredded; holes in the middle of stomachs; internal organs missing yet a heart still pumping; blindness; scarring; limping; screaming; tongues severed; wits lost; gaping mouths. One poor boy looked perfect until his head was turned and they could see that half his face was missing. 'Let me die,' he'd pleaded with them.

'The warfare,' Gustav reported, 'is like nothing experienced before; Stalingrad is being fought for by one soldier against another in hand-to-hand combat. It is a rats' war,' he said. The image of rodents scuttling around in brown uniforms was vivid in Annie's mind. 'They fight for every inch of street, every ruined building, factory, house, sewer, basement and staircase.'

'Yes,' agreed Otto. 'One side captures the bedroom but still has to fight for the kitchen.'

'And the cold,' Helmuth added. 'We think we have it bad here, shivering from house to shop to pub to work. But there, in Stalingrad, it is minus twenty-two and lower, and there is no hope of shelter or comforting food or the smile of a loved one to look forward to. There are so many cases of frostbite. Soldiers take their boots off after months of continuous wear and their toes come off with them.' He shivered with repulsion. 'I cannot imagine the pain and horror. And for what? One vile madman's egotistical pursuit of power.'

After they had sat in silence for a few minutes, probably contemplating, as Annie was, the suffering the soldiers were going through, she tentatively asked if any of them had come across a medic named Walther Wilhelm.

'Ah,' Otto said. 'Walther. His tour overlapped for a few days with my section. I didn't realise that he was the Walther you are keen on, Annie, or else I would have mentioned you.'

She was so relieved to hear of Walther, that a beam spread across her face. 'Well, I am so glad you didn't,' she said. 'Because he doesn't know about my involvement in our group and he would have been full of questions about how I know you.'

'Of course,' Otto said, putting his hand on Annie's shoulder. 'Perhaps when he returns we can sound him out to join us. What do you think? I believed him to be a good man when I met him.'

Annie was elated to have her perception of Walther affirmed, which was just as well as before he left for the Front, they'd acknowledged their feelings for each other out loud. And if they hadn't been close before that, things became very intense afterwards.

All the others in Otto's tiny flat were either reading, writing, making lists of references or folding paper in readiness for their fifth leaflet, Annie was trying to concentrate on proofreading, but images of what had happened between her and Walther after their declaration insisted on crowding into her mind. Glancing over at Fred who was scribbling intently, she wondered if he was having the same problem with pictures of Viola.

She had been happy to find out that Walther was as naïve as she was when it came to matters of love and what people did together, so she knew he hadn't visited brothels like a tomcat or tried his luck with other young women, which in her estimation made him most honourable – and all hers. They had fumbled and faffed for a while and then, true to their established dispositions, laughed at themselves and each other. They gave up that first time and Walther said, 'Let's just lie like this for now. It's enough for me. Is it for you, Annaliese?'

'Yes,' she said. Because it was more than enough to be wrapped in his strong, warm arms knowing that he loved her for her, not for what he could get from her.

There were two more, successful attempts after which Walther said that they were married in the oldest and truest sense and would make it official as soon as possible. Of course, they would have to obtain the approval of his parents and Fred, but she thought there was no doubt both parties would be agreeable. And when the wedding happened, she knew she would be thinking about her brother, whose father-in-law-to-be had said no and who pined for his Viola every minute of every day.

She worried too, not only for Walther's safety, but for how he would react to what he had seen on the battlefield. Would he be different? Of course he would. Who could not be moved by such sights? But she wondered how this would affect him over the years. He could become kinder, if that was possible, or angrier or he could be plagued by demons that would not allow him to sleep. Well, they would have to deal with those consequences if and when they arose. For now, the most important thing was that he returned home – that and the proofreading.

★

Annie could hardly believe what she had seen and heard. She felt as if she had been through the highs and lows of every known emotion – her heart racing, armpits clammy and legs trembling the entire day.

The Gauleiter of Munich and Upper Bavaria, Paul Giesler, had come to speak to university students in the Main Auditorium of the Deutsche Museum. That disgusting man had addressed the crowd of students who had gathered and proceeded to denounce all the men who were not serving in the army. He'd called them skulkers and shirkers and dared to say that they were not honestly clever and that their intellects were twisted. Then her jaw had almost hit the floor when he stated that the only real way of life could be transmitted by Hitler alone with his light, joyful and life-affirming teachings. The audacity of the man was completely and utterly unbelievable. The boys had started to boo and hiss and shout out to him that he was abhorrent and worse. Then he'd made obscene remarks to the female students, saying they were not doing their duty which was to 'service' Wehrmacht officers. Giesler had commanded his SS thugs to arrest the students, but other young people came to the rescue and fights broke out all over the hall.

Annie had been standing at the back with Fred, a few other members of staff and Frans, a lecturer who had recently joined their resistance group.

She became so excited to witness this act of rebellion that she moved to join in, but Fred put a hand on her arm and held her back. Disbelieving, she looked at him with a frown. He shook his head imperceptibly, something he had to do to her quite often, to warn her that it wasn't her place to join in. But how she itched to do so; every nerve in her body screeching out for her to raise her fists, pick up a chair and hurl it, kick the brute and his hangers-on, be a part of this orchestrated chaos.

Giesler was surrounded by his guards and whisked away, so the surging crowd tried to head them off at the side door or as they were getting into their cars or opening the gates. The rioters formed themselves into a group, marching and singing songs of protest until the police, armed to the hilt, forced them to go their separate ways. How wonderful it was to see the students' attempts; they looked and sounded like noble savages defending their territory from invaders when in fact, the barbarians were the ones being hunted.

It seemed that no one could settle back into their work after that, especially as they could hear chants and shouts from outside. So a number of their group convened in the dining hall. They knew, of course, who they could trust but they also knew that they could not express their concurrence with the student uprising in this public place. Instead, they drank tea and coffee and tried to convey their admiration by widening their eyes or subtly nodding their heads or nudging each other under the table. Very few people were talking. Some other members of staff looked terrified. One poor woman was pale and her friends were waving a handkerchief in front of her face. Others were shocked and Annie wondered how many, like them, were holding back on their true thoughts and feelings.

On the way home, Annie held on to Fred's arm and whispered to him, 'Do you think our leaflets had anything to do with the riot today?'

'It's hard to tell,' he said. 'And it doesn't really matter what or who is the source of that kind of resistance, the main point is that it occurred.' Then he smiled more broadly than he had for some time. 'But I like to think so,' he said.

She agreed, with a grin to mirror his.

When the authorities pompously announced that they had resumed Luftwaffe raids on London, Fred became even more afflicted with worry. Annie could hear him pacing up and down into the small hours and when they left each morning for work, he had dark purple pouches under his eyes.

Over a supper of stew, which Frau Wilhelm had brought round for them, Annie watched Fred pick the fat off the few bits of meat in his bowl and move them around with his fork.

'Eat that,' Annie commanded. 'You need it to keep strong.'

He pierced the lardy lump and held it up for her to inspect. It was thick and yellow and smelled a bit rancid. Her stomach turned although she had set upon all of hers with a fervour. 'This?' he said. 'Good for me? There is no nutrition in this, Annie.'

'Well, it will keep you warm.'

Without laughing he said, 'You sound just like Mum. And Oma.'

'That's not such a bad thing,' she said. 'So don't think that can insult me.'

He threw down his fork. 'I'm sorry, I am angry and frustrated and so worried about...'

'Vi,' Annie finished for him. 'I am in the same boat as you.'

'But unlike you with Walther, I have no idea where Viola

is. I hope she's still in Cambridge, or that she's returned to live with her parents. But then again I have no information about those places. They might be razed to the ground for all I know.'

'Why not work on the assumption that if they were, Hitler would boast about it without hesitation.'

'Wise Annie,' he said. 'But perhaps she's moved to London for work? We do know that city is on its knees and now the Luftwaffe is battering them again. My dear, sweet Vi.' He put his head in his hands and wept, one dry sob escaping from between his fingers. 'How I long to be with her and take care of her. I am the only one who can do that.'

Annie put her arm around him and rubbed his back. Then she took his plate away and scraped his leftovers into a bowl to reheat the next day.

20 January 1943
It must be lack of nutrition, but I have missed my monthly visitor twice. And the odd feeling in my breasts? I'm sure it is just the vivid imagination that Fred has accused me of having all my life. But I so wish Walther were here.

The fifth leaflet, written by Fred, was ready for distribution and they decided to circulate it far and wide instead of concentrating on the immediate vicinity. Annie volunteered, with Ilse and Gerda, to take as many as possible in their knapsacks to Berlin. Fred was against the idea, but Annie stood up to him saying that although she was pleased he was taking care of her, she sometimes felt as if he was treating her like a child. 'I'm a member of the group in my own right and want to do my part,' she said one morning before they left for work.

Fred huffed and leaned back against the sink. 'Annie.' His voice was pleading. 'Try to look at things from my point of view.'

'But you wouldn't say that to Gerda and Ilse. In front of everyone.'

'They are not my responsibility. You are.'

'I was. But am I still?'

'Yes,' Fred said. 'And like it or not, you always will be.'

'I'm sorry.' Annie softened. 'To be a burden.'

Fred rubbed his temples. 'You're never that,' he said. 'But who do we have but each other?'

When Annie looked at him, she saw how worry had eaten lines into his forehead. She reached up and kissed him on the cheek. 'I promise to take care of myself.'

'Okay.' He smiled. 'And I promise to try not to treat you like a baby, until the next time you behave like one. Which I guarantee won't be too far off.'

'Enough,' Annie shouted, flicking him with a tea towel.

Covering his head with his hands, Fred cowered away from her. 'Stop,' he cried. 'That's soaking wet. And you've just proved my point beautifully.'

Gerda, who was petite and very pretty, said they should have a plan in case the three girls were stopped by the SS or other authorities. 'We must say that one of us is recently engaged to a Wehrmacht officer and we are going to Berlin to buy wedding outfits. What do you think?'

Annie and Ilse thought that a good idea.

'Gerda, you must play the part of the bride-to-be,' said Ilse. 'You will be able to best get away with it. We will pose as your friends.'

'What if they check our knapsacks?' Annie asked.

Gerda looked up through her eyelashes and curled her lips knowingly. 'Then this is the first, and only thing they will draw out.' She produced a pair of lacy undergarments. 'That will please them and they will look no further. Believe me, those Nazis are very shallow and think of nothing except alcohol and what dangles between their legs.'

The other two girls liked the idea and said they would pad out their bags with their underwear. They would have to act a little bit innocent and a little bit worldly. Perhaps pretend they'd had a schnapps or two. And happy, definitely happy, that Gerda was romantically involved with a member of the regime. That thought made all three girls shudder.

'What will we do if they ask your young man's name?' Annie said.

'Look coy,' Gerda said. 'No girlfriend would want her fiancé to know she had been showing her intimates to other men, after all.'

They all giggled at that.

'And when we get there?' Ilse said. 'Do we stick together or go our separate ways and meet up again later?'

They turned to the men; for this they wanted a consensus and it was decided they stay together. 'Watch over each other and be ready to step in with an explanation or excuse for what might come across as your strange behaviour,' Carl said.

So on Thursday they would spread the word in Berlin and Annie told herself she wasn't afraid. It was the right thing to do.

The sights in Berlin were terrible to see, just as Frau Wilhelm had described and worse. Ilse nudged Annie's elbow and they watched an elderly woman pick her way over the rubble in front of her building with a shopping basket on her arm. Annie ran to help her, but she turned away without a smile or a nod. At one time, people would have thanked each other for offering assistance, but now everyone regarded each other with suspicion.

Keeping up their pretence of bubbly optimism, anything important Annie, Gerda and Ilse wanted to say to each other they did so under their breath. 'How will all of this ever be rebuilt?' Annie whispered to Ilse.

'I hope it never will be,' Ilse hissed back. 'Not as it was. That will only remind us of the dictator. And who wants that?'

They made their way through debris-strewn streets, past shells of churches and crocodile lines of women waiting for the dregs of nothing in shops. No one was dressed well or looked clean. Babies had sooty snot running down their faces and children were wearing dirty clothes that were at least two sizes two small or too large.

'What's that smell?' said Gerda.

'Which one?' Annie answered.

'I think it's smoke, burning, sewage, rotten food,' Gerda said. 'It's putrid.'

'If this,' Ilse said, 'is the Wehrmacht winning, then I dread to think what London is like. Now, stop talking and look happy.'

As they rounded a corner towards the university, they were confronted by three SS officials who sneered and leered at them. One of them, who had a scar running from the middle of his forehead to top of his mouth, asked them to identify themselves.

'Ilse.'

'Annie.'

'And Gerda.'

'Where are you lovely girls off to?' another officer asked.

'Yes,' his older companion said. 'It cannot be more interesting than sitting in there.' He pointed to a café. 'And sharing a drink with us.'

Annie was petrified. They had not practised for this eventuality. She felt her face drain of colour and she hiccoughed sick into her mouth.

But Gerda held her nerve. Batting her eyelashes, she said, 'I am spoken for by an officer and my friends are helping me to shop for my wedding requirements.'

'Oh ho,' the one with the scar sung out. 'His name?'

Gerda shook her head and pointed to her chin. 'Do you want to be hit hard right here?' she asked. 'Because you will be when I describe you to him.'

'What is in your knapsacks?' the older man said. 'Open them for inspection.'

Gerda shrugged and began to loosen the opening enough to expose a flash of white brassiere. 'Yes, okay. But he will be most displeased when he knows you have seen his wedding night surprise before he has. A beating will be the least of your—'

'Go,' the third officer said. 'Get out of our sight.'

They linked arms, with Annie in the middle and pretended to whisper and titter amongst themselves. Annie could feel the pounding of Gerda's heart on one side and Ilse's racing pulse on the other. Gerda was right, Nazi men were superficial and hollow. And stupid with it; all brawn and no brain and that was probably why they were so dangerous.

They found their way to the Friedrich Wilhelm University and left leaflets where they could. In the ladies' cloakroom, the library, the central hall, under other brochures on the reception desk, on tables in the dining hall, in the middle of books in the bookstore, under doors in the student accommodation blocks. Annie couldn't believe they were so bold, driven by a blind passion to make themselves heard and to reach others who may be thinking along the same lines as them; they must be out there and they must find each other as there would be power in numbers.

On the way back to the station, they stopped in as many bars and coffee shops and late-night dives as possible – to think, once upon a time, Berlin was known all over the world for its night life, now this was all that was left of those glory days. Wherever possible, they left a leaflet or two under tables or in hidden corners and got rid of the last few in dark cubbyholes. All that remained in their knapsacks was their snowy white smalls.

Annie wasn't sure if she would sleep that night as adrenaline was coursing around her body like an electric shock. Fred was so relieved when she returned safely that he hugged her to him with all his might. He listened to her recount the day and asked many questions. Then he fell asleep in a chair. Annie covered him with a blanket and hoped he slept for a few hours whilst she would try for the same in bed.

At the beginning of February, they had news that the German 6th Army had surrendered in Stalingrad. On her way to visit Frau Wilhelm, Annie felt as if fresh spring air was streaming into the heart of her, giving her all of those old Germanic attributes like strength and vitality and a sense of well-being. Perhaps Walther would be home any day now and it would all be over soon.

Frau Wilhelm greeted her at the door with a smile. They looked each other in the eyes and nodded. 'Now,' she said, 'I have made cake.'

'Oh, lovely,' Annie said. 'It's been a long time since I've tasted any of that.'

'Well, I had to substitute some ingredients, but here it is. Look.' She held up the plate and showed off the pale, golden squares, a proud look on her face.

It was not as good as Annie had tasted before rationing, but it was more than good enough. They mentioned Stalingrad but didn't go into details and they certainly didn't say, in words, how happy they were with the Allied victory. But at least half a dozen times, one of them said, 'Now Walther will be coming home.'

Later that day, she and Fred caught the train into Munich and went straight to Gustav's rooms. The others were already assembled. 'The sixth leaflet is ready to go,' Carl said. 'And it's perfect.'

'Good timing,' said Helmuth. He handed a copy each to Annie and Fred. It was written entirely by Professor Frans and was so eloquent that it put their previous efforts to shame. He was as articulate and impassioned on paper as he was in the lecture theatre where students from all disciplines listened to him criticise the regime in a clever, cloaked manner. But in the leaflet, he came straight to the point. *Fellow Students! The day of reckoning is upon Germany and the dead of Stalingrad are pleading with us to do something here.* It was as if he was holding a personal dialogue with each and every reader. He called for German youth to rise up, as they had done in the riot and fight for their freedom. It was a literary masterpiece. Not a single edit was deemed necessary and they decided that they must copy and distribute the leaflets as soon as possible.

'Are those the stencils?' Ernst pointed to the corner where five small, rectangular metal templates were poking out from under a curtain. 'How did you get them here without being seen?'

'We made them here,' Gustav said. 'Klaus Weber taught me how to do it.' He held up the stencils which spelled out *Down with Hitler* and *Freedom* and *Hitler is the Devil.* Annie's stomach dropped with fear then surged with excitement. Writing graffiti on walls seemed much more dangerous than dropping leaflets, but that was what it had been decided they would do. And they were going to start the next day.

18 February 1943
I can barely hold my pen. My hand and whole body are shaking almost uncontrollably. But I have three items

to list and not in any particular order of most to least distressing; all three are equally appalling and heart-rending.

Ilse, Gustav and Carl have been arrested by the Gestapo.

Walther is dead.

I am pregnant.

I I

April 1943

Pulling back the curtain a fraction, Viola looked out on the tall, lush trees in the front garden and the pink and purple tulips bobbing their heads at either end of the bench where she would sit later with Lillian. Beyond that all of London was bustling. Or at least she imagined it must be, but had no way of knowing for certain as she had been removed from everyday society and was waiting out her time in this cool, quiet convent with six other 'fallen women' and eight attending nuns.

The walls of her room, or cell as the nuns called it, were white. All the rooms were painted in the same stark absence of colour. The bedclothes and towels and soft furnishings were white. The staircases were white and the statues of Mary and the saints were white. Viola thought the colour scheme had been chosen specifically to remind the young women that they lacked the attributes that white traditionally symbolised – chastity, cleanliness, purity, innocence, spotlessness, restraint, virtue.

Mum had trudged around London on her own, vetting homes that Viola could be admitted to and said she had chosen this particular one because it looked so neat and clean and hygienic. Of course Viola was grateful to Mum, but she disagreed and thought her place of confinement antiseptic, impersonal and desolate – but in her position, she had no weapons with which to fight.

There was a soft knock on the door and a nun carrying a tray entered with soft, light, brisk footsteps. With a month to go, Viola was allowed several dispensations from the convent routine and breakfast in her room was one of them. Every morning Sister Marietta brought the meal in to her. Never granting a smile, she nodded to Viola and placed the white porridge, white toast and tea in a white teapot on the small white side table, made the sign of the cross and turned to leave so quickly that her veil billowed out behind her. It took all the willpower Viola possessed not to shout, 'I'm pregnant, not infectious!' at the disappearing figure.

The home was run with military routine and the nuns seemed to thrive on their tight schedule. Personal ablutions at six-thirty, breakfast at seven, cleaning at eight, laundry at nine, personal reflection at ten, exercise in the grounds at eleven, lunch at twelve, rest time at one, leisure time – which amounted to reading, writing letters or needlework – at two, doctor and midwife visits at three, visitors at four, tea at five, more reading at six, communal time at seven during which they listened to the news on the wireless, supper at eight, night ablutions at nine-thirty, lights out at ten. Viola had never thought of herself as rebellious or nonconformist, but she hated this rigorous timetable. It was a constant reminder that all her independence and ability to make choices and decisions had been taken from her. She was absolutely reliant now on Mum, Dad and these despotic nuns.

Viola stood, cupping her hand under her tummy to nurse some of her baby's weight. She had decided months ago that the active, kicking, rolling, punching baby was a boy. She looked down at herself, in her uniform of pale grey skirt and white smock and could not believe how much she resembled a barrage balloon. Her legs, under the surgical stockings the doctor had ordered, were a crisscross of lumpy, aching veins. Lillian had given her a pair of men's slippers to wear as her feet had swollen by two sizes and reminded her of pink, gristly sausages ready to burst their skins. No face creams or cosmetics were permitted either, but as mirrors weren't allowed in the convent, Viola had no way of knowing if the bare-faced look suited her or not. Lillian had offered to bring in a pocket mirror and help Viola to take a surreptitious look at herself, but Viola was worried that what she saw reflected back would cause her greater distress than she was already experiencing.

She wore her hair, which Fred had loved and stroked so tenderly, in a clasp at the nape of her neck as the inmates could not visit the hairdresser; one wash a week with the regulation bar of coal tar soap and a perfunctory comb-through, then the clip at the back was the limit of styling allowed. On Lillian's second visit, she had brought a pair of scissors with her and trimmed Viola's hair in the garden, the light, bronzed, wavy spirals floating down amongst the shrubbery. Viola had been chastised by a spying nun who told her in a quiet, disappointed voice that she must not allow herself to be vain. 'Yes, Sister,' Viola had said. But she would have loved to explain that her pregnancy had nothing to do with ostentation or conceit and everything to do with loneliness that cut deep into the centre of her being like the set of sharp, pointed blades that Lillian had held in her hand.

Stretching backwards as far as possible, Viola kneaded and rubbed into the small of her back. Tears pooled in her eyes when she imagined the gentle touch Fred would have used to massage her sore muscles if he was here and if he was the baby's father. Or Mum. She would have known the exact spots that needed relief. But her parents had been forced to abandon her, and Fred, when he returned, would surely renounce her, too. It didn't matter, either, how often she told herself that her defence was the alienation wrought by the war, she had to take full responsibility for her actions.

She eased herself down onto the hard-backed chair near the small table and pulled the bowl of porridge towards her. This morning the oats were runny and fell from the spoon in a river of tiny globules. Other mornings they stuck to the spoon in a huge lump. Either way it was served, it cemented itself to her throat as she tried to gag it down. But today she was not sure she could stomach it.

She dropped the spoon back into the gluey mixture and closed her eyes. In her mind, she could hear the nuns telling her she must eat. When Mum came to visit, she said the same thing. Of course, she knew it was important for her and the baby so she reached for the toast, which was always dry despite the margarine and jam the nuns scraped across the centre of the bread; like an obedient child, she bit into the crumbly slice and white powder rained down on the plate, the table, the surface of her grey smock. *I couldn't be in more of a state if I tried*, she thought, so with the help of the insipid tea she forced the rest down her throat.

Looking around, she thought the chaos she'd created was all she was good for now – making a mess of things for herself and everyone else. But dealing with the breakfast debris would be easy. At clean-up time she would borrow the carpet sweeper and run it over the floor and hey presto! All would be spotless again. *If only*, she thought, *I could clear up the shambles of my life so effectively.*

Every day she played out what had happened since she'd sealed the letter to Mum in an envelope and pushed it into the postbox. Mum had come straight to London and much to Viola's surprise and relief, had hugged her daughter hard to her. 'It's alright, it's alright,' she said over and over again, as if she was trying to convince herself as well as Viola. 'These things shouldn't happen,' she said. 'But they do. And there but for the grace of God...' Mum stopped short, blushed a deep crimson and turned away. Viola's first reaction was to ask for an explanation, a womanly confidence that would help her to feel less isolated, but she couldn't and realised she did not want to know about that part of her Mum and Dad's life. Or maybe she didn't want to be faced with Mum's near-miss partner not being Dad as the little boy growing inside her did not belong to Fred.

During that visit, Lillian had reiterated that if she were in Viola's position, she would try to abort the baby. Mum was not shocked, as Viola thought she would be, but neither did she try to persuade her either way. Like Switzerland, she remained neutral, saying she would help Viola in whatever decision she made. But Viola would not and could not be persuaded to change her mind.

'But why, Vi?' Lillian pleaded. 'It's not as if this Mike means anything to you. To carry and give birth to his baby and suffer the humiliation that entails. Well, it's stuff and nonsense to me.'

Viola looked down at her hands. 'I'm sorry,' she said in a feeble voice. 'But I couldn't bring myself to do that.'

Eventually, Mum put a stop to the discussion by taking Viola's hand in hers and saying, 'You have made up your mind, haven't you?'

Viola nodded.

'Then there are other decisions that have to be made,' Mum said. 'You will have to go into a special confinement home and therefore, Arthur will have to be told as he will have to decide whether or not to pay for such a thing. Are you prepared for that, Vi?'

'No,' Viola said, the thought of the consequences making her answers sound more and more childish to her ears. She had been hoping that Mum would insist she be allowed to wait out her time at home. But that ephemeral hope was blighted when Mum said, with tears in her eyes, 'I will pave the way with your dad as best I can and I truly believe that he will not see you destitute, Vi. Neither of us will.'

That simple statement made Viola's eyes fill in sympathy with Mum's. How she had let her down. 'Do you think he will want to see me?' Viola asked.

'I have no way of knowing,' Mum said. 'He might want to talk with you face to face or he might not be able to look at you for some time. I'll write and let you know.'

But Dad had wanted to see her and wrote himself to tell her so in no uncertain terms. *Viola Victoria*, his letter began in fierce black ink that almost tore through the paper, so violently had his hand pressed down on the pen.

Mum tells me you have disgraced yourself and are now in want of my assistance and indulgence. I cannot believe that you – my beautiful, intelligent, promising daughter – have got yourself into this unprecedented situation. Mum tells me it has become most common in this time of modern war, but you are not common, we are not common and, as a family, we do not lend ourselves to the histrionics and superficial displays of the age, no matter how horrific the era may be. But it would appear that you have given in to the loss of dignity that often befalls young people, in particular, during time of war, convincing yourselves that to live in the moment is justified. However, in most cases, living in the moment leads to a lifetime of living in shame and guilt.

I request that you come home so I can talk to you about my decision for your future.

Your father.

Viola had never felt so terrified. Her legs were stiff with fear and she had to fight for every breath, but she couldn't seem to force air past the top of her chest. If Dad disowned her she would be tossed aside and left to negotiate her way through this terrible trauma on her own. But Mum wouldn't let that happen – or would she have a choice? There would only be Lillian left for help and advice, and perhaps George, but they were as ill prepared, with no finances behind them, as was she.

After reading the letter twice, Viola tore it up into tiny

pieces and tossed it on the fire. On the same day, she also received a letter from Mum, explaining in more detail what Dad's reaction had been and preparing her for his questions and lectures when she arrived home. The most painful of his decrees being that the boys must not learn of their sister's disgrace.

Robert had acted in the precise way Viola had predicted. He had signed up for an engineering degree at Oxford, allowed himself to be taken there and settled into his rooms, then joined the RAF the following day. Mum's letter said that Dad felt as if, one by one, his children were betraying him. Therefore, she wrote, the hurtful things he said in his letter to Viola also pertained, in his mind, to Robert.

So that weekend she had to go home and face the music. But there would definitely not be any dancing to go with it.

First there was to be a week of lasts for Viola, which she didn't realise would be as difficult as they had been.

She handed in a week's notice at work, saying that her mother was in need of her at home. What she hadn't been prepared for was the number of people who stopped by her desk and told her, with genuine sincerity, that they were very sad and disappointed that she had to leave. She loved the job and knew that it was of great service to the war effort, but she was humbled when one junior minister said, 'You are, by far, our most outstanding German translator.' Another civil servant shook his head and asked her if she would please reconsider. The next asked if there was a possibility she would return after the crisis at home was resolved.

'Thank you,' she answered, her voice thin and feeble. 'But I think it will be a rather long-term situation.'

A few of the girls clubbed together and bought her two new books, which they signed with messages of good luck. She read them within the first few weeks of being in the home and often took them down from the shelf and looked at them, a reminder of how stunned she'd been to understand that she had been liked, by some of her colleagues at any rate.

And then the most remarkable thing had occurred. To this day and after all that had happened to her, she still could not believe the coincidence or the good fortune or happenstance or fate or destiny or miracle of the chain of events. She had no idea how to categorise the set of circumstances that fell into her lap and the deep meaning of their outcome for her.

Late in the afternoon of her penultimate day at work, a civil servant – or some such person – had rushed into the office with a couple of leaflets in his hand. He stood at the door looking frantic; he was jacketless, his tie unknotted, hair falling over his forehead. 'Miss Baxter?' His clear, booming voice belied his frenetic façade. 'I've been told to ask for Miss Baxter.'

Feeling a mixture of pride and agitation, Viola put up her hand and said, 'I am she.'

'Ah, Miss Baxter.' The young man made his way to her desk. 'I have been told that these must be translated immediately by you and only you and that they must take priority and precedence over all other documents.' He paused to take a breath. 'I am to give you one hour to type up the transcripts and then take them back personally to the PM. Understood?'

Viola took the papers from the man's outstretched hand and nodded. 'How many copies of each?' she asked.

'Three, if you please. I'll wait outside.'

Viola watched him leave the office with purpose and close the door behind him.

She opened the leaflets and propped them against her book rest, threaded a fresh sheet of paper into one of her typewriters, set the margins and poised her hands over the keys ready to begin. With the outline of a flower in the top left-hand corner of every page, she had never seen anything like these leaflets before. Reaching for them, she decided that initially she would read them from cover to cover to get the gist of what was written before beginning her translation. They were stained with tea or coffee cup rings and on one there was the imprint of what looked like the sole of a boot. A smear of dried mud swept from edge to edge of the first document and on the inside cover of the other, there were faint pencil doodles. Viola turned them over and over. Whatever were these? She wondered how they had come into Allied hands.

Then she started to read the mimeographed pages of the document entitled 'Leaflet V' and her heart gave a thump. It was resistance material of the most fervent, encouraging and intellectual kind. And the turn of phrase in the opening paragraph was so idiosyncratic that it could not be an accident or chance, no two people could write with such an unusual and distinctive style. There was only one explanation: Fred was the author of this leaflet. Her Fred.

All colour must have drained from her face because

Lillian was by her side, asking her if she was quite well. She dared not tell even her closest friend about this so hastily folded the leaflet again, drew her finger across her mouth and said, 'I'm fine, thank you, Lil. Just got a rush job on.'

Lillian nodded and hurried back to her side of the room.

Unfurling the battered, dirty page she willed that the remainder of the document bear evidence of Fred's mark. Each and every line, sentence, paragraph, statement, sentiment screamed to her that he was alive. Not only alive, but alive and well enough to be writing with such intensity against the Nazi regime and for the freedom of all. She longed to bundle the leaflet into her clothing next to the ring, but placed it with deference back on the book rest and read through Leaflet VI; there was no sign of Fred in the writing there, but she refused to give in to the fleeting notion that he hadn't written the sixth because something atrocious had happened to him after the publication of the fifth. She preferred to convince herself that the members of this group took it in turns to author their defiant literature so it would be less likely for them to be caught by the authorities.

Remaining calm and professional, she began to translate first Fred's leaflet and then the other. When she finished, she made four copies of each so that she could take one set home and compare the writing in Leaflet V with Fred's unfinished thesis that she had found in his college rooms. If caught smuggling them out of the building, she knew she would be prosecuted, but it was worth the risk to have that little of bit of Fred with her.

Before she let the junior minister take the three remaining copies from her hand, she held on to the pages with a fierce grip. 'These,' she said, holding his piercing gaze, 'are incredibly important and must be circulated widely amongst the German people.'

'How can you discern that, Miss Baxter?' the man said, pulling on the papers, trying to release them from Viola's hold.

She hesitated, wondering how much she could get away with without causing suspicion. Then, in an instant, she knew she had no choice. 'Tell everyone who needs to know, that I have been around German speakers and authors and scholars for a good deal of my life and I am assured that these have been written by resistance workers in Germany who are risking their lives to produce and distribute them. We must help them by any means we can.'

The man nodded and glanced at his watch, his spectacles creeping down his sweaty nose. 'Thank you, Miss Baxter, I'll pass on your message.'

'It's not a message,' she said. 'Look at me, please. It's a matter of life and death. Victory or defeat.'

The man narrowed his eyes, as if a sceptical thought had dawned on him. 'I should, perhaps, question you in greater depth,' he said. If he got it into his head to drag her in front of the higher-ups and question her about her formidable bank of knowledge, her story might lead to accusations of disloyalty or espionage. She might be sent to an internment camp, like Matteo, or be tried for treason.

Viola shoved the papers into his hand and said in a precise, firm voice, 'There's no time for that. Go now and relay my information.'

For a beat, the young man considered his course of action, then turned and raced towards his destination. Viola stood and watched him disappear, her legs too weak for her to do otherwise.

Now, Viola piled up the toast-speckled crockery ready to return to the kitchen then put her ear to the door and listened for the soft sounds of the nuns' cushioned footsteps. There were no locks on any of the doors and it was difficult to ascertain whether one of the wardens, as she called them, was creeping along the corridor, ready to burst in on her at any moment. When she was as satisfied as she could be that she wouldn't be disturbed, she pulled down Fred's thesis that she'd wrapped in plain brown paper, opened it and took out her copy of Leaflet V. Closing her eyes, she skimmed the tips of her fingers over the pamphlet, then read through every line for what must be the three hundredth time. Nothing anyone said to her gave her consolation like this one sheet of paper.

Then there was the last night in the flat she shared with Lillian and as a consequence, the last time she would be living independently for some time, if ever. Whilst she packed her belongings, Lillian had cooked them some sort of stew with their rations. It was richer and tastier than anything she'd had for a while and she realised that dear Lillian had used a good month's worth of shin beef, gravy browning and flour for the dumplings on this one meal. She had never been particularly fond of their accommodation, but now that she was leaving, every nook and cranny, dusty shelf, dripping tap, fraying rug and cold square of linoleum became a source of nostalgia. She tossed and turned that night, worried sick about the meeting with her father and the ramifications for her and her unborn baby. In the morning, Lillian went with her to the station and they said goodbye to each other and their life together as flatmates. Now June lived in Viola's old room and Lillian said it was, 'Alright, but only that.'

Mum had wanted to sit in on Dad's talk with Viola, but Dad would not allow that to happen. He said that Mum knew his decision and he needed to speak to his daughter alone. He wasn't cruel. Nor could he be called cordial or gracious. But he was benevolent. Although he asked Viola many questions, he stopped her from answering them by raising his palm in front of her whenever she went to speak. It became plain quite quickly that he wanted to talk to her, not with her. 'There is nothing you can ever say that will help me to understand how and why you have allowed this to happen,' he said.

Viola hung her head.

'Your wonderful mother and I have brought you up to comport yourself to a much higher standard than this. We have demanded that of you, have we not?'

'Yes, Dad.'

'Do not let me see those foolish tears. It's much too late for that. You have been reckless and immature and allowed London to turn your head, haven't you?'

Viola bit on her lip to quell her crying, but let her fingers stray to the contours of the ring beneath her dress. 'Yes, Dad,' she said.

'Stop fiddling. And that girl, Lillian, who we have welcomed many times as one of the family. Does she behave in the same decadent manner?'

'Dad, Lillian never—'

'Enough! Hold your counsel.'

'And now you come to me for financial aid. And what am I to do? Turn you away?'

'I beg you, Dad, please—'

'Quiet.' Dad's voice softened at last. 'I will pay whatever is necessary. Mum will sort out the arrangements. Now go.'

Tears of frustration and remorse clouded Viola's eyes. 'Dad,' she pleaded. 'Can we not be as we—'

'Go, Viola. Now. And I'm sure Mum has told you but I reiterate. Your brothers must never know about this.'

Viola took one more look at Dad before she closed the door of his study. His shoulders were slumped and his hair was thin, dry and grey. He looked like a man in mourning.

She and Mum took their meals together in the dining room and Dad ate alone in his study, so that meeting with him had been another last for Viola. When Mum travelled to London to vet confinement homes, Viola was not allowed to accompany her. She had to stay hidden at home and there, hidden from Dad's view. The following week, she packed a very small bag and Mum delivered her to this whitewashed, black-souled holding pen.

The most pitiful consequence was the letters from David that Mum brought with her when she visited once a month or so. They were full of what he was doing at school and how he wanted to follow in Robert's footsteps by joining the RAF; Viola had no doubt he would do so the minute he could. There was always a PS at the end of his letters asking when they could please arrange his visit to London. She had to reply as if she was still working, still seeing her friends, still sharing the little flat with Lillian and that his visit would be organised for some time in the vague future.

Every time Mum stepped through the door into the visitors' lounge, she broke down in tears. She wasn't the only one. All the visiting mothers seemed to spend their time in the same state of emotional collapse. Because of that, Viola tried to counteract Mum's overwrought reaction by pretending that her mother had chosen wisely and she could not be more content and calm and settled. When Mum's tears subsided and she could talk logically again, they discussed what was going to happen next. As Mum reminded her each visit, the baby would inevitably be born and then what? Adoption? Mum tentatively raised the idea. 'There is,' Mum said softly, 'no way you could ever go back into society if you keep the baby.'

But the more she thought about it, the more deeply Viola realised that back in society was the last place she wanted to be. During the scheduled periods of reflection and when performing tedious chores, Viola tried to imagine life on her own with her newborn. In her mind, she didn't see them in London; it was too built-up and crowded and dangerous. And she couldn't contemplate Cambridge; to live there without being a part of the academia would be impossible. Cirencester was definitely not a proposition, unless she wanted to give Mrs Bishop a heyday and Mum and Dad more grief than they were carrying around as it was. None of those places would be an option for her as a fallen woman. Her parents had all but forsaken her and Fred would do the same when he returned so what chance would she stand amongst ex-colleagues and acquaintances?

Money was, of course, the biggest stumbling block. She had none of her own and no access to anyone else's. Mum had implied that, although it hadn't been discussed in detail, Dad would not subsidise her if she kept the baby. It felt as if she was being hounded into submission, trapped into a corner like a cowering animal. That's what it felt like, when a wave of panic overcame her during a period of reflection or in the middle of the night – like she was recoiling from injury into the dark recesses of a cage, waiting for a cup of water or a morsel of food to be thrown to her. Other times, she felt stronger and determined to think until she came up with some kind of resolution. And when she did, she would fight doggedly, like a Spitfire pilot, to ensure her solution came to fruition.

It was nine o'clock, laundry time. With one hand she grabbed her bag of washing and in the other, she balanced her tray. Making her way down the cool, silent staircase, there was no relief from the alabaster surfaces. She washed her dishes in the sink, dried them and stacked them away, then she followed the sounds of hushed voices to the laundry room.

The rest of the day passed and then Lillian was there, like a faithful puppy, bringing news of the outside world. She looked beautiful in a pale green belted dress with a toffee-coloured collar and jacket. Her dark, shiny hair was pulled back off her face, her complexion clear and her grey eyes bright. 'You look fabulous, Lil,' said Viola, trying to keep an edge of envy out of her voice. Sitting opposite her friend made her cringe with the lack of grace she felt about her bump and ill-fitting clothes. 'Surely you haven't worn such a lovely ensemble just to visit me.'

Lillian couldn't stop a smile from taking over her face and crinkling her nose. 'Good old George is on leave and he's taking me to dinner,' she said.

'Oh, lovely,' said Viola. And she imagined the restaurant where they might meet; the food they might eat; the cocktails they might drink; the things they might talk about. 'Well at least it won't be somewhere as ghastly as The Whim, I hope?'

Lillian laughed. 'No fear,' she said. 'Not dressed like this.'

'Does George know?' Viola looked down at her bulge.

Lillian nodded. 'I told him in a letter.'

Viola blushed at the thought.

'He's been most sympathetic and non-judgemental.'

'As is his wonderful, time-proven manner. Lil, listen to me.' Viola took Lillian's hands in hers. 'Do not get yourself into this situation. It's horrendous. Please, promise me.'

'Oh, Vi,' Lillian said. 'I promise I'll be careful. And besides, I keep telling you there's nothing like that between me and George.'

Viola laughed. 'I think it's yourself you need to keep telling,' she said. 'I already know there is. Now, tell me all the news.'

Lillian told her about scooting behind some dilapidated buildings to avoid the crowds along Oxford Street and finding herself walking behind a beautifully dressed young woman. All of a sudden, from the hem of the girl's coat, a pair of knickers appeared. Lillian could see that the elastic waistband was torn and frayed, but the woman didn't bat an eyelid, she leaned against a post, slipped off the knickers and stuffed them in her elegant handbag. No one would be the wiser by looking at her. 'She was the epitome of that saying, "Fur coat, no drawers".'

Viola laughed so hard that her already stretched stomach felt as if would split open.

Lillian described going out with Harriet and June, the lift everyone was feeling after the Allied victories in Italy, some interesting things she'd concocted with her rations, how she'd replaced the collar on her pretty dress, the girl in the office who'd replaced Viola but who was not nearly as efficient. 'And yesterday I saw the saddest sight. A group of mums at the train station holding tiny babies and suitcases. Some saying goodbye to men in uniforms, others hugging their own mums or sisters. So heart-breaking.'

'But where do you think they were they going?' Viola asked.

Lillian looked amazed. 'They were being evacuated.'

'But I thought just the children were sent away and their mums had to stay behind and work or just get on with it.'

'Well, that wouldn't work for newborns.' Lillian shook her head. 'They need their mothers.'

Viola had never thought about that before. But when she did, it was the perfect solution to her dilemma. 'Lil,' she said. 'Can I kiss you?'

Lillian shrugged. 'Of course,' she said, offering her cheek. 'But why?'

'I now know how I will be able to keep my baby,' Viola said, and she could feel newfound energy pulsing into her hands, her feet, her mind and bringing a glow to her face.

Despite her swelling bump, Viola felt lighter once she knew there was a way for her to keep her baby and regain some control over her future; now all she had to do was hold her nerve. From that time on, she told everyone about her plan. Mum, who would tell Dad; the nuns; the other pregnant women; the midwives and the doctors. She did not waver from her decision. By the time she went into labour, a plan had been established. She would be taken to hospital, with all her belongings, in an ambulance. There she would give birth and lie in for six weeks. When discharged, she would be taken straight to the train station and evacuated to a predetermined place. She hoped it would be somewhere very far away, like Scotland, where the only person she would know was her child and they could start afresh.

Every time she ran through the arrangement in her mind, which was several times a day, she sighed with relief. Then her stomach would turn again and she would doubt her decision when she pictured her family and Lillian and the hundreds of miles between them and her.

If she thought she had experienced the deep pit of loneliness every day since Fred left, she was aware that the depths she could plummet to alone in some distant place, were unfathomable to her imagination. No wonder she'd heard about so many girls in her position who allowed their parents to bring up their babies as their own. But Mum and Dad hadn't put that forward as a solution, so she could see no other way than to move to Scotland or some other such remote place.

One of the advantages of the plan was that the government would pay for everything as she would be considered, even in her fallen state, to be a 'domestic soldier'. But more important to Viola was the fact that Dad would not be asked to provide for her. Mum said she would try to persuade Dad to telegraph money to her for a few little extras, wherever she might be, which would be lovely but, on the other hand, it would deem her more beholden to him than she was already.

★

When her time came, the labour was long and hard. Through the sweat and the agonising pains and the turmoil, she longed to think that Fred was in the corridor, pacing up and down waiting to greet their baby. She saw his face, looming in and out of her vision, but every time she reached out for him, he disappeared so she clutched and clawed at the ring instead. Doctors and midwives came and went, some encouraging, some scolding. She did her best to get the whole thing over and done with but the baby was taking his time. The cramping, the gore, the feral instincts, the sharp smell of iron was, she told herself, befitting and warranted. Then at last, at the apex of exhaustion, a mewl, a squall, a tiny form covered in slime. A girl, she was told. It's a girl. 'Do you have a name for this little lady?'

She hadn't made provision for this turn of events. She shook her head, a shower of perspiration bouncing around her. 'Frederika,' she managed to whisper. 'Hello, little Freddie.'

12

May 1943

Frau Wilhelm clung to Annie like a limpet, crying into her neck and leaving a trail of tears and slime on the shoulder of her jacket. But to Annie, her own grief for Walther felt soft and quiet and cushioned either by disbelief or by the baby growing inside her. There had been the telegram followed by the certainty that there had been a mistake, Frau Wilhelm and Herr Doctor's outrage, the panic about the baby she had to keep to herself, a short church service, black armbands to sew and position on their sleeves. There was no body to cry over, as Walther's was buried in the cold ground at the Russian Front, but Herr Doctor was making arrangements for a headstone in the local churchyard so they would have a place to lay flowers and ponder their lives without him.

Then terrible chaos and fear gripped Annie and Fred when Ilse, Gustav and Carl were arrested. And in the midst of all that, Annie told Fred she was pregnant. She sat and watched him tear out his hair – the short shocks, like tufts of grass, coming out in clumps in his fists. He stared at them, then threw them to the floor before searching his scalp to grab another handful. The first question Fred asked her, when he finished with his hair, was if the baby was Walther's. Humiliation washed over her. How dare he think otherwise. 'Of course,' she answered, careful to keep her anger under control as she was aware that she was completely at his mercy. But she couldn't help adding, 'Do you think so little of me?'

'I am sorry, Annie.' Fred slumped into a chair and held his grey face in his hands. 'But... how could you allow this to happen? You know how precarious our situation is already.'

Annie refused to hang her head in shame. 'I did not allow this, as you say, to happen. It just... did. And now I must face the consequences without Walther by my side.'

'Do you know, Annie,' Fred said, sitting forward and balling his hands into fists over and over again, 'that Vi and I had one night together? Just the one.'

Battling against a tightening in her throat, Annie said, 'Walther and I did not have many more.'

'For all I know,' said Fred, gulping another schnapps, 'there is a child. My child. Being kept from me by this bloody war.'

After a few minutes of heavy silence, Fred moaned. 'Oh, what to deal with first.'

'Perhaps,' Annie offered, 'our fellow freedom fighters?'

'I have already told you, Annie,' Fred shouted, beyond the end of his tether. 'You are not to go near that trial. I forbid it!'

None of them did. It might have been cowardice that

stopped them, but they believed that if they turned up in the gallery they would be questioned about their possible involvement with the resistance group and they had heard the rumours of the Gestapo using horrific means to get information out of people. And if they were arrested, too? What good would that do anyone?

But as it turned out, the trial lasted for just one day. One short, never-ending day during which Fred was in Munich, trying to ascertain what was going on and Annie was alone in the house, frozen in fear. Not daring to go to the window and move the curtain to peer outside, or visit Frau Wilhelm, or walk to the market for shopping. When Fred came home and told her what he had heard through prattle, she was incredulous. The judge was a puppet and Ilse had been brave way beyond the limit of the definition of the word.

'I heard she denied her complicity to begin with,' said Fred. 'Then made a full confession but refused to implicate any other members.' He shook his head. 'I doubt I could have been so brave.'

'Oh, Fred,' Annie said. 'Is anything worth this?'

'Ilse, I believe, would say there is. Annie,' Fred said, reaching out and holding her hands in his. 'Take a deep breath and steel yourself.'

She did as she was told. Then he continued, his voice thick and guttural, and told her that the judge, to make a warning of their three friends, condemned them to be executed by guillotine a mere few hours after the guilty verdict. 'I cannot even fathom it,' he said. 'It is all too horrific.'

Annie put her face in her hands and wept until she felt she could not wring out another tear. Fred poured both of them a drink with shaking hands and said, 'Someone reported that Ilse's mother tried to get into the court and when she told a guard that she was the mother of one of the accused the guard quipped, "Then you should have instilled better values in your child".'

Annie had never met Ilse's mother, but when she thought of her trying desperately to see her daughter for what turned out to be the last time, her heart felt as if it would break.

Wiping her nose, she remembered meeting Ilse for the first time in the university canteen, her welcoming smile and warm greeting. The way she clipped her hair behind her ear; the earnest way she listened to all sides of an argument and how swiftly that serious look turned to laughter. They had enjoyed, yes that was the right word, enjoyed their trip to Berlin. It had been dangerous and heart-stopping and precarious and although they would have given anything to live in a world where taking such risks was not necessary, they did what they had to do together, in high spirits and with high hopes.

Now, they could never do anything together again. Ilse had been disposed of as cruelly as if she were nothing more than a piece of dog mess on the sole of one of those big, black boots.

Annie and Fred spent the next week mourning and talking about Walther and their friends. So as not to raise suspicion, Fred continued to go into Munich each day but told Annie's office she was unwell and would return when she felt better; he passed the same message onto Frau Wilhelm. And it was the truth, she was sick with grief or pregnancy or both and racked with guilt that Ilse had been caught, but she was free; that Walther was in the frozen, unforgiving ground whilst she was feeling spring on her legs and arms; that she might have reeled off her comrades' names without compunction if she'd been arrested; that no matter how difficult the circumstances, she was expecting a child and Ilse would never get such a chance; that Walther would never be able to see, hear or hold their child close.

On the Friday evening, much earlier than expected, Annie heard Fred's key in the front door. Worried, she ran to the hall and found him sitting against the wall, pasty and exhausted. 'Fred,' she said, kneeling beside him. 'What's wrong?'

He asked her for a glass of water and after he drank it, Annie helped him to a chair in the living room. 'Fred, tell me what's happened,' Annie insisted.

It took him a minute or two to compose himself. 'Ernst, Otto and Helmuth—' he counted them off on his fingers '—along with a handful of others we never met from various places, were arrested yesterday, tried today and have been sentenced to death.' His voice rose on a sob. 'They're in prison awaiting execution.'

Fred's report cut Annie to the bone. She could almost feel the edge of the chilly, honed guillotine blade against her neck and wondered how those three honourable men, with their high moral standards, would meet their demise. With dignity, she told herself.

'How can this be?' she said. 'Shouldn't the Nazis be captured, put on trial and executed? That would be the right way around. Nothing in our world is how it should be. I will go into Munich with you on Monday and see those who are left. I know I won't be able to talk with them, but at least we can be together in quiet camaraderie. I need that, too. Fred, what do you think?'

But Fred didn't answer. He stumbled to the back door, threw it open and vomited down the drain below the downpipe.

Annie sat, her hands restless and fidgeting, asking herself over and over again if they had done any good whatsoever or if the promising lives cut short were too great a price to pay. But what about the people waiting to get on those cattle trains? The academics who disappeared and it was rumoured, were condemned to torture and death? *What about them?* she wanted to shout to anyone who would listen. Would she be able to do it all again? She hoped she would with Ilse as her heroine and when she had gathered her courage.

Fred came back in, filled a bucket and Annie heard him swill it around where he'd been sick. He flopped into the chair across from Annie, looking pale and waxy, a sheen of sweat around his moustache. Leaning his head back, he closed his eyes, took a deep breath and said, 'Annie, you will not be going into Munich for some time. Not for any reason.'

Annie opened her mouth to protest, but Fred held up his hand.

'There are now more pressing problems that we must sort out.' He pointed to her stomach, which she rubbed protectively. 'This will take all our time and attention for a good while.'

Fred sat forward in his chair and stared at a spot above her head for some time without moving a muscle or saying a word. Then he paced to the window and looked out at the vegetable patch – a few tomatoes, radishes, carrots, beetroot and onions basking in the weak sun. Next he went to the cupboard, brought out the bottle of schnapps again and gestured to her with it. 'No, thank you,' she said, touching the place under her ribcage. 'I am feeling nauseous.' He downed another measure of the clear liquid, then without warning flung his glass against the wall. Annie's hand went to her heart and she watched as the shattered pieces scattered on the floor. They reminded her of diamond chips in engagement rings that neither she nor Fred could lay claim to.

He poured himself another glass and told her to go to bed and rest.

'I will clear the glass first,' she said, wanting desperately to make amends.

'No,' he ordered. 'Leave it.'

Not wanting to be obstinate, Annie went up to her room but did not sleep; she lay wide awake and listened to the sounds of Fred pacing the floor downstairs.

Relief swamped Annie when Fred greeted her in his usual warm manner in the morning. Perhaps his long night of marching around the house had led him to some kind of resolution; or maybe the realisation that Viola could well be in the same position as her and would need help, support and advice had touched his heart and altered his thinking. After breakfast he said, 'Here is what I think should happen. Let us see if you agree. First, we should tell Herr Doctor and Frau Wilhelm about the baby.'

Annie was dumbfounded by what seemed to be an absurd and impractical proposition. 'Are you joking?' she said. 'How can I possibly tell them that I am expecting their dead son's child? And that he got me pregnant without us being married? No.' She shook her head until it ached. 'I cannot possibly put such a burden upon them.'

'But think about it, Annie.' Fred drew his face close to hers. 'Walther was their only child. As far as they are aware, they now have no one. But the fact is, they will soon have a grandchild and once they get over the shock, they will want to care and love and be involved in the child's upbringing.'

'But, Fred…' Annie wiped her sweaty palms on her skirt. 'Are you asking me to give up my baby to them?'

'I hadn't thought of that as a possibility, but in some ways it might be for the best.'

'No, it would not be the best for me or the child.' She set her mouth and crossed her arms over her stomach. 'I will not allow it.'

'No, Annie, in all honesty I did not think you would. But you will need protection now, you and the baby. More protection than I can give you.'

That statement made Annie shiver with apprehension. 'This is what we should do,' he continued. He said that they should put to Walther's parents that they band together for the sake of Walther's unborn child. Then, with the help of people Fred knew at the university, they could falsify a marriage certificate dated a few days before Walther was posted. Annie could wear Oma's wedding ring that she had left her and then the baby would not only be considered legitimate but would be the child of a Nazi war hero. Done and dusted. Protection for all of them.

'But people will ask why we didn't make the marriage public when it took place,' Annie said.

'Simple.' Fred had thought through all the loopholes.

'We just say that you and Walther were desperate to marry before he was posted and because it was arranged so quickly only immediate family attended. You had, of course, every intention of organising a bigger celebration upon his return, but that now cannot happen.'

It sounded almost feasible. Then for some reason, Horst's pink, turgid face came into her mind and with it, a sense of dread. 'But what if someone decides to pursue their questioning to the Town Hall and looks for the original marriage certificate there?'

Fred spread his hands wide and looked defeated. 'I suppose we can't cover every eventuality. But ask yourself who would do that and why? Everyone knows you and Walther were sweet on each other. Why else would both of us be wearing mourning clothes? And it is a time of war. People do impetuous things. So,' he said. 'I will pay them a visit and discuss all of this with them, steering them in the direction they need to take if they do not get there by themselves. After that, we follow what will, in effect, be their lead.'

Other than a few far-fetched misgivings, it sounded like the perfect plan – if Herr Doctor and Frau Wilhelm agreed.

Fred shaved carefully, dressed in a dark suit and adjusted the black band around his upper arm. 'Wish me luck, Annie,' he said.

She did, and silently thought he was going to need it. One hour passed, then two. Two and a half. Like a shotgun, there was a rap at the door that made goose bumps spike her skin. Fred had a key; there was no need for him to knock. Annie sat as still as she could, her hands twitching in her lap, neck stiff on her shoulders. Another loud battering on the door. This time she stood in alarm and looked around for somewhere to hide. 'Annie,' a voice called through the doorjamb. 'Please open the door.' It was Frau Wilhelm and besides sounding frantic to be let in, Annie could not discern her state of mind. She might be angry, disbelieving and insulted. Maybe she would draw back her elegant hand and slap her hard across the cheek. Or push her to the ground. But if she had run from her house in such an enraged state, Fred would have followed her to stop her from harming his sister.

Creeping to the door, Annie peered through the spyhole and observed her. She was breathing heavily and her eyes were swollen and red from crying for weeks, but there were no signs of rancour on her face. As she watched, Frau Wilhelm flung herself against the door and battered it with the flat of her hand. 'Annie,' she cried softly. 'Do not deny me.'

Taking a deep breath, Annie opened the door. Perhaps she was in for a chastisement or spiel about her lack of integrity, a cold shoulder or an interrogation into how she had led Walther astray. But what she had not been expecting was the usually well-composed doctor's wife flinging herself into her arms as if she were throwing herself on charity. In another time and situation, the scene that unfolded would have been most comical. In fact, Annie liked to think that Walther was looking down on them and laughing, encouraging her, as he always did, to join him in finding the humour in themselves. There in the hallway, as Frau Wilhelm tried to hug her and close the door behind her in one seamless movement, they lost their balance and fell to the floor, bringing down the umbrella stand and a potted plant with them.

'Annie, Annie,' Frau Wilhelm cried. 'Oh no, this is

impossible.' She gained her feet in the most undignified manner imaginable, unwittingly showing her bloomers and the rolled and knotted tops of her stockings in the process. Despite everything, Annie could not stop a giggle from escaping her throat. 'Annie,' Frau Wilhelm said. 'Are you hurt? Hysterical? I will run back for Herr Doctor.'

'No, no, I am in one piece,' Annie said, reaching for the bannister to help her to her feet.

'Give me your hands,' Frau Wilhelm said, in control again. 'You must not put any strain on yourself.' Two deep lines of concern formed near her eyebrows. 'Let me help you.'

Annie allowed herself to be pulled up, muttering all the time that she was absolutely fine. Then they stood, out of breath and awkward, staring at each other in their dark dresses and lack of makeup or adornment. 'May I?' Frau Wilhelm said, pointing to the living room.

'Of course,' Annie said, gesturing to one of the chairs beyond the door. 'Please make yourself comfortable. Would you like coffee?'

Suspended partway towards a sitting position, Frau Wilhelm said, 'But please let me get it for you. You shouldn't be running around after me in your condition.'

Again Annie told her that she was perfectly well. 'I will not be long,' she said, disappearing into the kitchen. But then Frau Wilhelm was there behind her, looming so close she could feel her breath and the faint odour of unwashed hair. *Oh no*, Annie thought. *If she and Herr Doctor grant me their acceptance and beneficence, she will hover around me like this for months and I'm afraid it will be all I can do not to scream aloud* – then she immediately felt guilty for the thought. She clamped her jaws together; Walther's parents were good people and she would need them to get through this difficult time. Turning to Frau Wilhelm, she smiled and said, 'Can you take the cups to the table for me, please?'

Frau Wilhelm seemed to be stunned out of a deep reverie. 'Yes, of course,' she said, happy to be asked to help. 'Annie,' she said softly. 'Fred has spoken to us of your predicament.'

Annie could not turn from the coffee pot. 'I am so sorry, Frau Wilhelm,' she said. 'That at such a time of terrible trouble, I have heaped more upon everyone I love.'

'Come. Sit down,' the older woman said. Annie noticed that Frau Wilhelm's hair, which she had envied for its thickness and dark shine, now appeared dull and uncared for. Annie supposed that brushing fifty strokes every night before bed was the least of anyone's concerns now. Both of their hands were shaking as they lifted the hot coffee to their mouths.

'I'm afraid I have no cake or even a biscuit to offer you,' Annie said.

Frau Wilhelm shook her head. 'I have no appetite at the moment.'

'Nor I.'

Then they both began to speak at the same time, but out of deference, Annie allowed Frau Wilhelm to continue. 'You have nothing to be ashamed of or sorry about.' Her eyes narrowed; her knuckles whitened around the handle of her cup. 'What is the one thing that makes this situation intolerable?' Annie didn't attempt to answer as she knew that was not what was wanted of her. 'The one and only thing that is regrettable is that Walther is not here.' Her voice caught in her throat and Annie knew Frau Wilhelm was struggling to continue, but she managed to do so with clarity, 'That my lovely son is... dead. There, that is the first time I have been able to say the word.' Annie reached for her hand. 'Dead,' Frau Wilhelm whispered into the distance. Her hand twitched in Annie's and she gulped in a long, silent, shuddering breath that she released through a gaping mouth.

Annie put her arms around her and held tight, wanting nothing else at that moment than to be able to give Walther's mother some comfort. When she looked down at Frau Wilhelm's face, cradled against her chest, there was a tiny pool of liquid quivering above her lip. With diminishing convulsions, Frau Wilhelm pulled herself together, wiped around her face with a handkerchief and said, 'It is the fault of... you know who and his comrades. How I despise all of them,' she spat, snarling her lips and baring her teeth.

'Yes, we agree on that,' Annie said. 'If Walther were here, then all would be well. I want you and Herr Doctor to know that things were settled between us and we intended to tell you when he...' Now it was Annie's turn to choke on what she had to say. 'Returned.'

They nodded at each other in complete accord.

'We know that to be true, Annie. Walther intimated as much to us the night before he was posted and we were most happy. But not surprised.' Then she cleared her throat and was business-like again. 'Fred came to us with an idea, but what do you want to happen now, Annie?'

'I do not want to give up my baby, Frau Wilhelm,' Annie said, wanting to make that perfectly clear before anything else. 'I will not terminate or surrender this gift from Walther. No matter how many people tell me one of those solutions would be the best thing to do.'

'You will never hear that from me, or Herr Doctor.' Frau Wilhelm's features looked as though they were set in stone. 'Do you know, that we thought we would have four children.' Annie raised her eyebrows in surprise. 'Yes, four or maybe even five. But fate stepped in and after I had Walther I could not have any more. So, imagine if I had, for some reason got rid of my beautiful boy? Herr Doctor and I would have been childless. Unimaginable.' She shook her head. 'A baby is always, in my opinion, a blessing.'

'If you have someone to love and help you,' Annie said, thinking of the girls in her position who might not have anyone to turn to.

'But you have Fred,' she said. 'And us.' She gripped Annie's hand with what felt like all her strength. 'We will stand by you in any way we can. Let us help you and our grandchild. I beg you. We will instigate Fred's marvellous plan. All we ask is to be a part of our grandchild's life.'

Annie could not believe how worried Frau Wilhelm seemed that she might accept her and Herr Doctor's help with the fake marriage and then reject their involvement with them beyond that. Of course she would not allow that to happen. She was blessed and fortunate and knew how very different things could be for her if Fred and this benevolent couple had decided to disown her. Not even the lowlife Nazis, who think of nothing but their own debauched pleasures, would want her. If she were in that dreadful bind, how could she possibly avoid getting rid of the baby? Her hand found her stomach and rubbed the tiny bump that had recently appeared. 'My most fervent wish for my child is that the little one would have had the chance to know his or her father,' Annie said. 'But given the circumstances, I could want for nothing more than that the baby have you, Herr Doctor and his uncle Fred. And I know that Walther would want the same.'

Frau Wilhelm wiped a stray tear from her cheek. 'Fred told me you would say so,' she said. 'But I had to make sure that this is how you want to proceed.'

Annie took a deep breath. 'I am positive,' she said.

Frau Wilhelm smiled. A broad, genuine smile that seemed to cut, momentarily, through her grief. 'I told my husband that if I did not return within the hour, he and Fred could assume that all was well and they could move forward with the grand plan.'

'The sooner the better,' Annie said.

Together they moved from the kitchen to the cosier living room and talked of the happier, light-hearted things that women discuss when a baby is announced. Did Annie think the baby would be a boy or a girl? Annie thought a boy and if that came to fruition she would call him Walther. Frau Wilhelm clapped her hands together and closed her eyes in near ecstasy when she heard that. What about baby clothes? They decided that after the false paperwork was complete, they would begin to knit and sew what was needed. Frau Wilhelm said that it would not be professionally possible for her husband to care for Annie or attend the birth, but he would ensure that she was put on the books of a doctor he recommended. And all being well, she would have the baby at home under the care of a midwife. In their attic, they had Walther's baby crib complete with drapes and linen. They would retrieve it, give it a dust and Herr Doctor would sand it down and varnish it. Frau Wilhelm would wash and mend the bedding. What did Annie think of all that? Annie thought it sounded wonderful. More than she had dared to hope for.

9 June 1943
Fred did not waste any time in getting the certificate.
There had never been a need for me to see such a
document, but even to my inexperienced eye, it looked
legitimate. Herr Doctor and Frau Wilhelm said it
appeared lawful and correct; no one would ever suspect
that it was forged. So, I have one copy, Fred another
and Walther's parents a third and fourth. Fred said we
needed a number because if we are bombed out or have
to get away quickly and we accidentally leave it behind,
we will not be able to go to the Town Hall like every
other married couple and get a copy.

So my dream has come true and I am married to
Walther. And if anybody asks I have the proof. There is
a ring on my finger and on the table in front of me, next
to his notification of death in action, is our marriage
certificate.

Annie spent her time in the house, preparing to give birth. She sewed, knitted, cleaned, kept her journal, cooked, read, tended the vegetable patch. She wandered to the shops or to see Frau Wilhelm who clucked around her like a broody hen – sometimes she wondered who was having this baby. Her time at the university with the resistance group seemed to have been another life. Fred still went off every day and he told her there was no longer any underground activity that he could discern, but she was not sure she believed him – he came home too late and was too agitated to have been lecturing and researching all day. She no longer questioned him because if he were to tell her he had resumed writing and distributing leaflets or spreading graffiti, she would go insane – because of her anxiety for him and because she could not be involved.

And tonight, of all nights, he was late again. The doors were locked and the windows latched, but still Annie jumped when the wind toyed with a loose window frame and she started at what might be a mouse scratching behind the skirting or when what should be the familiar sound of a creaking floorboard emitted a thin squeak. She sat on her bed, writing what she thought would turn out to be nonsense in her journal, grateful to have something to half-occupy her mind. Her knicker drawer was open so that if that despicable man Horst knocked, she could bury the evidence.

Earlier in the day, she'd had a pleasant couple of hours with Frau Wilhelm. They'd chatted and she was shown how to embroider a panel on a nightdress she was making for the baby. Herr Doctor had joined them during a break from treating patients and he questioned her about her health. Despite the fact he could not administer to her, he took her blood pressure, pulse, temperature, checked her ankles for swelling and pulled down her eyelids to scrutinise for signs of anaemia. She'd felt both manhandled and fortified when he had finished – and very relieved when he gave her the okay.

The walk home had been enjoyable; she'd admired

sunflowers, rhododendron, zinnias and peonies. A ginger cat sunned himself on the warm bricks of a wall. Two little girls and a boy scraped their toes through the dirt as they walked back to school after the midday break. She'd watched them for a long time, dawdling and picking up seeds and stones and leaves and inspecting them as if they were treasures. They'd made her laugh with their sleeves that were too short and their unruly hair. A plane flew through the light clouds overhead and only Annie had paused to look up. Nothing was going to get in the way of the children and their exploration of nature. *Who amongst us*, Annie had thought, *has got it right?* Certainly not the one adult present.

Then she'd rounded the corner to their little street and there he was – Horst – squirming with impatience and peering through the front window. Unfortunately, he'd spied her, too, so she couldn't turn and retrace her steps. He'd lifted his pudgy hand in a salute and called, 'Heil Hitler'. A few curtains twitched but soon resumed their smooth folds when they saw the big, bad, menacing figure of a Wehrmacht officer in their neighbourhood. *It's only Horst*, she'd wanted to reassure them, *you remember him, don't you? The little guy whose trousers never used to fit properly?* But recalling that hadn't reassured her, either.

Using her shopping bag as an excuse to only half raise her hand, she'd returned his salute. He'd seemed immeasurably jubilant with her response which made her, in turn, think he was more of a fool than she'd given him credit for. But a dangerous fool, she reminded herself.

'Hallo, dear Annie,' he'd called. 'I was about to give up for today.'

If only she'd stayed with Frau Wilhelm, or watching

the children for another few minutes, she'd thought, but then tried to rearrange her features to look as if she was somewhat pleased to see him.

He'd marched over and wrestled her shopping bag from her. 'I will help you.' Everything he said sounded like an order. Then he'd cupped his clammy hand under her elbow and marched her towards the house. How did he think she managed to get about when he wasn't there. 'Mutti told me about your situation. I am sorry for you, Annie,' he'd said, without sounding it. 'A bride, a wife, a widow and a mother-to-be all in the space of what – two months?'

'Yes,' she'd said in a thin voice. 'We live in bewildering times.' She'd opened the door and he'd followed her into the kitchen, placing her bag on the small table.

'You must find comfort in the Fuhrer's perfect plan,' he'd said. 'There is no confusion where that is concerned.'

He then plonked himself down in the nearest chair and watched her unpack her shopping, fill the kettle, get down the cups and make the coffee. 'Again no cake?' he'd said.

'Sadly, no. I find I'm not very hungry these days.'

He'd made no comment, but she could feel him appraising her from head to foot. 'When is the baby expected?' he'd asked. 'If that's not too intrusive a question?'

'Middle of September,' she'd replied.

'And tell me, Annie, why were we not invited to share your big day with you and Herr Doctor's son? Mutti was most upset not to witness you being married.'

Steeling herself to face him, she'd held tight to the coffee cups and placed them on the table. 'I am sorry that Tante Herte feels she missed out, but I did explain to her that Walther and I had every intention of celebrating with the family on his return. But…' She'd looked down at her feet and sniffed a couple of times.

Horst had picked up his cup and blown on his coffee. A curtain of steam hung between them for a moment. 'But why the hurry before he was posted?'

How dare he, she'd thought. He was an insensitive, callous brute. She'd put down her coffee cup and looked him straight in the eye, deciding to play him at his own game. Without blinking, she'd said, 'Our main consideration was that we plight our troth. Are you implying otherwise, Horst?' He'd broken their stare first and she'd felt a tiny twinge of victory.

But he couldn't leave it at that. He couldn't let her have that one win. 'As I said on previous occasions.' He'd leaned back on two chair legs, his chin in the air. 'You must call on me if I can help in anyway.'

'Thank you.' She'd tried to remain civil. 'I am lucky to have my parents-in-law, Herr Doctor and Frau Wilhelm. And my lovely brother.'

Horst had let his chair slam to the floor. His voice had become softer but more threatening. 'Fred?' he'd asked with mock innocence. 'But he will be away soon, too.'

The scant sense of having outfoxed him that she'd wallowed in a moment earlier slipped away in an instant. Fear had pricked along the length of her spine; adrenaline causing the pit of her stomach to drop and her legs, under the table, to feel numb and wobbly. She hadn't been able to decide if she might faint or be sick. 'I don't understand,' she'd said.

Horst had smiled, pleased to be back in what he thought was the superior position. 'He has been playing around in that university for too long,' he'd said. 'So I paid him a visit there today and told him it was time he joined up.' He'd waited for her reaction, but she had been dumbfounded. 'Yes, Oma no longer needs him here and you have Herr Doctor and Frau Wilhelm. A healthy young man like Fred is needed elsewhere. He must enlist, or before my leave is over I will frogmarch him to the recruitment office myself.'

Annie had placed her cup on the table with a rattle and wondered if she should beg Horst not to go through with his threat. Or perhaps try to reason with him. Remind him that German wasn't Fred's first language, plead that she needed him here, his students needed him at the university. But her tongue would not allow what was in her brain to be spoken.

Horst had kicked back his chair and stood, giving the impression that the conversation was finished. As he sauntered to the front door, he'd opened as many cupboards and drawers as he could and rummaged in bowls and behind books. She had not stood to see him out, but when he'd reached the front door, he'd turned and said, 'By the way, I am on leave for ten days only. Be sure to remind Fred.'

Annie had sat where she was for a long time after he left, playing the conversation over and over in her mind and worrying about how she could possibly have ensured that the outcome was different. If only she hadn't tried to outsmart him. But what else could she have done? She felt as though she'd had to stick to their story about her and Walther and their marriage. Her coffee grew cold. Shadows fell across the kitchen. She hadn't thought about dinner or dusting or washing or sewing. She'd been too stunned to move an inch.

When he came home at last in the early hours, Fred found her asleep on the floor. He put his arms around her and tried to lift her to a chair but she woke with a start. 'Annie,' he said. 'You should be fast asleep in bed.'

'Fred,' she sobbed. 'Never mind me. Horst has been here.'

'Shh, Annie. Take a deep breath,' Fred said.

She took several and he went into the kitchen, returning with a glass of water for her.

'He has been to see me, too,' Fred said. 'This morning.'

'He told me,' Annie said.

'Yes, he rounded me up with a few colleagues and told us the inevitable.' The anger and resentment that would once have been in his voice was replaced with a monotone of surrender. 'I… We have been ordered to join the Wehrmacht.' He looked up and his eyes were sad and defeated. 'Within ten days.'

'I know, but Fred…' she spluttered. 'Can he do that?'

'He and his bullies can do whatever they like.' He shrugged.

They sat in silence for a few minutes. Then she asked Fred what he was going to do about this latest crisis. How did he intend to fight the order? Could he put his case to someone higher up than Horst?

He put his hand on her arm. Shaking his head, he said there was nothing he could do. He must go. They must follow the initial plan they'd decided on four years ago and do whatever they needed to pretend that they agreed with the regime. That was the only way they could stop suspicion from falling upon them and hope to get out of this mess with their lives.

'No, no, no,' Annie shouted, beating a cushion with her

fists. 'I will not allow this. If you cannot stay here and fight against this, then you must run. Run away.'

'Where to?' Fred asked.

'I don't know. Switzerland. Or yes, I do know. I have it. You can hide in the attic. I will say you have run away. I will swear to it and I will say I am ashamed of your cowardice. That will convince them. Then I can take food and books and schnapps up you. When the Allies come to liberate us you can come down and you will be a hero of resistance.'

Fred started to laugh, but Annie did not join in. 'Too implausible,' he said.

'But so was your idea about falsifying my marriage and look,' she said, hoping her fervour would be catching. 'It worked perfectly. So will my plan for you and—'

He cut her short with a wave of his hand. 'Annie,' he said. 'Stop. The time has come. I must go. We have been lucky it has not come to this much sooner. Now, go to bed. You need to rest.'

She turned and marched up the stairs, unable to comprehend his complete and utter capitulation. Again, she lay in bed and listened to him pace the floor downstairs and knew that she would miss everything about his presence, even that.

They were able to talk more logically the following morning about what was going to happen next. Fred reassured her many times that Herr Doctor and Frau Wilhelm would look after her and that caused her to become exasperated. Yes, of course she was worried for herself without him, but she was also distressed and would be, every day he was gone, for his safety both physically and mentally. How, she wondered, would he be able to keep up the pretence of being in agreement with the Nazis when there was no respite from them? Could he possibly find like-minded men amongst his battalion or would it be too much of a risk to try to lure each other out of hiding; what kind of a fool would dare do that?

They discussed the possibility of him requesting a certain role in the Wehrmacht. Perhaps some kind of teacher, Annie suggested. 'Ha!' was his response. 'Education is the last thing any of those swaggering tyrants are interested in. The term all brawn and no brain was written for them. And any type of instruction from someone half-British would go down like a cache of bombs.'

She proposed he file conscientious objection, but he said he should have done so at the beginning of the war, not on the cusp of his recruitment. If only they had thought of that then. Or could he use her as an excuse? Say she would be left alone and vulnerable without him? 'If that were a good enough reason,' he answered, 'there would be no men at all in the Wehrmacht.'

At last they had exhausted every alternative and with much sorrow she, like Fred, resigned herself to the situation and decided to make the most of the time she had left with him as a civilian. How she loathed the thought of seeing him in that brown uniform and she knew that every second he had to wear it his skin would crawl with revulsion.

Frau Wilhelm invited them to dinner with her and Herr Doctor and she had been more creative than usual with the rations. They had a spread of pork knuckle, potato pancakes and sauerkraut followed by apple cake. Annie knew some ingredients had been replaced or stretched as not all of it tasted quite right, but it was laid out beautifully, like a condemned man's final meal.

Herr Doctor and Frau Wilhelm said they thought it would be best for her to stay with them, but she and Fred were anxious about leaving Oma's house untended and Horst laying claim to it. 'Then I,' Frau Wilhelm said, 'will come and stay with you. You must not be alone. Don't you agree, Erich?' She turned to her husband.

Herr Doctor nodded. 'Yes,' he said. 'From whenever Fred has to... When Fred is made to...' He cleared his throat. 'Leave. Temporarily.'

'You have done so much for us already,' Fred said. 'But I would be most grateful. Annie?'

'Thank you,' she said. And she meant it. Her gratitude to them came from the very bottom of her heart.

Annie watched Fred walk away towards the railway station in his stiff black boots and belt, a hard helmet pulled down over his freshly shorn head. On his back he was carrying a regulation knapsack that had in it a regulation flask, metal dish and cutlery, a shaving kit, his ID card with her details on the NOK form and a change of regulation undergarments. She knew it would upset him if she asked, so she didn't, but she presumed he would get his regulation gun when he turned up at his barracks.

His walking posture was one of a soldier, which she supposed was the essential effect of the uniform. Besides, he wouldn't want to draw attention to himself by walking with his shoulders drooping or his eyes on his obnoxious boots. 'Do not,' she warned him, 'say or do anything to make them think you are not happy to be doing your bit for the Fatherland.'

He laughed at that and said she should take her own advice as she was forever up to something questionable. 'Yes, but I am not under the scrutiny of the Nazis every hour of every day, as you will be.'

'Don't remind me,' he said. 'My English accent is going to be enough to make me stand out like a sore thumb.'

She turned her nose up when he put the helmet on his head and adjusted the chinstrap. He knocked on it twice and reminded her that the piece of moulded metal could save his life. She kissed her palms then and rubbed them all over the cold headpiece. Then there was nothing left to say except goodbye and Godspeed. Annie bit her lip and checked her tears as she didn't think it would be fair for his last image of home to be her, weeping. But at the last moment, she saw a puddle form and settle in his lids and she could not help herself – the crying started. Fred had to prise her hands from his arms finger by finger. He kissed each one, turned and did not look back. It took all her fortitude and the baby growing inside her to stop herself from running after him.

Alone in the house, Annie struggled to breathe and it wasn't because the baby was pushing up against her ribs. Her already splintered heart was crushed. She couldn't stop sobbing – loud, long, snivelling blubs that racked her from head to foot. She couldn't see or hear or feel anything other than the pain inside her. This was what it felt like to be broken-hearted not once, not twice but over and over again.

Fred – her protector, the older brother she put through so much, scholar, philosopher, gentleman, loyal friend, fiancé-to-be, honourable and ethical resistance fighter – had joined the Wehrmacht.

Later that evening, after Frau Wilhelm moved in, there was a heavy-handed rap on the door. Annie shuddered; she knew it was Horst again. She got up to answer the knock, but Frau Wilhelm stopped her with a hand on her shoulder. Straightening her skirt, she marched to the door. Annie leaned towards the hall and listened. 'Yes?' Frau Wilhelm said and Annie imagined her talking through a crack.

'Ah, Frau Wilhelm.' Horst's voice sounded less commanding when faced with the doctor's wife. 'It's me. Annie's cousin. Horst.'

'I remember,' she said without a trace of fondness. 'Herr Doctor treated you for hornets' stings one summer. Let me think. You were about seven at the time. Oh you did cry. Not a brave little boy at all.'

Annie had to hold one hand over her mouth, the other on her stomach to contain her laughter.

There followed indistinct mumbling from Horst.

'No, I'm afraid Annie is resting.'

'And Fred?' Horst asked.

'Do not pretend you are unaware of his whereabouts.'

Again Annie could not hear Horst's response, his usual booming voice reduced to a murmur by a middle-aged woman.

'Well, I am sure you're pleased your leave is over. Good

evening to you.' The door was closed and locked behind him. So, Annie thought, that was the way to deal with the odious Horst from now on.

When Frau Wilhelm came back into the living room, they laughed and retold the conversation many times that evening. Looking over at her mother in law, a wave of recently silvered hair falling over one eye, Annie thought about the meaning of bravery. Of course, nothing could ever take away from the courage of her compatriots in the resistance movement, but what about Frau Wilhelm and others of her ilk, taking every opportunity to be courageous and defiant whilst going about their everyday business. Nothing loud or big or showy or memorable, but a symbolic kick here, a metaphoric slap there, a challenging word, a token refusal to comply. After everything she had lost and stood to lose, she was willing to quietly let it be known that she was standing up to the aggressor. Annie put Frau Wilhelm on a par with Ilse and hoped that together with other quietly daring people, they could claim victory.

20 July 1943
I have no one to talk to so must get this down on paper. Ernst and Otto have been executed. I will never see their dear faces again and the world has been denied their wisdom and talent. Helmuth has been spared but remains incarcerated. I dread to think what the Nazis have in mind for him. He must feel so alone and frightened, locked up in a cell and wondering what his destiny will be. This might sound cruel, but if he is to follow the others in being executed, I hope it will be soon as waiting must be agonising. Helmuth – such a

kind, thoughtful, gentle man. I believe he was planning to marry. All our hopes, dreams, ambitions, lives have been snatched from us.

Fred, oh Fred. Wherever you are – Italy, Yugoslavia, Georgia – I hope this news does not reach you. It would bring you to your knees.

13

August 1943

Viola made sure all her belongings were in order, settled Freddie in her arms, touched the ring around her own neck, felt in the suitcase for Lillian's old brown cardigan, Fred's thesis, the German resistance material, the letters from Mum, and then checked her paperwork again. The funny hat she'd been given and told to wear made her scalp itch and she probed under the rim to ease the prickling. There was no point to it, she thought, except to tick a box to state she had been given a new set of clothes to see her on her way. Well, they were new to her but not brand new. She dreaded to think how many women had worn the old-fashioned, brown tam and tartan jacket before her. Both carefully chosen, she supposed, because she was going to Scotland. At last.

She had hoped they would have been there for a month by this stage and settling into life north of the border. 'But nothing seems to go to plan in my life, does it, little one?' she murmured, moving the blanket down from the baby's chin and absorbing every bit of the tiny creature her senses could handle – the sweet, warm, lacteal aroma of milk; the silky strands of dark hair that fashioned themselves into a quiff; the dark green eyes that, although they didn't focus on very much, seemed knowing in their depth; the impossibly tiny, shaped fingernails; the little marks on her translucent eyelids the nurses called angels' kisses; the steady breathing of innocence-induced sleep.

The day after Freddie was born, Viola had sent a telegram to Mum and one to Lillian. Both had replied, Lillian with a 'Congratulations!' followed by a visit; Mum asking if both were well. Hoping to entice Mum to come to hospital to see her and meet Freddie, Viola had written back: I AM RECOVERING STOP BABY PERFECT STOP. She certainly was perfect – and always would be. But Mum did not appear, thwarted Viola felt sure by Dad refusing to give his approval. Viola kissed Freddie's tiny nose and brushed the velvet fuzz on her earlobes.

She could not stop gazing at her, breathing her in, committing to memory all the little details that made her unique and yet familiar. This, she thought, was how Mum and Dad must have felt when she was born, at least she hoped they had. Then how could they bear to give her up? Viola looked at her armful of perfection and knew there was nothing Freddie could do to make her turn her back on her. She wondered if perhaps men felt parenthood through a different set of emotional channels from women that made their expectations for their children harsher. That, of course, would mean that Mum's suffering at having to follow Dad's lead in this would be cutting like a knife. Would Fred have presented with the same kind of behaviour towards any children they might have had if those children got themselves into a similar sort of mess? She refused to let herself imagine it and clung fast to the impression of the kind, magnanimous, loving Fred that she knew.

But she would never have the indulgence of knowing what Fred's view on wayward children would be; how he would grow old; whether he would be a stern or lenient father. The thought of what she'd had with Fred and allowed so easily to be lost, made tears fill her eyes again. The baby blues, the nurses called it, but she knew that her tears were for reasons that were a deeper shade of that colour than the act of giving birth.

Sitting up straight, she wiped her tears on a hanky. Now, were their IDs in the front pocket of her bag? She rummaged through to reassure herself. The ring nestled in its usual place? Freddie's birth certificate, the leaflet, the half-completed PhD. And their gas masks? How terrifying it had been learning how to place the horrible piece of kit over the tiny face and tie it under the little legs like a second napkin, but she had steadied herself, as she did with everything unnerving she had to get on with and thought of how she wished to mirror Mum's calm, steady countenance.

She leaned back against the chair and closed her eyes, but refused to allow herself to nap. After a two-month wait, she didn't want to miss the porter's call for her departure.

First, a minute piece of placenta had been left behind and by the time it was removed, she had become very poorly. She remembered nurses swimming in and out of her vision, offering her soup and soggy pieces of bread, bringing Freddie to her to be fed then taking her away to be topped up with formula and changed, doctors giving her injections and taking phials of blood to test. She winced, the pain still too raw to file away in a corner of her mind and forget. Worse than the pain was the dread of what would happen to Freddie if something happened to her. Despite the fact that the thought alone was difficult to form, when the crisis passed, she had talked to one of the nurses about provision should the worst occur.

The nurse's face had been soft with sympathy. 'I'm afraid that you need to specify a next of kin. If you don't, the baby will have to go into a home.'

In the back of her mind, Viola had thought that someone official asking her parents to have the baby would go down better than approaching them herself. 'But wouldn't the authorities try to trace someone in my family who would have her?' she'd asked in a weak, raspy voice.

'Yes, of course,' the nurse said. 'But it helps enormously if you've given them some kind of clue who to contact and if you have paved the way by asking that person to become the little one's guardian.'

As it stood, she hadn't petitioned anyone. Mum would but Dad wouldn't entertain the idea. Lillian's heart would tell her to agree, but it would not be practical and would be most unfair to expect Lillian to put the rest of her life on hold for Viola's mistake. When that word mistake came to mind, Viola clamped her hands over the baby's ears, as if Freddie could hear her unspoken thoughts. Viola put her face close to the baby's and brushed their noses back and forth. 'Never will you be made to feel that you were unwanted,' she said. 'I promise you.'

Then, when she was getting back on her feet, she had been told that it was proving difficult to find a place for her in

Scotland. Apparently, most women in her position wanted to stay as close to home as possible in case their parents decided to change their minds and offer help. Wouldn't she prefer Northfleet or Cleethorpes? She'd shaken her head. Great Yarmouth or Hornchurch? 'No, thank you,' she'd said. 'Scotland, please. The Highlands, if possible. Perhaps the Orkneys. Or Shetland.'

Those two islands had turned out to be dangerous places. Their close geographical proximity to Norway ensured that the sea around them was potentially teeming with enemy ships and submarines and the whole place was crawling with military. German planes used the sky above as their training ground. So, they could not accept evacuees as their own children were being evacuated. Other places in Scotland were reserved for babies, nursing mothers and children from the islands, Edinburgh, Aberdeen and Glasgow.

Of course, it hadn't been the nurses' job to find her a billet, but she'd been aware that when she regained her strength, she would have to vacate her bed and accept whatever accommodation was offered to her. Evacuation officers had come and gone from her bedside, sheets of paper and clipboards in their hands. One woman, who had looked harassed whenever she visited, would hold her pen so tight that her knuckles turned white. The skin on her hands was red and peeling with what Viola had thought must be eczema or dermatitis; Viola felt sorry for her, especially when she scratched with a vengeance and she'd hoped she wasn't contributing to the raw inflammation.

But that beleaguered woman came up trumps. 'I think,' she said. 'I've found you a place in Ayrshire. How does that sound?'

'Oh,' Viola said, propping herself up on her pillows. 'It sounds very good, Mrs Watkins. Where exactly is it?'

Mrs Watkins produced a map and pointed out the location on the west coast of Scotland. 'Sorn, to be precise,' she said.

Viola peered at the pinprick of a village.

'There's not much there,' Mrs Watkins said, a hint of apology in her voice.

Viola shook her head. 'I don't want much,' she said. 'The less the better.'

'Well, let's see. It's very rural. Close to the river, about fifteen miles or so from the reasonably sized town of Ayr. There's a castle, a pub, a general store and a motorcycle shop.'

That made Viola laugh. Mrs Watkins looked up from her paperwork, scratched her left hand with her right and smiled. 'Yes, incongruous, I know. But there in that tiny hamlet they do their bit by mending military motorbikes. Incredible, isn't it?'

Viola nodded.

'You don't have to decide just yet, my dear,' Mrs Watkins said. 'I can give you a couple of days to think about it.'

'Oh, no,' Viola said. 'I like the sound of it.'

'Good,' Mrs Watkins said. 'I thought you might.' She filled Viola in with the details. The billet was a croft on a farm owned by an older couple. It was available because the previous evacuees, a young woman and her baby, had decided to move back home to Glasgow. So, as an added perk, there was a cot, highchair, pram and various other pieces of baby furniture on the premises. Ready and waiting for her to use.

Viola could not believe her luck. Her jaw unhinged. 'It sounds… ideal,' she said. 'I'm so grateful. I can see us there already. Happy and—'

Mrs Watkins stopped her. 'Don't forget, Miss Baxter. There is still a war on and deprivation in the rural areas is just as rife as in the cities. So please do not become too complacent. You must remain wary and alert to any dangers.'

Chastised, Viola nodded. 'Of course. I will. When do we leave?'

Mrs Watkins capped her pen and told Viola not to rush things. 'Now that you've accepted, there's no need to worry. I'll arrange everything this end, get in touch with Mr and Mrs Barfoot, organise your transport. You concentrate on getting well enough to travel.'

Viola sat up and checked her bag to make sure she had all her tickets and the address of where she was going. It would be a long journey and despite her determination to be independent, Viola felt anxious. Her only experiences of travelling alone were short hops – Cambridge to Cirencester, Cirencester to London. The last time she'd travelled any distance was when, as a schoolgirl, she'd visited Germany with six other girls from her class who showed promise in the language. Then, the ignorance of adolescence meant she hadn't felt the least bit trepidatious. At that age, she hadn't been able to give voice or thought or imagination to the possibilities of what could go amiss and if anything did go wrong, Fraulein Konig and Miss Prescott would make it right. *That*, Viola thought, *is how little Freddie must come*

*to think of me, as someone who can be depended upon
without condition.*

The day was hot and humid, her ridiculous hat and
jacket irritating and fusty. She didn't want to insult anyone,
so suffered the discomfort, but couldn't wait to get on the
train and take them off. A bit of a breeze blew the curtains
back and forth and Viola turned her face to catch a swirl of
fresh air. Why, she wondered, had it seemed inappropriate
to allow girls and women to travel by themselves? Who
deemed it necessary that they needed to be accompanied?
What a load of old tosh, as Lillian would say. Surely it
would be better for everyone if women were taught how
to negotiate their way around those sorts of basic skills
and how to take care of themselves. The saddest reflection
to dwell on was that it had taken a war for that, amongst
other restraining customs, to be somewhat eliminated.

'Don't worry, my Freddie,' Viola whispered. 'I will teach
you not to be afraid of tackling anything on your own.' But
first, she thought, she must get used to facing everything in
life without Fred, without Mum, without Lillian, George
or her brothers. The enormity of what she was undertaking
washed her in cold sweat. If she was daunted about making a
train journey on her own, how would she face life hundreds
of miles from home? She breathed with Freddie – *in, hold
it, out, hold it*. She would pull it off, for Freddie, one step at
a time. But how she wished Mum or Lillian were with her.

Over and over again, Viola had to remind herself not to
get too comfortable – they would soon be on their way. But
repeatedly she could feel her eyes drooping; it had been a
difficult night with Freddie awake and fussing for most of

it. Then, a firm nudge on her shoulder. 'Miss, your taxi is here.'

All of a sudden there was no time to check her trappings again. She gathered the baby in her arms, said a quick goodbye to the nurses on duty, the porter grabbed her bags and together they went down the stairs and out of the door of the lying-in hospital, leaving behind the place she'd called home for the past two months. Her stomach lurched; it was happening too fast. 'Euston,' the porter said to the driver, bundling her bags in around her. 'Quickly, if you can. She's running late. Best of luck, Miss.' He gave her a half-hearted salute.

Part of her wanted to say, *Wait; take me back; I'm not sure.* She looked down at Freddie, wriggling herself awake and realised she hadn't had one minute alone with her baby since she'd been born. Could she manage? She had made her decision, so she would have to. The taxi accelerated and Viola looked out of the rear window at the signage above the door of the building. The British Hospital for Mothers and Babies, it read carved in stone – then the inscription and the home disappeared. Viola turned forward and bit her lip until she tasted blood.

As luck would have it the train was delayed, so Viola had plenty of time to find her compartment and seat. When she'd settled her things, she took the baby to the door and leaned out, ever hopeful that Mum, who knew all her travel arrangements, had come to see them off. But there was no sign of her. Lillian would have waved them goodbye, but she was busy at work. All around her people clung to each other as the platform clock ticked on regardless. Some couples kissed with passion and she looked away from the sight, knowing she would never be involved in anything like that again. Not even, she gulped down a lump in her throat, if Fred did return as she knew he wouldn't want her now. She would be repugnant to him.

The stationmaster blew a whistle, women were handed into the train, hankies were fished out of pockets for a final wave. The train pulled out of the station and Viola turned back to her carriage. What a failed experiment living in London had turned out to be. I hope, she thought, Scotland will be better. 'It has to be, little one,' she whispered to Freddie. 'I've got you to think of now.'

All the other women in the compartment smiled at her and the baby. There were two older women, one girl who looked in her early twenties, another woman of indeterminate age wearing a very smart suit and a woman of about forty who didn't seem to be able to stop blinking. 'How far are you travelling?' one of the older women asked. Viola noticed a circle of spiky hair that stood out from a mole on her jawline. 'Ayr,' Viola said. 'In Scotland.'

'Oh,' the woman said. 'That's a long journey on your own.' The others either gasped or nodded.

'You must let me help you,' she said. 'Although I'm not going that far.'

'Thank you,' Viola said. 'Does anyone object to me feeding my baby here? I have become rather adroit at obscuring the whole procedure under a large scarf.'

None of the women demurred. Grateful she would not to have to hide herself away in the lavatory, Viola conversely felt aggrieved that the question needed to be asked at all. As if the most natural and necessary act in the world should be disguised and undertaken in a furtive manner. *We are ridiculous people*, she thought as she covered herself and positioned the baby to feed as if under cloak and dagger. Of course, she could understand that men and boys might be embarrassed or offended, but why this behaviour was de rigueur with other women was a mystery.

Robert and David, averting their faces if put in a similar situation, passed through her mind. And that was another absurd state of affairs – Mum had written to say she had told the boys to send all their letters to Viola care of her and she would forward them on. Return letters from Viola to her brothers must take the same route. Viola had to agree, but she did ask Mum what the boys had been told to make them follow that chain without question. Apparently, Mum had told them Viola was being moved around the country with her secretive job. If it wasn't heart-breakingly ludicrous it would be funny. She and Freddie were being dragged down into a covert vortex where they were to be hidden from view until such time as Viola could make Freddie legitimate, by getting married she supposed. But that would only serve to enlarge the already enormous web of lies when birthdates were calculated and fingers were pointed. Viola wondered where all these lies, like the war, would end. In upset and resentment, she felt sure.

She had been so busy with Freddie and thoughts of her brothers, that other than a jolt forward, she hadn't noticed they had started on the first leg of the journey. But now that she had, an icy cold terror gripped her. As much to comfort herself as the baby, she jiggled Freddie with a soothing rhythm. This, after all, was what she wanted and what she thought was for the best, but worry about whether or not she'd made the right decision made her feel weak and indecisive. Sidings slipped away beside her, the backs of terrace houses became a blur, bomb sites rushed past on the periphery of her vision, the rhythmic sound of metal on tracks filled her ears. She was letting London go, although in reality she'd had about as firm a hold there as she had in Cambridge or the Cotswolds. And where would she go if she lost heart at the next stop or in Glasgow or Ayr or when she'd been in Sorn for a week, a month, a year? There was nowhere except an unmarried mothers' hostel where she would be bullied and nagged about putting up her baby for adoption and she could not bear to hear that.

In one of her letters, Mum wrote that Dad thought she was running away from her responsibilities, but Viola told herself she was not turning her back on her duties but was forcing herself towards a place where she could be single-minded about living up to her obligations. For a split second she closed her eyes and thought, *Oh I do so hope that's the truth of the matter.*

Freddie fussed and Viola turned her so she could suckle on the other side. When she'd had her fill, Viola lifted her onto her shoulder and rubbed her back until the tiny mite released a huge bolt of wind. All the other women laughed. 'What's her name?' the woman with restless eyelids asked.

'Frederika,' Viola said. 'But I call her Freddie.'

'Unusual name,' commented the smartly dressed woman. 'Especially for this time and...'

Viola looked the woman in the eye, but couldn't maintain the stand-off as Mum had done with Mrs Bishop. She reddened first and had to look away. Gathering a few things, she excused herself to find somewhere to change the baby and give them a chance to talk about her.

When she returned to the carriage, the atmosphere was frostier and none of them shared any other information about themselves, reducing their communications to polite pleasantries. A sourness hung over the carriage for the remainder of the journey and, although passengers alighted and were replaced by others, the spoilt milk atmosphere remained.

The plan was that Mr Barfoot would collect them from the station at Ayr. But when Viola stepped off the train into the cool, pure Scottish morning, there was no one on the platform who looked to be a likely candidate. The stationmaster said something to her but she had to ask him to repeat himself three times before she understood he was offering his help; it would take time for her to tune in to the broad accent. She told him they were evacuees and were waiting to be escorted to their billet in Sorn. All she could understand of his lengthy reply was something about slow roads due to tractors, puddles, cattle, sheep or fallen trees. At least she thought that was the gist of it. He picked up her things and led her to the ladies' waiting room, saying it would be more comfortable for her there. She flopped down in a chair with relief, as if she hadn't been sitting on and off for hours on end.

Again, she had to be woken up; she blinked and tried to cover her embarrassment by checking on the baby. The stationmaster was introducing another man to her as Mr Barfoot. 'So pleased to meet you.' She held out her hand and when they shook, she moved the blanket from the baby's face and said, 'This is my baby, Freddie.'

'Och,' Mr Barfoot said in a deep voice, thick with the same rich dialect as the stationmaster's. 'Pleased to meet both of you. Your carriage awaits,' he said, pointing towards the front of the station.

She followed the men towards the exit. Mr Barfoot was younger than she'd expected from Mrs Watkins' description of him and his wife as an older couple; he was forty at the most and dressed, rather uncomfortably, in a dark brown suit, grey tie, white shirt that had seen better days and tan brogues. She supposed there wasn't much call for formal clothing on a farm. A grey, bashed-about trilby, which he'd taken off to greet her, was now back on his unruly hay-coloured hair. She had to stride to keep up with her two escorts, who were chatting like old friends. Well, walking fast was one way of keeping out the cold that cut through her despite it being August. It was a good few degrees colder here than in London; she shivered and drew her arms a bit tighter around the baby.

Parked at an angle to the kerb was an old, mud-spattered vehicle that looked as if it had been cobbled together from bits of cars and lorries and tractors and motorbikes, with a couple of pushbike components hammered on in random places for good measure. The back seat was already occupied by three collies who pressed their interested noses to the windows, smearing them with glutinous streaks, so she was directed to sit in the front passenger seat. The two men swung her baggage into the trailer fastened to the rear of the car with a rope, Mr Barfoot fiddled with some levers, there was a bang as loud as an incendiary and they pulled away.

The collies bickered, with wagging tails, to have sniff and snuffle rights to her neck. The persistent moist noses made her giggle, but she drew the line when they tried to extend their inspections to Freddie. Their smell and wet tongues brought back memories of Pitch, who Mum had written was getting old, deaf and arthritic; she had loved that dog so much, but now she doubted she would see him again – another fixture in her life that was disappearing as fast as the train that was now heading back to London.

'Lassies.' Mr Barfoot sounded firm without raising his voice. 'Down.' As one, the dogs circled three times, lay down and put their long noses on their front legs.

Mr Barfoot smiled at her, taking his eyes off the road for far too long for her liking. 'We were told the baby was a girl,' he said. 'But it's a wee Freddie.'

'Oh, Freddie's a nickname,' Viola said. 'She is a girl. See?' She caressed the pink blanket as if that would prove a point.

'Just as well, as the last lassie we had with us also had a lassie, so some of the clothes and blankets she left behind are for girls.' He said the last word as if it was two syllables: ge-rels, with a trill across the r. She wanted to ask him why he and his wife accepted evacuees, if all of them were mothers and infants, how they were affected by the war so far away from London, if they had any children of their own, what they would expect from her. Instead she commented on the scenery and he pointed out sights such as the castle in the distance and the river.

'Jeanie will tell you everything you need to know about living in the croft,' he said.

'So kind,' she said. 'Thank you both very much, Mr Barfoot.'

'You can call us Finlay and Jeanie,' he said as if it was the most ordinary thing in the world.

'Oh, I don't think I could possibly,' she muttered, thinking of her parents and how they addressed people they'd known for years with their appropriate titles.

'Well,' he said with an ease she was unused to. 'When you're ready.'

The landscape was pretty, but very different from London and the flat countryside around Cambridge. And not as ambrosial as the Cotswolds, which she always thought the quintessential perspective of Britain. But although officially Britain, she had to remind herself, this was a different country so what was considered beautiful or evocative or resonant in one place, might not be in another. She had a lot to learn, but wanted nothing more than to take a back seat and observe, keep herself to herself and get on with what she had to do in peace and quiet. More than that, she did not want to offend or do anything that would turn people against her and Freddie; she would rather remain an enigma than antagonise anyone.

Mr Barfoot was talking and she realised she had to give him her full attention in order to decipher what he was saying. 'Aye, winter comes early here.' He took both hands off the steering wheel, scratched his nose with one and pointed to a scene in the distance with the other. 'Those fields yon? Soon they'll be covered in frost. Then snow.'

'Every year without fail?' she asked.

'Aye.' He nodded, turning to check on the dogs in the back.

'Sometimes we get snow in London. Other years, nothing.'

'Well, I hope you've got some sturdy boots with you,' he said with what Viola thought was a touch of amusement.

The baby stirred and Viola knew that any minute she would start crying for a feed. She joggled her gently, although the commotion of the car making its way over potholes and through puddles would cancel out the soothing movement.

'My footwear is probably all terribly impractical,' she said, looking down at her lace-up brogues. 'I shall have to look into purchasing a pair of sturdy boots and some woollen socks.'

'Och, no need to bother,' he said. 'Jeanie will have some you can borrow.'

There were a lot of sheep around and Viola wondered if they stayed out in the snow. Perhaps she would ask when she knew Mr Barfoot better and he might think her less of a fool. Or she might wait and see when the time came.

Then, during one of the many times he took his eyes off the road, she thought he hazarded a glance at her ring finger. In her mind, she beat her fist against her forehead. Why hadn't she asked Mrs Watkins what these kind people had been told about her? Did they know she was an unmarried mother with no prospect of a returning father for Freddie? Or were the Barfoots not given any information and it was left up to Viola to tell them what she would about her situation? And would it matter to them if they did know?

Turning her face to the window, she worried at the place on her lip she'd bitten earlier and tried to decide on a version of her story that would cause Freddie the least trouble. Before she was conscious of what she was doing, she secreted her ring finger under the folds of the baby blanket and felt around it with her thumb. She could have bought a cheap ring and worn it, then no one would have taken a surreptitious peek at her hand, no questions would have been asked, no whispers in the small shop or after church. But she had decided against that as to do so would have been a denial of how the war had robbed her of Fred and their future together. Besides, the only ring she wanted on her finger was the one that had been waiting, but would now remain, around her neck. She supposed that if pushed, she could say she had been widowed and taken off the ring as officially she was no longer married. Each narrative she considered seemed more complicated than the last. Of course, she didn't want herself or Freddie to be ostracised, but she decided that she would not offer any explanation at all until asked outright and then she would tell the truth about Fred being in Germany and about having Freddie because she had been lonely. When she turned back, she smiled at Mr Barfoot and asked about the running of his farm.

'Och,' he said. 'Partly arable – spring barley, winter barley and wheat, potatoes. And the ubiquitous sheep.'

The thought of lamb and mint sauce caused saliva to pool in her mouth, followed swiftly by a hollowness in the pit of her stomach when she remembered the last meal she'd had with Fred in her parents' house on the night of their failed engagement, the plate of untouched meat and the yellow fat, congealing around the outside of her plate as the gravy grew cold. 'We don't see much lamb in London,' she said. 'Mutton, but that's not the same.'

'Aye well, it's requisitioned to the government,' he said. 'So I donnae know where it ends up, but we're not short of lamb chops, roast lamb, lamb casserole and lamb fricassee here. We're all sick of it and you will be, too. Believe me.'

She wondered if that would be the case.

'Baaa,' he blurted out in an alarming way. 'See? I've turned into a lamb I've eaten so much of the stuff.'

Viola laughed out loud and Mr Barfoot seemed pleased with her response. *This*, thought Viola, *is going to be alright.*

Another few meandering miles rolled past. Mr Barfoot drew Viola's attention to a number of bonnie burns, a vivid heather-covered glen, the back green of Mrs McKenzie's cottage and countless flocks of sheep who were owned by various farmers. How Mr Barfoot could tell one from another she did not know.

'There.' He pointed to a large, white house in the distance, an ancient, gnarled tree standing guard next to it, snowy sheets and towels blowing in the breeze in the garden. 'There's our Ould Aik Farm.' He sounded as if he was talking about a person he loved very much.

'What does the name mean?' Viola asked.

'Old Oak.'

'Of course. I can see where that comes from.'

'And if you follow the track with your eyes, up the hill and to the left, you will see the roof of your croft. Your new home.'

Nestled between two dips, she could make out what was probably a thatched roof, a strand of smoke disappearing into the sky from a chimney, two small windows set in a whitewashed wall. From this distance it looked cosy and welcoming, but she hadn't expected it to be so far from the main house and so isolated. Then again, she hadn't known what to expect and now it was too late to turn back.

Without any warning, Mr Barfoot brought the car to a halt. 'Just in time,' he said. 'The wee one's chewing her fists so she must be hungry. Wait there, Mrs Baxter, I'll come round and help you out.'

So, Mrs Baxter it was. Perhaps that was how Mrs Watkins

had filled in the forms she sent on to the Barfoots. Or maybe it was a presumption on their part. Either way, it solved a dilemma for her and she had no intention of correcting them at this point.

Mr Barfoot opened her door and offered his hand for her to lean on. At the same time he somehow managed to release the dogs, who shook themselves then sat at his feet, waiting for their next order. 'Jeanie,' he called out. 'Here they are. Safe and sound.'

A lovely, round woman in a white apron appeared in the doorway. She had fair hair drawn back in a loose bun, dark brown eyes, flour on her forehead and hands. 'Och, Fin.' Her voice was a soft sing-song. 'I was getting worried. I thought you were driving home via Aberdeen.'

Mr Barfoot laughed. 'Hold your whisht, woman,' he said. He cupped his hand under Viola's elbow and steered her towards his wife. 'Jeanie, this is Mrs Baxter. And Freddie.'

Mrs Barfoot wiped her palms with vigour on her apron, then grasped Viola's hand. 'Welcome,' she said. 'And to Freddie.' She peered in amongst the blankets. 'We were told you had a baby girl.'

'Freddie is a girl,' her husband said and shrugged. 'London ways are a mystery to us, Mrs Baxter.'

Oblivious to their new surroundings, the fuss being made of her, this huge change in their lives, Freddie started to wail for a feed. Viola thought this must be what people meant when they said life went on.

'Och she's hungry,' Mrs Barfoot said. 'Come in, come in. You must be, too, hen. And tired.'

She was exhausted, light-headed and a tiny bit faint.

'Sit here.' Mrs Baxter showed her to a rocking chair. 'You

take care of the baby. I'll get us a cup of tea. Dinner is on the go. I hope you like lamb?'

Mr Barfoot bleated another disquieting 'Baaa' and laughed from his boots at his rendition. His wife rolled her eyes but smiled broadly.

Viola had thought Mr and Mrs Barfoot would waste no time in showing her the croft and leaving her there, with Freddie, to settle in. But it seemed they had the entire afternoon mapped out for her in the main house with them. They could not have been more accommodating and their easy, relaxed manner made Viola feel rather stiff and reserved. But, she reminded herself, this was their home, their territory, and she was the guest. She realised as the time went by that the Barfoots were jovial with each other, with her and with the farmhand who knocked on the door a couple of times. So, she presumed that was the way they communicated all the time. It was lovely to hear them, talking so naturally and gently chiding each other. They gave everyone their full attention when they spoke as if they truly valued what others had to say. When listening intently, Mrs Barfoot had an endearing way of tilting her head to one side, which gave her an aura of being understanding and sympathetic. And it was all so genuine.

After the baby was fed, topped and tailed, Mrs Barfoot insisted on taking the dirty napkin and washing it in her big, stone sink. Her hands looked pink and sore when she took them out of the water, but she dried them on her apron and didn't seem to notice. They had tea and cake, a short walk around the garden and outhouses, she was introduced to Donald, the hired hand who tipped his hat at her and said something indecipherable and then they went back into the house for dinner. Mrs Barfoot had conjured up lamb and vegetable pasties, mashed swede and turnips all covered in gravy. To follow, there was a blackberry and apple crumble with custard. Not one word was spoken about the war other than referring to her as being an evacuee. Mrs Barfoot reiterated what her husband had said about calling them by their Christian names; again Viola said that would be difficult for her, but added they must feel free to call her Viola. Or Vi.

'Another London way,' Mr Barfoot said.

'Have you ever been to London?' Viola asked.

They both shook their heads. 'I've been to Glasgow twice,' Mr Barfoot said. 'And Edinburgh once. But I was glad to get back.'

'And I've been no further than Ayr,' Mrs Barfoot said.

Viola felt her eyebrows arch in surprise.

'Och, I know,' Mrs Barfoot said. 'I'm not very adventurous, am I? But I've got all I want here.' She spread her arms wide and Mr Barfoot smiled at her. 'Now, tomorrow we can walk into the village and I'll show you where to get your rations and then you can cook for yourself in your little croft. But the wee lassie we had above often used to come here, which we enjoyed. So we hope you'll feel welcome to do that, too. No need to give me advance warning or wait for a special invitation, just turn up. Fiona and little Heather used to spend more time down here with us than they did up there, but of course that will be your prerogative. We also used to go into Ayr together for the shopping we can't get here and I'd certainly be glad of the company if you would.'

Viola nodded and tried to take it all in. She had longed for solitude and peace and wondered how obliged she would feel to follow in Fiona's footsteps. But when Mr Barfoot said he would drive her up the hill so she could settle in before it was dark, she felt a lurch of anxiety and knew she would miss the warm kitchen, Mrs Barfoot's lilting register, her hosts' easy manner and their company. When she, Freddie, their bags and the three dogs were once again bundled into the car and she'd waved goodbye to Mrs Barfoot, the little croft looked a long way away.

'How long does it take to walk down?' she asked.

'Well...' Mr Barfoot thought about his answer as he veered around a small flock of sheep who stared at them as if they were trespassing. 'Depends. Twenty minutes or so, I'd say. Going down. Going back up you'd have to add another five minutes. Then again it takes longer with a baby carriage. Of course if it's raining, snowing, sleeting, windy or otherwise inclement it takes longer. And if the girls are in the way...'

'The girls?'

'The sheep,' he carried on. 'Then you sometimes have to detour around them or wait for them to move or forget your trip for the day.' He said all of this in a nonchalant way as if it was the most ordinary situation in the world. Well, for him it must be, she supposed.

'If they do get in your way, you can clap at them and they will usually scuttle off, but you cannae scare them if they're lactating as their milk might dry up.'

'How will I know?' she asked.

'You have to look at their undercarriage,' he said and again he sounded slightly amused at her lack of knowledge about the natural world.

'Of course,' she replied, trying to come across as knowing.

'Now, here we are.' He pulled up without slowing down. His driving seemed to consist of go and stop, nothing in between.

Viola was taken aback to see that no key was involved in opening the door, in fact there didn't seem to be any kind of lock worked into the wooden panels. She stepped straight into a small sitting room, a fireplace at one end in which glowed the ends of an earlier fire. Next to it was a scuttle full of what looked like clods of earth. 'I've filled you up with peat,' Mr Barfoot said. 'And the lean-to is about to burst open with the stuff so you won't go cold. Here, let me stoke you up again.' He bent over the open fire, threw in a couple of blocks of fuel, blew on them with the bellows, stood up and brushed his hands on his trousers.

'Do you have to blackout here?' she asked.

Mr Barfoot nodded. 'Everywhere,' he said. 'You'll hear German planes flying over, but they donnae bother with us. Well, never have. And we donnae want them to notice a speck of light and think they'll have a go, do we?'

'Of course not,' she said.

'This is the kitchen.' Viola followed him into a small room dominated by a type of range she'd never seen before, let alone used. Mr Barfoot opened a drawer built into the side of the black stove and told her that was where the peat went. 'I'm afraid you have to boil a kettle or saucepan for hot water.'

'Oh.' She tried to sound more confident than she felt. 'I'm sure I can manage that.'

'To get you started, there's a small loaf, dried milk, an ounce of tea and matches in the press.'

Then she followed her host upstairs, bobbing when he

did under the low ceiling. In a room at the top of the stairs, a bed was made up and next to it was a crib. A green-patterned bowl and jug stood on a washstand, a bar of soap and towel next to it. 'Jeanie put a hot stone in your bed earlier,' Mr Barfoot said. 'But it might be cold now.'

'I can't thank you enough,' Viola said.

'There's not much we can do,' he said. 'For the war effort. Except this and the lamb and the barley. It's really not onerous.'

At the front door, Mr Barfoot chucked Freddie under her chin and said goodnight to Viola. 'You must let us know if you need anything or if you cannae find things. And hopefully we'll see you tomorrow.'

Viola nodded and wished she could think of a question now, to keep him here for a few more minutes. 'Is there a torch?' she asked.

'On the table in the kitchen,' he said.

'And where do I... you know. Where are the facilities?'

'There's an outhouse near the back door and a pot under the bed.'

'And a door key?'

He looked bemused. 'You can latch yourselves in,' he said. 'But that's the closest any of us here have to a lock and key. Down, girls,' he addressed the dogs. 'Goodnight, Viola and Freddie,' he said. Then he put the car into gear and was gone. Viola watched until the last trace of him disappeared down the hill, pulled Freddie close to her, went in through the minuscule door and latched it behind them.

For the first time, Freddie drifted off and slept for a good six hours, but although Viola's whole body ached with exhaustion, she could barely sleep. It was much too quiet for her liking. There wasn't simply a lack of noise, but a sense of calm and stillness she'd never experienced pervaded the outside world and permeated the croft; it was like a heavy blanket covering her head and shoulders and making it difficult to breathe. So overpowering was the silence, that she found herself on edge waiting for something that would break the spell. That did happen occasionally in the form of an owl hooting, a sheep bleating, a scuttle here, an animal cry there. Then the peat in the fireplace would shift and she'd sit bolt upright wondering for a moment what it could be. A few times she thought she heard the latch on the door being lifted, but then she reminded herself that she'd wedged a chair under it so if someone did try to get in, she would hear it scraping along the floor. She knew, of course, where she was and why, but she reeled with disbelief every time she realised that she was alone, in the wilds of Scotland with a tiny baby to care for.

She was grateful when Freddie woke, crying for a feed. Viola grabbed her from her crib and, sitting up in bed, pressed her close. The window was within touching distance, as was almost everything and she dared to lift a corner of the blackout and peek outside. Dawn streaked grey and violet across the sky and she could make out the looming shapes of sheep and hillocks, dark and foreboding against the pastel glow. As Freddie drained her breasts, the tension flooded from her. In its place was a sense of elation – she'd made it through the first night and now that hurdle was over, she hoped she would go on to feel stronger and more settled.

Despite her lack of sleep, she was full of energy. Making a cocoon out of a couple of blankets, she laid Freddie safely on the floor to sleep. First, she needed to empty the pot and then relieve herself. The lavatory was a hole in the ground which she stood and gawped at, her mouth as round as the one she was supposed to crouch over. Next to it was a bucket of water, a couple of insects skating over its surface, which she guessed should be used to flush. Steeling herself, she squatted. A couple of uncomfortable minutes passed during which she shuffled on her aching legs and peered into the abyss beneath her. When at last the stream started, water splashed on her legs so she scrambled closer to the hole. Strips of newspaper hanging on a nail had to suffice as toilet paper and the scrunch of it on her intimate parts made her shudder. But, when she finished and gathered herself together, she burst into laughter at the whole process. Lillian would love that story.

By the time she was dressed and had changed the baby again, light filled the sky and she could pull the blackouts and begin to get herself organised. She set about finding a bucket in which to wash dirty napkins. Next she lit the stove to boil water for tea, looked for kitchen utensils, pots and pans to consider meals, pulled an old clothes horse out of a cupboard and set it up ready to dry wet clothes, scrubbed the kitchen table, sorted out bedding and towels, unpacked her belongings and put them away in cupboards and sideboards. Feeling satisfied with what she'd accomplished, she prepared another cup of tea to drink whilst she sat on the couch and fed Freddie. She would have to decide whether to try to get to the village for rations or ask to eat again with the Barfoots.

Here at least, she could feed the baby without having to pander to convention. She unbuttoned her blouse, rearranged her vest and pulled Freddie close. The only sounds were the snuffles of the baby as she settled to the serious business of feeding. Then there was a soft knock at the door, followed by a subdued, 'Yoo-hoo.' Mrs Barfoot's soft voice, rather more solemn than yesterday. 'May I come in, Vi?' She peered around the door.

'Of course,' Viola said, grabbing a woollen blanket and placing it over her chest.

Mrs Barfoot's jolly face had been transformed by a look of concern. Deep lines pulled her mouth down rather than up; the twinkling brown eyes were clouded. Instead of a white apron, she wore a dark skirt and cardigan. 'Vi, hen,' she said, as if they'd known each other for years. 'I fear I'm bringing you bad news.'

Sitting as close to Viola as she could without disturbing Freddie, she held out a telegram bordered in black. Viola's hand clamped her mouth, but not hard enough to stifle the strangulated sob that seemed to come from a place she'd never needed to delve into before.

14

October 1943

From Annie's first pain to the moment her beautiful baby boy Walther greeted the world was a matter of two and a half hours. And he gave her no trouble, waking only when he needed to be fed and changed and waiting with utmost patience if it took her a few moments to get to him. Frau Wilhelm had not stopped telling her how lucky she was.

As a consequence of the short labour, she had been in shock for a day or two but other than that, no ill effects for either mother or baby. In fact, she had so much energy that lying-in proved to be a frustrating experience. On a number of occasions she tried to get out of bed, tiptoe across the bedroom and set about doing something – folding napkins, changing linen in the crib, opening a window, rearranging flowers in a vase – anything to occupy her restless limbs. But Frau Wilhelm would burst into the room, order her back to bed, take over whatever chore she was attempting and make her feel like an insubordinate schoolgirl. 'Please, Annie,' she would say, one hand on her hip, the other pointing to the bed. 'Do as you're told.'

And Annie would turn, shuffle towards the bed and allow herself to be hoisted back in between the sheets. Then, more often than not, Frau Wilhelm would lift Walther from his crib, place him in her arms and tell her that all she should be doing for six weeks was feeding and cuddling her baby. They'd spent so much time staring at each other that it would be reasonable to think she'd had her fill of him. But she held the baby at every opportunity and studied him with a fascination that seemed to intensify with each day she had been his Mutti.

As soon as Walther had been born, Frau Wilhelm sent a telegram to the forwarding address they had for Fred, telling him that he had become an uncle and Annie was well. There had been no reply, so Herr Doctor thought he had probably been posted to Italy where the Germans had occupied Rome, rescued Mussolini and allowed the dictator to re-establish a Fascist government. They boasted about this in the papers and on the radio like small, swaggering boys bombast about cuffing each other on the way home from school.

A few days later, sitting up in bed, Annie had written him a long letter describing his nephew in detail.

We call the dear little boy Walti, which stops us from having to ask each other whether we are talking about Big Walther or Little Walther. He looks so like his Vati that it takes my breath away. His tiny ears are flat against his head, which is covered in the most abundant amount of dark hair that spikes in every direction. And do you remember the little line that ran between Walther's nostrils? His son has inherited that feature but his eyes are a hazy blue, which is the colour Frau Wilhelm tells me all babies are born with, so they will probably change to the same pale hazel as Big Walther's in time.

She had felt happy, but at that point in her letter a tear had plopped onto the paper and sent diluted ink running through the words. She could have started again, but they must not waste paper and why shouldn't Fred know she had cried? She didn't doubt that he shed tears, too, even if he had to swallow them down and not allow them to manifest themselves where others could see the evidence of all his sadnesses.

So, she'd explained that her tears were for him, whose introduction to his nephew was delayed until a future unknown date. And for Walther who would never get to meet his son. But more than that, she cried for the baby, who had been deprived of both of those strong, handsome, wonderful men who should, by this time, be a significant part of his life.

She had written about how kind and attentive both Herr Doctor and Frau Wilhelm had been to her since he left and how much she appreciated and loved them. Yes, it was true. She did love them, not as her own parents, but as outstanding replacements. They could not do enough for her or the baby and she knew she would do whatever she could for them.

Luckily, the midwife was in Ulm when the baby started because if Herr Doctor had to drive to another town and collect her, she would probably have been too late. He stayed downstairs and the way he walked up and down, backwards and forwards, reminded me of your pacing, Fred, when you had a problem to think about. Which was often. Frau Wilhelm stayed with me and I was worried that her presence would be overpowering, but she did whatever the midwife asked of her – nothing more and nothing less. Most of the time, she stood next to me and pressed my hand, telling me how strong and brave I was. And she did not attempt to have the first cuddle, but she did look at her grandson with longing in her eyes when he was wrapped and given straight to me. She busied herself then, helping the midwife to clear up, but I held the baby out to her after a few minutes and watched as she wrapped her arms around him as if she was holding a precious, fragile treasure. Herr Doctor was called upstairs to join us and he, too, admired the baby, with a visible lump in his throat.

But there was always a but in life, she told Fred. And as her six weeks of confinement went on, Frau Wilhelm remained helpful and attentive but she had become more of a clucking hen. Apart from not letting Annie leave her bed, she organised everything – cooking, cleaning, sewing, burping Walti, changing him and shopping which she'd designated to a friend's little girl so she would not have to leave the house. Watching and listening to her from the bedroom made Annie feel tense.

But Annie had at last, after much discussion, persuaded Frau Wilhelm to go into Munich to see her sister who was recovering from a stomach complaint. It would have been more beneficial if she had gone earlier, but she insisted on waiting until her sister was somewhat better as she didn't want to bring illness back to them. She was the epitome of thoughtfulness. So, how could it be that Annie was weak with relief and excitement to see someone so kind and caring turn her back on the house, walk down the path and leave her alone with the baby for eight or perhaps ten joyful, carefree hours? She was ashamed to say that when she waved for the last time and disappeared around the corner, Annie put her palms together, said a thank you to the heavens, then jumped and clicked her heels together. Right away she felt guilty, peered into Walti's crib, put a finger to her closed mouth and told him that her reaction would be their secret.

She waited to make sure Frau Wilhelm wasn't going to pretend to miss her train, then made herself a cup of coffee, fished out her journal, pulled the crib close so she could keep an eye on the baby, ignored the full nappy bucket, the dry garments on the clothes horse, the potatoes, carrot, half a cabbage and slab of pork on the sideboard waiting to be prepared for dinner and sat down to write.

She set out how she was longing to go into Munich and show Walti to her ex-colleagues at the university, but when she mentioned the possibility of such an outing, Frau Wilhelm had been horrified. Her face drained of colour and left behind two amethyst stains under her eyes.

'Annie,' she had said, shaking her head.

'What?' Annie was bemused by her reaction.

Frau Wilhelm's head continued to shake for some minutes. 'Walther told us you had grown to be a determined, strong-willed young woman and I have come to understand that about you. But that suggestion is beyond...'

'Did he?' Annie asked, a tiny piece of forgotten biscuit between her fingers. 'Beyond what? I don't understand...'

Frau Wilhelm sat next to her on the couch, bundling the blue and white blankets she had been folding onto her lap.

'You must not go anywhere,' she said. 'You must stay here.'

'Oh, but my confinement is almost over.'

Again, the older woman's head moved from side to side in an almost mournful manner. 'It is more treacherous in Munich than it is here – you know that,' she said. 'People are trying to run from the worst of the war, not towards it. And definitely not with a tiny baby.'

That comment made Annie prickle with shame. 'But I am so proud that I want to show him off. And I cannot stay cooped up here for, well, I don't know how long.'

Frau Wilhelm took a deep breath and exhaled for a long moment. When she spoke, there was the slightest edge of irritation in her voice, something Annie had never heard before and that, more than her previous remark, filled her with humiliation. She could feel her neck and face redden. 'We are all in the same position, Annie,' she said. 'Do you think any of us like the way we are being forced to live?'

When no reply was forthcoming, Frau Wilhelm dipped to look Annie in the eyes and prodded again, 'Well, do you?'

'No,' Annie said.

'No,' Frau Wilhelm echoed. 'That's right. But we all have responsibilities towards our loved ones, especially when they are too helpless to look after themselves.'

'Yes.' She nodded. 'I know you're right.' Annie grabbed at her hand. 'I'm so sorry,' she said.

'No need to apologise. I am sorry, too, that you are young and have to go through all of this.'

'It's not just the young,' Annie said. 'As someone wise told me – we're all in this together.'

They laughed then and Frau Wilhelm continued folding and smoothing the blankets. 'Perhaps when you are well and truly on your feet,' she said, 'you can go into Munich on your own and leave Walti with me for a morning or afternoon. Or maybe we can go together.'

'Thank you,' Annie said. 'Either one of those will be something to look forward to.'

Walti started to murmur and thrash his little fists about for his feed, so Frau Wilhelm brought him to her and went into the kitchen to continue her daily tasks there. The living room was quiet, apart from the gratified sounds of Walti's greedy sucking, and Annie was left to think about what had been said. She closed he eyes against the guilt she felt but when she opened them, the feelings of remorse continued to nag at her. *That's not a bad thing*, she thought, *to be brought down to earth by the truth*. She did have responsibilities now, not only to Walti but to Frau Wilhelm and Herr Doctor and to Fred and as such, she had to mature and live up to them without sulking or complaining or figuratively stamping her feet.

30 October 1943
What surprised me most, though, was understanding that Frau Wilhelm was fed up and disgruntled, too. Other than the tragedy of losing her only son, I thought

she was content with her lot. How dare I harbour the assumption that she wanted nothing more for her life than to be a wife, mother-in-law and grandmother here in Ulm. Of course, I know her political leanings and understand she would like to go about her business without being under the control of the Nazis, but I presumed that was the extent of it. Then I remembered her telling me about dancing and visiting nightclubs in Berlin and realised that what we see of Frau Wilhelm now is the tip of what constitutes her. Who knows what ambitions she had for this time in her life that have now been quashed? Maybe she had envisaged herself creating an award-winning garden. Or writing a Kuchen recipe book. Travelling to Paris or London or further afield with Herr Doctor when he handed over the practice to Walther. In my mind, Frau Wilhelm had taken on other dimensions – not merely those I had fashioned her into for my convenience. She has a right to her own aspirations, too, or at least to the longing for them. And I have a duty to honour and respect her for them.

Walti stirred, so Annie picked up the notebook and, taking the stairs two at a time, made her way up to the hiding place in her bedroom. A knock on the door cemented her to a step, enough evidence to execute all of them on plain view in her hand. The last time there was someone at the door whilst she was on her own it had been horrible Horst. But even he wouldn't let himself into a feeding mother's home, would he? 'Who is there?' she called, wondering if she could make it up to her bedroom and back without him noticing.

'Gisela,' a small voice answered. 'I've come with the rations, young Frau Wilhelm.'

Annie's heart thumped so hard that she hoped the stress wouldn't turn her milk sour. That was what Frau Wilhelm said could happen.

'One moment, Gisela,' she called back. She wanted to let the little girl think she was buttoning her blouse or making sure the baby was safe in his crib, not scrabbling to hide a lethal document.

By the time she opened the door, her breathing had returned to its usual rhythm and she was composed enough to offer Gisela a benign smile. The child skipped away, none the wiser, her long, thick ponytail streaming down her back.

As the weeks went by, Frau Wilhelm and Annie began to take Walti for walks in his baby carriage until at last, Annie was allowed out with the baby on her own. It took so long to bundle him up that she thought he would need his next feed before they stepped out the door. But then they were walking in the crisp, autumn air and the sting of it on her face made her laugh out loud. If she hadn't been in charge of the pram she would have taken off her hat and gloves, perhaps her coat, and run into the biting wind. As it was, she turned down the finger sleeves on her mittens and ran her fingers along the hoar frost on the top of a low wall, enjoying the tingle of cold needling into her flesh.

So many people stopped to admire Walti and Annie dutifully pulled back his covers a tiny bit and let them peep at him. How they oohed and aahed. Everyone knew Herr Doctor and his family, so they all had an opinion about who the shape of the baby's face resembled, or how Walther's hair had stuck out in the same pattern of disarray as his son's, or how his nose had the same curve as Frau Wilhelm's. There was no mention of how the baby might take after her or Fred or Oma in some small way – the tilt of his head on the pillow, the arch of his eyebrows, the translucence of his skin. She didn't feel resentful about that and preferred that he favoured Walther as that would be a lifetime's reminder of the man she had loved.

But then to a person they offered condolences about Walther and said what an illustrious young hero of a man he had been for dying in service to his country and how proud she should be of him as he would be of her and the baby and on and on in that vein. Her stomach wrapped itself around in a tight twist when she realised that most of them knew Walther better than she did, or at least had known him for longer, and she had been robbed of that chance. But did they know him? She had to stop herself from scoffing aloud when he was called a war hero time and again. He hated the war, the Nazis, the regime and was posted only as a medic and that was against his wishes. Her initial feelings of invigoration seeped from her and she wondered if Walther, with his good humour and optimistic outlook on life, would find anything here and now to laugh at. If so, she wished he could somehow point it out to her.

Something had shifted in Ulm from before she gave birth and had been confined to the house. At first, she thought her overstrung imagination was at work again as she could not grasp what the difference was. Then she began to piece together what she observed and came to some conclusions. Many people were beginning to look very shabby, as if they could not keep mending over the mending they had already used to mend their clothes. A number of women were stockingless, a sight that would never have previously been seen, whatever the weather; the shine on men's trousers was so glassy, she could have used it to make sure her hair was in place. And all the colour had been washed out of the clothes – no black, brown, beige, lavender, blue – everything was a variant of grey.

That was the colour favoured for faces, too. Gaunt, ghostly and sunken with bones more prominent than flesh. Shopping bags hanging off spindly wrists were less than half full, no loaves peeking out of the top or cabbages balancing on bulging bags of flour. Her tummy rumbled as she walked closer to the market, reminding her that despite having a few more rations as a feeding mother, there seemed to be less on her plate for each meal. Herr Doctor and Frau Wilhelm's bowls and spoons seemed to hold even less than hers. She thought she had been so on the ball after having the baby, but she must have been somewhat foggy or ensconced in her own world staring at Walti, that she missed or misjudged what was going on around her. Vaguely, she recalled hearing the end of a hushed conversation between Frau Wilhelm and Herr Doctor about 'nutrition' and 'making sure she gets enough' and having another look for vegetables tomorrow.

She reasoned that she had a voracious appetite because she was producing milk, but today, wandering through Ulm, she realised that rations were dwindling. Icy, agitated fingers moved through her chest and settled in her stomach. If she couldn't feed Walti what would she do? Reaching under his canopy, she tucked the blanket closer around his chin.

But she listened to the radio and read the papers. They were being told there was more than enough for the entire population. They had the fat of the conquered lands. Their gardens and vegetable plots were overflowing. The cows were bellowing to be milked and begging to be slaughtered – if only the farmers could get around to them. Of course, the people were ordered to believe the military got most of the food and that was right and proper as they were defending the Fatherland. How she wished she had the right to express herself freely. If she did, she would let it be known that she, for one, wished all the fighting men had only just enough to keep them alive so the Axis would surrender to the Allies and put an end to this insanity.

The marketplace was a sorry sight – there were a few chickens running around to choose from, but they looked as if they were being offered for sale only because their laying days were over. One had a bald patch on the side of her scrawny body, another a sore, swollen eye. Annie stood and watched as the poor thing tried to relieve the itching by rubbing its face in the dirt. No, she thought, even if there was enough meat on either of them to eat, she would not be able to force it down her throat.

She moved on through the jostling crowd, all probably looking for the same things she had on the list Frau Wilhelm had given her to try to procure. The baby carriage certainly helped in forging a way through, but twice her toes were trodden on, once she bumped her knee on the edge of a wooden table, then she took an elbow to her ribs and a fist landed on her hip. Or was it the flat of a hand as it felt more like an intrusion than an accidental dig? She stopped and stood on her toes, trying to see over the crowds to who might have touched her in such an intimate way, but there were only the usual housewives, Wehrmacht soldiers, diesel factory workers and it could have been any one of those. Or, she shrugged, none of them. But as she worked her way through the stalls, the place above her bottom burned with the heat of unwanted attention.

Irrational pride swelled in her when she handed over rations for three eggs, powdered milk and a small tin of soap flakes – Frau Wilhelm would be so pleased. Beetroot was on the list, too and she presumed her mother-in-law wanted to make Herr Doctor's beloved Borscht but had used all that had been grown in their gardens. Then tucked away in the far corner, she noticed an elderly woman wearing a headscarf and frayed gloves who had a handful of wilting beets left on a trestle table. *My life has come to this*, she thought, as excitement surged through her when she laid her hands on the purple roots and claimed them for her own.

'A baby!' the woman cried. 'May I see?'

Annie nodded and the woman left her station to peer into the pram. 'Boy or girl?' the woman asked.

'A boy,' she said. 'Walti.'

The woman explained that her daughter-in-law in Berlin had recently had a baby girl and she hoped to be able to see her soon. They both gazed at the baby for some minutes before Annie made a move to readjust the pram cover so she could move on. Then she was distracted by a leaflet or brochure caught under the wheel, a torn corner flapping against the spokes. It looked familiar, but she couldn't think how at first.

'Oh,' the woman said. 'Those have been all over the

market since last Monday.' She pointed to a neighbouring stall. 'Herr Muller says it's filthy British propaganda. Here, let me…' She reached down to grab the piece of paper from the wheel.

'Don't be silly,' Annie said, beating her to it. 'I'll get it.' Without glancing at the writing, she crumbled the leaflet and put it in her pocket as if it meant nothing to her. 'British propaganda?' she said. 'But how did it get here?'

'They drop them, those nasty RAF pilots, on the way back from bombing raids. I hope they rot in hell.'

Handing over her rations, Annie shook her head in what could have been interpreted as a show of unity and returned the woman's Heil Hitler.

Hunching her shoulders and ploughing ahead with the pram, Annie could feel her heart beating against her ribs and the pulse in her neck ticking like a time bomb. She hoped not to meet anyone else on the way home, friend or foe. Her fingers kept straying to her pocket to check if the crushed leaflet was where she had put it. It was, and she longed to stop, take it out, smooth the page and see if her suspicions were correct. But she knew she must not be foolhardy and sneak behind a tree or around the back of a shop and get the paper out in public; if she was not a mother now she would not have been able to stop herself, but she kept calm by thinking of Walti's safety.

Frau Wilhelm met her at the door with endless questions about her walk, who she had met and what they had said to each other, if Walti had cried, the produce or lack of it on the market, which routes she had taken there and back. Annie replied with all the right answers in all the right places, but omitted to mention the unsettling occurrences

– the sense of that unwelcome touch and the leaflet. Frau Wilhelm tried to help her off with her coat but, with a smile on her face, Annie said she was perfectly able and hung it on the coat stand. Her mother-in-law's gratitude for the purchases she'd made would have been touching if Annie wasn't so anxious to get upstairs and look more closely at what she considered to be the most important find she'd appropriated that day.

They went into the living room, Frau Wilhelm cuddling Walti and babbling in a sing-song voice about how much she'd missed him. 'I will get us coffee. Then the baby will need his feed, won't he? You must be tired. Sit.' She pointed to the couch.

'Yes, thank you,' Annie said, sitting in her place. Then she jumped up as if something was bothering her. Covering her chest with her arms, she said she thought her milk had leaked and she needed to change her vest.

Frau Wilhelm's mouth turned down and she looked sorry for Annie. 'So uncomfortable,' she said. 'I remember. Go. We'll be fine here.' She dandled Walti on her knee and began to take off some of his many layers.

In the hall, Annie reached into her coat pocket then bounded up the stairs, closed her bedroom door and made a lot of noise opening drawers on the pretence of taking out fresh undergarments. When at last she unfolded the scrunched leaflet, her hands were shaking. Then her legs gave way and she had to sit on the edge of the bed. She had been right – it was their fifth leaflet. Exactly as they had written it with the addition of an introduction by the Allies saying that it had initially been written and distributed by German citizens in Germany. *Join forces with your own resistance!* it said. *You are not alone!*

She clutched it close. To think – their humble leaflet had been to Britain and back again. If only she had some way of letting Fred know that this most unlikely chain of events had happened. She looked out of the window, beyond the garden, across the fields, towards the horizon. The wide world was out there, working to bring the atrocities of this war to an end. Her spirits bubbled.

Annie could have legitimately stayed at home and cared for Walti, but she felt she owed it to Fred, Walther, the RAF pilots who dropped the leaflets and of course their fellow resistance fighters who had lost their lives to the cause, not to allow herself to become too comfortable or complacent. So she brought up again the idea of going into Munich and oh, the decisions and arrangements and excuses that had to be made.

Frau Wilhelm wanted her to wait until the baby was much older and then go by herself, but Annie countered with the argument that Walti was the reason she wanted to see her ex-colleagues in the first place.

'Well,' Frau Wilhelm said when every option had been pulled apart, 'there is only one thing for it if you insist on this trip, Annie.'

'Please,' Annie entreated. 'I do not insist. I just want to feel like any other new mum in normal times.'

Frau Wilhelm sighed in much the same way Fred had done at her petitions.

'But we don't live in normal times. These years are extraordinary.'

'I know,' she said. 'But… just this once?'

'Alright,' she acquiesced. 'I will come with you. I will leave you at the university for an hour or so and visit my sister. That should be a good solution for both of us.'

'Thank you,' Annie said, barely able to stop herself from skipping and jumping around the living room.

'It is, how do you say in England, killing both birds with just the one rock?'

'Yes.' Annie laughed. 'That's it exactly.'

Preparations lasted for the best part of a week. Times had to be agreed upon, tickets bought, a bag packed for Walti, warnings given. 'This is really quite precarious, Annie,' Frau Wilhelm insisted. 'The streets in Munich are barely passable and we will be stopped by soldiers at every turn. God knows what they could want with two women and a pram, but they will find some excuse.'

Annie nodded and agreed and said they would be vigilant and careful. It was on the tip of her tongue to tell Frau Wilhelm, during one or other of her discourses, that Ulm had become dangerous and threatening for her. But every time she almost blurted it out, something stopped her; she didn't want to worry her mother-in-law or put her under the added pressure of thinking she had to do something to help Annie. At least until she was more sure of what was going on.

The pat on her hip had not been her imagination. It had happened again whilst she was leaning over Walti's pram outside the bakery, but that time a hand had brushed her breast. She'd started, unable to believe what she felt. But scanning the crowds and the queues, she could not pinpoint who it might have been. Everyone had looked both innocent and guilty. A few days later, someone had rubbed the small of her back whilst she was carrying Walti into the dry goods store. Whirling around, she was sure she would be able to spot the degenerate and when she did, she was going to give him the full weight of her tongue in a very loud voice. Again, she had been too late or too unobservant or too reluctant to accuse.

Now she saw shadows moving out of shadows when she left the house; heard rustling and footsteps following her; could sense breathing close to her ear. She took to buying enough food to last two or three days so she wouldn't have to leave the house, telling Frau Wilhelm she was tired and asking her to take Walti out instead. And she was pleased she wasn't going to Munich on her own, as she would be terrified if her unwanted pursuer followed her there.

If Annie thought people in Ulm were beginning to look downtrodden, Münchners had taken on a most unhealthy pallor. There, too, no colour seemed to exist – the bleached grey dominated buildings, clothes, hair, skin, the barks of trees, pavements, birds, dogs. And no one was smiling – not one person in the train or on the streets or in the café where she and Frau Wilhelm bought a dingy cup of coffee and a slice of mouldy cake. Everyone hurried with heads bent, intent on getting wherever they needed to go, except the dreaded Wehrmacht soldiers, SS and anyone in uniform who strolled along, presenting themselves as smart and well-fed, arrogant and entitled.

It was horrible and Annie found herself walking at the same clipped pace as everyone else, keeping her gaze on her feet or the pram wheels, not smiling or nodding or engaging in any conversation with Frau Wilhelm other than the necessary statements such as: 'We turn right here' or 'Mind your footing there'. Again, in startling contrast, the soldiers laughed too long and talked too loudly amongst themselves as if trying to convince everyone of their courage with shows of bravado. For a second, she lifted her eyes and they faltered on one young Wehrmacht officer standing next to, but apart from, two of his comrades. His gaze cut towards her and there was nothing coming from him – no sense of self-righteousness or pride, no bluster or bluff. He was in the same position as Fred, she thought, before they both blinked their eyes elsewhere. She wondered how many of those young men despised their lot in the same way both he and Fred did. If only they could band together and rise up against the regime. But they, like all of them, must keep their eyes averted and the truth in their hearts hidden.

At the university gates, Frau Wilhelm asked Annie if she would be alright. She wasn't sure she would be, but of course she couldn't say that having dragged both of them all that way.

'Two hours?' Frau Wilhelm asked, holding up her fingers. 'Is one enough for you?'

Frau Wilhelm seemed surprised but said, 'Of course.'

Annie watched her walk away, then made her way to the department she used to work in. She didn't recognise anyone and was asked by several people how they could help her. She mentioned a few names but they shook their heads at each one with explanations such as the person had married and moved away or joined the military or was working elsewhere. One girl who she had particularly liked had died when her house exploded because of a gas leak. She had been young enough to still wear her hair in plaits across her head and her arms had been covered in freckles. It was so sad to think that whilst she had been giving birth, that young woman had her life blown out of her. Sadder, though, was the matter-of-fact way the news was divulged.

Next, she walked through familiar corridors to the dining halls. It was always cold through those dark, chilly passageways but it was more than the draughts that made her shiver. She remembered the times she had walked side by side with Fred or Ilse or Gustav, making their way to share lunch together, deep in thought about the next moves within their resistance group. After so many of their comrades had been imprisoned and executed, she had wondered if their efforts had been worth the outcome. How dare she think that such a paltry gathering of inexperienced young people, with nothing going for them but their idealistic attitudes, could make any difference? But tucked in next to the journal in her underwear drawer was their leaflet, evidence that their attempts at rallying others had reached the hands and minds of those far beyond the immediate vicinity and their most outlandish hopes.

A few people turned and stared at her, a woman with a baby carriage coming into the dining hall – not a usual sight in a university. Scanning the tables and benches, she quickly ascertained there was no one there she recognised so turned the pram and headed back the way she'd come before any questions could be asked. She felt lost and out of her depth and decided she should admit a foolish defeat. She would wait by the gates for Frau Wilhelm.

A group of men, gesticulating and talking about something that seemed deep and serious, stepped to one side to let her pass. 'Thank you,' she said without looking at them. Then a hand, spotted with irregular brown marks and sprouting wiry hairs, reached out and touched her arm. Reminded of the recent undesirable advances in Ulm, she drew back as if she'd been stung. 'Fraulein Scholz,' the man said. 'Annie?'

When she gave herself a chance to look, she saw it was one of their old comrades.

'Professor Frans.' She breathed out, her hand reaching out to meet his.

He glanced at the pram. 'I heard you were expecting a baby.'

'Yes, yes,' she said. 'This is my Walti.'

He continued to scrutinise her instead of looking at the baby. That was something she wasn't used to. 'And I heard that the father, your husband, died in Russia.'

Again she said, 'Yes. He was a medic.'

Professor Frans nodded knowingly and in his narrowed eyes there was such a familiar depth of understanding that Annie thought she would cry without being able to stop.

'Come into my office, Frau...?'

'You can still call me Annie,' she sniffled.

'Wait one moment.' She watched him catch up with his colleagues who were waiting for him at the end of the hallway. They exchanged a few words and then he turned back towards her with a rather jaded stride.

'Here,' he said. 'This door.'

He ushered her into a leather chair and manoeuvred the pram to where she could see Walti, breathing in and breathing out; Annie mirrored the rhythm of the baby's shallow puffing and felt, if not as peaceful as him, at least a bit calmer.

'Would you like a snifter of brandy?' Professor Frans asked.

That broke the tension she had been feeling and she snorted in a most unladylike manner. 'Thank you, but I am meeting my mother-in-law and she will not let me out again on my own if she smells alcohol on my breath.'

He laughed with her. 'Well, coffee?'

She considered, then said. 'No, I will have that brandy, thank you.'

'Good,' he said.

Whilst he rooted around in his filing cabinet and took out two glasses and a bottle, Annie looked at the books piled on his desk and leaning lopsidedly on the shelves. Their dark green, blue and burgundy covers were comforting, reminding her that there had been better times than this and that there would be time, in the future, to concentrate on thoughts and ideas other than how and when this war would finish. Professor Frans put a glass in front of her and lifted his in a toast. 'Ahh,' he said after his first sip and she nodded in agreement.

Never one to miss a trick, Professor Frans realised she had been surveying his array of books because he swept his hand towards a pile and said, 'These are not mine.'

'Then whose?' she asked him. 'Are you storing them for a colleague?'

He shook his head and leaned in closer towards her. 'My

books were stolen from me by the…' His index and middle finger went under his nose and his arm shot out in front of him. When he finished with the salute they all hated, his nostrils flared as if a putrid smell had filled the room. 'Years ago they marched in, raided my library and burned my books along with many others. Thomas Mann, gone. Erich Maria Remarque, gone. Émile Zola, Jack London, gone, gone, all gone. These,' he said, spittle gathering in tiny dots on his bottom lip, 'are what they left in their stead.'

He thrust a black bound edition of something or other by Werner Beumelburg – who she knew wrote about camaraderie and good times to be had on the front line – towards her. He ran a finger along another pile and held up the dust for her to see. Again he inclined his head. 'I refuse to read them and when this war is finished I will take them outside and burn each and every one of them.'

'I will join you. If I may.'

'Yes, Annie. You may.' They each sipped their brandy, then Professor Frans asked her bluntly why she was at the university with Walti.

She hesitated. Although very unlikely, it was still wise to consider everyone as if they might be in the pay of the SS. But she decided that she didn't want to be that sort of suspicious person. She drew herself up tall and told him about finding the crumpled leaflet Fred had authored.

He seemed to turn over the information in his mind and smiled as if he was thinking about an old friend who conjured up happy memories.

'It was on the ground in the marketplace. In Ulm. Someone told me it was dropped by the RAF and I wanted to verify that was a fact.'

'Yes,' he said. 'That has been happening. It's good.'

'It is. And I wanted to see if I could help. In any way.'

But before he replied, Annie knew what the answer would be. She could tell by the atmosphere in the university, the weary, rather cynical tone in Professor Frans' voice, the lack of old contacts. 'Do you remember Helmuth?' he said.

'Yes, he has been in prison for eight months, so I believe.'

'Well he was, but I thought you might have missed the news during your confinement,' he said. 'He has been executed.'

'I cannot believe it.' Anger and sadness churned together inside her creating a foul-tasting bile that rose from her stomach.

'Oh, Annie,' he said in that same fatigued tone. 'I do not think that is the case. Even you must, by now, accept this as normal. Is that not so?'

She nodded. It was true. She knew that the regime would undertake any barbaric, uncivilised or brutish deed in order to remain in power.

'There is no one left here that I can put you in touch with, Annie,' he said. 'They are all gone, other than old men like me. Go home, take care of your baby and pray that your brother returns.'

She finished her brandy in one gulp, turned the pram and then stretched across the desk to formalise their goodbye. He took her hand in both of his and said, 'You have done so much already.'

She shook her head.

'You have no idea, but you have been wonderfully brave.'

Outside, Frau Wilhelm strode towards her with a smile

of relief on her face. 'Did you see who you wanted to see?' she asked.

'No,' Annie answered. 'They've all gone. How is your sister?'

'Weak. And fragile.'

Like this city, she thought and the people in it.

23 November 1943

This morning my unwarranted suitor revealed himself in the most improper manner. I thought I was being cautious and wary, but as I drew level with the passageway that leads to the butcher's shop, a man in a diesel factory uniform stepped out in front of me. My heart somersaulted and landed hammering in my throat. Then I recognised him as a boy who Fred sometimes kicked a football with during the summer. He stood, hands in pockets, smiling at me in a rather fatuous way. He called me by my name, but I struggled to remember his, then it came to me – Dietmar.

Not wanting to unfairly denounce him when I didn't know if he was, in fact, my tormenter, I nodded and made to walk around him and carry on with my business. But he blocked my way and shoved me into the alley. I kept one hand on the handle of the pram, dragging it behind me and cried out, but there was no one to hear. I'd heard about girls who were violated by soldiers or interfered with by drunken men, but never thought I would be in their position. Everything in me was electrified and I wanted to kick, punch, bite, spit but Dietmar pushed me against the wall and whispered that he'd liked me since we were small and now that Walther was gone, he wanted to have me. Two of his teeth were black and his breath smelled of rotting pork. I flailed around, bashing the back of my head against the wall and tried in desperation to knock the chassis of the pram into the back of his legs. Rather than frighten him off, that only served to make him laugh and explore the skin under my scarf with his scratching, dirt-encrusted fingers.

Then, just when I thought I would have to suffer his molestations there was the sound of boots, clumping on the flagstones and a flash of brown from the other end of the passageway. I don't know where my presence of mind came from, but the intrusion gave me enough time to kick Dietmar hard in the shin and duck out from under his grasp. I took one, cursory look over my shoulder to make sure he wasn't following me and I caught a glimpse of two Wehrmacht officers, the first pinning Dietmar's arms to his sides and the second pressing his forearm hard into the assailant's windpipe. All I could think about was getting away with Walti, so I wasn't convinced, but I thought the tallest and heaviest-handed officer was Horst. And the more I think about it and turn the episode over in my mind, the more certain I am that it was him. Horst, of all people, was my hero and the upholder of my dignity.

The letterbox rattled and Frau Wilhelm and Annie looked at each other, thinking the same thing – it was Horst again. Frau Wilhelm must have presumed Annie wouldn't want to see him, so she drew back her shoulders, fastened her cardigan, set her mouth in a straight line and gave Annie a look that meant she would get rid of him.

But Annie had thought long and hard about what had happened with Dietmar and made up her mind that when next Horst called, she would thank him and try to rekindle the feelings she had for him as her younger cousin and make sure she found him a piece of cake.

Both women made it to the door at the same time to find no one on the other side but there was an envelope, facing down, on the mat. Annie gasped when she turned it over, the half-crossed Ts and looped Gs enough for her to know it was from Fred.

Annie held it close, desperate to open it but wanting to savour the moment. She and Frau Wilhelm sat close together in the living room and Annie slit the envelope with care. Inside were two pages of regulation army writing paper. She unfolded them and read with reverence.

Congratulations and well done to you, my Liebling Annie. Although I have not seen him yet, I have formed a perfect picture in my mind of my little nephew Walti from your description. I know that your husband died a hero for the Third Reich, but I want to reassure you that you and your child will always have my love and protection.

Annie had to read through that paragraph again to believe her eyes. Icy cold fear churned in her bowels. 'Has he been brainwashed or indoctrinated into the ways of the regime?' she asked Frau Wilhelm.

'No, no, of course not,' Frau Wilhelm said. 'He is protecting himself and us. Now, read on.'

I long to hold you both close and tell you this in person, but that is not possible at the moment. Just know it in your wonderful heart, Annie. For me, you and Walti and my fiancée mean more than anything in this world and I will fight for all of you.

Give my special thanks to Herr Doctor and Frau Wilhelm for all they do for you and I hope that in victory, we can share a glass of schnapps together.

Here he did not state whose victory, but she knew what he meant.

The second page was more about logistics and had been heavily censored.

I am in -----, having been posted here from -----. We have -----, -----, ----- and ---- for our rations and ----- blankets to keep us warm at night. I am well and very happy to be doing my duty for the Fatherland.

Please write to me, Annie, as your letters are such a comfort; I keep them together in my Bible and have read them so many times over that the paper has worn thin. I will write as often as I can, but as I'm sure you know, the post from here is slow or perhaps non-existent in some cases.

As a Wehrmacht soldier on the -----, I can assure you we will all be together again soon and I will take my proper place amongst you as brother, uncle, friend,

*benefactor and patron. Especially to our Walti who I am
already devoted to completely.*

   Heil Hitler!
   Your loving Brother
   Frederick

They read and devoured the letter three times and ended
up with tears in their eyes. 'He is alive,' Annie said.

'Yes, and let's hope that his predictions about the end
being in sight come to fruition.'

'I wish I had your faith,' Annie said, realising that in the
last two minutes they had mentioned faith and hope.

But what about charity, the most important of the
three virtues? That was apparent in the love and devotion
expressed in Fred's letter to them. And in Horst's unforeseen,
unexpected but most laudable act of chivalry.

15

December 1943

There were two weeks until Christmas. In Scotland, Jeanie told Viola, Christmas was a quiet affair, but Hogmanay was a different matter altogether. The Barfoots would invite as many friends and family as they could fit into their farmhouse and there would be food, drink and reels. Of course, Viola and Freddie were invited and although it was difficult for Voila to imagine such wild revelry during these austere times, she was looking forward to the occasion.

But, she thought as she opened the back door to shake out a rug, she would like to do something to celebrate Freddie's first Christmas. That day was, after all, a huge part of the baby's heritage and it was awful enough that they would be missing their family let alone the traditions she was used to observing.

Like a fascinated child, Viola puffed frozen billows of mist into the air and watched as they gradually dispersed into thin silvery wisps. It was bitterly cold; snow covered the ground and it was only possible to pick out sheep in the distance when they moved. She smiled when she remembered one of the first questions she'd had about the surroundings when she moved here – where do the sheep go when it snows? Nowhere, was the answer, except those on very high ground that can be rounded up and moved to lower pastures where it might be a bit warmer. Pulling Lillian's old brown cardigan around her, she shivered in her stockinged legs. The rug would have to do, she thought, retreating to the kitchen and closing the door behind her.

Viola tiptoed to the crib to look in on Freddie, sleeping on her side with her thumb in her mouth. After that first night when the baby had slept through, there had been arduous months of trying to settle her into a proper routine and Viola had worried the baby might have assimilated much more than she was given credit for about the circumstances of her birth and their evacuation to Sorn. But now, with perseverance and the help of that little plug of a thumb, life was easier and more structured. What light there was from the heavy sky cast a shadow of Freddie's eyelashes that played, for a moment, across her cheeks; the contours of her face, fleshing out and caving in with each fierce pull on the substitute teat; her hair, dark and thick fell about her ear and neck in waves. In that moment, Viola wanted to pluck her from sleep, wake her and savour every bit of her. But that would be madness, especially given how often she had longed for the little mite to sleep and give her a break. And how many times Jeanie had taken over for an hour or two and instructed her to have a lie-down.

As quietly as possible, Viola took dry napkins from the clotheshorse and replaced them with wet clothing. Not for the first time she wondered what she would do without Jeanie and Finlay. She didn't know how or why she had been so lucky to have landed firmly on her feet with those two. They could not have been more welcoming or accommodating; it was almost as if the only reason they needed to be magnanimous was that she was a human being who required comfort and help – it was humbling.

After the telegram from Mum had arrived telling her about the news of Robert's death in action, she had been beside herself with anguish. She had tortured herself with the fact that he hadn't known he was an uncle and that her letters to him, via Mum, had been based on a lie. Her dreams, when Freddie had allowed her to sleep, had been focused on her brother. Often, they would be running around a tennis court, serving aces or producing drop shots from the net, chasing after poorly aimed balls. Sometimes David would appear, too, hanging around waiting to play the winner. And there, on the side-lines, was Pitch, tongue lolling, alert and following every rally with a swivel of his regal head.

In one particular dream that she'd experienced a good few times, she'd seen Robert as he had looked when they'd last been together at his eighteenth birthday party. Tall, handsome, angsty, brooding. Waiting to join the RAF even if it was against their father's wishes. He'd wanted to be a hero and now he had fulfilled that longing in the most conclusive manner possible. She had once read that it was no good thinking about what-ifs when someone dies as those possibilities simply do not exist – there was never anything else on the cards for that particular person so their death, when it came, must be accepted. That theory had seemed logical and sensible when she was yet to experience the death of a loved one and she had thought she could implement that wisdom when the time came for her to be bereaved. But it had been anathema to her after Robert died. All she could think about was the person he had not had the chance to become.

She had wanted her mum, Fred or Lillian. Even David or Dad would have had their arms tight around her and she could have cried on their necks. But instead there had been the devoted Jeanie who had come up to her every day during that month, bringing food that had only to be heated, lighting the fire, washing napkins, jiggling the baby. Jeanie had told her that she and Finlay, try as they might, had not been able to have children.

'There's still time, surely?' Viola had asked.

'Oh, aye.' Jeanie had shrugged. 'There's a wee bit of that. But Fin and I decided that we cannae let it stop us being happy. So we find comfort without bairns.'

Easier said than done, Viola had thought. But that had given her some insight into their attachment to each other and the fun that was always present when they were together.

After much deliberation, Viola had told Jeanie about Fred, Mike and how Freddie had come to be. Her head on one side, Jeanie had listened without making any outward sign or murmur of disapproval. But when she'd finished her story and Jeanie had not responded, Viola had felt a tingling of fear crawl down her arms and into the tips of her fingers. Perhaps she should have kept that information to herself; the Barfoots were, after all, churchgoers and might have been offended by a fallen woman in their croft.

'Och, hen, so sad,' Jeanie had said at last, distress lacing her voice. 'We knew you weren't married, but we didn't know the surrounding circumstances.'

'But you both called me Mrs Baxter from the first time we met.'

'We thought that would be the most befitting course of action.'

'Yes, of course. It was. Is.'

'Do you want people to know otherwise?'

Viola had shaken her head with conviction. 'No. I don't think others would be as understanding as you.'

Jeanie had agreed but said she didn't know why as she could name a fair few around Sorn and Ayr who had been in the same position and had then gone on to marry the father or another man who turned a blind eye to the indiscretion – her own dear, deceased mother for one.

But now, Viola was beginning to feel better. Not any less bereaved, but resigned to the process that bereavement would take – she wasn't sure where her grief or dreams or thoughts and feelings would take her, but she would follow them down their natural paths and deal with them there. Knowing that she could do that gave her strength and she needed fortitude and tenacity to be a good mother to Freddie.

Her dreams, too, no longer centred on Robert alone, but had reverted to Fred, which was comforting as during her waking hours she was alarmed to find that his image in her mind was becoming a pinprick. It was as if he was in the distance, watching and waiting for her still, but try as she might she could not bring him closer, where she longed for him to be. At night, though, when she closed her eyes he was there as he had been when they were courting in Cambridge. She could see his startling blue eyes that were never tempted away from gazing at her, almost feel his thick brindled hair between her fingers, breathe in the musty scent of his soap and a warm spring day on his skin. His breath on her neck, his hands on her hips, the shape of his fingernails, the warmth of his mouth on hers. Sometimes she woke with a start, certain that he was there with her, only to be crestfallen when what she had been convinced was his side of the bed remained cold and uncrumpled. In the morning after those dreams had visited her, she opened Fred's incomplete thesis and the resistance leaflet and stroked them or held them close to where the ring glanced her chest.

Jeanie came to the croft less often now, but insisted Viola and Freddie spend as much time as possible with her and Finlay in the main house. Initially, Viola had thought she might be intruding but soon felt comfortable enough to come and go as she pleased. Finlay was often busy with the sheep and the farm and when he was at home for meals and a bit of rest time, he was amiable and easy-going, fitting in with whatever Jeanie was doing. If dinner was a few minutes late, that was fine; if the floor had that minute been scrubbed then he would use the other door; if the baby was fractious then of course he would walk up and down with her to give the two women a break.

With Jeanie, a profound friendship had taken root and grew in depth with the amount of time they spent together. Viola felt such ease with her hostess that they were able to talk about many things in great detail and to laugh at themselves, each other and the world at large; she knew that no matter what happened after this stage in her life, Jeanie would always be a part of it. Of course, no one could take Lillian's place, she thought, stroking the faithful cardigan, but there was room in her heart for more than one intimate friend. Besides, in time she hoped that Jeanie and Lillian would meet and get on well; she felt certain they would.

Careful to avoid creaks and squeaks on the stairs, Viola went into the bedroom to tidy up. She opened the curtains and wiped away the half-frozen condensation on the inside of the window then opened it a crack to let in some fresh air. The glacial mist had not lifted and she wondered if she would, as planned, walk down to the house. She wondered that every day when the weather was so cold and inhospitable, but was pleased when she wrapped up and headed out.

Lillian was on her mind so much this morning. She longed to see her and talk with her like they had on countless occasions. But for now, letters would have to suffice and there were plenty of those flying backwards and forwards. Viola kept every single one in a special drawer, along with letters and cards from Mum and the boys. At the bottom of the pile was the black-edged telegram that told her she would never receive another letter, card, smile or touch from Robert.

The most exciting news from London was that Lillian and George had become engaged. Viola wrote back immediately.

I knew it. You tried so hard to keep it hidden, but you can't keep anything from me! Besides, it was plastered all over both of your faces.

Lillian had replied:

Honestly, Vi, I promise I was not trying to hide anything from you. But I think I was trying to conceal my true feelings from myself. However, now that I've let them out into the open, I couldn't be happier. But my sympathy and understanding of your plight is so much more acute now. I know that to have no knowledge of my Good Old George's whereabouts or any contact with him would tear me apart. I weep for you.

That had made her cry. For herself and for the injustice of the situation. She had shared the letter with Jeanie and they had dabbed at their eyes together.

Mum wrote that David could not wait to join the RAF next year and Viola knew that she would be beside herself with fear and worry about his safety when the time came, as would she. She and David exchanged letters in the same convoluted way Dad had decreed and she was tempted to suggest to Mum that perhaps now David could be told the truth, but she didn't want to give her parents any more heartbreak to deal with. When she wrote to Mum, she used the opportunity to mention Freddie's smile, or how she grabbed Viola's finger and held on as if it was something of great value, her efforts to roll over, the dimples in her knuckles. And Mum acknowledged those anecdotes with exclamations of delight. *What a clever girl! You used to do that. I can picture her perfectly.* Although it was never mentioned, Viola hoped Mum shared the letters with Dad and that the little stories would begin to soften him.

In her last letter, Mum mentioned coming to visit during

the summer. Viola's heart thumped, seemed to miss a beat, then thumped again. She longed to have Mum here, to be folded in her lovely, plump arms and be a child again. No date was suggested, but Mum had thought about it in some detail because she wrote that she'd been in touch with Lillian to enquire if they could make the demanding journey together. Mum and Lillian visiting at the same time – it was more that she dared to hope for. She had written back that same day and let Mum know that she would be delighted to see both of them whenever they were ready to travel.

With Freddie fed and changed, Viola piled on two scarves, the silly brown tam o'shanter, which she hated to admit was very warm and handy to have, woollen mittens, a thick coat, hand knitted knee-high socks over her stockings and a pair of Jeanie's wellington boots. By the time she dressed Freddie in layer upon layer of cosy bonnets and matinee jackets and covered the pram with every blanket they possessed, it was impossible to make out the baby underneath. She laughed when she thought it could just have easily been a lamb nestled amongst the comfy material.

Lamb, she thought as she pushed the pram down the potholed track, was a dichotomy for her. The meat here was wonderful, but she had to steel herself to eat it because it reminded her so vividly of Fred and that awful last supper. Fin had said she would grow tired of lamb and his prediction had proved correct, but the guilt that went with that was overwhelming. How Mum and Lillian would have loved a slice of tender, mouth-watering lamb instead of the fatty, tough as old boot leather mutton they had to put up with when they could get it. But here they ate it, in one guise or another, almost every day and even though

Jeanie was inventive, the taste had become monotonous and tiresome. She supposed there would be some form of lamb for dinner today and that it would be the highlight of the Hogmanay buffet table. She sighed, not so much at the thought of lamb, but at the impatience she felt with her own grumbling dissatisfaction. *How churlish and ungrateful of me*, she admonished herself.

'Shoo.' She gently encouraged a small flock of the creatures out of her way. 'Go, girls,' she said a bit louder. 'Just for a minute so I can get past.' With a mixture of defiance and ignorance on their faces, the creatures chewed nonchalantly and stared at her. Sighing, she moved back onto one hip and her foot dislodged a stone. That startled one sheep into bolting and the others followed. Remembering Fin's warning not to spook them, she hoped they hadn't been too shocked.

Then she thought of chicken and her mouth watered. She could have, or should have, been worrying about the baby. Or the war. Or Mum, David, Fred and Annie. But of all the things to dwell on, she was stuck in an endless loop of intertwining thoughts about lamb, chicken and Christmas. She would love to invite Fin and Jeanie to the croft for a typical English Christmas dinner and that would involve serving chicken. But she couldn't ask her hosts for one of their own chickens, which they kept solely for eggs, so on the quiet she would have to find someone she could negotiate with for one of the feathered creatures. And that would be difficult as since Robert's death, Jeanie insisted on going everywhere with her.

When she came to a line of Scots pine trees, their dark orange bark and blue-green needles colourful against the white winter scene, she knew she was halfway to the farmhouse. In the distance she could see the slate-coloured bricks that walled the garden from the farm and the chimney puffing out plumes of grey smoke into the leaden sky. The oak tree was stripped bare and stood with its arthritic, snow-heavy branches reaching for any light in the sky. Viola thought she had never seen a more welcoming sight.

'Yoo-hoo, hen,' Jeanie sang when Viola turned the door handle. Protected as she was under a mountain of bedding, the noise didn't startle Freddie. 'Och, you poor thing. It's such a murky day.' She dusted her hands on her apron and helped Viola in with the pram. 'Do you get freezing fog like this in London?'

'Sometimes,' Viola said. 'But never as cold.'

'Take your things off, hen, and warm yourself by the fire.'

'Thank you, Jeanie. I was is in two minds about whether to come or not.'

'I would have been up that hill after you if you hadnae,' Jeanie said. 'Now, I cannae offer you tea as that husband of mine has had the last leaves in the tin. And here's me, dying for a cup.'

'I could have brought you some of mine, if I'd known,' Viola said.

'Aye, well, we'd need to sort out carrier pigeons or smoke signals or flag semaphore first.'

Viola laughed. 'Actually, that wouldn't be a bad idea.'

'So, hot milk?'

'Yes, thank you, that would be lovely,' Viola said. Then an idea occurred to her. 'Why don't I walk into Sorn and get us some tea?' She unclasped her handbag and peered into its depths. 'I've got my ration book with me,' she said.

'You cannae do that,' Jeanie said. 'You're like a block of ice as it is.'

'I've warmed up a bit,' Viola protested. 'And I find that walking in the cold air gives me a sense of well-being.'

Viola could tell that Jeanie was swayed by her longing for a cup of tea, so she seized the advantage. 'Besides,' Viola said. 'It will do me good to go to the shops by myself. It will give everyone the chance to see me as part of the scenery and start to get to know me.' Without making eye contact with Jeanie, Viola replaced her gloves and wellingtons and kept up a steady flow of chitchat. 'Anyway, I haven't taken off my coat yet so I'm ready to go.'

'I'm not sure,' Jeanie said. 'If we wait until after dinner we can walk down together.'

Viola stopped then and smiled. 'Please allow me to do this one little thing for you,' she said. 'A tiny payment for all your kindness to me.'

'We donnae want anything; we've told you that so many times.' Jeanie smiled in return. 'But a cup of tea would be so nice.'

'Won't be long,' Viola trilled over her shoulder as she headed out before Jeanie thought of another excuse to get her to stay.

The freezing fog danced in strange shapes over the fields and in front of the sheep's faces when they breathed out. Viola kept her head down so she could avoid hazards in the snow, but was spurred on by the thought that this might be her only chance to acquire that chicken. But from whom and how could she pay for it?

A large sheet of paper pinned to a sandwich board outside the newsagent's shop had come loose on one corner and was hanging limply in the still, icy air. Stopping, she folded back the edge to read the whole headline: LARGEST RAID ON BERLIN. It was hard to keep up with the news here. She didn't have a wireless and the Barfoots rarely tuned theirs in. But surely this was good news? The Allies must be making tremendous headway if they had, at this point in the war, the capacity and the manpower to produce such an immense push? Of course her next thoughts were for Fred and Annie but they were in Munich, not Berlin, so she presumed they were safe.

The realisation that she was kidding herself overwhelmed her in a rush. For a second, the path seemed to ripple under her and she had to lean back against the cold brick of the shop. How could she have any idea where Fred and Annie were or how they were? If alive, they might have moved to Berlin, or one or other of them could be in hospital, or they might be in the forests of Germany or Austria or Switzerland, trying desperately to escape back to England. But the leaflet told her that Fred was alive, at least until recently, and she told herself that she must hold on to that. Feeling for the ring under her layers, she prodded it until the skin on her chest felt tender, then she gathered herself together and went in to buy a copy of the *Daily Record* to read later.

At Grannach's Groceries she joined the queue and waited to be served, wondering all the while about how she could broach the subject of procuring a chicken. 'Hello, hen,' Mrs Grannach greeted her. 'On your own today? Our Jeanie not unwell, I hope.'

'No, Mrs Grannach, Jeanie is perfectly fine, thank you. I've volunteered to get tea as we're all desperate for a cup at the farmhouse.' She handed over her ration book to be stamped.

'Och, well, it's tea that'll win this war,' Mrs Grannach said, reaching to lift down a canister from the shelf behind her. 'How's the wee bairn?'

Viola smiled. 'She's coming on beautifully. Thank you for asking.' She leaned forward a bit. 'Mrs Grannach, do you know where I can get a chicken?' she asked.

'A chicken, hen?' Mrs Grannach said, unaware of how funny the question sounded. 'You won't have enough rations to buy one, I'm afraid.'

'No, I thought as much. I was going to try to bargain for one. It's for a surprise Christmas dinner for Jeanie and Fin.'

'What a lovely wee thought. Well, there's Mr and Mrs Selkirk right on the other side of town; they might be persuaded. Or there's young Bryce at the motorbike shop.'

'Chickens at the motorbike shop?' Viola asked.

'Oh, aye. Bryce lives with his parents on the premises and they keep quite a few.'

Viola thanked Mrs Grannach, apologised to the queue for taking such a long time and stepped out into the whitewashed cold. She thought about her two options and based on proximity, decided to try the motorcycle shop first. Besides, she was fascinated to see such an incongruous set-up as chickens alongside motorcycles. Oil next to corn feed; the twin sounds of clucking hens and revving engines; feathers and tyres lying next to each other.

She and Jeanie had passed this way on numerous occasions, but because the premises lay back from the road she had never scrutinised them to any degree. As she walked in off the pavement, she could see marked bays on the concreted forecourt and each of them housed one or more militaristic motorcycle in some stage of repair. The building was signposted with boards telling drivers which way was in and which was out, where to go for spare parts and a door that announced itself as 'Reception'. 'Cameron Motorcycle Repairs' was emblazoned in red lettering across the front of the building.

She had expected to hear machinery and grinding metal and the clanking of tools, or to see men in overalls peering into the depths of engines. But it was eerily quiet and there was not a feathered fowl in sight. Standing still, she listened for the sounds of pecking and clucking and to her amazement, could make out soft chicken noises from around the back. And when the light, misty breeze shifted, the distinct smell of chicken muck wafted towards her.

She had hoped to ask someone to point out Bryce to her and then to approach him here, but she had no other choice than to go into the reception area as if she was an official visitor. The thought of the superficial reason for her visit made her blush especially when the work being undertaken here was so vital. Nevertheless, she squared her shoulders and tried the door handle. It was then she saw the handwritten sign saying reception was closed for the dinner break and please try later. She checked her watch and hesitated, wondering if she had enough time to make it to the Selkirks' and back without Jeanie worrying about how long she'd taken to buy tea.

I'm halfway there, she thought, marching back the way she'd come, *so in for a penny, in for a pound.*

'Hello,' a voice stopped her. 'I heard your rattle.'

Turning, she saw a young man leaning out of the door, wiping around his mouth with a cotton cloth.

'I do beg your pardon,' Viola said, aware of how out of place she must look. 'I didn't mean to interrupt your dinner. I can come back another time if more convenient.'

Bryce, or so she presumed, stepped out and shook his head. 'No need,' he said. 'My afters can wait.'

He was wearing a blue, chambray shirt and unbuttoned grey overalls with the sleeves hanging around his waist, probably to allow him to eat without spreading dirt over his food.

'Bryce Cameron? My name is Viola Baxter.'

'Aye,' he said. 'You're billeted with the Barfoots.'

'Yes, I am.'

'Pleased to meet you. How can I help?' He folded his arms and looked bemused, waiting for her reply.

He was rather short, but stocky with well-built arms and his blue-black hair was slicked back off his forehead with what Viola thought might be some kind of mechanical grease; his dark, heavy eyebrows looked oiled into place, too. The skin over his cheekbones was taut and his nose was a little bent, as if it had once been broken. His half-smile was generous, so steeling herself, Viola said, 'I was told... Well, I asked and someone said that... I'm trying to get hold of a...'

'Motorcycle part?' he offered. 'This is the place for that. But if you don't mind me saying you don't look as if—'

'A chicken.'

'A chicken,' Bryce repeated. 'Aye, well. I cannae say that's an everyday request.'

Viola didn't know what else to say, so watched him and waited for a response.

'And that might be a bit more difficult. Can I ask what you want to keep one for? Eggs? The feathers?'

Viola sighed and blinked her eyes closed against the tension of the conversation. 'I don't want to keep a chicken, Mr Cameron,' she said. 'I want to cook it and serve it to the Barfoots as a Christmas surprise.'

Bryce seemed to be at a total loss, but said, 'Aye, well. We're having lamb.'

'Yes, and that's what the Barfoots would be having but I want to thank them for how kind they've been to me. With a chicken.'

Viola could hear a rough, sandpaper scuff as Bryce rubbed his face with his hand. 'We usually trade our chickens,' he said.

Viola made a decision. 'Look,' she said. 'Thank you ever so much and I'm dreadfully sorry I bothered you, but I think perhaps I shouldn't have asked. I'll stick with lamb like everyone else.' Raising her hand to say goodbye, she turned towards the road.

'Mrs Baxter. Wait.'

When she looked back, Bryce was hurrying towards her. 'I'm sure we can come to some arrangement,' he said. 'And I think Fin and Jeanie would be delighted with your idea.'

Viola walked back into the forecourt. 'It's just that, I cannot imagine I have enough rations, or money to pay you.' She raised her hands skyward in a helpless gesture.

'Then never mind. Let's break the rules for once. We've got a few hens, so I'm sure we won't miss one.'

It was, of course, the perfect solution but Viola didn't like to think he was doing her such a huge favour. 'What can I offer in return?' she asked, racking her brain. 'I'm quite good at paperwork, or filing? I'd have to bring the baby with me but—'

'I donnae expect anything, Mrs Baxter.' And he sounded as if he meant it. 'I'll deliver the bird on Christmas Eve in time for you to get her ready.'

'I can't thank you enough,' Viola said, then realised she had never done anything more with a chicken than pop it into the oven. 'But what will I have to do to prepare it?'

Bryce crossed his arms and gave her the same partially amused smile as Fin when anything was said about a rural way of life. 'Would you like me to wring its neck, pluck, quarter and hang it for you?'

Viola felt sheepish but nodded her head. 'Yes, please,' she murmured. 'I wouldn't know where to start.'

Bryce laughed out loud then extended his hand to shake on the arrangement.

Jeanie in particular had protested before accepting Viola's invitation for Christmas Day, then Fin had joined her in saying it was too much trouble, the croft kitchen was too small and they thought she needed rest rather than running around after them. But eventually they caved in and said yes graciously. When Bryce knocked at the door and handed her the fat, succulent chicken, she gave him a hand-knitted scarf wrapped in paper on which she'd drawn sprigs of holly. It was a token gesture that she had deliberated about as she didn't want to give him the wrong impression. His eyes grew large with surprise. 'There was no need, Mrs Baxter.'

'Well, I am most grateful and wanted to show my appreciation.' And she hoped that would be that.

In between feeding and tending to Freddie, Viola spent Christmas Eve preparing. She filled the chicken's cavity with homemade stuffing then sewed the pitted flaps of skin over the hole; she boiled gizzards for gravy; peeled potatoes that she intended to mash and roast; parboiled parsnips and carrots and fashioned what would pass as a Christmas pudding. With the leftover sultanas and peel she made skew-whiff lattice-topped mince pies. There would be a spoonful of custard each and a shot or two of whisky. When Freddie was in bed for the night, Viola turned her hand to laying the table, cutting out paper crowns and hanging a wreath of pinecones on the door. She was glad to be busy as it kept her from brooding too much about how she longed to be making these preparations for Fred and her family.

By the time the Barfoots arrived after the morning church service, Viola was ready and excited. 'Happy Christmas, hen,' Jeanie warbled.

'Happy Christmas to both of you,' Viola said, kissing her friends on their cheeks.

Fin and Jeanie took it in turns to remark on every detail of Viola's preparations, sounding genuinely surprised and pleased to have such a fuss made in their honour. 'The smell,' Jeanie said. 'Och, no. It cannae be...' She looked at Fin, her mouth open as if waiting for the first forkful.

'Is it chicken?' Fin asked. 'I havenae noticed any missing from the henhouse.'

Viola ushered them in, took their outdoor clothes, poured whisky for all of them and told her story.

'Well done, Viola,' Fin said. 'Very resourceful.'

'Aye,' said Jeanie. 'And very secretive.'

Viola had taken beads off an old jumper and sewn them around a plain hairclip, which she wrapped and gave to Jeanie. For Fin, she had scrubbed and polished a round, blue-veined stone and said she thought he could use it as a paperweight or doorstop. He turned it over and over in his hand, admiring the colours and heft. 'Thank you, Vi, you are resourceful indeed,' he said.

'I'm going to save my gift to wear on Hogmanay,' Jeanie said. 'It will match my dress perfectly. This is for you.' She held out a tubular-shaped parcel wrapped in brown paper.

The shape was intriguing as was the light weight. 'Whatever can this be?'

'Open it and see,' Jeanie demanded.

When Viola did so, she saw a piece of thick, rolled artist's paper. Unfurling it revealed a full-length pen and ink drawing of her pressing Freddie to her face. In the background was the oak tree in full leaf. Watercolours had been used to highlight sections of the picture – pink-washed cheeks and lips, green leaves, a yellow blanket and sapphire sky. Viola gasped and her hand flew to the ring beneath her collar. 'It's beautiful. Much more than that,' she said. 'I don't know what to say.'

'We thought it would always remind you of your time in Scotland,' Jeanie said.

'I will never forget Scotland or either of you.' Viola threw her arms around Jeanie's neck, then Fin's. 'But who is the artist? You, Jeanie? Or Fin?'

'Neither,' said Fin. 'It's by the equally resourceful Donald.'

'Well, I never,' Viola said. 'He's a dark horse.'

'Aye, well. A lot of his paintings are hanging in houses

around and about so we thought we'd commission one for you.'

Viola couldn't take her eyes off it. 'It's perfect,' she said.

After dinner, which went down a treat, Fin held Freddie whilst Viola and Jeanie cleared the dishes. 'Bryce,' Jeanie said. 'Such a nice young man. Hardworking and from a good family.'

'Are you trying to set me up, Jeanie?' Viola asked playfully.

'I wouldn't dream of interfering, hen, I'm just mentioning what a good catch he is.'

'But there's Fred.' Viola suddenly felt defensive.

Jeanie put an arm around her and Viola could smell a light, heathery perfume and alcohol on her breath. 'I'm sorry, Vi. It's just that… I'm ever so fond of you and want you to be happy.'

Viola knew she could never be happy without Fred. If he wouldn't have her, then she would make a life on her own with Freddie. She looked into Jeanie's eyes and saw nothing there but good intentions, so hugged her back then stepped around the house closing the blackouts. 'Who's for a game of charades?' she said in a cheery voice, wondering again if she had somehow overstepped the mark with Bryce. But then she pushed the thought to the back of her mind and the evening returned to a jolly celebration.

The party shouted, 'Flowers of Edinburgh!' And when the fiddlers started up Bryce grabbed her hand and in a group of four, Viola soon picked up the repeating steps and for most of the number, held her own. When the reel finished, they stood in a square, gasping, laughing and congratulating themselves on their prowess. The dance had been so energetic and she'd had to concentrate so hard, that it wasn't until it was over that she wondered if perhaps Bryce was thinking along the same lines as Jeanie.

'Thank you for the scarf, Mrs Baxter,' he said. 'It's a treat to wear in the yard during this weather.'

He touched her elbow and turned in the direction of the buffet table, but before she could follow his lead she saw that he was distracted by a group of new arrivals. Amongst them was a slender young woman with auburn hair and an uptilted nose; Bryce couldn't take his eyes off her. Nodding, Viola excused him from his gentlemanly responsibilities and watched him make his way with a jaunty stride straight to the young woman, whose side he didn't leave for the rest of the evening. Viola allowed her shoulders to drop and she breathed out – no harm done, but she told herself she'd have to be very careful in the future.

The blackouts were drawn against any enemy operative, but if there was a gap in the material, Viola wondered what a German Messerschmitt crew would make of Hogmanay. She knew from her German exchange trips and conversations with Fred that Germans loved their Karneval and Oktoberfest, too, so perhaps they would peer in through the window and then, out of a deep-rooted sense of shared humanity, let them get on with it.

All the men wore kilts; the women a sparkly dress or blouse or necklace. Lit candles stood in various holders. There were a few elegant silver sticks that looked as though they might have some value, sentimental or otherwise, metal chamber sticks and old jam jars housing snubs of wax and wonky wicks. There was no room for a sit-down meal, but the buffet table held lamb, of course, corned beef and spam fritters, cauliflower cheese with bacon lardons, shortbread, cheese and potato dumplings, fruit shortcake, potato scones, oat macaroons, apple chutney, root vegetable mash and Viola's leftover mince pies. Everyone had brought a dish to share and most had donated a bottle of something to drink. This was so very different from the parties that Mum and Dad had hosted, with Mrs Bishop chipping away to excavate information that she could use to humiliate others and people comparing their children's so-called talents and ambitions and everyone addressing each other with formality. Here, people called each other by their Christian names, slapped one another on the back and linked arms to walk from one end of the room to the other. They enquired about health and happiness, not the accruement of money and rank.

Then she remembered Mum defending her, Mum visiting her in London and the fun they'd had, Mum dragging herself around mother and baby homes to find one she thought would be best. And Dad. Looking back she felt sure he had not allowed her engagement for the best of reasons, to protect her; she could see that now she had Freddie. *Perhaps*, she thought, *we are all nothing more than the product of our surroundings and the limits of our environment.*

'The Hamilton Jig!' Another cry went up and Viola was plucked from the corner of the room by the vicar. Then it was the Gay Gordons, which had Viola laughing from start to end. When it finished, she found herself clapping for the fiddlers with Fin. 'Did Jeanie give you the card?' he said in puffs.

'No.' She shook her head and wondered who it could

be from, she'd had cards and letters from everyone she expected to send Christmas greetings.

'Och, in the excitement Jeanie must have forgotten.' He steered her towards his wife who was in deep conversation with Mr and Mrs Selkirk.

'Are you enjoying yourself, hen?' Jeanie asked, the embellished clip sparkling in her strawberry-blonde hair.

'Very much, thank you,' Viola said. 'It's all fantastic.'

'Jeanie, did we forget about the card that arrived this morning?' Fin asked.

'Och, aye. Oh, Vi, I am so sorry. What with one thing and another...'

'There's no need to apologise,' Viola said.

'It's behind the clock in the kitchen. You know where that is. Help yourself.'

Viola found the white envelope sandwiched between a shopping list and a note from Donald. It had Mum's writing on it so perhaps it was something extra from David. Tearing open the envelope, she drew out a small card with a picture of a girl in Victorian dress skating on a pond. Inside, Mum had written *Season's Greetings to Vi and Freddie. We are thinking about both of you all the time. X.* But Viola didn't dwell on the lovely sentiment because her eyes darted to the bottom of the page where there was a note from Dad. Seeing the writing was like a jolt and she had to steady herself on a wooden stool. *Dear Vi,* he had written. *Dear!* She could not believe her eyes. *As Mum says, you are constantly in our thoughts. May the New Year be good to all of us. X.*

Viola put down the card, then picked it up again. She read and reread both messages. How had this come about, she wondered. Even though Dad had fallen back on Mum's words, probably after ruminating for ages about what to write, he must have had a change of heart. Perhaps the war rumbling on had made him think about what was important to him? Or maybe losing Robert shocked him into thinking he could not waste what he did have – her and Freddie included. She shook her head; it didn't matter how it had happened, the most important thing was that it had and Dad was handing her an olive branch, which she would accept with both hands and her heart.

'"Auld Lang Syne", hen,' Jeanie called into the kitchen. 'Where are you? You must join in.' Jeanie stopped short when she saw Viola, so Viola suspected she looked pale. 'Och, not bad news?'

'No,' Viola said, standing on shaky legs. 'Quite the opposite. I'll tell you all about it tomorrow.'

'Jeanie. Vi,' Fin was calling from the main room.

She took Jeanie's outstretched hand and they joined in the circle as midnight struck. Her voice, when she joined in with the lyrics, was loud and strong and hopeful.

If the weeks before Christmas had been cold, then the months after were what Viola imagined to be arctic. Walking to the farmhouse every day, Viola compared herself to Roald Amundsen trekking to the South Pole. She smiled when she remembered how pleased Dad had been with a book of the explorer's expeditions that she had given him for his birthday one year.

There had been no further communication from Dad, but Mum wrote about him in a softer way, so Viola hoped the Christmas card, which said so much, had been a turning point.

After consuming the newspapers that Viola occasionally brought in, Fin took to buying a daily copy. Together the three of them read about how the Germans were taking London by surprise again with night after night of bombing; the reports sounded devastating and Viola worried for Lillian. Then they cheered and congratulated themselves when the first daylight bombing raid was carried out on Berlin.

On a fresh day in April with buttery daffodils dancing in bunches by the sides of the roads, Jeanie and Viola looked over Fin's shoulder at the headline: USAAF AND RAF JOINT BOMBING OF MUNICH AND SURROUNDS and underneath in smaller type: ALLIES CLAIM HUGE SUCCESS WITH CARPET BOMBING STRATEGY. This time there was no cheering, although Viola knew the Barfoots' initial reaction would have been to celebrate. She knew Ulm was one of Munich's surrounds but said there was every possibility that Fred and Annie might not be there now. 'Besides,' she said, trying to stabilise her smile, 'they will want an Allied victory as much as all of us. And they will want it as soon as possible.'

Jeanie made tea. Fin went out to see to the sheep or a fence or talk to Donald. Viola read through every word of the article and for the rest of the day she could not get out of her mind that fifty per cent of Munich had been destroyed. If Fred and Annie were in that city they had a fifty-fifty chance – their destinies narrowed down to a roll of the dice.

Mum wrote that she and Lillian would depart from Euston on the fifth of June and arrive, via the overnight sleeper to Edinburgh, on the sixth. As with her and Freddie's arrival, Fin would pick them up from Ayr and drive them in the rickety car to the farmhouse. For weeks prior, the croft and main house were a hive of activity. Hair was permed, rooms cleaned with vigour, clothes scrutinised and mended, previously unexplored corners dusted, cakes and bread baked, glasses and cups polished, bedding arranged. She sang to Freddie whilst she undertook the chores and in her own way, the little girl joined in.

Freddie had barged her way through the crawling stage and was now pulling herself up on sturdy legs and following Viola around by holding on first to the couch, then a chair, then a stool or table. Everything had to be moved out of her reach. She had three front teeth and another on the way; her dark hair had turned fair; she could wave and say words that sounded like Mummy and Jeanie. Much to everyone's amusement, Fin was teaching her to shout, 'Baa!' They'd had a small birthday tea in May when Freddie turned a year old, but Viola was planning something more elaborate for when Mum and Lillian were visiting. The baby was adorable, everyone loved her and Viola felt sure her grandma and Auntie Lillian would be besotted, too.

Viola decided to stay at home the day before Mum's arrival; she wanted to fuss over details in the croft and make everything perfect. The front door was open to let in the fresh flowery air, so she heard the old car long before it pulled up outside. She picked up Freddie and waved at the two figures in the front seat – neither waved back. Pulling Freddie close, she felt a chill push past the heat on her arms. 'Is something wrong?' she said as soon as the car doors opened.

'Hen,' Jeanie said. 'There's a telegram.'

Viola felt faint and Fin took Freddie from her.

'It's not trimmed in black this time.' Jeanie held it out, but drew her arm through Viola's.

```
TRAIN  CANCELLED  NO  REASON  GIVEN  MUM
LILLIAN
```

Equal measures of relief and disappointment swamped Viola. But by the time the Barfoots had driven them all down to the farmhouse for the night, the latter emotion won. Viola could not eat or sleep. All she could muster was the energy to care for Freddie.

The following morning Fin appeared and with a triumphant flourish, opened the paper on the kitchen table. They all stared speechless at the headline and then at each other as the reason for the train cancellation became apparent. And it was being called D-Day.

16

So much had been made of that failed attempt on Hitler's life. The radio and papers were full of nothing else for months, most of which Annie disbelieved as propaganda. The authorities obviously thought they were mushrooms – best kept in the dark and fed manure. What she did regard as true, was that the Resistance had been involved. But they had not been told the names of individuals or groups who might have assisted in the plot so she couldn't know if any of their old comrades were under suspicion.

Another aspect she had no doubt about was that as a backlash, the Gestapo arrested seven thousand people and of those, executed almost five thousand. And they boasted about that. She imagined the monsters in uniform walking blindfolded through crowds of people, their arms outstretched, stomping over and mowing down anyone who got in their way. They were eliminating everyone who dared to say, 'this is not right' or 'there is surely a different way' or 'let me think about that'. They kept trying to brainwash them with the idea that they were creating a pure, Aryan race.

Well, Annie for one hated the thought of living in a world where everyone looked the same and agreed with each other. And she knew there were many others like her who craved the opportunity to be challenged in their thinking and learn about others' ideas, philosophies, cultures and religions that differed from their own but were equally credible. And that was what she wanted for Walti, too. How she abhorred the thought of his little arm saluting Hitler or his chubby legs being taught to goosestep. She could not imagine any set of circumstances in which she would allow that to come about.

She also believed that Rommel had been involved in the plot and had not died of natural causes – either a heart attack or cerebral embolism from the injuries he suffered when his staff car was strafed some months previously, or so they were told. When he returned to his family home in Ulm after the assassination attempt, the town was suddenly swarming with SS watching his every move. And he was not posted elsewhere after that; he stayed at home for three months, which was unheard of for the Desert Fox. If he had remained in Hitler's good books, he would have been buried in Berlin. As it was, he was laid to rest not far from the Minster, with his son saying that was his father's request. It was, though, a full state funeral and a hero's burial with a day of mourning. Annie was relieved when the citizens of Ulm were not rounded up, as she thought they might be, and ordered to stand outside the cemetery and look heartbroken. She knew she would not have been able to do that and her protestations could have led to a great deal of trouble.

There was so much she didn't believe. They were told day after day that Germany was winning. Annie wasn't a war historian, but she didn't think the side close to victory would look as thin and ill and haunted as they did. Their food could not be rationed further, their clothes were in shreds, and often there was no electricity or water, cold or hot. They were scared, but couldn't muster the energy to display how daunted and dogged they were.

They were still gathering a few potatoes and carrots from the garden, but it was not enough. So every day either Annie or Frau Wilhelm went out to look for food – sometimes two or three times a day. More often than not it was Annie, because Frau Wilhelm had become too emaciated and Herr Doctor was trying his best to treat patients. Annie had the boldness and determination to find something, anything, to feed Walti whose appetite was insatiable. At a little over a year old, he kept all of them amused with his cheeky grin and endearing ways. Last week he'd knocked over a cup that Herr Doctor had left on a low table and toddled to get the dustpan and brush and tidy it away. 'Mutti,' he'd lisped. 'Walti sweeped.' They'd all laughed and Herr Doctor threw the little boy up in the air, his hair flopping over his forehead as he landed safely in his Opa's arms.

It was lovely, but Annie had a stab of anguish straight to her heart when she thought that it should have been Walther throwing and catching his baby son. He looked more like his Vati every day, too. Frau Wilhelm and Annie remarked on it all the time, perhaps too often for their own good as they inevitably become mournful again. But how could they avoid what was so obvious and what they wanted to see? The little boy's eyes were the same pale hazel as Walther's; his nose had the same ridge running between the nostrils; his hair was the same dark brown. Even at this young age he had the same build as Walther and, best of all, Annie was convinced he had the same sunny personality and love of fun.

Last week, she'd found Frau Wilhelm crying in the kitchen. She had a cloth in her hand and although tears streamed from her eyes and her nose was running, she had not faltered in her duty of wiping away the aftermath of the vegetables she had been scrubbing. 'What is it?' Annie had felt chilly with alarm. 'Are you unwell?'

Frau Wilhelm had sniffed and shaken her head. Annie could tell that her mother-in-law felt embarrassed to be caught in such a state of distress.

Annie had taken her by the shoulders, looked into her face and asked her again, 'Dear mother-in-law, what's wrong? It's okay. I still cry for Walther, too.'

'Yes,' she had conceded. 'It is for Walther and...'

'And?'

'Selfishly, for myself.'

'You are the least selfish woman I know,' Annie had said. 'So please tell me.'

At last Frau Wilhelm had rinsed the cloth and left it to dry next to the sink. 'I worry that one day you will meet someone else and Herr Doctor and I will become insignificant to you. And Walti.'

Then it had been Annie's turn to cry. 'Oh, no,' she'd

managed. 'Never. I would never allow that to happen. Look at me,' she'd said in a firm voice. 'We will always be one and the same family. Do you understand?'

Frau Wilhelm had wrung her hands and looked agitated. 'It's not that I don't want you to find happiness again. But whoever your next husband might be, he probably won't want us.'

Thoughts of a potential future husband had not crossed her mind. Now that she took a moment to consider that possibility it seemed highly unlikely. There was no longer any contact with her comrades from the university and she never spoke to any of the men who worked in the truck or diesel factories, especially after her frightening experience with Dietmar. Despite seeing another side to Horst, she shuddered when she thought of the Wehrmacht or the SS and knew if there were no other men on earth they would have to claim her screaming and kicking. 'If,' she'd told Frau Wilhelm, 'I meet such a man one day, he will have to accept my situation completely or I will not accept him.'

'Liebe Annie.' Frau Wilhelm hugged her and held on tight.

'And for now,' she'd said, 'Walti, Fred, you, and Herr Doctor are more than enough for me to concentrate on. And, of course, my memories of Walther.'

They'd smiled at each other, wiped their noses and gone back to their chores.

Annie left the house early in the morning in the hopes that she could avoid the queues and find something edible to bring home. She thought the same thing every morning, but was inevitably faced with lines of weary women, hunger, fatigue and worry etched on their faces. Walti had begun to cry for food and it was the most sickening sound she had ever heard. She rocked him, gave him most of her rations, turned him on his tummy over her knees and rubbed his back hoping to give him some comfort. Other times he was quiet and listless, too tired to kick a ball or turn the pages of a nursery rhyme book. At night they slept in the same bed to keep each other warm and she lay awake, panic surging through her.

She joined line after despondent line of women waiting and hoping, like her, for some kind of sustenance to take home. At Lange the Baker's she stamped her feet, eager for the queue to creep forward. The woman in front of her had thinning hair that smelled sour and huge white flakes of skin on the shoulders of her coat. When she turned suddenly, Annie had to control a sharp intake of breath. Her eyes were deep in their sockets and ringed with purple stains, like squashed summer berries. Averting her face, Annie caught sight of her reflection in the empty shop window and realised that her own eyes were at least as ghoulish.

Of course none of them thought for one minute they would get a loaf of wheat bread or rye or pumpernickel. What they were hoping for was much more basic than that. A teaspoon of yeast or a handful of flour or the crust of a three-day old bread roll left over from either the barracks or one of the factory canteens. But not today – Frau Lange locked the door from the inside, turned the sign to read closed and shook her head; Annie thought she saw her crying. So they turned en masse and made their way to join the queue plodding towards the entrance of the next shop along. She craned her neck to see if the women coming out had anything that looked worthwhile and there did seem to be the promising shapes of tins and packets in their bags, so she waited patiently.

She knew that this general store would not have had much delivered but would be dependent on handouts for most of their provisions. It was not possible, though, to go on like this much longer as the Wehrmacht themselves were looking rangy and bedraggled. A group of them, trying to walk like bulls despite their lack of meatiness, pushed into the store and came out rattling tins of coffee and pressed pork under the women's noses. A bent, frail woman, older than Frau Wilhelm, broke the line and shuffled towards the market, but the soldiers circled her, taunting her with filthy, degrading names. One of them held out a tin of peas and just as the woman made a grab for it, the despicable man pulled it back. His comrades cheered him on and he repeated the nauseating show with all the goods he had stolen from under their noses. Annie felt as if she would vomit, but strode up and pulled the woman free. 'How would you like that to happen to your own mothers? Or grandmothers?' she chastised them. 'Shame on you,' she shouted, her chin in the air.

For a split second they did look humiliated, but then they turned on her with jibes of what they thought she would do with them to get her hands on a packet of dried egg. She felt very frightened, her prominent bones rattling in her thin frame, but she held her nerve, huffed at them and steered the older woman away. 'Thank you, thank you,' the woman repeated, bowing her head. Annie watched her hurry away and wondered what she would do next time if no one came forward to help her.

Then she tried her luck at the newsagent's where they sometimes had goods like biscuits and tea for sale. The queue was only eight-deep so she thought she might be successful. The woman before her was a clerk in the Town Hall who used to be the type never to have a hair out of place – plump and well-turned-out. Now she was neither. She began to chat to another woman and the gist of their conversation was that they didn't hold out much hope of anything at the newsagent's, but mentioned foraging in the forest. Annie's eyes widened and she listened closely – she'd never heard of such a thing. It sounded feral and dirty and... godforsaken. Was that what they were now? Forgotten people scouring the back roads like animals? Stooping to pick through roots and branches for anything to put in their mouths? If they had come to this, she thought, then she was truly frightened for their lives and their souls.

She couldn't listen to any more so made her way to the marketplace. Nothing there either. Guilt and remorse ate through her when she recalled how she had refused to buy the scrawny, ulcerated chickens on display there last year. If only they were available now, she would take one without hesitation.

There was nothing left for her to do. So with a heavy heart and a growling stomach, she made her way to the forest. And what she saw there was truly shocking. The day was already darkening when she arrived and as she stepped into the undergrowth, all light seemed to be left behind. She waited for her eyes to adjust and when they did, she could make out grey shapes bending and stretching behind every copse of trees. There were scuttling sounds and the crack of twigs breaking, the low murmur of voices pointing out fallen nuts and festering mushrooms. 'There!'

'Where?'

'By your foot.'

'I cannot see.'

'There. Quickly, before someone else gets it.'

Steeling herself, she moved towards the dense interior and made herself known. Women with children, a few older or disabled men, stopped for a minute and stared. One or two who she'd seen around the town nodded then resumed their hunt. She joined them, finding acorns, berries, digging roots with her hands, pulling up weeds, brushing leaves and thorns away from her face and out of her hair. A man whose trousers were held up with a piece of string caught a mouse and without any compunction, bashed its head against a tree. The creature let out a thin squeal and its captor threw it into his bag.

It began to rain, but they carried on until they couldn't see a thing. Then she followed everyone back to Ulm feeling repulsed and proud of herself in equal measures.

'Annie!' Frau Wilhelm was beside herself when she came in cold and dirty and pale. 'We have been so worried. What has happened?'

Annie tried to play down her retelling of the queues, the soldiers, the forest but Frau Wilhelm was horrified. She ran for Herr Doctor who said he thought she was in shock so she was dried, fed thin soup by the trace of a fire and in lieu of hot, sweet tea, told she would have to make do with a shot of brandy. At last, she thought, something was going in her favour. It did the trick and helped her shivers so, happily, Herr Doctor prescribed another.

Whilst Frau Wilhelm fussed and fretted, Herr Doctor told them he had heard about the foraging from patients attending his surgeries with stomach cramps, headaches, skin rashes and vomiting.

'We must do all we can to make sure you do not have to do this again,' Frau Wilhelm said.

'I thought we had,' Annie answered.

Frau Wilhelm did not say anything, but took the bag into the kitchen, emptied the contents into the sink and picked over the spoils of her hunt. She did not throw any of it away.

Annie's feet remained blocks of ice and she was sent to bed under as many blankets and eiderdowns as Frau Wilhelm could find. With sagging eyelids she listened to Walti calling, 'Walti wants Mutti.' But Frau Wilhelm shushed him with promises of a story and the last of the watery soup.

Before she succumbed to sleep, Annie forced herself to write about what she had seen and heard, felt and undergone that day. If she didn't, she might convince herself in the morning that she had dreamt it, rather than knowing she had lived through a most horrendous nightmare.

31 December 1944
I refuse to insult this book with writing the trite message we used to greet each other with on this date every previous year. There is no time or energy for such

superficial sentimentality. Herr Doctor is under the dust
and debris of his surgery. Most of Ulm has been razed to
the ground. The rubble is so thick and deep that walking
through it is almost impossible. God alone knows when
or what we will eat next.

Despite her grief, Frau Wilhelm carried on with household
duties and minding Walti whilst Annie spent most of her
time looking for food. They had to, there was nothing else
they could do. Frau Wilhelm spoke of Herr Doctor with
great sadness and when she had time to sit, she wrung her
hands in agitation. They both tried not to cry, but kept soggy,
balled handkerchiefs up their sleeves as without warning
they would fill up with tears. All of their men had been
taken from them and poor Walti was growing up without a
father, grandfather or uncle to look up to.

Frau Wilhelm also cried for her cherished, spotless, old-
fashioned home. The one she'd lived in for most of her life
with Herr Doctor and Walther. Annie knew she dwelled on
everything they shared there together and how she built
such a warm, comfortable sanctuary for them as a family.
Annie remembered how she generously gave up her trinkets
and cuckoo clock, dark patterned carpets and much-loved
kitchen to spend time helping her after Walther died. It
must have been difficult enough for her to do nothing more
than pop backwards and forwards to her own territory, but
now there was not a brick left of her house to go back to.
Nothing. Not a photograph or teaspoon or door handle or
towel or rake could be salvaged. And not a trace of Herr
Doctor although they know he had been there when the

bombs hit, treating patients with what little he had. How Oma's little house – Annie's little house – escaped the devastation they had no idea, but they did not take that good luck for granted.

Amongst the wreckage in the streets, Annie sometimes glimpsed minute pieces of life as it had been lived – the handle of a coffee cup, a torn bookmark, a length of string very like the one that man in the forest had used instead of a belt, a dog's collar, part of a brooch, a child's bone teething ring. Somehow those things made her cry harder than the colossal demolished pit that used to be Ulm.

She could not comprehend that terrible air raid. Although the authorities would never admit it, they all felt sure it was nearly over so why did the Allies decide to punish them in that way? If they weren't worth bombing years ago then why now when they were already on their knees with hunger and illness and exhaustion? If they could see them as they were in their everyday lives – dragging themselves around, living from hand to mouth, frightened, cold and on the brink of madness, they would take pity on them. But they were human beings so they must surely be able to imagine their plight?

Frau Wilhelm reminded her that the bombs destroyed the Gallwitz barracks. 'Isn't that a good thing?' she asked, trying to convince herself as well as Annie.

'It would have been, when the men in the barracks were more than starving spectres,' Annie retorted, thinking of the Wehrmacht wandering around, what left of their torn uniforms hanging off them, looking disorientated and rudderless. She sighed and flopped into a chair, bouncing Walti on her lap. 'I don't know any of the thinking behind it,' she said. 'None of us do. But couldn't they have made a show of it instead of retaliating in such a cruel way?'

'I know, Annie,' Frau Wilhelm agreed. 'A couple of military hospitals were obliterated, too. Herr Doctor—' she choked when she said his name '—would never have sanctioned any hospital being bombed. All those poor helpless people. All the medicine and bandages and equipment. The nurses and doctors. It's unthinkable. Herr Doctor could have used all of that in his surgery if it hadn't been... If he wasn't...'

She could not carry on and Annie hugged her, knowing the conversation would have to come to an end. But her mind kept racing and to herself she acceded that the truck factories and diesel plant were fair play – if it was nearly over then wrecking those kinds of places would accelerate the process. But their homes, shops, the market, their friends, their families, what little they had – everything was dust. Thank goodness the Minster was relatively unscathed and could offer a roof to the thousands who had lost their homes. That was where she would go to beg for some of the minute portions of food being distributed to the most needy. She would take Walti with her to prove she had a child who must be fed.

As always there were those worse off than them. They, at least, had a house to live in, a fire to keep them warm when they could get fuel and a kitchen to cook in when food was available. Of the thousands left homeless after the air raids, some sheltered in the Minster, some in any sort of makeshift shelter they could find or build, others had taken to walking towards places they thought might have more to offer like

Munich or Berlin. Annie had seen them with the little they owned on their backs or in sacks, barely able to put one foot in front of the other. How they had the strength to get anywhere was a mystery to her. And others set up camp in the forests.

She'd seen them when she'd been foraging. They lived in industrious groups, clearing away swathes of undergrowth and using bits of sheets and tarpaulin to provide cover. Or they sat in twos and threes around fires on which they roasted creatures she couldn't identify and didn't want to think about. Most regarded her with hungry indifference, some looked antagonistic until she passed by without exchanging a word. One woman had picked up a large, pitted stone and stood with it primed and ready, daring her to intrude on her space. 'There's nothing here worth having,' she'd shrieked. 'Go away.' So Annie had turned and hurried away as she'd been ordered.

But one afternoon she heard a shout, 'Young Frau Wilhelm.' Annie didn't recognise the voice and couldn't see anyone so spun around and around until a waif pushed her way through a clump of bushes and appeared in front of her. It took her a minute to recognise the child as Gisela, the little girl who'd helped them after Walti was born by delivering their rations. But gone was the thick hank of hair and in its place was a shaven scalp, which she scratched until Annie thought it would bleed. The pink cheeks were replaced by sallow hollows, the dimpled knees by bones so sharp they almost pierced her skin. Her mouth was stained green.

She held out her hand to Annie and said, 'Come with me.'

To Annie's shame, she hesitated. For one thing she could

see the child was filthy and crawling with lice. For another she wondered if she was taking her to where she would be assaulted for the few berries and nuts in her bag. But that was not the way she wanted to live her life, by being suspicious and insular. That was not how she wanted the world to be so thought she must make a stand based on her principles and morals. She squared her shoulders, beckoned for Gisela to lead the way and followed at a short distance.

They stumbled over fallen tree trunks, through muddy streams, around crudely built camps. 'Gisela,' Annie said. 'Why is your mouth green?'

Gisela turned, wiping her face on her ragged sleeve. 'I am sorry, young Frau Wilhelm. It is grass.'

Alarm surged through her. 'Grass?' she said. 'You have been eating grass?'

Gisela nodded her head. 'Sometimes we have nothing else.'

Nestled in between a square of four trees was a shelter built from long strips of tree bark and hung with old blankets and rugs. Three men, who looked like brothers, were trying to make the structure more sound. Gisela introduced them to her as her father and uncles and Annie to them as her friend. That made her heart feel heavy.

'Where is your Mutti and your Tanten?' Annie asked.

Gisela shook her head and started to cry. Still trying to avoid touching the poor mite, Annie squatted down to her level and said, 'What do you want me to do for you, Gisela?' knowing full well there was very little within her power that could help.

'Can you ask Herr Doctor to give me something to make my head stop itching?' Gisela asked.

Of all the things she could have requested – her mum, books, a dress, food, a clean bed, shoes, all she could think about was having her most uncomfortable present dilemma soothed.

'Herr Doctor is dead,' Annie told her in a gentle voice. 'And all of his medicines have been lost in the air raid. But I will ask Frau Wilhelm if she knows of a cure for you. Alright?'

'Thank you,' Gisela said and looked down at the dirt covering her thin, summer sandals.

'I will come back,' Annie promised, raising her hand in farewell.

She hadn't gone far when she was startled by a rustle behind her. Ever wary that Dietmar might be lurking and waiting to grab her again, she gasped, turned and saw Gisela's father. They both stood stock-still and sized each other up; Annie could see the pulse under the whiskers on the side of his neck hammering like a machine gun and she could feel that hers was a match for his. Through the slant of her eye, she looked around for a stick or branch she could use as a weapon.

Then, in a hoarse voice he said, 'Take her. Please.'

Annie felt shocked and appalled. 'I cannot do that,' she said in an uncompromising voice. 'She is your daughter.'

'I have nothing to give her. She will die. I give her to you.'

'But... But...' Annie could not find the words to express her dismay. 'I have very little, either, and she needs to be with you.'

'What she needs is the chance to have a life. I give you my daughter so she can live.'

He must have been able to see that she was horrified, but took a step closer and said, 'I am begging you.' There were tears in his eyes.

Annie refused to continue the discussion, so started to run backwards, stumbled, turned from him and crashing through the forest, made her way home.

'He is mad,' Frau Wilhelm said. 'How can we take care of another child when we can barely take care of ourselves? Perhaps you can take her to the Minster and ask the church to look after her?'

Annie shook her head. 'Her father could have done that, but he wants her to be with a family.'

'What's left of a family, you mean,' Frau Wilhelm said.

'A family nevertheless.'

Frau Wilhelm sighed and found a fine-toothed comb and said that the best thing for head lice was to pull it through the hair and over the scalp every day. Then they would need to pick out each other's lice and crack them between their fingernails. Herr Doctor used to give the patient something they could paint on their scalp, but that was gone now with everything else that might have helped.

The next morning, armed with the comb, Annie made her way back to the forest determined to show Gisela and her father how they could treat each other's infestation – that and nothing else. But each step of the way she doubted her resolve and felt as though what she was actually doing was condemning the little girl to death. Or worse. If her father and uncles became ill or died, she might latch on to someone dishonourable, like Dietmar who would abuse her or sell her to the Wehrmacht who would ruin her completely. For the rest of her life she would wonder what had happened to Gisela when she abandoned her and not knowing would be torture.

If she had any indecision left when she arrived at the squalid camp, it disappeared when Gisela ran towards her, grabbed her hand and said, 'Vati told me I am going to live with you.'

'Where is your Vati?' Annie asked.

'They have all gone to look for food,' Gisela said, but Annie could feel her father somewhere close by, watching and waiting. 'Vati knows I will be gone by the time he gets back.' She looked up at Annie eagerly.

This time Annie took her hand and said in a loud voice, 'Yes, Gisela. You are coming home to live with me, Frau Wilhelm and baby Walti.'

At home, Annie and Frau Wilhelm scrubbed the little girl, picked over her hair, fed her a small bowl of soup, put her clothes with the rags and, after dressing her in one of Annie's nightgowns, tucked her up in Oma's old bed. Annie thought the worry of having another mouth to feed would keep her awake that night, but she slept better than she had done in ages.

Annie and Frau Wilhelm had been happy to have their house intact when so many others had lost theirs; now they found some comfort in the corner of their house that remained standing. They were reduced to living in one bedroom, part of the sitting room and a corner of the kitchen. They dug a hole in the garden to relieve themselves as the privy was in ruins and they washed when there was a bowlful of water from the taps.

But it was a miracle they were alive. Annie went over and over the air raid in her mind, tormenting herself with how different it could have been. Frau Wilhelm had been on her way to the Minster when the raid started and she'd picked up Walti and run the remainder of the way with him in her arms. 'Oh, how funny he thought it was,' she'd reported. 'Bouncing along next to my chest, pointing at the planes, laughing at everyone running. And minutes before I had almost turned back for a scarf. Thank goodness I...' She'd shaken her head in disbelief.

Annie had been with Gisela in a different woods to forage for food as she hadn't wanted the little girl to catch sight of her father. But they had heard the planes overhead, a swarm of locusts destroying everything in their path. Smoke had gathered over the city, obscuring the rooftops so they had no inkling of what was being destroyed underneath. Even from that distance, the noise had been terrifying and they had cowered and covered their ears. It must have stirred up a memory in Gisela's mind about her mum dying in the last raid, because she had clung to Annie's skirt and cried for her mother. Annie's first instinct had been to run back to Ulm to find Frau Wilhelm and Walti, but she'd steeled herself to think logically and stay where they were. Frau Wilhelm would protect little Walti. Her heart told her she would put his life before her own.

As soon as she'd thought the danger had passed, she'd

grabbed Gisela's hand and dragged her along as she ran towards home. Crowds had appeared from the woods all going in the same direction.

Streets that had been strewn with detritus from the last raid were now completely inaccessible. People with glazed eyes were wandering as if they had suddenly been planted in a place they had no recollection of seeing before. An old man, his vest in tatters, had lurched towards them and they'd scooted around him, only to see his ear hanging by a thread. A woman in a stained apron, with nothing on her feet, dragged one body after another from a bottomless heap. Against the remains of a wall, a man had sat slumped, his leg gone below the knee. But they hadn't stopped; they had to find Frau Wilhelm and Walti.

The pile of rubble that had been their house hardly registered as Annie took one look at it and refused to believe her beloved son and mother-in-law were inside. She and Gisela had held on tight to each other and, blocking out the stinging from their torn, bleeding feet, flown to the Minster. There, hunkering in the corner of a pew, they'd found a trembling Frau Wilhelm cradling Walti on her lap. Relief had flooded through Annie and she sank onto the kneeler in front of them, slowly and deliberately. Candles shuddering in waves of aftershock cast shadows on the walls, the boarded windows, their hollowed faces. Gisela had put her arm around Annie's neck and with her other hand, stroked first Frau Wilhelm's arm, then Walti's.

If she had only heard it the once she would not have been convinced, but it was repeated by so many different people she knew it must be true. Annie was out with Gisela and Walti scavenging for materials to use to breach their bombed house, when a woman joined them on their heap of bricks, clawed at her arm and said, 'He is dead. It's the truth.'

Annie's initial thought was that the woman had gone insane, but in a gentle tone said, 'Who is dead?'

Then it was the woman's turn to look at Annie as if she was demented. 'Hitler.' She nodded and closed her eyes when she said his name. 'Haven't you heard?'

'Let's leave our pile here and collect it on the way back,' Annie said to Gisela. 'Come and hold Walti's hand.'

She thought it best to go to the Minster and ask someone there if what the woman had told her was truth or rumour. But on the way she heard others shouting out the same information to each other. One man told another he'd heard it on the wireless. A crowd was dancing what looked like an impromptu hokey cokey. Rags were unfurled and waved out of what was left of windows. Then she allowed herself to believe it was true. A smile took over her face and her heart somersaulted. Taking the children, she raced for home. Without making a sound, the words played across her lips over and over again until she threw herself into the house and shouted to Frau Wilhelm, 'Hitler is dead! It's the truth.'

Later that evening, Annie and Frau Wilhelm were cleaning the last few bits of serviceable crockery as best they could and stacking them on the coffee table that was now put to use in the kitchen. It had lost a leg in the bombing, but Annie and Gisela had fashioned a new one out of a tree branch and it was less wobbly than they thought it would be. Walti had tried to help, but they had to keep a close eye on him to make sure he stayed safe. The little fellow loved Gisela and followed her around saying something that sounded like, 'Gisela, Gisela. Walti wants.'

Gisela was never impatient with him, but treated him with fondness as if she were his big sister, which she was in every way except by blood. One, two, three she counted each spoonful she fed him and encouraged him to repeat the numbers after her – which he did in a little sing-song lisp. And she pointed out colours to him although now there wasn't much to see except grey.

'Do you think they will come for us?' Frau Wilhelm asked. 'Or will they think we colluded with the Nazis and leave us to die?'

'They will come for us,' Annie said. 'They will understand we have been innocent civilians.'

'Where do you think they will put us whilst they rebuild?'

At that moment it hit Annie that she and Frau Wilhelm had never discussed what would happen when the war finished – all they had kept in their sights was what had, for years, been the elusive end. Now it was tantalisingly within reach and their peculiar situation meant they would have to make decisions about the future. Well, Annie had decided on her options but she supposed the time had come to share them with Frau Wilhelm.

When they were sitting with their mending, Annie broached the subject and told her mother-in-law that she had been thinking about her earlier question. 'I do not know where they will want to send us during the clean-up,' she said, keeping her eyes on her stitches. 'But I will stay in this shell of a house until Fred comes back. Because he will not know where to look for me otherwise.'

'Yes, of course.' Frau Wilhelm nodded and Annie was glad she took Fred coming back as a given, as did she.

'Then he will want to go back to England to his Viola.'

'That would be the best thing for him to do.'

'And I will go with him.' Annie put down her sewing and looked at Frau Wilhelm's drained, gaunt face, tiny lines feathering out from her lips and eyes; unruly, greying eyebrows; a chipped, brown front tooth. But before she could find any words, Annie told her that she would be applying for her and Gisela to go with them. 'Can you bear to leave and start over again in England?' Annie asked. 'I cannot imagine life without you.'

Frau Wilhelm's hands quivered when she reached for Annie's and for an instant she was as she had been, before the war began and took its toll on all of them. The cloudy film lifted from her eyes and she smoothed her hair with her fingers. 'I told you once upon a time,' she said, 'that I love having adventures and that has not changed.' She sighed in a manner that could almost be described as contented. Then they both picked up their mending again, stopping periodically to exchange a grin.

There was a soft knock at the door, followed by a pounding. Frau Wilhelm and Annie exchanged a look, trying to convey their anxiety to each other without passing it onto Gisela who was up late waiting for her longer hair to dry.

'Horst?' Frau Wilhelm mouthed.

Annie shrugged. Part of her longed to see him if only for a few minutes to let him know she was proud of him and so grateful that he rescued her from Dietmar. But a shiver crept up her spine when she wondered what he might want now. So many Wehrmacht soldiers were wandering the streets, wraithlike and aimless, looking for homes that had been flattened and families that no longer existed. She felt nauseous and wondered what she'd say or do if Horst and his comrades forced their way into the house and confiscated it for themselves.

Gisela and Frau Wilhelm stared at her, looking for guidance and reassurance. 'I will go,' she said and mumbled something about someone losing their bearings and wanting directions.

The pounding came again followed by a deep voice. It was Horst, calling her name. 'Annie, Annie. Open the door.' She pretended to fumble with the broken furniture they used for security. 'Horst,' she said. 'Are you on your own?'

'Annie,' he commanded. 'Do as I say. Now. I must see you.' And then in a lower voice he said, 'I mean you no harm.'

Pulling open what was left of the door, Annie was taken aback to see nothing outside but the black night. This was not the time to be playing schoolboy pranks, she thought. Then she could see that Horst was standing like a statue at the end of the path. He moved, jabbed his finger twice at the ground in front of her, turned up his collar and made to hulk off into the shadows.

'Horst, wait,' she said as she bent down to what looked like a pile of rags on the ground. But the bundle shuddered and she plucked open what was left of a brown, ripped, muddy coat and there was Fred, her brother, on the verge of drawing his last breath.

Disbelief, dread and elation hit her at once. 'Frau Wilhelm. Gisela,' she screamed. 'Help us!'

As they were lifting Fred's poor, skeletal body into the house, Annie caught sight of Horst's shadow slinking away. 'Horst,' she called out. 'Twice you have done the right thing for us. I will never forget that. Or you.'

He stopped for a moment and touched his hand to the brim of his cap, then he was gone.

Fred was so diminished and frail that he took up a fraction of the space in Annie's small bed. There were fresh wounds and old scars all over his body and something was very wrong with his left arm – it hung at an angle and he winced whenever it was moved by accident or out of necessity. Try as they might to get him to eat, he could not drink much nettle soup and gagged after three small mouthfuls. But that seemed enough to sustain him because his breathing became steadier and before he closed his eyes to sleep he whispered, 'Annie.' It was the sweetest sound she had ever heard.

Annie stayed awake all night, staring at the brother who she told herself she had helped to keep alive with hope. Dawn broke pink and mauve and blue above their ruined city, and still she could not take her eyes from him.

By the end of May, Fred was well enough to come downstairs and sit, upright, in a cushioned chair. Walti loved him and took every opportunity to sit on his lap and pretend that his uncle's whiskers scratched the tender skin on his palms. Gisela, shy at first, began to join in the games they played.

Annie left them to it and went out for food but came back with chewing gum and stockings. She tore open the packaging and told them about the American soldiers in their huge tanks and jeeps, throwing out treats to anyone who could catch. On the verge of hysteria, they laughed with the relief that came from knowing they had lived through the worst and that help was close enough to touch.

26 July 1945
I have dreamed about writing these words so many times, but now they are a reality. We are going home.

17

September 1945

Viola spent months battling with the dilemma of whether to go back to London or the Cotswolds or to settle in Sorn. Lillian, David, Mum, Dad and George all got in on the act of convincing her to return, telling her that she would be better off close to family and friends who would help her and Freddie.

She listed the pros and cons, considering each point in turn. For Freddie to be near her grandparents, uncle and two of her dearest friends would be good for the little girl and she deserved to get to know them and for them to spoil, advise, scold, feed and watch over her. And for Viola to have the comfort of knowing her family was close by, after yearning for them for so long, created a pull so strong that she could almost feel her heartstrings tauten to breaking point.

Certainly there would be better prospects for her and for Freddie in England. She could go back to work there; here there was not much hope of that other than a few hours in the post office or behind the bar in the pub. In Sorn, there was one school for all the children up to leavers' age; in London she would have the choice of a number of good establishments. And, as he had relented with such magnanimity, Dad would no doubt help with a private school like the one she had benefitted from.

But there were other things that, at this moment in time, seemed more important. It was difficult to list them as she found it almost impossible to shape her feelings into words. When she walked through muddy lanes and around harvested fields holding Freddie's hand, avoiding as best she could the all-pervasive sheep, she sometimes thought she had made material her vague thoughts, but then they would slip away again like the wispy threads of mist that so often hung over the landscape.

So she allowed herself to feel rather than think and she realised that here, in Sorn, she had found a peacefulness and calm she knew she wouldn't be able to reclaim in London. She imagined her life there becoming more complicated, rushing to the Tube for work, hurrying home to Freddie; shopping for makeup and clothes to keep stylish; booking hair appointments; asking Lillian and George, David or Mum to mind Freddie so she could go to a club or out for lunch with friends; being set up on dates by well-intentioned people, only to find the man others thought perfect was neither funny, interesting or ambitious – no match for her Fred.

Here, there was time to collect leaves in the autumn and daffodils in the spring and make collages with their efforts; to watch the old oak tree move through the seasons; to learn everything there was to know about sheep and laugh at Freddie when she said, 'Baaa'. The little girl had so much attention that she was talking in complete sentences; if they were to go back to life in the south, she would not have the time to pursue such worthwhile activities with her child to the same degree.

Jeanie and Fin had asked to her stay and said they would charge a peppercorn rent for the croft now that the billeting payments had ceased. Fin had great plans for renovations to the little house that included an indoor bathroom, windows that were sealed against draughts and replacing the thatched roof. And Jeanie was like a sister to her plus an aunt, cousin, and grandmother rolled into one for Freddie. The Barfoots adored the little girl and Viola knew that if anything happened to her, they would put Freddie's interests above their own. And they were not like family to her – they were her family and had been for almost two and a half years.

Then of course, as always, there was Fred. He had never been part of her life here, so apart from her memories there were no associations with him. To knowingly churn up all that emotion again, in London or the Cotswolds, was more than she could bear to put herself through.

She penned all of that in letters to Mum and Lillian and stressed that her decision was set in stone, but she was waiting for their long-promised visit.

The return letter from Mum arrived so quickly, that Viola sighed when she opened it, sure it would contain countless reasons Mum thought Viola better off at home. But what she read blasted her decision to pieces like a bomb reducing bricks and mortar to scree.

My dearest Viola

You will never guess who has been here today, chatting with me and drinking tea. No, don't try to guess, you never will, so I will tell you – Annie! Yes, Annie. Fred's sister.

My goodness, how she has changed. But so have we all during the long war years. Do you remember her as a young girl? She had long, wavy hair that would not stay in the pins she adjusted over and over again. And she used to find it so hard to keep still, jiggling and giggling her way through conversations and high teas. Well, she is remarkably beautiful with hair that does as it's told and a lovely, calm, rather intense demeanour. I couldn't decide whether her prominent cheekbones were the result of lucky genetics or deprivation. Certainly her razor-sharp shins beneath elegantly crossed legs would have me believe the latter.

I came to the conclusion that she had been through a lot – at least as much, if not more, than you and I have experienced – and been incredibly brave to boot. She mentioned a few occurrences like foraging for food in the forests and watching hordes of Germans take to the roads in search of shelter and sustenance and a group of young people she and Fred were involved with who wrote and distributed resistance material. Two or three times she referred to a journal she kept for the duration of the war and said that everything they had gone through was written in its pages. She did not elaborate on any of those events and I didn't feel inclined to probe as there was something so painful churning deep in her eyes that I was loath to stir it up. But I would love the chance to be privy to that notebook.

I was amazed that when she gets settled, she said she would like to go to university and learn how to help people overcome what she called social injustices. That sounded like a difficult aspiration for anyone, let alone a young woman. Well, I thought, Bevan could use someone like you and said so. Her head bobbed up and down when she confirmed, as I thought she would, that she agreed with his proposals for social reform. Conviction and determination were etched into the set of her features, the earnest way she spoke about her vision for the future, her fist that pummelled into the opposite palm every time she made a point. She is convinced that people have more in common than they have differences and that the world should bear that in mind.

'Yes,' she said. 'All of us have experienced war. We have been men and women at war and we must recognise the similarities amongst us. We must listen to the ordinary people and understand what binds us together rather than what drives us apart. Then we might not ever allow such a wide gulf to open between us again.'

Then she told me she has a little boy, not much younger than Freddie and no husband, but she was wearing a wedding band. Also in her care are her German mother-in-law, a young girl who she has taken under her wing and – please sit down for this, Vi, and if you are sitting make sure you are well supported – Fred! He was injured and malnourished but is making good progress in St Thomas's. Annie said he would probably be discharged within the next two or three weeks.

I told her you had been billeted to Scotland with your

little girl, although I did not offer any more information about that as I didn't think it the appropriate time or place or indeed my call.

I do not know if you want to pursue this, Vi, but will you now please come home and see if this flame you have carried for Fred can be reignited? It seems, from what Annie intimated, that Fred has never ceased in his affection for you and yes, I know, that was before he learned of your indiscretion. But the war has changed attitudes so he may accept Freddie as his own. If Dad could have such a change of heart, then anyone could.

Lillian and I are going to arrange tickets for the middle of October to come to Scotland and, given that you will have had a month or so by then to think about this news, bring you and Freddie back with us.

All my love to you
Mum X

Never before had Viola been so glad to follow Mum's advice. If she had been standing or sitting on the edge of the chair, she would have passed out. As it was, she had to put her head between her knees until the giddy spell passed. 'Mummy?' Freddie asked, putting her little hand on Viola's arm. 'Freddie get a cup of tea?'

Viola nodded and sent her daughter to play out her latest game with miniature cups and saucers and spoons. She read the letter again, following each line with her finger. Whether she and Fred had a future together was up in the air, but he was alive and without that certainty there had been nothing but a black abyss. Now, at least, there was a chink of hope.

That night she laid out her treasures on the bed. The

pamphlet that she now had no doubt was written by Fred; Lillian's comfy cardigan, now more hole than wool; Freddie's birth certificate; the card signed by Dad; letters from Robert and David; the portrait of her and Freddie under the oak tree; Fred's thwarted thesis. There was the ring, too, resting in the dip between her collarbones. Each one of them a memory that symbolised a part of her whole. If these outward trappings were the sum total of her life, then it was not too bad a tally. But was it wrong to want and hope for more?

She didn't think it was, but she had seen and heard and learned enough to know that her life was not always under her dictate alone. Of course, she could not begin to harbour thoughts that Fred might want her and Freddie until she told him about every aspect of her ill-fated relationship with Mike and the result of that assignation. Mum was right – Fred did, after all, have a right to learn the truth and it was her responsibility to tell him the whole story. When Freddie was asleep, she spread out her writing paper and pen and started at the beginning. She did not spare him any of the details, but emphasised that she had acted out of loneliness and regretted how immature and selfish and destructive her behaviour had been.

It is you I love, Fred and always have. I wear your ring close to my heart and your heart in mine. Not an hour of any day goes by when I haven't ached for you and I am mortified that I ruined what we had together.

If you could begin to understand what happened or to forgive me, I would be forever grateful.

Always your Viola. XXX

When she lifted Freddie to post the letter, both she and the little girl kissed the envelope. Watching it disappear into the red box, her heart dropped, too. If felt as if the tiny glimmer of hope she had been keeping aflame all this time was inevitably about to be extinguished. And as the weeks went past with no reply, she had to convince herself that what had been between her and Fred could never be rekindled.

At the first sound of tyres on the path, Viola stood on the doorstep with Freddie in her arms. The banger had been old when she was first billeted to Sorn, but now it was ancient and spluttered and wheezed its way up the hill. At last she could see it, fumes puffing from the exhaust. Freddie was pointing out the birds, the sheep, the car in the distance. But all Viola was aware of was the hammering of her heart and the snakes twisting and turning in her stomach. Mum and Lillian were nearly here and she was beside herself with excitement and trepidation. Then, as luck would have it, a flock of sheep skittered across the path and stood, vacant and nonsensical in front of the car.

For a moment she didn't know what to do. *Fin will shoo them away*, she thought. *Or should I make my way down to meet them?* But she was wearing house slippers and didn't want to miss their arrival by taking precious time to change into wellies.

In the time it took her to hesitate, Fin hopped out and opened the back door to help Mum, Viola supposed. But he had his hand under a man's elbow. A tall, rather thin man who seemed to have his left arm in a sling. Fin leaned into the other side of the car and appeared with a young woman clutching what looked like a red notebook. Viola's mind flashed between knowing it was Fred and Annie and refusing to believe it was possible. As if caught in time and space, they all stood motionless, staring at each other, registering recognition and disbelief. For a split second Viola recalled her perfect day in the family garden six years earlier, when she thought the path of her life was unalterable and would bring her the epitome of happiness. This setting was nothing like that and yet, in these blotched surroundings and as one of these flawed people she knew she had never experienced happiness before.

The spell broke and in a frenzy, they all moved at once. Fred scooped up a small boy who looked about the same age as Freddie, leaned on Annie and with one determined step after another made his way up the hill. Somehow, Viola's trembling fingers released the ring from under her blouse to where it bounced in between her heart and Freddie's and she ran without stopping towards them.

Acknowledgements

A special thank you to my lovely daughter, Kelly Collinwood-Erdinc, who read each chapter as it was written and provided me with invaluable feedback and advice.

I would like to acknowledge how grateful I am and how lucky I feel for the love, support and encouragement I receive from my husband, Don Gilchrist, my son, Liam Collinwood and my stepsons Tom Gilchrist and Danny Gilchrist.

Thank you, also, to my wonderful family members Ozzie Erdinc, Arie Collinwood, Sonia Gilchrist, Sue and Gerald Ward, Duncan and Lisa Gilchrist, Ally and Sharon Gilchrist and my fantastic friends Nick Abendroth, Lizzie Alexander, Jo Bishop, Helen Chatten, Penny Clarke, Breda Doran, Fiona Emblem, Jo Emeney, Steve Farmer, Natalie Farrell, Chris Holmes, Paula Horsford, Jan Hurst, Maureen John, Nick John, Liz Kochprapha, Katy Marron, Tom Mathew, Liz Peadon, Dave Pountney, Liz Prescott, Jenny Savage and Martin Shrosbree.

Thank you from the bottom of my heart to Peter and Kathleen Casey and my Galway family for their encouragement and love, to my supportive family members in Turkey and to my sister, brother-in-law, nieces and nephews in the United States.

My thanks go, as always, to my grandchildren Toby, Kaan, Ayda, Alya and Aleksia for bringing endless joy, laughter and happiness to my life.

I am so grateful to Rhea Kurien, my fantastic editor at Aria Fiction who has been committed to this book and to me as an author; I'm going to miss you, Rhea. Thank you, also, to my very helpful and dedicated agent, Kiran Kataria at Keane Kataria Literary Agency.

Thank you to the National Centre for Writing in Norwich and to the Creative Writing Department at Anglia Ruskin University for their on-going support.

Perhaps this should have been mentioned first rather than last, but I am deeply grateful to the White Rose and all young people, on both sides of the channel, who put what they believed to be right and just above their personal safety and thoughts for their own futures.

About the Author

J AN CASEY was born in London but spent her childhood in Southern California where she was inspired to become a writer by her teachers and regular visits to the impressive Los Angeles Central Library.

Before becoming a published novelist, Jan had short stories and flash fiction published and achieved an M.A. in Creative Writing from Anglia Ruskin University in Cambridge.

She was a teacher of English and Drama for many years and is now a Learning Supervisor at a college of further education.

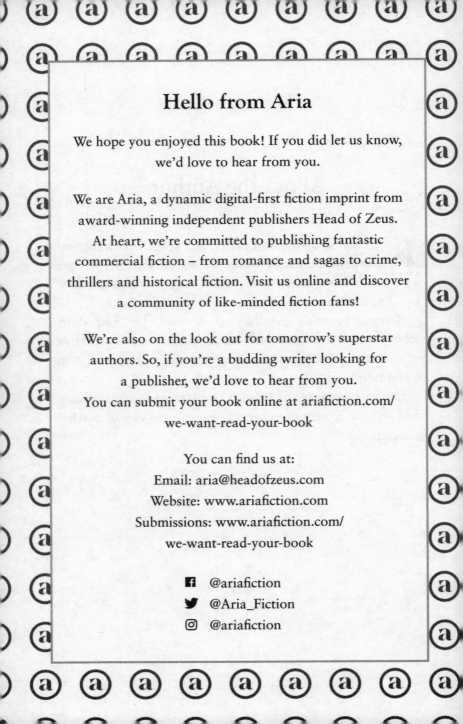

Hello from Aria

We hope you enjoyed this book! If you did let us know, we'd love to hear from you.

We are Aria, a dynamic digital-first fiction imprint from award-winning independent publishers Head of Zeus. At heart, we're committed to publishing fantastic commercial fiction – from romance and sagas to crime, thrillers and historical fiction. Visit us online and discover a community of like-minded fiction fans!

We're also on the look out for tomorrow's superstar authors. So, if you're a budding writer looking for a publisher, we'd love to hear from you. You can submit your book online at ariafiction.com/ we-want-read-your-book

You can find us at:
Email: aria@headofzeus.com
Website: www.ariafiction.com
Submissions: www.ariafiction.com/ we-want-read-your-book

    @ariafiction
    @Aria_Fiction
    @ariafiction